SWORD OF ALLAH

MIDDLE EAST ESPIONAGE AND LOVE STORY

ROBERT THOMAS FERTIG

SWORD

OF

ALLAH

SWORD

—OF—

ALLAH

Middle East Crisis Espionage & Love Story

ROBERT THOMAS FERTIG

ISBN: 978-1-961677-77-7 (Paperback)

ISBN: 978-1-961677-51-7 (E-book)

Library of Congress Control Number: 2024908040

Printed in the United States of America

Published by:

info@thequippyquill.com
(302) 295-2278

CONTENTS

PREFACE

This is a "Historical Novel." It is a sequel to *Quicksand,* published in 2014, *Gathering Storm in the Middle East,* published in 2010. Many of the events and political characters described herein are real. However, the main characters are imaginary. The opinions expressed in this novel are solely the opinions and views of the author and do not represent the opinions or thoughts of the publisher.

The author has represented and warranted full ownership and/or legal right to publish all the materials in this book, and exercised his imagination, *combined with actual historical events,* to foretell happenings and actions that he believes have a high probability of becoming a reality. Photos are from author files.

Places and incidents are mostly *historically accurate.* Some names are changed to protect the innocent. The violence, sex and language used by the author is to provide a realistic portrait of the characters and events, and may not be appropriate for less mature readers. It is easier to write about the "reality" of historical events, and key actors who played a major role, especially by name, in this work of "historical fiction."

To Miriam, my loving spouse of sixty years, devoted mother of our three children, passionate educator, whose editing, support, patience, and understanding made this challenging work possible.

Teacher Miriam Fertig at Greenwich H.S. Graduating class of 1999

INTRODUCTION

"What is history, but a fable agreed upon?"

—Napoleon

Readers must know that this writer believes that ALL religions that teach love of God and love of neighbor are always respected. On the other hand, one cannot expect anyone to respect "religious radicalism," that teaches death to all who do not support their *fanatical or fundamental* beliefs, be they Christians, Jews, Hindus or Muslims.

Any single racial, ethnic, or religious group no longer defines America, in the 21st century. WASPs (White, Anglo Saxon, Protestants) do not dominate any longer. African-Americans, Asians, Germans, Irish, Italians, Poles, and many others, especially Hispanics, make up our population. While Protestants remain the religious majority, they represent many different dominations and sects. Catholics are the largest *single* group, representing a quarter of all religions in the U.S. today. The United States of America is an extremely diverse, multiethnic, multicultural society, with a strong national identity. We are a "melting pot" of every race on earth. Nevertheless, we retain our "primeval" ethnic identities as families. Moreover, there are disruptive forces of "tribalism" that have, and will continue to cause political and racial adversities, in America and worldwide.

Many of these tribal societies are in the Far East and Middle East. Muslim majorities, for example, refuse to *assimilate* into Western society. The main reason is that Islam is not just a religion— it is a "way of life" for families and tribal communities. Islam represents less than two percent of America, but they are over 10% of UK and EU populations, and growing very rapidly. If present population trends continue, Muslims may become nearly one-third of the world's population, by 2050.

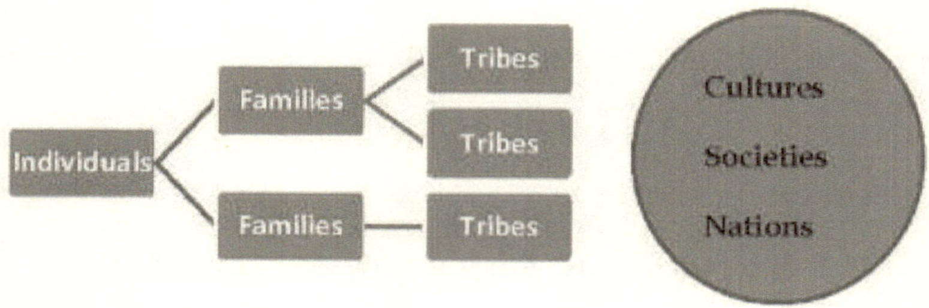

The Boston bombings, the Fort Hood shootings, the events of September 11, and terrorist activities worldwide, are only new to uninformed people or those who have a limited sense of history. Our earliest founders, in 1805 were familiar with *radical* Islamists. Thomas Jefferson, who was serving as the ambassador to France, and John Adams, the Ambassador to Britain, met in London with Ambassador Abdurrahman, Tripoli's ambassador to Britain, in an effort to negotiate a peace treaty. Peace for Islamist means, *"Surrender to Islam."*

Everlasting peace would cost $160,000 plus the mandatory commission. Moreover, this only applied to Tripoli. Other Muslim nations would also have to be paid. The total amount came to $1.3 million (big money at that time). There was also no assurance that the treaties would be honored. In vain, Jefferson and Adams tried to argue that America was not at war with Tripoli. In what way did the United States provoked the Muslims, they asked.

Ambassador Abdurrahman explained the finer points of Islamic jihad to Jefferson and Adams. In a letter to John Jay, Jefferson wrote, "The Ambassador answered us that it was founded on the Laws of their Prophet, that it was written in their Koran, that all nations who should not have acknowledged their authority were sinners. It was their right and duty to make war upon them wherever they could be found, and to make slaves of all they could take as prisoners, and that every [Muslim] who is slain in the battle was sure to go to Paradise."

Abdurrahman was paraphrasing the Koran's *"rules of engagement"* found in the Surah 47: *"Whenever you encounter the ones who disbelieve [during wartime], seize them by their necks until once you have subdued them, then tie them up as prisoners, either in order to release them later on, or also to ask for ransom, until war lays down her burdens."*

Unless a nation submits to Islam, that nation is, by definition, at war with Islam. Jihad means, *"To Submit."* A nonaggressive nation is still at war with Islam as long as it has not embraced Islam. Islam's goal is to conquer the world, either by the submission of one's will or by the **Sword of Allah.**

When President Jefferson refused to increase the tribute demanded by the Islamists, Tripoli declared war on the United States. A U. S. navy squadron, under Commander Edward Preble, blockaded Tripoli from 1803 to 1805. After rebel soldiers from Tripoli, led by United States Marines, captured the city of Derma, the Pasha of Tripoli signed a treaty promising to exact no more tribute.

Jefferson, embroiled in a war with Islamic terrorists in his day, commented, "Too long, for the honor of nations, have those Barbarians been suffered [permitted] to trample on the sacred faith of treaties, on the rights and laws of human nature!"

President Obama, in his Cairo speech in 2009 (See the Appendix) *rewrote or misunderstood* history when he stated, "I know, too, that Islam has always been a part of America's story. The first nation to recognize my country was Morocco. In signing the Treaty of Tripoli in 1796, our second President John Adams wrote, "The United States has in itself no character of enmity against the laws, religion or tranquility of Muslims."

Political and violent Islam goes back to Muhammad, in the seventh century, who massacred the Qurayzah tribe and the Jews of Khybar.
In Medina, he started waging war against non-Muslims, and he explained to his followers that they should offer non-Muslims three choices: "to convert to Islam; or submit as inferiors to Islamic rule, paying the tax and accept the discrimination that Islamic law mandates for non-Muslims in the Islamic state; or die."

The Qur'an says Jews are the "worst enemies" of the Muslims (Surah 5:82), saying that Allah cursed them and turned them into apes and pigs (Surah 2:62-66; 5:59-60; 7:166). In 1066, four thousand Jews in Granada were slaughtered by Muslim mobs. The Muslim chronicler Abdu Allah said that the mobs "put every Jew in the city to the sword and took vast quantities of their property."

In 1291, Isaac ben Samuel, a Palestinian Jew, said, "In the eyes of the Muslims, the children of Israel are as open to abuse as an unprotected field."

The philosopher Maimonides said: "You know my brethren that on account of our sins, God has cast us into the midst of this people, the nation of Ishmael, who persecute us severely, and who devise ways to harm us and to debase us. ... No nation has ever done more harm to Israel. None has matched it in debasing and humiliating us. None has been able to reduce us as they have. ... We have borne their imposed degradation, their lies, and absurdities, which are beyond human power to bear."

What was the reason for the 9/11 attack on the United States by Osama Bin Laden? It was on 9/11 in 1683, when the Ottoman Turks lost their most significant battle to the Christian King of Poland, and European forces, at the Gates of Vienna. Osama's *primary* motive, I believe, was vengeance for this major historical defeat.

A "sample" of some of the key Islamic beliefs, teachings and acts in the Koran are Allah [God] is Radically Transcendent, Unapproachable, and Unknowable. Allah is not Father, but Master, and Orders [all] slaves to obey His rules. Men are above Women because Allah made Men Superior to Women. Paradise to Muslims is a place of Milk and Honey, Women and Sensory Pleasures. Muhammad should forgive infidels (Surah 15:85); Muhammad should not forgive infidels (Surah 9:73). People of the Book—the Jews and Christians, shall be saved (Surah 5:69).
Salvation is only for Muslims (Surah 3:85). Allah's words do not change (Surah 6:15); Allah's words change [as we choose] (Surah 2:106). Allah dictated the Koran, through the Angel Gabriel to Muhammad (Surah 81:25). Some are contradictory Sarah's; however, Muhammad could not read or write, and depended on followers to document his thoughts.

In 2017, the White House released a list of 110 terrorist attacks in the United States during the last five years. Samples of acts of terrorism includes worldwide terrorism, such as the Marine Barracks attack in Lebanon; Lockerbie Airline explosion; USS Cole explosion. Domestic terrorism attacks or attempts includes: the 9/11 terrorist attack in NYC, D.C., PA; the LA Airport attempted attack; NJ Army Base attempted attack; Shoe Bomber and Underwear Bomber attempts; Fort Hood and Chattanooga killings; NYC Christmas terrorism attempts (twice); the Boston bombing; the San Bernardino; and Orlando, Florida attacks.

Have Americans become blind to the power of *fundamentalist* Islamic tribal forces? When groups feel threatened, they retreat into tribalism, to become insular, more defensive against their perceived enemies, such as recent Sunni vs. Shia sectarian battles. *The West had better wake-up to this reality!*

**

DREAM OF EXPLOITS

*"Dare to live the life you have dreamed for yourself.
Go forward and make your dreams come true."*

—Ralph

An exceptionally large, pale full moon lingered in the west, as the bright crimson sun emerged on the horizon, through the haze in the east. Something was different, puzzling that morning, as Vincent Renaldo looked up at the mysterious sky from his St. Regis hotel window overlooking Central Park in New York City.

At 9 AM, Vincent arrived at the Javitts Center, a little nervous. He was the keynote speaker at a technology conference. His speech focused on a popular book he helped to create, *Waves of Change*. It would be the most important presentation he would ever make. He grasped his topic better than most experts did. He meticulously prepared. More importantly, he totally believed in what he would say. That conviction would be contagious to the thousands of delegates there.

Vince did not want to leave the audience with merely a list of general technology trends, but something more, something to connect these worldwide developments to that which they would be able to personally appreciate and relate to. Vince ended his speech with a summary of the actual impact various technologies will have on each person, within our society, in the 21st century:

Nature, as we know it, cannot exist without ants, he said. If you study ants, you will find that they all have specific functions in life. There are worker ants, food gatherer ants, defender or warrior ants, babysitter ants and the queen ant. If one could interview worker ants and ask them what they contribute to the anthill, the workers would reply, "We do not know anything about the structure of the anthill; all we do is walk around and if anyone sees a grain of sand fall down, we put it back on top." If you converse with food gatherer ants, they would answer, "I don't know anything about anthill building. All I know is that when I find food, I leave a chemical trail to inform the other food gatherer ants and we all bring it back to the anthill." If you ask a defender or warrior ants, they might answer, "My only job is to look out for invaders. When I see any, I inform my fellow warriors and we attack them."

None of the millions of ants knows anything about the entire structure and function of the anthill. Yet, they all contribute to the success of the anthill, *without* any global blueprint or central plan. In essence, the Web, and the Internet "cloud," and all of our financial systems are similar to an anthill. It is a large, complex system, where no single person or group is in charge of controlling its vast overall operation. Yet, millions of user clients and thousands of network server programmers (worker ants) are constantly accessing the Internet Cloud, working to expand its capability. As we begin this new millennium, the fundamental engines of change are:

Globalization: The emergence of over half the world's population into the capitalist system, especially China, India and Middle Eastern countries.

Demographics: Aging of the population in developed countries, especially in Japan, Europe and the United States, and the immigration of Moslem populations into the UK and the EU, will have a *profound impact* on political systems, on local economies, on crime rates and politics. "Echo Boomers"—children of Baby Boomers, will also represent a new market and huge force.

Technology: global competitiveness will force more companies to restructure themselves, outsource nonessential activities, and downsize to remain competitive. Microcomputers and communications will have widespread implications for how we work and live together. Telecommuting (working at home) will increase as 5G communication networks improve significantly.

Terrorism: Radical Islam and other "brain washed" terrorists will have oil money and technology (Weapons of Mass Destruction) and cause orders-of-magnitude damage to our Judo-Christian societies, on a worldwide scale.

After the conference, Vincent agreed to meet the chief executive of a software and consulting company, for lunch. Charley Lansky, the CEO of Computer Techniques and Systems, reminded Vincent of a dwarf version of *Lenin*, with his perfectly trimmed goat tee beard, shiny almost baldhead, five foot-five frame and charismatic personality. Those dark-brown eyes seemed to penetrate ones' soul. He sensed immediately if you are *for real*, or just another bullshit artist.

Vincent reminded Charley of himself, when he was just starting out to establish his company ten years ago. His presentation perfectly harmonized with many of his own ideas about the future direction of technology and the information industry. "Maybe he is too conservative, Charley thought. Would Vincent be willing to take risks? Does he have that adventuresome spirit which I had at his age?"

During lunch, Charley immediately got to the point. "That was a great presentation! Why don't you join me at CTS? I really need your perspective, your strategic vision ... your creative ideas in my firm."

"Well ... thanks Charley. I really appreciate your sincere compliments. I do not think I could go back to the hassles of New York City, after being away for so many years. Look, I have a big mortgage, a spouse in the healthcare profession, and two kids; both of them expect to start college next year. I can't afford such a drastic change."

"All your arguments all seem to point to money. Naturally, I'll give you an increase that will more than meet your needs."

"Thanks, but it's not just about money. I cannot up-root my family at this time. Besides, how would I really fit into your organization? What could I *actually* contribute to your business?"

"You will report to me directly, as my new strategic planning executive, and also help me with my speeches. I will increase your salary by ... say fifty percent. That should cover any cost-of-living concerns. You can also use one of the CTS empty apartments in the city, until you move your family. What do you think?"

Charley Lansky was not the kind of person to accept no for an answer. His style and guts gave him the competitive edge over much larger, more rigid, and predictable firms, like AT&T, GE, IBM, and Microsoft. His success in business was based on his keen human and business instincts. Charley explained that he started CTS with only $5,000. He grew the firm to a multimillion-dollar enterprise, in only ten years. He hired all sorts of bizarre people: young bright kids just out of college, immigrants from Israel, Europe, Russia, and Iran. Some did not have much college education, but they were willing to learn if given a chance. He gave them a chance; he took the risk and those opportunities he offered them resulted in a very dedicated and intelligent work force.

Charlie's job offer began to intrigue Vincent. "What specifically would I do for you and your firm? Do you have some kind of job description?" he inquired.

"Write your own job description. I want you to setup a technology-planning group. Let's call it, TAG, for Technology Analysis Group. It will be your own profit center, and I'll give you 10% of the profits. It doesn't have to be located in the 'Big Apple' either."

Charlie's proposal was direct. He cut through all the crap, and got right to the important aspects of the deal. I was impressed with Charlie's unorthodox approach, his instincts and his ability to make quick decisions. Maybe this is the challenge I have been looking for. Perhaps an executive position with a much smaller firm is the answer to my urge to break out of my mundane job. Am I compatible with his temperament and personality? Would my business methods conflict with his way of doing things? I should insist on an employment agreement to protect my ass, in case I do not fit.

"If I accept your offer, it would mean a total change for my wife Susan and me and the kids. It is going to disrupt all the plans we made. Would you be agreeable to some kind of contract? Perhaps a two year agreement?"

"*Absolutely!* Sure! I'll fax a draft for your lawyer to review today,"

"I don't expect any guarantees. You know I can't just up-root my family, without some assurances ... I need to know the exact role I would play in your organization."

"Of course! I understand what you're saying, entirely. Do we have a deal?"

"I'll have to discuss it with my wife, Charley. Please send a draft of the employee contract and give me a few days to consider your kind offer."

***

The next night Vincent awoke early from an intense nightmare. He could still remember faint, obscure mental images from his turbulent dream. There were mental pictures of a wild, crazy escapade. It involved a misadventure in a foreign country. An extremely sexy woman, with sad green eyes, tried to seduce him. He could not resist her. Suddenly she turned into a weird creature with a long tail, which was pulling him down. The more he fought, the more her long tail kept pulling him in deeper and deeper, like *quicksand*.

All at once, a brilliant heavenly woman appeared. He could not see her face clearly because of the radiant white light, but he remembered her golden hair and deep-blue eyes. Her blouse was white with gold trim. She held rosary beads of bright blue crystals. The dazzling light from the beads caused the creature to recoil and run away. The only message from that celestial person, which he could still remember, that he *could not forget, was "Always remember, I love you. The Master will be coming. I will be with you again, very soon."*

Fig 1. Heavenly Blond Woman

Light from the blue crystals then shined much brighter, which jolted him awake. That nightmare left him in a cold sweat, restless and anxious. He had intense dreams in the past, but they were merely disjointed fragments of events that did not make much sense, which quickly faded from memory.

As Vincent finished breakfast in his room, he watched people below his hotel window rushing to work, just like thousands of worker ants. Ants have a well-regulated social structure, he thought. They are like tiny, preprogrammed robots, where each has a specific function—and they all cater to *a single queen.* I am just like one of those ants, he thought. I am a slave to the queen ant, called Corporate America.

While shaving he looked into the bathroom mirror. His thoughts quickly shifted to his uneventful existence: We are born, spend decades getting educated, find a job, get married, procreate, reach maturity—and finally die. Our children and grandchildren repeat that same cycle. Is this what human existence is all about? I just turned forty-five. I am at the prime of my life. What in hell have I really achieved? What is missing from my dismal life? Why can't I be content like most people?

Vincent had grown up in Brooklyn, New York. You had to be "street-smart," and tough to survive in Brooklyn. As long as he could recall, he rarely followed the crowd, or accepted the prevailing opinions of others. He was independent, a loner—always a maverick. He was *"a wild duck that would not fly in formation."*

His late father, William, experienced the Great Depression and gave him one piece of advice that he *rarely* followed. "If you feel like criticizing anyone," he remarked, "remember that many people in this world haven't had the advantages and opportunities you've had."

The family was relatively poor. Vincent did not have all the benefits that many of his peers had, so he did not understand what "advantages and opportunities" his father was promoting. His dad also taught him that all truth begins with lies. "Everybody lies," he said. "You must inquire, question, scrutinize everything. **It's not what people say—it's what they do that really counts!"**

That was advice that Vince generally followed. When he did not follow these words of wisdom, or did not trust his basic instincts, the result was usually unpleasant. His close friends knew him to be logical, decisive, honest, and also a bit unpredictable or radical, but *very humane.*

Unlike most of his peers, Vince was a virgin, at that time. Perhaps it was his faith, but he could not regard any woman as merely a "sex object."

When Vince was in military service, his friends took him to Nogales, a border town in Mexico to have a good time, and get laid. When they arrived in the local bar, the women were dressed in low-cut blouses and short dresses. They looked them over and joined them at their table. These were aggressive prostitutes. They began feeling him under the table. Vincent did not like this vulgarity or the woman with bad teeth and garlic breath that sat next to him. He noticed a more attractive, taller blonde-haired female near the bar. He went outside to get a shoeshine from some kid, which was just an excuse to get away from that repulsive prostitute. Upon returning, Vince selected the cute bleached blonde-haired person. After he bought her a few drinks, she immediately took him upstairs to a private room. Vincent asked, "Please change the soiled sheets on the bed."

Bewildered by his strange request, she changed the linen anyway, and undressed at once, as if her "meter" was running. Vincent tried to talk with her, but she pretended she did not understand, except when he asked her why she did this kind of work. Her reply was simple, "My baby needs milk."

How could he criticize a mother struggling to feed her baby? She had a great ass, although her young breasts drooped a bit. He took out a sketchpad from his satchel and began drawing her. "That will cost extra," she said.

He tossed a twenty on the bed. "I don't like quickies." Again, she did not understand. It turned out to be a crude experience without feelings. Because he was afraid of VD, he did not have sex. After that tasteless, crude experience, Vincent promised himself that he would never get involved with prostitutes—*never ever again!*

***

When Vincent Renaldo completed military service, he accepted a job at Columbia University, in upper New York City. During a Halloween party, he met Susan at a college dance. Her dark alluring Spanish eyes, her rosy lips, her lustrous black hair and exotic beauty attracted him. As Vince grew to know Susan better, her charming personality, remarkable dancing style and fantastic shape impressed him even more. She had a congenial personality and a natural smile that made everyone feel at ease.

He and Susan dated as often as their studies allowed, typically once a week. They often met at the NY library, on 42 Street. He helped her with homework. They kissed passionately, but her religious faith restrained them from going all the way. At the relatively young age of twenty-six Vincent finally proposed to Susan.

It seemed ridiculous, but he agreed to ask Susan's stepfather for her hand in marriage, as she requested. Vince wanted a simple ceremony, but ultimately conceded to her wishes for a big church wedding. *Amazingly,* a white dove (symbol of the Holy Spirit) came into the church and flew over their heads, during the wedding service.

After the reception, they arrived at their apartment in upper Manhattan, the Washington Heights section of the city. It was a simple, one-bedroom apartment. At that time, they only had a bed, a couch and kitchen table. Nevertheless, that small flat had a great view of the Hudson River and George Washington Bridge.

Vincent got into bed. As he reached for Susan, he was surprised that she still had her clothes on. "What's this?"

"I'm still a virgin, you know. Vince, let's go slowly, okay?"

"Sure, but at least take off your dress." She removed her dress under the sheets. They talked for hours about their plans, before he finally took her in his arms.

They struggled for years and gradually, moved up the economic ladder. In time, they saved enough to buy a charming home in suburban Philadelphia. Their first girl, Amy, was born one year later, followed by a son, Robert, eighteen months afterward.

As new parents, they made one major mistake, which did not become evident until it was almost too late. That mistake was sending their first child to an elite private pre-school, which spoiled her. Amy demanded *things* that her schoolmates had and she could not appreciate that her parents were not in the same economic league. They pulled their son out of that exclusive school before he developed similar traits.

As the children became teenagers, Susan did not think they were spoiled. She said, "We should thank God! In comparison to other children, our kids are good. After all, they don't have sex, drug, or drinking problems, and all the other foolish hang-ups that other kids have in today's society."

"That's how they should be!" Vince responded. *That's the norm!* What have they done that goes beyond these basic traits? Why should we lower our standards to conform to others? I didn't have half the economic benefits that they have today." (Then he remembered what his dad told him decades ago: "If you feel like criticizing anyone, remember that many people in this world haven't had the advantages and opportunities you've had").

They were opposites in many ways: Susan saw the cup half-full; Vincent saw it half-empty. She emphasized the positive; he was not cynical nor negative, but was more pragmatic. She was sentimental; he was the "deep thinker"—more systematic and discerning in his thought processes.

The loss of their third infant, a boy born three months premature, affected them both terribly. The doctor found a noncancerous tumor in Susan, and removed both ovaries *without* Vincent's knowledge or consent. He was away on business overseas at the time. After he learned about her inability to have more children, it disturbed him *enormously.*

The children had now grown and both were in college. They would be alone together for the first time in twenty years. Now, at forty-five, Vincent was going through a kind of "mid-life crisis." He awakened that day in New York City, and *questioned everything:* Why am I here? What am I doing with my life? What's my purpose? His mind was perplexed, everything was in question; all was disorder, and his reaction against that disorder caused more disorder, more confusion. He was disgusted with everything about his routine, predictable, suburban life.

Vincent knew he had to breakout of this mundane existence in which he felt ensnared. After ten years working for the same company, he felt *trapped.* He was tired of the internal politics and all the corporate infighting. The web of management politics and intrigue stifled his mind, as it would repress any creative mind. The arrogant president of the corporation surrounded himself with "ass-kissing" executives, who were afraid to tell him the truth about the *real* state of the business and the competition.

Those make-no-waves managers only told the boss what he wanted to hear. They filtered-out analysis, especially anything negative. They presented the CEO with sugarcoated reports. Vince knew that information, more precisely **intelligent information was**

real power. To know what is going on, or better yet, what is likely to happen, gave one more power than any other sources. Management, nevertheless, said his competitive views and forecasts were *too onerous:* "Vincent, you must tone down your competitive assessments," his boss Josh, demanded.

"You hired me for my expertise, for my experience at intelligence gathering ability. Why don't you let me do my job? You know the quality of my sources. Why should I water down my candid analysis of the real facts?"

"It's your subjective analysis that management doesn't like. Just provide them with objective raw data, and leave out your interpretations. Let the executives determine what is important, not you. They are the decision-makers. They see the big picture. Every time you write this kind of stuff, you piss-off important top executives."

"Look, everybody knows that raw data, without any context, without intelligent analysis, is *really crap!* Raw data can be easily misunderstood," Vince argued.

"Do you recall that old story about 'the messenger that brought the king bad news?' He lost his head, didn't he?" Josh answered.

Vincent grasped his point. Office flunkies must cow-tow to loftier executives. He was a maverick in a corporation that was increasingly anti-intellectual, conformist, and bureaucratic. He had to get away from this "crap-trap." His talents were wasted. He debated within himself about changing jobs, after ten years with the same firm. Yet he knew that job security with a bigger firm was really *an illusion.* Many larger corporations, such as leading financial and technology firms, Citicorp, AT&T, and IBM had been downsizing, and thousands of talented dedicated employees lost their jobs. Would his company be next? With his reputation for fighting "the system," he might be the first to go, when the inevitable downsizing ax falls.

Vincent Renaldo finally made a *crucial decision.* He would accept Charley's job offer. It was a great opportunity. *He could not refuse this new and exciting adventure.*

***

PARISIAN BEAUTY

"What you do, the way you think, makes you Beautiful."

—Scott Westfield

He could not keep his eyes off her during the concert. Her oval face with its pale pink hue did not reveal a single blemish, for a Parisian woman in her mid-twenties, except for an exotic intriguing small black mole that harmonized with her soft mouth. The mouth was perfectly sculptured; its lips formed sensuous ruby curves, with only an illusion of lipstick. Her long golden yellow hair glimmered with silky highlights that reflected the light. Those large deep-blue eyes glistened and seemed to hint that she knew your inner secrets.

While her expression was a little sad, she engendered great hope whenever she smiled. Her demeanor was humble and courteous, yet she appeared to be quite confident. There existed an overall feeling of *mystery* about this woman, as if ordinary humans could not explore her "cosmic nature."

The tall naturally tanned young man, with dark wavy hair sat one row behind her, to her right. She felt his eyes on her. When she finally sneaked a glimpse of him over her shoulder, she thought he looked like the late handsome actor, Tyrone Power. Anne could not conceal her adoring smile. It was an innocent, impulsive reaction.

During intermission, he finally got up enough courage to introduce himself. "Hello. I am Armin. I saw you sitting alone and thought you might like to share a glass of champagne with me."

"Bon Jour. I am pleased to meet you. I'm Anne," she responded, with a captivating, enchanting smile. "S'il vous plait, I would love some champagne."

He guided her to the reception area. His fascinating seductive black eyes did not deviate from her as they talked. Instant rapport existed between them, without any need for words. Armin explained that he was an Iranian alien, a student in Paris who desperately wanted to stay in beautiful, exciting France, when his visa expired next month.

"I have good contacts in the government. Maybe I can help in some small way. That is, if you want my assistance,"

"But you don't really know me," he replied. "Why would you want to help a stranger?"

"Do we ever really know anyone, *completely*?" she asked. "Do you have any employment opportunities lined up after your courses finish?"

"No, but I certainly will look for something, if that's required."

"But of course. *It is essential.* They will not extend your visa without a job or other means of support you know. Why don't you meet me tomorrow? We can discuss it further."

The bell rang for the concert to start again. Anne hastily wrote her phone number on the back of an envelope. She could not let him slip away, if she could do anything in her power to prevent it. Anne was a virgin in her mid-twenties, which is remarkable for a young beauty, especially in easy-going Paris, where early sexual experiences were so commonplace.

The following afternoon, they talked for hours over coffee at a sidewalk cafe, near Notre Dame. Their eyes and body language spoke more than any words could express. She arranged everything for him: a small apartment on the left bank of Paris, temporary residency status and employment as a real estate clerk, when his classes ended at the end of the month.

Fig 2. Paris at night

Anne's eighty-year-old, very traditional mother and father *totally disapproved* of Armin because he was of the Islamic faith. She would secretly meet with him anyway, almost daily. They spent hours together talking and holding hands in the park and cafes. They were decorating his apartment together. It was a small one room flat, with a kitchenette and pull-out bed hidden in the sofa. It was located on the left bank of Paris, near her former art school and it had a nice view of the Seine below.

She served lunch, which she had bought from the local market. Cold chicken, salad, bread and wine, with a mixture of different cheeses were the menu of the day. They talked about the beauty of Paris, about all the historical places to see, her particular interest was in the fine arts, woman's fashions, and import-export trade.

He said, "I received my French passport, thanks to your efforts. I'll be looking for a better job, as soon as my final exams are over." That afternoon, he held the ladder for her as Anne hung the drapes she carefully altered for his windows. They both became a little tipsy from the red wine, which affected her more than he did. Armin began kissing her bare foot. "Please don't do that, Armin," she pleaded. Her voice betrayed that she really did not want him to stop.

He ignored her pleas. His stimulating touch and kisses aroused feelings in her that she had never experienced before. Armin carried her off the ladder on to the sofa. His kissing grew more aggressive. She could not stop him—she did not want to stop him. The delicate texture and smell of her soft skin and hair reminded him of pink rose pedals. His gentle touching awakened intense passionate feelings that had remained dormant in her—far too long. Her heart began beating like a drum. She thought he might hear its rapid loud pounding.

"Armin, I must tell you I'm still a virgin. Please understand, I must remain untouched until I'm married, my darling."

"Don't worry Anne, I'll be gentle and respect your wishes."

Never did she experience such exhilaration, such passion. Shivers ran up her body as he reached her breasts, cupping them in both hands. "Turn over so that I can massage your back," he instructed.

She promptly obeyed. His sweet gentle manner caused her body to become more relaxed. "I'm sorry, Armin darling, you're getting me too excited. Please stop!"

He ignored her pleas. Anne quickly regained control over her emotions. *"Stop!"* she demanded.

He was frustrated, but stopped. They fell asleep in each other's arms.

Thereafter, Armin attempted to dominate her life. He told her how to dress, where to go, what to do, and she nearly followed his dictates, without question. Anne became utterly devoted to him.

Seven weeks later, they traveled to Iran to meet his mother and father, to announce their engagement, and receive their blessing. While in Iran, Anne immersed herself for many hours and days studying their language, traditions, customs, history, and the lifestyles of this strange country. She wore the traditional black dress and veil, as *he instructed* her to do whenever they walked in the city. Her loyalty and devotion to her lover *became* absolute! Anything he wanted or needed, she granted without the slightest hesitation, *except sex.*

Anne's parents said they would cut her out of their will, when she shocked them by announcing they planned to marry. Since her thriving electronics import/export, and fashion business made her independently wealthy, she did not care. In spite of her youth, Anne was an exceptional businessperson. A single big order from the United States would earn her 500,000 Euros. She learned how to skillfully trade and close big business deals from her grandfather, the late Count du Chardonnay.

The following summer Anne and Armin traveled together to Southern California. They rented an apartment for the week near a beach in La Jolla. One of Anne's biggest clients had a chain of fifty-six stores throughout the States, and she had important business meetings with them in San Diego. She had to leave Armin alone in order to consummate one of her biggest trade deals.

Finally, after three days of intensive effort, Anne successfully completed the business transaction. To celebrate her success, she stopped to buy Armin a gift and a bottle of champagne. As she entered the apartment, strange sounds came from the upstairs living room. She climbed the stairs quickly. It sounded as though he was struggling with someone, and in great pain. What she saw shook Anne to the roots of her soul. Her fiancé was having sex with the young hotel domestic worker on the living room couch. Anne screamed and threw the gift at him.

The shocked girl quickly put on her clothes and departed, as Armin tried to console Anne. "I'm so sorry, darling. You left me here all alone in this strange country. I became lonely and happened to meet someone from my country. All men need sex; it is natural. It is not my fault. She seduced me! She doesn't mean anything to me."

"Right, blame it on her. You had nothing to do with it, I suppose. She is just a 'female object' who seduced you. *You're a real bastard!"*

Anne regained her composure, and packed her bags. Armin got down on his knees and begged her to forgive him. She caught the next flight back to Paris, *alone.* Her first romance came to an abrupt tragic ending. How could the person she adored so much, destroy everything? Anne finally understood that his love for her was *conditional, selfish love,* which is not real love at all.

*****

New York City: Vincent Renaldo left his steady secure job as a senior competitive intelligence and planning analyst for one of the largest computer firms in the world, to join a much smaller software and consulting firm, CTS in mid-town, New York City. After tough negotiating, Charley Lansky nearly doubled his salary and provided a company paid apartment on the upper eastside, on 82nd Street, until he relocated his family. It was a once in a lifetime opportunity that was difficult—*impossible to refuse.* The employment agreement seemed reasonable. It gave Vincent a two-year guarantee, a sense of security, in case this new relationship proved to be short-lived.

Vincent was surprised to find that he enjoyed the big city, after being away from it for so many years. It was adventurous, especially at night. The cosmopolitan lifestyle also caused him a kind of haunting loneliness, which he felt in others who sat all alone, wasting the most precious moments of their lives.

He arrived the first day at his new job, at 53rdrd and Madison Avenue. His first thoughts were about his "VP executive status," his private office, the personal secretary that he would hire. He was exhilarated, excited, and eager to establish new friendships and business relationships. There was not any welcoming committee. Nobody seemed to know that the new executive, the vice president had arrived. "What's going on? Where's my office?"

Everyone seemed puzzled by his questions. He went immediately to see Charley. Before he could express his disappointment, Charley interrupted.

"Vincent, very glad to see you ... welcome on board! Do you have a passport?"

"Sure, I got it renewed last month. Why?"

"We're going to Iran together, *right now*. Pack your bags!"

"What's it all about? I'll have to call Susan."

"I'll explain later. Call her at the airport."

On the way to the airport, Charley explained that CTS has a large staff of software specialists in Iran, working on their computer system. Iran was the fourth largest military power in the world. The Iranian finance minister refused to pay CTS some five million dollars of long-overdue invoices for software development work they completed, months ago.

"Charley, I really don't know anything about Iran ... Why don't you send someone with more knowledge, more experience?"

"You don't need to know anything about this *bullshit* country. You're a strategic intelligence expert ... Right now, I need some kind of strategy ... I need your strategic planning skills."

They traveled together in first class, which was nearly empty. (It was not a popular tourist vacation spot, even during those earlier years). The flight to Tehran would take about 18 hours. The long trip gave Vincent an opportunity to study Charlie's way of thinking and his novel approach to business. He freely offered his candid points-of-view on many, many things. Vincent kept occupied studying business documents and Iranian travel brochures, at a distance, but could not ignore Charlie's off-colored jokes with the passengers. This person is outlandish, he thought.

Ultimately, Charley got around to telling Vincent the whole story and history of CTS, and its involvement in Iran. Some years ago, before our State department put limits on dealing with Iran, CTS won a fifty-million-dollar contract to develop an inventory control system for Iran. The first phase was completed about two years ago, and Iran paid $25 million. The second phase also finished, almost on time, but the final payment was three months over-due. The Iranian officials came up with all kinds of delaying tactics. Charlie's street-smart sense told him there *must be* "other reasons." He would find out what they were.

They arrived at Mehrabad International airport at 10 AM. Guards with machine guns were stationed at all strategic points and exits. They examined them scrupulously before their passports were finally stamped. After arriving in the city and checking into the Hyatt Crown Regency, Charley directed that they should drop off their baggage and go to the computer site, immediately.

The city looked very clean. Traffic was light (there was a shortage of gasoline) as the cab driver explained, as he took them to the computer site, about fifteen minutes away. A staff of fifty-one engineers, mostly software types, was anxiously waiting for the boss. The office had skimpy furniture and looked very messy with lots of boxes containing computer printouts, everywhere. "What's our status? *I don't want any bullshit!* Give it to me straight," he demanded.

The chief software engineer, Jon Cooper, obviously a native New Yorker from his accent, explained the situation. "The government is having a lot of internal problems. They are holding back on payments to all contractors. Some kind of religious fanatic is causing lots of trouble with foreigners, especially Americans, after the CIA discovered a new nuclear facility near their holy city. The U. S. is pressing for new stronger sanctions against Iran. As a result, the military leaders and government of Iran are pissed.

"The Iranian finance minister, Ben Amir, who controls the purse strings, arranged a meeting, yesterday. You remember him Charley, don't you? He's the guy with a big head, long mustache and short legs."

"Yeah, that's the cagey *son-of-a-bitch* who has been bullshitting me." "Ben Amir told me that CTS must pay him $50,000 in cash, *immediately,* and put another $50,000 in his confidential Swiss bank account, by next week. Then he *might* authorize the final payment due us. Can you believe that crap?"

Reasonable bribes of about five or six percent of the contract is common, "normal" in *all* Middle East business deals. However, CTS profit margins was only about 25%. This sizable payoff might screw-up the bottom-line. In addition, Charley had no guarantee that this bastard would actually approve the final payment, or maybe the Iranian check would bounce.

After Charley heard the full story from his staff and better understood the real situation, he arranged to setup a meeting with the Iranian Minister. Ben Amir. Charley knew that the Iran secret police bugged *all* foreign hotel rooms, so he insisted on a private rendezvous, out-of-town.

The Iranian concluded the short meeting by stating firmly: "It would be in *your personal* interest, and good for the health of your people, if you confirmed the cash in my account by next week, *at the latest.* No payoff, no check!" was Ben Amir's statement.

Following that meeting, Charley arranged a confidential conference over dinner, with Vincent and selected members of his staff, away from the hotel, which he knew was bugged. They drove to a quaint little restaurant just outside of the city.

The fresh roasted lamb and spices was strange to Vincent's taste, but exquisite. After hours of discussion of possible alternatives, which did not resolve anything, Charley said emphatically, "I'm not going to pay any bribe. Unless someone has a good idea to save the situation, we better plan on closing our operations here ... *immediately.*"

Vincent then came up with an idea, a strategic plan, which he called "Trojan Horse." He explained that their software experts could plant destructive program codes in the military computer system, which would become automatically activated, in the event of threats to the staff, or if they failed to pay any money due by a definitive date.

"Exactly how would that work?" the boss asked.

"Their supply system is highly centralized, right? They depend on this computer system for locating all the components and subassemblies, for maintaining aircraft, tanks, trucks, electronic equipment—*everything.* The idea is simple. A software virus is *covertly* planted in the inventory control system. It has a timing mechanism that will automatically trigger and scramble the database, the application software programs, and then self-destruct. Naturally we must also erase all back-up copies of any files as well with a strong magnet."

"What if they put our asses in jail until we fix it?" Charley asked.

"If anything happens like that, we can claim it's *merely* a software bug, and send for backup copies from New York. At least that will give us a good bargaining position, and buy us more time," Vincent answered.

"Look, there is a good possibility that the current leader might be over-thrown by the radical Muslims anyway, right?

President Ahmadinejad had warned Western leaders against their military adventurism. Government beatings, arrests, show trials and killings have nevertheless failed to discourage Iranians from taking to the streets in protest."

Charlie added, "The destructive virus would give CTS and the U.S. the ability to destroy the entire computer supply system, especially if it falls into the hands of those fanatics." He immediately approved the plan. "If they don't pay us for services rendered, those swindlers will lose everything. We had better pay Ben Amir his initial $50,000 right away, to avoid suspicion. Start planning our exit strategy, before that 'software bug' starts ticking."

It was late January, when the escape plans were completed. It was just in time, since the government had begun stirring-up the religious fanatics. Meanwhile, Charley arranged to purchase a used bus to take his CTS team out of Iran, over the border to Turkey. "We will all act like tourists returning home as a cover-up for the trip," he ordered. "If you don't have a camera, buy one. I want most of you to wear baseball caps, sneakers and typical tourist clothes."

A second revolution or major battle between the voting youth (about 70% of the population is under 30 years old) and the older Imam Government controlled party was quickly brewing over the "alleged fixed election results." Charley's team could be caught in the middle of this political storm.

The *Wall Street Journal* wrote, "The Obama administration is increasingly questioning the long-term stability of Tehran's government and moving to find ways to support Iran's opposition 'Green Movement,'" said senior U.S. officials. "Cutting off foreign gasoline supplies to Iran was being considered."

Leaving from the airport was too risky. Government agents would wonder why such a large group (especially Americans) that worked in Iran for years was abruptly leaving. Besides, some of the exit visas for the local staff were *counterfeit.* Operation *Trojan horse* would go into effect in 72 hours. The fanatical Iranian leaders would have trouble finding a screwdriver, even a fuse, never mind the tens-of-thousands of spare parts needed for their huge war machine. We would be doing America and Obama's administration a big favor.

Although he did not ask us to do it and probably would not approve of our actions.

At about that time, President Obama was an "apology tour," where he told his Cairo audience, America was acting like "colonialists" during the Bush administration. He told the French, "America has shown arrogance and had been dismissive, even derisive" toward Europe, and showed reservations about support for Israel, especially if they did not stop housing construction, without any requirements for Hamas to stop their terrorist activities. (Hamas has been in control of Palestine since 2007. During the past five years, the Obama administration gave $3.5 billion to Hamas terrorists). In Prague, he said, "America has a moral responsibility to act on arms control because only the U.S. had used a nuclear weapon."

Obama chanted the opening lines of the Muslim "Call to Prayer" in Arabic, with what Nicholas Kristof, in his interview on March 6th, 2007, says is a first class accent, and then, Obama goes on to volunteer that this is *"One of the Prettiest Sounds On Earth At Sunset."* Here is what this "Call to Prayer" says:

> "Allah is Supreme! Allah is Supreme!
> Allah is Supreme! Allah is Supreme!
> I witness that there is no god but Allah
> I witness that there is no god but Allah
> I witness that Muhammad is his prophet…"

This opening section incorporates the *Shahada,* the Muslim confession of faith, and many Muslim say, ***"if a person recites these lines, a person thereby becomes, for all time, a Muslim."***

Surely, this is something Obama knows based on his early education in Indonesia, from the age of six to ten. He also bowed to the Saudi King on his trip to Saudi Arabia. He did not show such reverence to the Queen of England, or the Pope.

***

Escape to Turkey. That weekend, all of the CTS staff took picnic lunches and only essential bags, and prepared for their hasty trip to Turkey.

Charley shouted commands, like a general: "Make sure everybody goes to the bathroom; we're not stopping for anyone to take a leak. Mike, leave that gear here; we have no space for your stereo. Jon, be certain that no one has any marijuana. We do not need any unnecessary problems at the border. Vincent, where's your damn baseball cap?"

The roads were good the first hundred miles or so, to Qazvin. Beyond this point, it was a two-lane blacktop road to Tabriz, which is about three hundred miles from Tehran. The bus became extremely hot as they made their way over desert like roads, until reaching the snowcapped mountains. The group had to stop to repair a blown tire. The bus stopped at two checkpoints along the way, but their papers appeared to be in order. Water was running low because some asses used it to wash and cool their faces.

They finally arrived near the Turkish border, at Barragan, some twelve hours later. There were two Iranian guards that one could see from the top of the hill overlooking the border. Everyone was extremely apprehensive about the counterfeit exit visas. "What if they stop us? Would they check with Tehran?" Charley asked. "That computer virus could have been discovered by now."

After discussing possible alternatives, everyone agreed on the next move; they had no other option. Charley said, "Stay cool! Act normal! Remember, you are merely tourists returning home. Take many pictures! Tell them how much you loved their wonderful culture and the illustrious history of Persian Iran."

Some of the staff took pictures with their arms around the guards, who seemed proud to pose with them. The guards searched the bus and found nothing to cause alarm. The chief sentry tried to call someone in Tehran. Everyone became *extremely frightened.* He could not get through due to massive strikes that existed throughout the city. Finally, after nearly an hour of discussion, our papers checked out and the guards waved the bus on. The no-man's-land between Iran and Turkey was about three hundred yards. It was the most anxious 300 yards they had ever driven in their lives.

In Turkey, they made their way from the city of Van, to the capital, Ankara, which was another 500 miles. The snowcapped mountains were beautiful. The group was not interested in sightseeing, however. The first five hours were *extremely* cold.

The bus climbed over steep dangerous mountain roads. Some of the passengers huddled together to stay warm.

Roadblocks were everywhere during the next sixty miles of the initial Turkey leg of the trip. Security guards stopped them frequently, checking for bandits, smugglers, or Kurds. The three Iranians who insisted on leaving with them, caused most of the delays. Passports were examine closely, with very *suspicious* eyes. There were no gas stations for about a two hundred-mile stretch of road in Iran and nearly one hundred miles in Turkey. They were lucky to have an extra 55-gallon drum of fuel under the back seats. That was Charlie's idea. He saved our asses.

Finally, the group arrived in Ankara. The stench of the city was overwhelming from garbage, pollution of coal fumes, and sulfur dioxide. Unfortunately, the next available flight to Europe was the following afternoon. They were forced to stay overnight at a dirty, roach infested hotel. Turkish roaches were the biggest, most aggressive bastards they had ever seen.

The airport the following day was a madhouse, with swarms of pushing, shoving humanity. Hours later, they boarded the flight to Paris, with connections to New York. The flight arrived at De Gaulle airport in Paris. The TV in the airport lounge showed the "newly elected" crazy leader in Tehran, with about two million screaming Iranians greeting him.

President Obama totally ignored the pleas of the hundreds-of-thousands of voting youth who pleaded for American support. They objected to the fraudulent election, but the Iranian Revolutionary Guards beat them into submission. We looked at each other in utter amazement. We had escaped just in time from a country that was about to go through another traumatic rebirth—a birth of *absolute lunacy.*

Meanwhile, CTS was in financial trouble. The company had lost $25 million from the sudden pullout from Iran. "That's about 30% of our total corporate revenues and over 50% of our expected profits this year," Charley announced to his assembled top executives. In addition, forty-seven people were now jobless, but at least they are not hostages. Charley found positions for eight of the key individuals; the rest would receive one month's pay, letters of recommendation and best wishes from the boss.

Vincent thought of another wild idea: Why not sell essentially the same or similar inventory control software to the Iraqi government. He learned from the software gurus, who have close contacts with their peers at other computer sites, that the Iraqi support system was extremely antiquated. Moreover, after the Iranian upheaval and the resulting economic chaos, Iraq, with enormous American aid, had become one of the largest military forces in the region. The United States government and its major allies sold them tens-of-billions of dollars' worth of military equipment, even though they *had not* updated their archaic inventory control system.

After some deliberation and debate with his executives, Charley accepted Vincent's proposal. He was sent off to Iraq, with a beautiful woman called Myram. Charley claimed she knew the Iraqi President and his family, *personally.* NSA and the State Department, under Hillary Clinton, also approved their plans.

On the flight to Iraq, Myram told Vincent that she was the former spouse of a diplomat in Iran, who became Ambassador to Switzerland, when the previous government was in power. "How did you escape?" he inquired.

"They imprisoned me in a small cell without any windows or light, for four months. When they finally let me go, I could not see for almost a week. These extremists shot my husband. They also confiscated our estates," she lamented, as her black eyes glazed over. "They finally allowed me to leave with my children and the clothes on my back, as these fanatics took over my country."

In spite of such a tragic experience and suffering, Myram still maintained her dignity and graceful style. Her jet-black hair, light olive skin, dark eyes and Persian features reminded Vincent of *Ava Gardner,* that exquisite actor that he remembered from the *Bare Foot Countess,* among other great movies. Myram became Charlie's new International Public Relations executive based in Milan, Italy. She spoke fluent English, Italian, French, German, and of course Arabic and Farsi. This widow of a diplomat knew most of the rich and powerful leaders, and key bankers of Europe, personally.

At the President's residence in Iraq, Myram introduced Vincent to the top leaders. Saddam insisted that CTS staff the project with some of his technical people, even though they really did not know shit about the design of the software system. Saddam's son-in-law would be to be in charge of the project. The Iraqi computer hardware was not compatible with the Iran's IBM system. A software conversion effort would be required. CTS would receive $60 million; a third paid in advance.

On the way back, from the meeting, Myram warned Vincent: "Please don't let *anyone* know that Charley Lansky is a Jew if CTS hopes to keep that contract."

***

Paris, France: The golden blond beauty rushed to catch a taxi in the pouring rain. To Anne's surprise, she found an attaché case on the floor next to the back seat, which someone had obviously forgotten. She opened it and was *astonished*. The case contained an American passport, thousands of dollars and Euros, a packet of gems, and important business papers. The driver noticed her find from the rearview mirror and *insisted* that he has to take responsibility for lost goods found in *his* taxi. Anne refused to yield. "No thanks. I'll handle it myself."

After many hours of calling telephone information service in New York, Anne finally reached the father of the person named in the passport, Robert E. Mellon, Jr. Mr. Mellon, Sr. was elated! "My son is very fortunate that such an honest woman found his attaché. I will call Robert in Paris, immediately. Bless you, my dear."

A few hours later, a very tall, distinguished looking individual, with salt and pepper gray and black hair, arrived at Anne's apartment overlooking the Eiffel Tower. His intelligent bright hazel eyes discreetly looked Anne over from head to foot. "Madam, please excuse my intrusion. I understand you found my attaché."

"Yes I found it in a taxi. Do you have identification?"

After he proved who he was, Anne immediately turned the briefcase over to him. Robert Mellon was thrilled. "If any other person found such a fortune, you could be sure that they would keep it," he said.

The next day, a courier from *Cartier* arrived at Anne's apartment. He presented her with a fantastic necklace. "What's this?" Anne was shocked.

"A small gift, a token of appreciation from Mr. Mellon," he answered.

"He doesn't have to give me a reward. Please thank him and take it back."

"But … Madam, I … I have *explicit* instructions from Mr. Mellon. He insisted that I leave this gift with you, *no matter what.* Why don't you return it to him yourself? Here's an invitation to meet him at Maxim's, tonight at 8 o'clock."

Anne agreed to meet Mr. Mellon for dinner. She wore her black velvet low-cut dress, to provide the best contrast for that exquisite diamond and ruby necklace, which she just might keep. She guessed his age to be about forty-five, nearly twenty years her senior. Despite his age, after her earlier bittersweet experience, Anne was ready to accept any decent, mature and *sincere* man that might come into her life.

After the fantastic dinner of cold poached salmon, topped with caviar, and magnum of Moet Champagne, Robert said, "I know you probably heard this before, but it's true—*you're really beautiful!* Your radiant face and golden hair reminds me of an angel. How come you're not married?"

"Well I almost was married about a year ago. I nearly made the biggest mistake of my life. It is a long story. Anyway, I found out that he was unfaithful—*just in time.*"

"How can any person be unfaithful to such a heavenly angel?" he answered.

After Robert convinced her of his sincerity, she kept the exquisite necklace.

Over the next six months, the relationship blossomed. Unlike Armin, Robert Mellon treated Anne with total respect. He did not tell her what to do, or how to act, and where to go, or otherwise dominate her life. His love for her was *unconditional love.* He put her on a pedestal, like a kind of princess.

They shared the simple things of the life, like walking in the park holding hands, going to church together, having a coffee while talking for hours, at the local sidewalk cafe. They kissed good-bye each evening and gradually became lovers, although they agreed that sex would *not* be part of their otherwise perfect union, until God blessed their marriage in church.

Robert Mellon was the only son of one of the biggest "old money" family banking institutions in the United States, the Mellon Banking Investment Company. Wedding invitations went out all over the world. This would be one of the biggest high-society weddings in New York City history.

A few close friends organized the Shower party for Anne, in Paris, two weeks before the wedding. Her aging parents were there and they voiced how pleased they now were with her new choice. Not only was he handsome, mature and very rich, he was a *Christian.*

Her girlfriends wanted to know where they planned to spend their honeymoon. "In the Swiss Alps," she explained. "Robert likes to ski and I bought him a new outfit for our trip. I also bought him a new Porsche, while we were in New York. He loves that car so much." They planned to live mostly in Paris, at least when Robert did not have to travel to the States on business.

Just as the group sat down for coffee and dessert, the phone rang. Her mother answered it. "It's from New York dear," she said, as she handed Anne the phone. The long-distance phone call was from Robert's father.

"No! No! My God, it's not possible!" Anne cried, as her body crumbled and fell to the floor.

Anne finally awoke in the hospital, the following morning. They eventually told her the whole story. Robert Mellon was traveling in his Porsche, at very high speed on Route 80, in Pennsylvania and hit a parked truck, which had no emergency lights on. The front-page news reports of his death said that his head was decapitated from his body. She became extremely depressed, *utterly devastated.* No one could console her after such a horrible unexpected turn of events in her life.

***

Connecticut: Vincent and Susan settled in Stamford in a charming house near a park. His daily commute to New York was not that bad. Vincent learned a lot from Charley, but after nearly two years, the future of CTS looked very shaky, again. Under financial pressure, Charlie's personality changed. He became extremely dictatorial. He seemed more brusque and hostile than on previous occasions – a man whose nerves were beginning to fray and pressure was mounting. Why it took so long to discover this side of him, Vincent wondered. He dominated all staff meetings with his executives. His vice presidents were afraid to speak up or refute the boss.

During one weekly staff meeting, Charley seemed to lose control. He asked the marketing executive, "Why are your sales down *again,* for the second straight month?" Not waiting for a reply, he threatened him with dismissal if he did not do better next month. He then barked: "What asshole produced this company brochure, *without* my approval?"

Vincent decided not to take any of his crap, especially in front of his peers. "I designed that brochure," he announced loudly. "What's wrong with it? Charley, if you have a problem with my work, see me when you are in a better mood." He immediately walked out of the staff meeting, which shocked the others. Maybe they did not have an employment contract, but he did. Vincent was not about to put up with this kind of personal abuse.

The following afternoon, Charley invited Vincent to his office. He seemed to respect Vincent's quick response to his earlier unbridled insults. He offered him some chocolate chip cookies that he himself baked, as Vincent sat down. "Sure, thanks, it's my favorite," Vincent answered.

After he consumed two cookies with coffee, Charley warned him, "Take it easy, I baked them with *grass,"* he said, laughingly.

"Grass? ... You mean marijuana?"

"Exactly!"

"You're joking with me. I never heard of baking cookies with pot."

"I used *my best stuff,* so take it easy," he cautioned.

Vincent had to go to Long Island to celebrate his mother's 70th birthday. The traffic was heavy that evening. About three quarters of the way there, he gradually began to feel numb all over. His senses seemed to slow down; the brake pedal appeared mushy; the steering wheel seemed as if it over-reacted to his slightest movements; and his eyes could not concentrate on the road.

Vince remembered Charlie's cookies. Shit, he *really* baked them with grass. He never smoked marijuana, had not heard of anyone using it for baking, and was completely naive about its effects. He stopped and bought some black coffee. It did not help. Somehow, he made it to his mother's house before the full effects of the drug finally hit him. Vincent's mother said she never saw him in such a happy, silly state. "You made jokes about everything that anyone spoke about last evening."

The following morning Vincent stormed into the CEO's office. "Charley, did you know you almost caused an accident?"

"What are you talking about?"

"Your damn cookies really screwed me up while I was driving to Long Island. That's what I'm talking about."

Charley began laughing. "You're an *idiot,*" Vincent shouted, slamming the door to the CEO's office as he left. This little *"Napoleon"* dictator gave him his first big opportunity—but Charlie's *"Waterloo"* was about to happen.

Vincent ran his own profit center, and Charley promised him 10% of all profits, at the end of the fiscal year. His Technology Analysis Group (TAG) made nearly $10 million in sales, with one-third profits, during the second full year of operation. At later meetings, the CEO praised Vincent in front of the other executives, which became embarrassing. "Charley, please stop comparing me to the other VP's. It's not good for my personal relationships with my peers," Vincent urged.

When the year ended, Vincent went to accounting to pick up his 10% share of the profits. "Sorry, we are a little slow in closing the books. Our final accounting has not been completed yet," was the accountant's answer.

"Why don't you get a computer and use all that great internal software expertise," he responded. It was a classic case of the "shoemaker going without shoes."

A month later, Vincent complained again: "where's my profit-sharing check?"

"Oh, you really didn't make that much profit," the accountant explained, with a crafty grin. "What do you mean? What kind of crap are you giving me?"

"We had to add *all* the 'corporate overhead' to your department."

"Corporate overhead! I don't remember headquarters helping me last year," was Vincent's indignant response. "I'm the one who *actually* helped this company."

"The President says he supported you by speaking at your client meetings. He says he provided *very valuable* assistance. See it's all there," said the 'bean counter,' with a shit-eating smirk. "Do you want us to tell the boss that his services were not appreciated?"

"Let me see that report. What is this screwy charge? QE II boat trip to Europe ... for two ... *first class?*"

"Don't you remember? That is when Charley made that speech for your conference, in Eze, France, last year. You know the boss only goes first class, and always travels with his spouse," he replied.

"Accounting has no right to change the rules of the game, *after* the game is over," Vincent insisted.

I was really screwed! The boss spent my profit-sharing bonus, and I had no support for my case. Besides, it did not pay to fight this battle and lose the war. If that's how he wants to play the "corporate game," if he's going to screw the executive who took all those risks and made a *major* contribution to his company's bottom line, then I'll establish my own business. I do not need this kind of *bullshit overhead.*

Vincent plotted his next move. As he finalized plans to leave CTS, his attractive Swedish born private secretary and he had lunch at an exclusive Italian restaurant, to celebrate his planned departure and new business venture. After the luncheon, Vincent paid with his American Express. Minutes later the manager came to the table with a concerned look on his face. "Sir, I'm afraid your corporate card has been canceled."

"What do you mean? That is not possible! I used it yesterday."

"So sorry sir, your credit card was recalled by your company today." The sly smile suggested she knew what was really happening. She offered her plastic to pay for the lunch. He assured her he would repay her the next day.

Hours later, Vincent found out that his lovely secretary, *covertly* spied for Charley. He did not know that they jogged together, almost daily, near Charlie's country estate. She became his "secret agent." She reported *everything*—all of Vincent's private plans and meetings, the new business venture activities, and his future spin-off plans.

During what was to be the last meeting, Charley became *extremely pissed* that one of his key executives would *dare* leave him. "You schemed behind my back, when I gave you the opportunity of a lifetime," he shouted.

"Well, if your phony corporate overhead hadn't screwed me out of my bonus, there would be no need to make any plans," Vincent responded, rudely.

"I see you're not used to running a business. Every firm has corporate overhead. All the other departments paid the same. What's your gripe?"

"You changed the rules of the game with accounting, *without* informing me. How about that QE II trip? Why should my group be charged with that huge expense?"

"Get out! Charlie shouted. "I want you out of this firm in an hour. You hear me?"

There was no turning back now. After I burned the bridges behind me, my only alternative was to try to make it on my own, *regardless* of the consequences. My contract had expired. Charley threw me out of CTS, without paying my last month's salary. He also threatened to sue me. Suddenly I found myself without any income, with a huge mortgage, two children who expected to enter an expensive college, while facing a lawsuit from CTS for $550,000 for allegedly stealing away clients-*all at the same time.* Vincent saw his entire career, which he nurtured through many years of effort, suddenly *shattered* in small unrecoverable pieces at his feet.

All business ventures need capital. Financing a new business can be a formidable task. Forget the so-called credit banks; they only give credit to people and businesses *that do not need any.* Where are your balance sheets? What assets do you have? He tried to explain to the bank executives that it is a *new* business. By definition, any new venture has no record of accomplishment, or assets. "My assets are my management ability, many years of experience, and my technical skills," he said.

"We're not in business to take risks," the bank executive answered. "You need to have some tangible assets."

"What about all those bad sub-prime mortgages given to poor clients, and loans to South America and the Middle East?" Vincent replied.

The bank executive claimed that those loans were "fully guaranteed" by U.S. government institutions. Sure, but that did not make them risk-free. Look at the hundreds-of-billions that were written-off, because of bad mortgage loans. The real estate "bubble" of 2008-2009 had finally busted. Many of the failed investment banks, and AIG, required immediate Federal bailouts? It did not matter how good your business plans are, or the quality of the management team, nor the fantastic financial projections for the new venture—they were *not* going to give him any credit.

Maybe Venture Capital firms will be more flexible, Vincent thought. He soon discovered that they wanted *absolute control* of the firm, and they insisted on telling him when he could write a check, and for what purposes. In their view, the most important thing is *not* the idea or invention, nor the business plan, but the record of accomplishment of the management team. In addition, they wanted him to pay back their investment ASAP, with significant interest, plus a *big* slice of the company shares. Venture firms claim only one-out-of-ten new ventures are successful. As a result, they try to make up for the other nine bad deals, by bleeding the present successful business venture dry.

Vincent decided to take out an equity loan against his home and avoid all those financial *swindlers*. In his consulting and research business, all he needed was a small office, a good part-time secretary, some phones and a computer. Another positive aspect of his type of business was that most of the clients paid part of the consulting fees up-front, and he did not need any costly inventories. Charley settled the dispute out of court. Vincent agreed not to make contact with CTS clients for two years, unless they contacted him first. Nevertheless, most clients did exactly that.

***

TWIST OF FATE

*"There's nowhere you can be that isn't where
you're meant to be ..."*

—John Lennon

Paris: He came up to the tranquil young woman who was quietly reading her book on the park bench. Instinctively he sensed that she would help him. He attracted her attention. Immediately she recognized his distress and promptly gave him some of her bottled water. "Where are your parents," she asked.

He did not understand French or English. Confidently he continued to sit by her side. He knew that this kindhearted person would take care of his every need. A sudden commotion distracted her. They came running towards her.

They were ecstatic. "Marc, she found you!"

"He seemed lost and thirsty. I gave him some water and he sat with me," she explained, as the young boy jumped up with delight.

"Pardon us Madame, my son must have left our car while we were shopping and got lost. We are so happy you found him. I should have known it was too hot for him to stay in the car."

"You are right! It is *cruel* to leave any child in a hot car.

"You don't know how delighted we are that you found him. Marc must have been desperate," the distinguished man added. The tall, tanned person had a long mustache and some kind turban on his head. He introduced them. "I'm Brigadier General Ahmad and this is my son Marc."

"Bon Jour. I am very pleased to meet you. I'm Anne Marson."

"May I invite you for some lunch, Madame?" he asked.

"Merci beaucoup. I already ate and I'm late for an appointment."

"May I propose lunch on Sunday then?" He insisted.

"You don't have to treat me to lunch because I helped your child."

"There are crazy people who would kidnap a child today," the General said.

"Il est possible. Où est-ce que nous nons rencontrerons? Where to meet?" "How about the restaurant near the Louvre? I think it is ..."

"I know the place. You mean the Metropole?"

"That's it! Say by noon?" He suggested.

"Oui. I may be a little late. See you then," she said. "Au revoir. Bon voyage."

***

Paris Noon Sunday: After nearly one hour of polite conversation, while feasting on roast duck and a magnum of French champagne, General Ahmad finally asked Anne about her business. "You told me you are in the import or export business. What kind of goods do you trade?"

"Woman's fashions mostly. Also advanced electronics, like microcomputers and communications equipment."

"How did you get from women's fashions to electronics and computers?" He inquired. "That's a strange mix, isn't it?"

"Oui. That is something I really did not plan doing. You see I met an electronics engineer at a conference who introduced me to some clients one evening. Anyway, they were complaining that electronics products, sold in France, are two to three times the cost of the same products in the States. I recalled that I knew executives in Hong Kong, who dealt with such equipment. I thought that maybe they could get them cheaper, directly from my contacts in the Far-East."

"What happened?" General Ahmad continued to probe, showing intensified interest.

"They agreed to test my idea with a small order for personal computers, backed by letters-of-credit. Later, my acquaintance in Hong Kong said that he could only meet their price if they imported the computers as spare parts or modules, and were willing to assemble them in France. That is a legal way to get around high import duties and trade restrictions. To make a long story short, they agreed to the deal. Later I received an order for two thousand sets of microcomputer modules. So, I suddenly was in the electronics import/export business."

General Ahmad explained that the Revolutionary Guard leaders recently appointed him the new head of the Iranian army. He went on to discuss some of the history of the region. "Did you know that our people are Persians, *not* Arabs?"

Anne knew that, but pretended not to know. In spite of her Master's degrees in history and the arts, she was an unpretentious person, especially with strangers.

"Arabs have traditionally been considered nomads, epitomized by the Bedouin of Arabia. Some oft-repeated portrayals of Arabs today use the image of the nomad or tribal sheik *with prejudicial intent.* Bedouins are less than ten percent of the total Arab population. Most Arab societies today are urbanized, particularly the oil-rich states of the Arabian Peninsula."

Anne politely interrupted. "That's right, especially in France; foreigners tend to also *generalize* about Parisians." She continued: "The typical Parisian, unlike my ancestors who have lived here a thousand years, are *not really* Parisians at all. Most came from Algiers, Belgium, from small towns and villages. More than ten percent are from the Middle East. Still others are temporary tourists, who can't really appreciate the beauty, the culture, language, and long intriguing history of Paris."

The General agreed. "You're absolutely right! There are also important differences in political and religious outlook among Arabs and Persians. In the midst of such diversity, the two basic elements uniting most Arabs and Iranians are Arabic, the Farsi language and Islam. While both speak Arabic, it differs greatly from country to country. However, written language forms a cultural basis for all. Arabic is the language of the Koran, the revealed word of Allah, delivered through the prophet Muhammad."

"My former boyfriend was from Iran. He was a Shiite," Anne remarked. "How many Shiites are there?"

"The majority of Iranians are Shiites," he explained. "The division of Islam into two main branches is the result of a dispute over succession to the Caliphate that goes back to the 7th century. This has led to doctrinal differences between the two branches. Major Shiite countries are *non-Arabic,* such as Iran. There are large numbers of Shiites also in Iraq, where they now form a *majority.*

Shiites are now one of the biggest single religious group in this region. Shiites, are considered the economic underclass in many Arab nations, and they are discriminated against by the Sunni."

"Do you feel that your country is better off politically and economically, after the new Imam leader came to power?" she inquired.

"*Absolutely!* He unified our people and brought them back to their *fundamentalist* Islamic traditions. Although conventional tribal life has nearly disappeared, tribal values and identity retain great significance, especially when linked to Islam. Anyone from the clan of the prophet Muhammad, or from one of the first tribes to accept Islam, carries *great prestige.* Many villages and towns contain prominent families with common links to tribal ancestors. Blood ties contribute to the formation of political tribal factions. Leading families seek to inter-marry to preserve tribal bonds and many urban families retain patronage ties to their villages."

Anne interrupted. "When I was in Iran, I especially enjoyed visiting your small villages. The people there *are so natural.* They have maintained their historical traditions, without Western influences."

"Oh, you visited my country? When was that?"

"About three years ago. I was engaged to a young man—it didn't work out—but I loved the natural generosity and kinship of your people."

"The importance of tribal kinship," the General continued, "has been weakened by the rapid expansion of urban society, by modern educational systems, by the creation of centralized governments. Those bureaucracies are the major source of employment. Except for oil, there are few natural resources for development. Productive land is scarce in many regions because of the lack of water. Droughts have increased the possibility of conflicts over water resources shared by neighboring countries.

Fewer opportunities in agriculture, together with social change have caused young people to flock to major cities seeking education and employment."

Anne asked, "What percentage of the population are young people? That's important for my fashion business you know."

"We have a large number of young people. About 70% are age thirty or less. Population trends also suggest great potential for social unrest. The failure of secular regimes to fulfill their promises of economic wellbeing has contributed to the increasing association to Islam, by young people.

"Arab inability to regain the territories lost in the 1967 war with Israel led to questioning of the secular doctrines. A growing gap exists between rich and poor, and the spread of education increased demands for greater collaboration in largely undemocratic political systems."

"What about the influence of Western culture on Arabs, and also Iranians?" she questioned, with genuine interest.

"The key individuals who led the Arab independence movements were non-clerical. Some of them, such as Egypt's Nasser, were Arab Nationalists who advocated the creation of a single Arab nation. They believed it vital that their countries adopt many aspects of Western civilization, such as secular laws and representative government. Such views *seriously threatened* the primacy of Islam in everyday life. Islamic law makes no distinction between religious and secular power. Muslims believe that *all law* derives from the Koran. God's word must apply to *all aspects of our life.*"

Anne reacted, "Many Christians also believe that God's word should apply to all aspects of life, you know. It's not just part of the Islamic faith."

"Some do, but most Christians don't really follow the teachings of their Bible. Muslims see the West as a direct threat to Islamic faithfulness. Most see Israel as an *agent of the West,* depriving Palestinian Arabs of their rightful homeland. Non-clerical Arabs fear reintroduction of a Muslim power structures. They often feel enraged at what they perceive as Western ignorance and insensibility towards Arab problems.

"The Palestinian uprising created a new appreciation of our problems. Anti-Israel statements often served to create a *false* impression of unity, when real agreement was lacking. The Arab League has become a forum for Arab sparring than a framework for cooperation. Arabs genuinely feel common bonds based on language, a shared historical and cultural legacy, but they also identify themselves as Iraqis, Syrians, Iranians or Egyptians."

The General then got into a very *emotional* discussion about Israel: "Israel is a direct consequence of Hitler.

Without Hitler, there would have been a colony of people, who would have liked to live in Palestine, but they would *never* have been a success, and they would never have achieved nationhood. *Hitler created Israel.* Dr. Bruno Kerensky, *a Jew,* and former Chancellor of Austria, made that statement. If an Arab or non-Jew were to make that observation, there would be immediate allegations of anti-Semitism."

"You're right. You can't criticize the Jews without them labeling you," she agreed. (Anne *intentionally* supported the general's position to draw out his anti-Jewish views). It worked. The general was captivated by her remarks.

Anne told him a few facts about Israel that she recently read about: "The undeniable record from the UN and the United States State Department '*Report on Human Rights*,' including the *Israeli Judicial Commission of Inquiry,* is very revealing. Thousands of innocent Arabs have been tortured, jailed (without trial), and killed (without cause). Former Israeli Supreme Court President, Landau, *confirmed* that Israeli secret security police (*Shin Bet*), had for years, illegally used physical and psychological torture to coerce confessions from persons suspected of hostile terrorist activities.

"A *secret* annex to the commission report *exonerated* the military courts for accepting sixteen years of *perjured testimony,* and further recommended that no one be prosecuted for practicing torture and brutality, during that period. The commission established this as an irrefutable fact. I think that's appalling," Anne stated.

The General was surprised by her knowledge and graphic memory. Clearly, she is *"no Jew lover,"* he thought. He then added, "To remember the holocaust also means not to act like the Nazis. The evil perpetrated against the Jews during World War II *cannot* justify evils committed by Jews on the Palestinian race."

By intentionally adding fuel to the fire of his deep-rooted hatred for Jews, she *completely conquered him.* He was delighted by her anti-Semitism attitude. "Why don't you come to Tehran, as my guest? I'm sure our people need clothes, and electronics," he proposed.

"Thank you for your kind offer. I am sure you're very busy with all the important changes that are happening in your country. My small business should not be of any importance to you."

"It would please me very much if you considered my offer. Of course, I will make *all* the arrangements. You can stay at our Grand

Hotel. I will *personally* pick you up at the airport, so you do not have to go through all those silly administrative nuisances," he insisted.

"I'll think about your very kind offer. How can I reach you?"

The General gave her his personal card and wrote his private phone number on the back. He completely understood her unspoken concerns—a woman is *not allowed* to travel unescorted in any Muslim country. He kissed her hand, as they departed. He then shouted: "Please be sure to call me. I'll make all the arrangements."

***

London. Vincent sat at the Savoy Hotel bar and ordered a scotch with soda on the side. The cocktail lounge overflowed with British and international high-society people having their afternoon tea, cakes and spirits. A jittery waiter approached him with an expression on his face that indicated something was wrong. "Sir, pardon me, but I really can't serve you here, without a collar. So sorry! Its house rules you know."

"You mean shirt and tie? That is ridiculous! I never heard of such an absurd rule in any international hotel bar." (The Savoy is one of the most distinguished "blue-blood" hotels in London). Vincent went up to his room and put on a more conservative dark blue suit, light blue shirt and stripped red silk tie. Upon returning, he again ordered another scotch. Minutes later, an older man sat next to him at the bar. He began drawing something on the back of an envelope. "Excuse me sir that looks like a computer system. Right?"

The ruddy-faced man, with a large head, capped with thinning gray hair, stared at him with a surprised look. His gold rimmed, slightly shaded spectacles, partly masked eyes as steel gray as his hair. His intense eyes riveted on Vincent. "How did you know that?" he questioned with astonishment.

"Sorry to interrupt your concentration. That is my business. I'm a computer systems software and network consultant"

"So pleased to meet you, I'm George Dubois. I'm a retired part-time inventor."

After they shared a drink together, George explained: "I was born in Belgium but now live in France and Monaco. I'm working on a new type of medical device that's connected to a computer."
This casual meeting could happen anytime, anywhere. George Dubois showed Vincent his crude drawing. It was some kind of fiber optic

cable, with led light source on one end, and camera on the other end. It's inserted down the patient's throat or up their rectum, to probe for tumors. Then, images of the body interior organs are sent over telecommunication lines to a computer, for further analysis and diagnosis.

"I think there's an easier and far less costly way to do that," Vincent suggested. "Why don't you simply interface the output images from the camera, directly to a personal computer, and save the facsimile images on a disk?"

"Fantastic!" he said. *"That's an excellent idea!* You really know your technology. Why don't you join me and my wife for dinner, so we can discuss this further?"

The Savoy was a bit rich for Vincent's budget. He figured that he would be George's guest. "Sure, why not. I have to go to a business meeting. I'll see you, say ... about eight?"

Francine was at least twenty years younger than George's sixty plus years. Her excellent command of both English and French suggested she was well educated, and her demeanor clearly indicated her "breeding." George promptly boasted about Francine's career as a French actor. Vincent had never heard her name nor seen her in any movie. They explained that they lived in a villa near Eze, and spent a few days each week at her apartment in Monaco.

Vincent remembered having a management conference in Eze, with Charley as the keynote speaker, some years ago. He could not forget that place, where his boss charged the *entire* boat tip to his cost center, including Charley's underwear, and thereby screwed Vince out of his profit bonus. The ancient castle at Eze sits on a mountaintop overlooking the sea. It has a fantastic four-star restaurant and small pool. Strangely, hundreds of cats took up residence in that thousand year old French village.

As a citizen of Monaco, Francine provided her spouse with significant tax benefits since this small country does not have any taxes, whatsoever. They get most of their revenues from gambling and tourism. She seemed to be the total opposite of George, in both her manner and interests. This discriminating French woman talked vividly about the arts, culture and the theater. Her spouse concerned himself only about his invention, business and finances.

The discussion turned to the recent wave of terrorist activities in Europe. "Assassins led by Abu, with support from Iran, recently tried to kill the Israeli Ambassador," George noted. "Did you see the *London Times* today?"

"No. But I read in the *Financial Times* that a Colonel, from the United States, was recently assassinated by Lebanese terrorists in Paris." Vincent replied, "I think these religious fanatical assassins set back their own purposes, whatever they may be, by these foolish acts."

George added, "What's it all about? Different groups seem to be involved in assassinations, bombings and airline hijackings. There does not seem to be any common link. Maybe they are connected with the Hamas, or splinter groups in the Middle-East."

"I don't think that they will achieve anything significant. They are killing many innocent people," Vincent said.

"Actually, I think it hurts their cause and objectives." Francine said, "You're right. People are outraged by these senseless acts. It caused the Spanish government to change; now it has become more socialistic."

George reviewed his invention in far more detail than Vincent ever expected to explore, at this stage in their relationship. He's pumping me for all kinds of technical details. Near the end of the dinner, George asked, "Why don't you and your wife be our guests in Monte-Carlo, Monaco? I am thinking of planning an International Healthcare conference there to present my invention. Your thoughts about my planned technology meeting would be most helpful."

When George picked up the considerable dinner tab, Vincent was sure his proposal was serious. "I'll have to discuss that with my wife, Susan," he replied, although she usually deferred to his judgment on these matters.

"If she approves, let me know soon. Hotel reservations are impossible in the summer," Francine emphasized. "I would really enjoy meeting your wife. I'll show her the *real* Monte Carlo."

***

Nice, France. Vincent decided to accept George's offer. He and Susan badly needed a long overdue vacation.

George met them at the Nice Airport. He took them to the Beach Hotel just outside of Monaco.

The principality was *positively spectacular.* Immense pastel colored hotels and apartments surrounded the clear green-blue sea and harbor. Streets near the beach were lined with tall, elegant palm trees. The classic structures and exotic semi-tropical parks suggested a very rich and classical history. The overall image is that of an elegant peaceful city with a distinctive ambiance.

"Monaco has remained independent for nearly 800 years," George said. "It's a land of green-blue sea, clean beaches, half-naked bathers, theaters with great music, and of course, our famous casinos and the Grand Prix. There are no taxes for the Monegasques and foreign residents. It's also a very safe place to live."

Francine quickly chimed in. "If you ever meet 'real' Monaco natives you will find them to be warm, humble and friendly. Did you know that there are only about 7,000 Monegasque nationals in this country, which is about the size of your New York Central Park?"

"No. I didn't know that."

"The other 28,000 inhabitants are foreign residents, or visitors. Tourists expand our population to over 100,000 during summer."

George added. "Your movie actress, Grace Kelly, put this sleepy village on the world map, by her marriage to His Serene Highness, Prince Rainier. She also cleaned-up this Principality by forcing out the prostitutes, drug pushers and Mafia criminals.

Fig 3. Princess Grace of Monaco

"Her tragic death unfortunately occurred before her mission was accomplished," Francine pointed out. "There are many facts that *don't* support the 'official' conclusion that Princess Grace 'suffered a stroke,' which caused the 'accident' while she was driving down from her villa at Roc Agel. Did you know a truck driver was directly behind her car? He saw it zigzag and observed that the brake lights *never* came on as they approached the most dangerous turn in the road. The ambulance arrived at the scene in five minutes, when it takes twenty minutes to climb that mountain road."

"How come the driver was never interviewed?" Vincent asked.

"Princess Stephanie said that her mother panicked—she didn't know what to do—she lost control. Monaco officials *refused* to allow the French police to inspect the vehicle, until sometime later. Suicide is unrealistic! A woman would not load her Rover with dresses to be altered by her couturier, or take her daughter with her if that was her plan." George claimed.

Vincent remembered reading that the brother of Princess Grace died from a heart attack soon thereafter, while jogging in Philadelphia. It is preposterous to believe that two deaths can occur in the same family, at the same time. Drugs could have been used to induce a heart attack. Drugs have been used in both cases.

According to some press reports, Prince Rainier III was having extramarital affairs in Paris, and at his villa near Monaco. In addition, Princess Caroline's father-in-law was *allegedly* a Mafia chief in Milan. Sometime later, Caroline's chauffeur was caught smuggling drugs across the border of Italy. Monaco has a very serious drug problem. The rich and powerful need a steady source of drugs for their parties. Monaco is certainly safe—and a secure tax-free haven for dirty money.

"We may never learn the complete truth of these *strange* events, leading up to that tragic day, but speculation continues," Francine declared.

If there is such a thing as a perfectly safe, secure county, Monaco *claims* to be it. However, the scandals abound. During the wedding of Grace Kelly to the Prince, her mother's jewelry was stolen, at the palace of all places. The noted publisher, Matthew H. McCloskey, also lost $50,000 worth of jewels at the "very secure" Hotel de Paris.

A *Wall Street Journal* article, titled *"Crime in Monaco,"* reported that thieves removed an 18thth century painting belonging to Prince Rainier from the Salle Garnier Opera house, and held-up a jewelry shop in November of that same year.

Vincent decided to do further research himself to explore all he could about the history and current events of Monaco. He talked to the locals and studied a few old books in the library. He learned a few fascinating historical facts about the Principality:

Phoenicians established a settlement in Monaco, attracted by the natural harbor. Subsequently, Greeks, Carthaginians, and Romans held it. In 1162, the city-state of Genoa took control of Monaco. In 1297, Monaco became the property of the Grimaldi family of Genoa. In 1304, the first Grimaldi Prince ascended to the throne of Monaco. In 1792, during the French Revolution, the Grimaldis' were deposed. In 1814, they regained the throne.

Monaco is a totally urbanized state, about the size of New York's Central Park. The Principality includes four distinct areas. Monaco-Ville, the official capital, is on the flat top of a rocky promontory extending into the Mediterranean; the 16th-century ruler's palace, government buildings, and the cathedral (built in 1876-90). La Condamine is the commercial port area. Monaco's light manufacturing industries are concentrated in Fontvieille. Monte-Carlo is the major tourist center where the beaches, hotels, opera house and the gambling casinos are located.

More than 35% of Monaco's annual revenue comes from tourism. The casino is only for tourists. Citizens of Monaco are not allowed to gamble there. Monaco has encouraged an influx of private and corporate capital by providing a *very favorable* tax structure that does not tax most corporate or personal income. Instead, various indirect taxes, including excise, estate, and export taxes are levied. Foreign corporations are strongly encouraged to establish their headquarters in Monaco. Many firms, particularly American, have done so. Banking has become a second significant revenue source because of their effective privacy laws and their total lack of taxes.

After further in-depth research, Vincent discovered an *amazing secret* about the history of Monaco: During the 14th century, a rejected mistress of the Prince cursed the Grimaldi family. She put her "curse" on *all future royalty, declaring "... none will ever enjoy a happy marital relationship in the future."*

Susan and Vincent spent the next few days swimming, sunning and people watching. Topless women, with high-heel shoes, paraded around the pool area. This mid-day fashion show, with bare bouncing boobs, kept Vincent amused. The green-blue sea was so clear that one could see fish darting from place to place. Tents placed along the beachfront gave it an ancient Arabic romantic setting. Semi-nude women and men took in the sun outside their tents, while their children played in the sand nearby.

Service at the Beach Hotel was first class. Waiters in their stylish white uniforms served drinks and coffee on the terrace near the pool, and they *always* remembered the customer's last name. They did what they were trained to do best: they served guests in the finest tradition and professional manner. They took exceptional pride in their craft. All provided the best of service at all levels—housekeepers, waiters and the concierge. Nothing was artificial. Vincent was not used to such personalized pampering, which unfortunately appears to be a lost art in much of America, although exceptions certainly exist—if you have enough dough.

For the conference planning, George and Vincent agreed to meet at his villa near Eze, about thirty minutes south of Monaco. The villa was more extravagant than Vincent and Susan expected, with Spanish tiled roofs, and a white stucco structure, overlooking the blue-green sea below. Tropical trees and flowering plants surrounded the kidney shaped pool. It was a semi-tropical paradise, compared to the urban setting of Monaco.

George introduced them to his charming Italian house cleaner and cook. She was one of the best *chef de cuisines*. She prepared a fantastic lunch. After the feast, they agreed to schedule an International Congress together next year in Monte Carlo. The theme would be, *advanced technology in medical sciences*. George would be the chairperson of the steering committee, and Vincent would handle all the technical aspects, including finding leading edge research doctors and prominent information technology speakers.

After the meeting, Vincent became exhausted due to the time change, endless refills of red wine, and especially the luncheon feast. He went back to the Beach Hotel, got into his shorts and relaxed in a chair on the terrace, overlooking the sea. Susan went up to the hotel room to read a book. Vince spent much of his professional life handling technology questions, and typing research reports.

For this vacation, he wanted nothing to do with technology—just the sea and the sun. He expected to spend the next six days drinking by the pool, while working his way through several novels, occasionally raising his gaze from his chilled daiquiri, to watch the swaying hips of topless women in high-heels, passing his way.

Nearly an hour into his first novel, from the corner of his eye— an anxious pink blur was all that he saw. The woman he was deliberately trying to ignore was throwing her small dogs' sugar cubes. "That's not good for their health you know," Vincent said.

"Je suis un expert du chien! Je sais ce qui est bon pour eux! Je dois faire attention à mon possède de l''affaire." With his limited French, Vince thought she tried to say, "I'm a dog expert. I know what's good for them." In other words, why don't you mind your own business? The sexy blonde was dressed in short soft pink suede. The one-piece outfit caused Vincent's imagination to wonder what kind of intriguing body she concealed under that skimpy covering. It is more than creature lust that attracted him to this person. There was something about her style, her movements, and naturalness that would inspire any man to want to know more. Her sad green eyes reminded him of *someone from his past..*

In Vincent's romantic view, *some* women represent a prime example of God's most beautiful creation. Since he's not blind, why should he ignore a prime example of His finest specimen? While he had many opportunities and narrow escapes during his frequent business trips, he invariably resisted all of those temptations.

The woman thought that her quick response to this interesting and attractive stranger might have been a bit too harsh. She apologized in French, and introduced herself: "Veuille m''excuser, peut-être j'étais trop sarcastique. Mon nom est Eva Billiere."

"Sorry, my French is limited. I'm Vincent Renaldo. Pleased to meet you." She ignored the language problem, and continued to speak in French. "Tu aimes avoir un café avec moi, ... by that umbrella covered Terrace?"

"Have a coffee with you? You mean where all those beauties are baking themselves around the pool?"

"Oui! It's cooler there." She clearly had no inhibitions talking to strangers.

"Please excuse me, I'll be right back. Why don't you reserve us a seat." He went up to the room to invite Susan to join them for coffee. It seemed the most sensible thing to do. Susan was deeply involved in her book and declined the invitation.

"No thanks! I am tired and busy reading. You go along and have coffee with her,—*if you really want to.*"

"Listen, it's a unique opportunity to meet an interesting French person, who might tell us more about the *real* Monte Carlo."

After twenty-one years of marriage, they had reached a plateau in their relationship. The children were away in college. They were alone for the first time in many years of living together. For some unknown reason they did not take the time or make an effort to try to understand the *true feelings* of each other. You can live with someone most of your life, and not really know them. Susan appeared to be pissed over some petty issue. Something important was missing in their relationship and Vincent did not understand what it was. At that moment, he did not care.

After sharing a coffee, Eva looked at him squarely in the eyes. She made a quick determination. "Pourquoi ne te fait pas rencontre et voyage à Nice avec moi?"

"Why don't I meet you later? You want to travel to Nice. Is that what you're suggesting?"

"I must buy things for my dog grooming business. Je te montrerai quelques endroits très intéressants' in Nice. Excuse my French. I said I'll show you some charming places in Nice."

"How long will it take?" Vincent asked. "I have a business meeting later" (which was not true).

"My English is good, oui? We can be back in few hours. Before six o'clock."

Vince was a bit apprehensive but his intuition, his gut feeling said, why not take a chance with this interesting woman? He explained to a disinterested Susan that he was going to explore the village in Nice, and take in some of the sights. "Would you like to come along?" His real intention was to keep a rendezvous with that sensational, enchanting individual, named Eva. He was pleased that Susan did not care to go. He was not about to avoid such a harmless and interesting adventure.

"Are you going with that French person?" Susan abruptly asked, as he started to leave the suite.

"*Of course not!* She merely gave me ideas about what might be of interest to us."

***

Vincent arrived at her flat at 3 o'clock sharp. It occupied the entire top floor of an older building, on avenue St. Charles. Her apartment seemed modest in size by American standards. Its main attraction was the huge terrace that surrounded most of the rooms, with a spectacular view of the sea and city below. It was one of those charming buildings built during the beginning of the 20th century. It had very high ceilings and full-length French doors that opened onto the terrace. The combination living and dining room area was huge with lots of plants and palm trees that complimented the ornate Persian carpet.

It would certainly make an impressive office. One of the two large bedrooms had a unique green silk wall covering, with textured flowers. It was an extremely feminine bedroom. The furniture consisted of a mixture of Louis XV antique chairs, gold leaf framed mirrors, with a more contemporary sofa and dining table. Obviously, she is a collector of antiques, and she knows how to mix the old with the new.

Her sad green eyes studied Vincent as they talked. After they shared a coffee and chatted for a few minutes, Eva changed clothes for the trip to Nice. She wore tight-fitting jeans and a simple white tee shirt that made her large breasts standout, like two protruding headlamps. Eva drove her small white British Mini as if she was in the Grand Prix. She raced across bridges, in and out of traffic, up steep hills and flew around mountains—that did not have any guardrails. What a wild reckless ride! Vincent became a little frightened. He could see the newspaper headlines: "American computer executive found dead in automobile accident with a sexy blond French woman."

No parking spaces existed anywhere as they arrived in Nice. That did not stop her. Eva swiftly parked her small mini halfway on the sidewalk. She then looked at him and asked, "Est-ce que tu aimerais 'acheter une robe?"

"Would I buy you a dress?" He quickly regained his composure, in his limited French, he said, "Bien sûr."

Eva tried on many outfits. Each change revealed a female who had too much of everything, which any normal healthy man would certainly appreciate.

"You like?" she asked, coming out of the fitting room in a dark-blue classic dress, with many small white flowers printed all over it.

"Très magnifique!" meaning the dress and everything else he saw before his eyes. Vincent's pulse quickened each time small glimpses of that partly naked person exhibited herself behind the curtain. He did not have much cash and hoped they would accept plastic. They did.

Then, she suggested, "Maybe matching shoes are necessary, don't you agree?"

"Bien sûr!" he said, again. That special outfit looked fantastic on her, with dark-blue high-heel shoes to match.

Upon returning to the Beach Hotel, they agreed to meet the next evening to sample the nightlife of Monte-Carlo. He wondered what kind of excuse he could give Susan. As the sun set that beautiful Saturday evening, Vincent found that he did not have to invent any fake excuses. Susan claimed she had a migraine headache and did not want to go out. Was she testing him? If so, that was a lot of crap. That would not stop him. Hell, they were here on vacation. He was not about to spend it in a hotel room watching another dumb TV program, in a foreign language neither understood.

The classic casinos, the lively discos, the exquisite restaurants, and the well-mannered people would fascinate any visitors to this city. Nothing could compare to the glamour and nightlife there. Everybody delighted in dressing up, showing-off his or her clothes, jewels—and *everything else.* They arrived in Mercedes, Rolls or Jags, with well-dressed male escorts. They met at *Jimmy's club,* the most extravagant and exclusive club in Monte-Carlo.

Eva dressed seductively, yet she had a classy look, in that dark blue dress with small white flowers. The dress seemed molded to her body. It complemented her short blond hair, clipped in a pageboy style that set off her cheekbones, and sad green eyes. All eyes seemed to focus on us, as she strode over to the table, with the air of a *Vogue model* walking the runway. Eva radiated a fresh engaging vitality. Many heads turned for another glimpse at the resilient dance movements of this sexy woman.

The club with its open panorama view from all sides, allowed us to see the bright stars above, which the candle lit tables did not diminish.

Music consisted of tropical themes from the Caribbean, and popular Latin numbers from Italy and Spain. Eva was a marvelous dancer, although she liked to take charge, and he willingly followed. The seductive rhythmic sway of her hips, and set of stunning breasts, only partly concealed in that low-cut dress, sent him persistent signals all evening.

The inquisitive woman's questions finally came: "tu est marié?"

"Yes, twenty-one years married," he answered.

"You have children?"

"Yeah, Oui. Two, both are in college."

"Eest marié heureusement?"

"Am I happily married? Well ... not really," he replied, as they finished the last glass of the champagne.

"Ce qui t'apporte Monte-Carlo?"

"I'm involved in planning a conference in Monaco, for next year," he answered. "How about your situation? Comment est-ce que vient une belle femme comme est-ce que tu n'es pas marié? I don't see any wedding band."

"I haven't met the right man yet."

"Are you so difficult to please?"

"Je ne pense pas donc. Excuse me. All I want is a sincere man that *I can really trust*. I'll know who he is when I find him."

Her green eyes sparkled in the candlelight, and started to swell up with tears from some past melancholy thoughts. Her expression suggested that I might have hit a sensitive nerve. "Did I say something wrong?"

"No! ... Not really. I just got out of the hospital. I had what you call miscarriage."

"I'm so sorry. It must have been very difficult. Expérience difficile?"

"Oui. I was four months pregnant from my former fiancée. They also discover a tumor in my breast. I'm still waiting for test results."

"My God, you really had a rough time. I read that most breast tumors are not malignant. Try not to worry. Essaie de d'inquiéter ne pas. When will your doctor get test results?"

"In two days. Sorry to spoil your evening with my personal story."

After two magnums of champagne, Vincent was feeling no pain and was in the mood for *anything*.

Back at the apartment, Eva offered Vincent more drinks. He willingly accepted some Scotch, to drown his guilty feelings. As she handed him the drink, their eyes met. The message was clear. He took her in his arms. Her lips parted ever so slightly, as he held her firmly in his embrace. They kissed—a very passionate warm kiss. Her vivacious tongue slowly teased his, giving him the exhilarating sensation of having intercourse, mouth-to-mouth. He kissed her bare shoulder. He admired her deep cleavage.

Somehow, in spite of his drunkenness, Vincent summoned up enough courage to break away from her. "I'm sorry, but I don't want to take advantage of you during this time of your emotional stress." (The truth is Vincent was afraid of his own vulnerability). "Besides, it's getting extremely late."

Vincent arrived back at the Beach Hotel feeling *guilt-ridden*. As he walked back into the room he asked himself, why did Susan refuse such an *innocent* request to share a coffee with this stranger? Why wouldn't she come with him that night? Susan must be testing me; that's the result, he concluded. He slipped into bed, she turn in her sleep in the bed next to his.

"Where were you last night?" Susan asked, with an irritated expression, the next morning. "You were very late returning."

"Yeah ... I got lost in Nice, after a late dinner. I did not realize ... trains do not run after midnight. By the time I found a taxi, I guess it got pretty late."

"Did you have a good time?"

"Sure did! Why do you look so annoyed? You know I invited you to go out with me last night."

The fire, the passion had gone out in their relationship. He was weary of all the artificial crap, tired of her petty friends, bored by the mundane routine of his life. What middle-aged man's ego would not be flattered by the gestures of a beautiful younger woman? After all, this *minor affair* did not lead to anything of consequence.

Vincent was not ready to blow everything that he worked all his life for, or wreck his family over this *trivial* occurrence. He felt guilt-ridden because of this secret meeting with Eva.

He could not stop turning it repeatedly in his mind. Susan is a devoted mother, and an excellent nurse, who cares for God, the children, her patients, and me—*in that order.* That's the problem. Her priorities are wrong. God should be first. Why couldn't he be at least second or third?

They had all the commonplace challenges of American life. Both were workaholics, struggling to pay the mortgage and other considerable bills. He was conscientious about his new business. They were constantly squabbling about what is right for the children. Family life was important to him, but he thought that adults also have a right to enjoy life. Have we created a society, a generation of self-centered children? When one focuses and centers everything on children, they come to believe the world centers on them, and this warped attitude does not change with adulthood. Have we forgotten that the greatest gift we can give to our children is *not things?* It is our love for one another. When our kids become more important than our marriage, we create egocentric kids. We give children what they want—*not what they really need.*

Then Vincent's thoughts shifted to Eva. Why did he give any credence to this stranger? Why do we seem to belief people we just met, often trusting them more than family and friends that we have known for years? Was it her unusual personality?

Was it her free spirit? Was it her extraordinary passion for life? There is a reason we are attracted to, and fascinated by strangers. We are attracted because that person has something we need in order to feel *whole.* It may not be the person itself that arouses our interest, but "it"—that something we need. Some quality that we lack. In Eva's case, it was her *incredible free spirit.*

***

MISSION OF MERCY

*"You cannot conceive, nor can I, of the appalling
strangeness of the mercy of God."*

—Graham Greene

Anne would soon be arriving in another world, a world of strange customs and unfamiliar traditions, of very particular political and religious beliefs, a *very different world.* Her knowledge of Iranian culture and language was limited. Would she be able to conceal the *real reason* for her trip? Anxiety over the possible consequences consumed her, as the jet began its decent into Tehran.

The General impatiently paced back and forth, waited at the airport for Anne's flight to make its final approach and landing. She had accepted his invitation about one month ago. Dressed in his best uniform, he wore colorful medals adorned on his chest. The limousine and bodyguards came directly up to the plane.

"Bienvenu à Iran, my dear. How was your flight?" he asked, while checking his long carefully waxed mustache.

"Très bon. Thank you for meeting me. It really wasn't necessary." (Actually, she was extremely tense during the entire trip, and *very, very apprehensive* that he might not be able to meet her at the airport).

"My staff will take care of your bags. Give them your tickets, and come with me," he commanded. "I reserved a beautiful suite at the Inter-Continental for you."

"Excuse me general," she whispered softly. "I have a special gift for you and I don't want it to break or be seen by your soldiers. You know your favorite whisky is strictly forbidden here." (Among her things was a case of Johnny Walker Black Label Scotch. She knew it was against the Islamic religion to bring liquor).

"Merci, mon sucré. You're right! My troops might even steal it for themselves. I'll direct them to put your bags in my limousine, *immédiatement.*"

It was hot as hell as she stepped from the air-conditioned limo. The general and his aid escorted her directly to the suite. The huge main marble rooms of the suite overlooked the city, with its tall prayer towers, gold covered Mosques and bustling open markets, directly outside her window. Freshly cut flowers decorated all the rooms. "I'll let you rest and get yourself together after that long trip. We shall see each other at dinner. Say ... about eight. D'accord?"

"Oui. You're very kind and considerate, très gent'l general," Anne said, with an enchanting radiant smile.

"You may call me Ahmad, except of course when my troops are present, my dear. If you need anything at all, my personal aide will be in the lobby. His name is Captain Omar."

"Oh, general ... I mean Ahmad, s'il vous plait, let me give you that case of scotch before someone finds it."

"Wonderful! It is impossible to find such quality whiskey in my country. Merci mon sucré." He called his aide to take the covered box. "Au revoir. Do take a rest. I will have my aide fetch you later at eight."

Anne was sweating profusely. It was *not* merely because of the hot sticky weather. Her bags also contained a *very risky* package, carefully camouflaged in a hidden compartment. Her Iranian friends in Paris persuaded her to smuggle items into Iran to save their compatriots who were trapped there, and marked for death. She was instructed that a waiter at the hotel would pick up the package, when you ask for afternoon tea. Ask for *green tea* (the code word). If the waiter says, we only have *Jasmine* tea, it's your signal that he's ready to take the package. 'Jasmine' is the counter code word," they told her. Afraid that the housekeeper might find her package, she hung the "Do Not Disturb" sign on the door.

At sundown, the sound of loud prayers by the muezzins in the long minarets of the city's mosques woke her. Anne took a long cool bath. Then she ordered some *green* tea. The voice at the other end of the phone said, "Sorry, Madame, we only have *black* tea. We expect *Jasmine* tomorrow." At least my contact is in the hotel, she concluded.

The general's handsome aide arrived promptly at eight to take her to dinner. His deep black eyes studied her from head to foot. Anne wore a very conservative dark-green, full-length dress with long sleeves that covered *everything*. She had a single string of pearls around her neck. Anne understood the traditions of the country. As far as attire is concerned, every part of a woman's body *must* be covered including her hair.

Dinner was at the general's residence, a relatively small palace with armed guards stationed at every exit. The general and his son greeted her graciously as if heralding a visiting princess.

"Bon Jour, Madame, did you have a nice rest? You remember my boy from Paris ... that craziness, don't you?"

"Bon Jour. Of course, how I couldn't forget your handsome Marc."

The general introduced Mrs. Ahmad. The stout woman of about fifty was dressed in traditional Iranian black with a veil, although she did not have to cover her face at home. (I 'm not going to sell many Parisian fashions in Iran, Anne concluded).

They served lamb with special spices, wrapped in grape leaves, together with rice, followed by fresh figs and fruits. After dinner, the general's aide, Captain Omar, joined them for coffee and trade discussions. The handsome Captain wore a long robe. His perceptive black eyes examined Anne, frequently. However, Omar carefully avoided speaking, unless the General asked his opinion on something, although *his eyes spoke more than any words.*

Anne tried to avoid his look but she could not evade their concealed message. Iranian custom teaches that a man *must not* look directly into a woman's eyes, *unless* he desires her. Anne knew such traditions and understood that this was a kind of seductive proposal. She decided to tease him back—just a little—with her big deep-blue eyes.

During desert and coffee, she listened politely as the General continued to ramble on about his point-by-point knowledge of Iranian history. He then spoke to Anne about business opportunities in Iran. "My country needs many things, and can trade them for oil, chemicals, or caviar. Our caviar is the best in the world. It is worth its weight in gold, you know."

"I understand the good quality of your caviar. It is certainly the best in the world.

Nevertheless, il peut être difficile ... I mean it is difficult to do business, without cash. Many traders are naturally concerned about the temporary instabilité au Iran. They will request 'letters-of-credit' confirmed by your international bank."

The General asked his aide to look into the letter-of-credit possibilities. Captain Omar responded immediately: "Sir, I'm sure LC's could be arranged for certain *important goods.*"

"Okay ... Provide a list of what's needed and terms and conditions for our guest. Have it ready tomorrow," he ordered. An urgent phone call for the General interrupted their coffee.

"Please excuse me my dear. It seems that everyone is afraid to make decisions without me. *They are like children!* The Captain will see you to your hotel. Good night, until tomorrow."

Anne took the Captain's arm, as he escorted her to the awaiting car. "Permit me to say how attractive you are, Madam. Please excuse me for staring at you this evening. But your eyes ... they are like the color of our beautiful Caspian Sea."

"Merci Omar, or should I call you Captain?" she replied with a *very sensuous* smile. Anne knew that she might need his support if the smuggled goods are discovered. What is better than the top General of Iran's aide on her side?

"Omar is fine. May I call you Anne? It's such a charming name."

"But of course, Omar! Do you have you a large family?"

"Most of my family was killed ... by the Shah's secret police, I am sad to say."

"Oh, je suis donc désolé ... Please excuse my personal questions, Omar."

They arrived at the hotel. She invited him up for the coffee he did not finish at the General's house. Anne noticed the "Do Not Disturb" sign was *not* on her door. She became frightened, but quickly regained her composure and immediately phoned for coffee and cakes. "Excuse me while I change into something more comfortable. This dress is much too warm ... for your hot evenings."

Anne quickly checked to see if the concealed package was disturbed. It was not touched. It is so hot. What can I wear? This light-blue soft cotton dress might do. It should go with my eyes and compliment my shape. She thoroughly powdered her body so that the dress would not cling to her extravagant curves. It did not help; the humidity was too much. Looking into the full-length mirror, she let her long golden blond hair down to her hips, and brushed its silky strands. *Perhaps this dress is a bit too revealing. So what! Let me tease him a little, as he did all night with those seductive eyes.*

Coffee arrived before Anne finally came out. The captain looked up with astonishment at the gorgeous beauty before his eyes. After she served him, she intentionally sat a safe distance across from Omar sat on the sofa. As Anne crossed her long shapely legs, his eyes *suddenly* shifted. The sight of her white bikini panties caused him to spill his coffee.

"Oh, my dear Captain, look what you did to your beautiful uniform. Let me help you. I understand that if we put some cold soda water on it right away, the stain should come out."

She knelt down next to him with a wet towel, and started rubbing his pants leg. Her rubbing motions with the cold soda water, near the top of his leg, caused excitement, especially when she inadvertently touched his genitals. He ran his fingers through her smooth silky hair, raised her head, and kissed her lips gently.

She opened her receptive mouth wider. He kissed her delicate mouth more generously. Slowly, gently, his large strong hand slid down the deep crevice, reaching the soft smooth mounds of her breasts. She was scared, but gave him a warm smile of encouragement, that concealed her fright.

Abruptly the phone rang. The sound startled her. The loud ringing allowed her to regain control over her fear. It was for the Captain. The General ordered him to report to headquarters, *immediately.* They kissed again. "Urgent affairs of state required that I leave you for now, my dearest."

"Must you go right now?"

"Yes!" He abruptly pulled away. "Stay warm for me, my sweet."

Captain Omar could not return that night. Anne had difficulty sleeping. Omar reminded her so much of her former Iranian boyfriend. She was innocent then, completely naive, *but not now.* Armin was her teacher—an expert. Never since that time in Armin's apartment did she experience such intimate passionate feelings. Back then, he was her master, and she a willing slave. Amorous thoughts continued to engulf her.

Anne wondered how she could be so susceptible to the charms of Omar, or any man. *How can I be so vulnerable? Why am I so weak, so careless, and foolish?*

The next morning, Anne ordered green tea again. The waiter arrived promptly. "Sorry, Madame, we only have *Jasmine* tea today." (This was her counter-code word). She gave him the concealed package. He quickly placed it under the serving cart and covered it with the white tablecloth. He kissed her hand intensely and left, without another word. Anne could now relax. She did her duty at considerable risk to her personal safety. The rest of the plan was up to the secret underground to handle.

That evening Omar delivered the list of goods needed by the government. Surprisingly, it included some special microcomputer modules, along with a large request for 100,000 pairs of jeans, and a draft of the proposed letter-of-credit, with very reasonable terms and conditions, as the General requested.

Anne told Omar that she received an urgent call from France. "My aging father is very sick. Unfortunately, my dear, I must leave on the next available flight. Could you please help me get a speedier exit visa and airline reservation?"

"Consider it done. But the next flight is not till morning," he said. "Why don't you relax and I'll tell the General about your situation."

"You're so sweet ... Tu es donc sucré, Omar. I do not know what I would do without you. Please come this evening and let me spend my last few hours with you. Oui?"

"You know I'll do my best to get free tonight."

Omar had to report for active duty that night. He delivered her tickets and exit visa. She started to ask, "What's happening?"

He signaled her to be *quiet.* His response confirmed to her that the hotel room was bugged. They kissed passionately and he departed hastily.

The next morning, General Ahmad sent Anne a basket of fruit, candy and nuts, with a short note: *Dearest Anne, I am so sorry to hear about your father. Unfortunately, the affairs of state prevent me from saying good-bye, in person. However, I know we will meet again very soon, in Paris or Iran. If you need anything, please feel free to call me or send a fax.*

I know you will follow-up on the list of items needed by my government. I am sure we can do some profitable business together. I am always at your service, General Ahmad.

She breathed a long sigh of relief, as her jet headed out to sea, the next morning. Anne felt like a modern day *"Mata Hari,"* except this spy was not executed. The fresh fruit looked delicious. Something shiny caught her eye. It's was a pearl broach hidden in the basket. It was a magnificent gift from the General.

Weeks later Anne learned that most of her former supporters escaped. The counterfeit passports and exit visas she secretly delivered to Iran saved them.

***

Monaco. Beyond the terrace of the Beach hotel, the sun had dropped below the mountains bathing the far side of the city in shadow, while the foreground silhouette of Monte-Carlo was brilliantly lit. Vincent gestured with his glass of wine to the shadow-shrouded sentinels of the mountains and the wash of blazing orange sunset behind them. It was a very different world from the States. He was *captivated* by its charm, its affluence, its old world culture, and spectacular beauty. Planning for the conference and exhibition required Vincent to return to enchanting Monte-Carlo, alone.

In the morning, George Dubois, the chairperson of the steering committee, picked Vincent up at the hotel for their meeting at his villa. When they arrived, Vincent was introduced to the other members of the planning group: Jacques was the head and chief surgeon of the Princess Grace Hospital; Danielle was a Public Relations executive, who would be responsible for the entire PR for the conference; Professor Martin knew all the leading medical researchers, and he would select the papers to be presented.

As the meeting progressed, George turned out to be an arrogant ass who insisted on doing things his way, which was the *only right way.* He had a hyperactive personality—always projecting energy— always trying to show that he was in command.

"Everything must be first class," George said. That included all the best Monaco hotels. The speakers must be only from the elite circles of the medical world. "It must be *exceptional,* since the Sovereign Prince himself will be attending our conference."

Vincent was in charge of finding expert speakers from the States, as well as responsibility for the technical program, and the essential computer demos. George would take responsibility for printing and mailing the invitations on official Monaco letterhead with its impressive princely seal. Some of the best and brightest stars of the technology and medical research world would attend and present their papers.

There was only one key problem, the limited funds contributed by the group and expected ticket sales did not match George's *exalted* plans for the Congress. He would not listen to the steering committee concerns about staying within budget. George argued, "All the major European vendors will be delighted to contribute, when they see what a wonderful meeting we put together. They will beg us to participate!"

It was difficult for Vincent and the other members of the planning group to disagree with George, after we learned that his lovely wife Francine was dying from cancer in the Princess Grace hospital. He had a great imagination, and worked long hours to make the congress a success. He also invested his own money in the project.

After all the speaker invitations went out, Vince encountered an unexpected problem. Some of the scientists and expert speakers threatened to decline to attend, if their *first class* travel tickets were not paid *in advance,* for them, their spouses, or other "escorts." At this late stage, Vincent decided to save the congress from pending disaster by using his own personal credit card to pay for some of the keynote speakers.

The Worldwide Congress and Exhibition opened a few months later. It was a huge success, in terms of attendance, and the quality of the technical papers presented. The conference made all the major international newspapers. It also turned out to be *one of the biggest financial flops* in Monaco history. There was another surprise—the Prince did not come. He sent his sister to represent him. The Princess greeted the speakers and important guests during the cocktail parties.

George finally paid Vincent's credit card charges, but there was no money left to pay for his consulting, or travel and living expenses. Many of the hotels were not paid either, and smaller contractors were left hanging. The very prestigious conference ended, with a loss of about 500,000 Euros. Other members of the planning committee, including the leading doctor, had to make up for the shortfall; otherwise, the entire group could be banned from Monaco.

George's spouse, a delightful human being, died of cancer, several days after the conference concluded.

***

During those warm summer days, in beautiful Monte-Carlo, as Vincent tried to take care of his convention responsibilities, a petite woman often took the sun *topless,* some distance from his window. Later that day, she came close enough on the beach for Vincent to see her. It was Eva. She did not expect to hear from him or see him ever again. Eva had all the characteristics and personality that most sensible men would probably avoid. She was too sexy, too compulsive, and *extremely unpredictable.*

On an impulse, Vincent tossed sugar cubes to her two small dogs from his terrace. Eva looked up and gave him a radiant smile. "Come down and join us," she said.

"Give me a minute to put my shorts on. I'll be right there."

"I never expected to see you again, especially at the Beach Hotel. What brings you to Monte-Carlo?" she probed.

"I was helping with the planning for a conference. I'm sorry I didn't leave you a note or something when I departed..." She interrupted. "We just met and spent a few hours together—*that's all!"*

"Yeah, but I should have at least have called. Will you forgive me?"

"Don't be silly," she laughed, showing a flash of clear white teeth in her sun-golden face. "It's I who must be *very grateful* to you for that beautiful dress and shoes you bought me." Eva turned over to give him a better view of her tanned breasts.

His enchantment with her was unrelenting. Two hours later, they both returned to his suite to take a shower. As they washed each other's backs, Eva knelt down. He stopped her just in time. She laughed and suggested they continue on the bed. She knew all the right buttons to push. Vince had never experienced such unbridled sex. She finally had a convulsive-like climax. They rested in each other's arms, talking for hours about life's experiences.

Eva explained that she grew up in Lille France, near the Belgium border. "It's a small coal town with no character, and definitely no night life," she added. Her mother suffered greatly during the Second World War.

Eva went to an all girls' Catholic school where the nuns were strict. She claimed she was very shy and timid as a child. All that dramatically changed, after an *incredible* experience. Her boyfriend, André, her first love, raced his motorcycle down a steep hill and twisting road in a canyon, with Eva holding on to him in the backseat. As they came around a sharp curve, they hit a fallen rock on the road and instantly crashed. André's head was completely smashed inside his helmet.

It took six months for Eva to recover from her broken bones, a serious concussion and the emotional shock. Her personality *totally* changed, when she finally awoke from the almost a yearlong coma. She was no longer "shy Eva." From that day on, she would live each day as if it was her last.

Eva moved to Monaco because the dry arid weather was good for her broken bones, which healed completely. They still hurt when it rained. It *always* rained in Lille. With her insurance money from the motorcycle accident, Eva bought a small dog grooming shop in Monaco. She had a natural gift and talent for handling dogs of any breed or size. The young woman of twenty dyed her hair blond. She looked like the twin of Olivia Newton John, the famous singer and performer.

The Monte-Carlo "jet set" quickly accepted her. Eva was not only remarkably sexy, but also a fantastic dancer. It is as if she was *reincarnated,* with a new much more dynamic personality and free spirit. In those days, jeans and a simple tee shirt was the fashion of the day. Short skirts and dresses were the accepted style for the evening. Eva stood out from the crowd with her large breasts and feminine curves. Men clamored for her favor, but she was a very independent person. Jewels, fancy cars, and gifts did not give anyone "a right" to sleep with her. If she liked your looks, style, and your eyes, you might become her partner for the night.

Vincent was somehow excited that other men claimed to love Eva, in the past. It increased her value in his eyes. Subconsciously, Eva wanted to be the *number one* beauty of Monte-Carlo, a Princess, *without royal blood.* Her looks were exceptional, and she knew it, but she was no princess.

The following day Eva asked Vincent to go with her to the Hotel de Paris. She had to take care of a dog housed *permanently* at the hotel. This extremely huge St. Bernard dog was the mascot of a very wealthy man who was away on business. He paid her to feed, exercise and look after his mascot.

They climbed the majestic white marble stairs of the hotel leading to the hallway carpeted in plush light green, with walls surfaced in rose silk. Upon arriving at the suite, Eva opened the door, and this black longhaired animal, at least twice her size, and weight, jumped up with joy and licked her face. She saw him more often than the master did, thus she controlled this beast better than the owner did. He obeyed her every command.

They took this enormous dog to the park, and he ran with her off his leash. When this huge St. Bernard encountered another small dog, he would intimidate the dog and its owner. Eva would then give him a firm command to sit. He stopped abruptly! What is incredible is that most animals seemed to understand and trust her, as if she had some kind of *mysterious power* over them; a power that gypsies seem to possess. She made a modest income from this small animal grooming business.

All these extraordinary experiences had an impact on Vincent. He admired her ability to survive in this crazy, difficult "human jungle," without losing her exceptional enthusiasm for life. Most people would have become despondent or cynical, by such tragic experiences.

Vincent remembered one extemporary experience during his third trip to Monaco. He bought an expensive dress from an exclusive shop and left it at her apartment as a surprise gift, with a note: "Rencontre à de l'"hôtel Paris." He was having drinks with friends visiting from California at Hotel de Paris. All of a sudden, Eva arrived in the bar dressed in jeans, with the box under her arm. Looking angry, she said a brief hello to the guests, and abruptly yanked me from my chair and took me outside.

"Pourquoi est-ce que tu as perdu ton argent sur cette robe chère?"

"Calm down, I don't understand your French when you speak so fast."

"Why did you waste your money on this expensive dress? Don't you know I can get much better at half the price?"

She forced Vincent to return to the shop and get his money back—*immediately.*

From that experience, among others, he believed Eva was not a "gold digger." Culture and language differences were a struggle, but he was willing to deal with such formidable challenges. He was an incurable romantic, who continued to believe that, *love could conquer all!*

Vincent departed Monte-Carlo, and returned to conservative Connecticut. He again left Eva abruptly, without even calling to say good-bye. He did not want to give her any "false hopes," about a lasting relationship, or the possibility of life together.

On the next trip to Monte-Carlo, the following month, Vincent became more and more committed, however. He could not continue to ignore his feelings for Eva. He began drinking to cover-up his *profound guilt.* He knew that Susan was deeply in love with him. She was a devoted mother, and he still loved her and his two children. That made his situation enormously awkward. How could he possibly hurt such a good and loyal person? A person who was so fragile, so devoted, whom he lived with and shared everything with intimately, for nearly half his life?

Why is it that the one you care for most, you seem to hurt the most? Europeans, especially French and Italian married men, have a "normal" family life and a mistress on the side. They never mix those two lives. As a good Christian, which Vincent *thought* he was, he believed that one woman at a time was the only way to live. After all, marriage was a "special sacrament," blessed by God—*isn't it?*

Vincent could not continue to live a dishonest life, with two women. Because of his guilt complex, he would typically consume a half-bottle of scotch in one day and night. Eva found him smashed one evening as she returned from her pet shop. She screamed and threatened to throw him out of her apartment. He pleaded with her to pardon him. She threatened to hit him over the head with the bottle the next time he indulged. He knew she was quite capable of such fierce behavior. Her temper, during times of emotional stress was *extremely potent.*

Eva made him face reality. She said, "If you are not happy with your workaholic routine life, then you must change it," she insisted. "You're wasting your life. Stop complaining! You just have to find the will power to change it. It will not be easy but your career and health is now in jeopardy. *Am I not worth the effort?"*

She was right. After that encounter, Vincent finally decided to support Eva. He had to accept some responsibility for her future welfare. He paid for her apartment, maintained the car, insisted that she get insurance, and tried to convince her to give up the "black market" business, importing clothes from Italy *without* paying any duty. She ignored all his arguments and warnings, until one fateful day when Eva got caught by customs, crossing the Italian border with a trunk filled with illegal contraband, mostly cartons of cigarettes and clothing. After Vincent paid the duty and penalties, they released her.

***

One evening, Vincent waited for Eva at her apartment. Her phone rang often. The answering machine took the messages. Most of the callers were men, who spoke French or Italian. One voice was *clearly British.* "Hi, Eva, I'm back in Monaco. You can reach me at Hotel de Paris. Do you have anything for me? Remember, I like them very young, and blonde-haired women. Call me around tea time, if you have what I like."

That message *stunned* Vince. Eva is running an escort service! She's providing sexual services for the rich, famous and powerful of Monte-Carlo. No wonder they treat her with such favoritism. Eva is a *professional madam!* He quickly searched the apartment, and found her "little black book." He got out his pocket French—English dictionary and began translating some of the more revealing parts. He ran through the names in the notebook. Some he recognized; many he could not. The ones' he recognized contained explicit details about their "special sexual needs."

One patron was a well-known movie actor. Two were prominent business executives. Another was a government official who only liked "young girls." A judge was also on her special list, as well as a nationally known television personality. The Monaco police chief himself is listed; his specialty was black women. *Shockingly,* even the father-in-law of Princess Caroline had his particular needs as well. All used her professional services. Now he knew why Eva had such excellent connections, and such superb benefactors in Monaco. They were afraid that she knew too much about their shady private lives. *They were right!*

Hotel de Paris was the central meeting place, the "headquarters" for all those high-class call girls. The escort service was well organized. Some of the hotel staff were her "special agents."

They knew who was in town and what kind of "score" they desired. They discreetly made arrangements, and received their "piece of the action." A typical night might cost 500 to 1,000 Euros. Some of these high-priced women of the night drove Jags, Rolls, and Bentleys. They wore designer clothes from Christian Dior, Oscar de la Renta, and Givenchy. Their elegant jewels were from Cartier and Tiffany.

Her agents arranged most of the events for the evening, except for the selection of girls—that was Eva's *specialty*. A night on the town included dinner at the best restaurants, followed by dancing at *Jimmy's,* or the *Living Room,* or the other exclusive clubs. The evening would end at the casino, before they jumped into the sack together.

Monaco is a small village and everyone knew what was happening. It was good for business, and that was all that really mattered. There were very few scandals since that would be bad for business. The police were everywhere, and they knew everyone and everything that was going on, but rarely arrested anyone. If a dispute occurred, it was of course the fault of the prostitute, regardless of who was the guilty party; she became *persona-nongrata,* and could not enter the Principality again. If the client became a problem, he was quietly escorted out of town. None of these scandals were reported in the local press. Anything that might hurt the *"good image"* of the Principality, or the Prince and his family, or the tourist trade, was *absolutely taboo.*

When you checked into any hotel in Monaco, within minutes the police knew who you were, and what you did for a living. All the casinos had a detailed dossier on every potential customer. It was "a highly computerized network." Vincent knew since the SBM hotel chain sought his advice on how to upgrade their IBM mainframe computer system. Cameras installed on top of the buildings, the lampposts and in the hotels, allowed the police to zoom in on anyone, anywhere, anytime. It was a police state! Still, the police made extraordinary efforts to eliminate many of the drug dealers.

When she arrived, Eva could tell immediately that something was bothering Vince. He could not conceal his annoyance. The anguished expression on his face, his body language and demeanor was very evident. "What's wrong? Why do you look so irritated?" she asked.

"You didn't tell me about your 'other' business," he said. "Your escort service."

"How do you know about that?"

"Never mind how I know. It's all documented here in your black book."

"Give me that! You have no right to search through my private things. It doesn't concern you."

"Your British client called, that's how I know. What kind of crap is this? How long have you been providing girls for these sick men?"

"Look, it's not like that. I simply arrange for my girlfriends to meet interesting wealthy men. *That's all!"* Eva answered. "What they do afterward is not my concern. It's their private business."

"Don't bullshit me! You get money from them, don't you?"

"It's a professional dating service. Why shouldn't they pay for my services? How do you think I paid for this apartment, this furniture and my clothes, all these years? You have escort services in the States, don't you? It's a legal business—*isn't it?"*

They argued for more than an hour. Then Vincent *demanded* that Eva stop this crazy racket, which could seriously hurt both of them. It was difficult for her to change. It was easy money. Vincent gave her an ultimatum! "You quit this business *immediately,* or I leave you *right now!* The choice is yours!"

In the past, she had been a high-priced courtesan, and very good at it. Part actor—all "ladies of the night" are actors—she could enter into the client's desired fantasy with complete conviction. Yet part of her mind would always remain detached—observing, despising them. The lords of commerce and aristocrats sought her favors. She was a good-natured madam with witticism. A woman who knew her time of pleasure giving would be limited. In any case, her personal tastes were *quite different.*

Vincent gave her an opportunity to stop such activities, which she knew did not have much of a future anyway. She became frightened that he *really* meant what he said. She did not want to lose the *only* man in her life that gave her a sense of security. She promised to stop. "I'll even change my phone," she said firmly. "I love you Vincent, *please* don't leave me, darling."

He wanted to be convinced. When the phone calls ended, over the next few weeks, he then began to believe her.

He tried to provide alternative activities that she could take pleasure from; something that would give her a sense of self-esteem, something to keep her busy. She needed some kind of *legal trade.* She needed a chance to be proud of herself once more—to be *respectable.*

After weeks of deliberating and searching, Vincent found a small shop, just off Monte-Carlo, and bought it for her. She was very pleased by this charming shop. Woman's fashions were one of her "passions."

"I could sell new and pre-owned women's fashions," she said. Many of her friends wore a brand new expensive dress or suit, once or twice, and they would sell it to her later, at a fraction of the original price. They made plans together to decorate and furnish *her shop.* Contractors were hired, stock was selected, and advertisements were placed in the local paper. She named her fashion shop, *"Troc Affaire."*

Their lives together became enjoyable once again. They made frequent trips to picturesque villages throughout France, Spain and Italy. One day, they found themselves lost while driving to a beautiful Italian mountain village called *Saint Vincent.* Tired and hungry they ultimately arrived at a charming family restaurant in the middle of a lush green forest. It was about two in the afternoon. The owner informed them that the kitchen had just closed. "Please try to accommodate us. We're starving," Eva pleaded.

She looked them over, and then escorted them to a table in the corner. The people seemed so natural, so humble and the food tasted great. The luncheon feast included roast pig, fresh Italian vegetables, assortments of cheese, and exceptional desserts. Wood burned in the fireplace, as musicians played romantic Italian songs. The local wine was also exceptional. They were in no condition to drive back to Monaco. A little old woman, one of the owners of the place, who must have been eighty, said, "Why don't you sleep in those hammocks," pointing to the woods outside.

"That's a good idea," Eva responded. "May we pay you for using them?"

"No! Don't be silly, young lady. You tipped me too much already."

They took a long very welcomed nap outside, in the cool peaceful woods.

They found peace and happiness together, more deeply with each of their trips. Eva must really love me, Vincent thought when she showed how *extremely* jealous she could be, whenever he happened to merely look at another woman. "All healthy men look at other women; *it's normal,"* he said. In his case, it was *totally innocent.* He did not care for anyone, other than Eva, Susan, and his beloved children.

She spilled hot coffee on him once, when his eyes happened to drift to another charming woman sitting at a table in a restaurant. Never had Vincent experienced such extreme jealously. They were fighting over something that was, in his view, *completely normal.* After many similar episodes, Vince concluded that Eva must have a serious "PMS problem." She acted strangely, a few days before her period. She became irritable, emotional, and argued with him, as well as others. He finally told her that she had a PMS problem; there were pharmaceutical products that might help her.

"Je n'ai pas du problème, and I don't need any drugs," was her quick-tempered reaction. Eva never told Vincent that one of her former lovers was a drug dealer from Naples. After she learned about his secret activities, she dropped him at once. In her past, she saw many cases of drug addicts, in Italy and Monaco. These tragic incidents affected her deeply. She refused to take any drugs—not even aspirin.

***

Cannes, France. The French Rivera, where the International Film Festival takes place every summer, is in Cannes. Actors and performers meet there to receive their awards. It is like Oscar night in Hollywood. It was a perfect place to have a fashion show. It was an opportunity to demonstrate to the famous that you have something *special* to exhibit.

Eva knew the owner of the *Pink Panther* nightclub in Cannes, and he agreed to let her show her fashion collection. Models would have to be selected. Clothes must be carefully chosen. A program had be designed and printed. It was a huge undertaking. Vincent did not know anything about how to organize this kind of show. Moreover, he had to tend to his consulting business in the States.

Vincent flew to the States and left Eva alone to run her show, which would start the following week. They called each other every day. Usually her voice came on the phone as something fresh and cool. This time it seemed harsh and dry. They talked for a while, and then abruptly they were not talking any longer. "Why are you so moody?"

"It's just the … the show, I guess. It is a lot of work you know. Besides, you left me here all alone to do everything by myself," she said.

"Well I'm also working here alone, to make money for us. I'm not here just to have a good time."

Vincent did not know who hung up first. He sensed that something was not right. Call it instinct; a kind of *sixth sense*. He felt that something serious, something *strange* was happening thousands of miles away. You can perceive when someone is fibbing by the tone of his or her voice, and the way they avoid talking about things. There was something wrong in her behavior.

During the fashion show, Eva introduced her models to Greek sailors who were staying at the same hotel. She became enchanted with the leader of the group. A Greek Captain who seemed to, *"only have eyes for her."* He did not care for the younger, sexier models— *only her.* Perhaps she was going through some kind of mid-life crisis. Eva had just turned thirty-five. She was worried about her looks. Did she still have what it takes to attract the opposite sex? Here was her *"Prince Charming,"* Captain Demetri, who cared about her personality, her character—not merely her sexy body.

Demetri, a relatively short man, with wavy black hair and large black eyes, claimed to be a humble sailor, who built his fortune the hard way; *he earned it.* "My father was a fisherman. When he died he left me only a small old boat."

"My, that's remarkable. You're very young to be a Captain," she said.

"I'm twenty-four. My brothers helped me a lot. However, I had the idea to change from fishing, which is a very unstable business, to a more profitable shipping business. Now I have a fleet of three ships."

Later Eva told her models, "have you seen his rippling muscles and dark youthful good looks ... il est donc parfait ... his body is so wonderful, I can't help wondering what he wants from me." After all, if he just wanted sex, the other girls are much younger and sexier, she thought. "Just look at him. *Be honest.* Don't you want to jump in bed with him? Can't you imagine getting it on with him?"

"We may be younger," they said, "but you have a more interesting, outgoing personality."

"Men think that they control everything," she told her models. "They don't realize that the woman who controls a man's genitals *actually controls the man.* After all, Eve seduced Adam into eating that forbidden fruit. And Samson, with all his strength, became as weak as a baby, in the arms of Delilah."

Her models interrupted her, "why don't you take him up on his offer to show you his new boat tonight? Everything is now ready for the show tomorrow."

The sun sank lower spreading its last rays of light over the sea. Demetri showed her his new yacht, the evening before the big fashion show. A few drinks of strong Ouzo relaxed them as they talked about Greece, her shop, and program for the next show. She had been in Athens many years ago and knew something about the country. "You know, I visited Athens about ten years ago."

"It's beautiful, isn't it?" Demetri asked.

"It certainly has lots of history. But the people are too traditional."

"Yeah, I know what you mean. They are very conservative. We do not have any topless bathing in Greece. Why did you visit my country?" he inquired.

"Well, the truth is ... I went there to have an abortion. My former boyfriend got me pregnant. I could not get an abortion in France, at that time. You see the father of the baby drank a lot. After six months, I did not gain any weight and the baby did not move in my belly. I thought the fetus might have been affected by his drinking."

"That's sad. Was the baby deformed?" Demetri asked.

"No, it would have been a healthy baby boy. The doctor was *very angry* with me. He said he would never again do another abortion, after this experience."

Eva wore one of her latest fashions, a soft white, long summer silk dress that complemented her dark tan skin, and short blond hair. She did not wear under garments during hot summer nights. That would alter the smooth flowing lines of the dress, and conceal her bountiful breasts that bulged through the thin material.

Eva smoothed out the long white dress that accentuated the tapered curves of her body. She knew what turned-on men. She played her seductive role like a professional. It was getting dark outside. "Let's have some food and drinks in the cabin," she suggested.

"That's a good idea. It's also getting a bit cool," he agreed.

Long shadows from the last rays of the sinking sun, accented the fine bone structure of her exotic tanned face, and lit up her sad green eyes. As she stood up ahead of him, lights from the cabin shined through the translucent dress, illuminating the exquisite shape of her buttocks. She turned to serve him a drink and noticed that his masculinity became more prominent in his tight-fitting jogging trousers. The swaying yacht made her a little dizzy. She fell back on the long cushioned chair. Demetri came over to assist her and knelt down by her chair. "Are you all right, sweetheart?" he asked.

"It's just the Ouzo, I guess." She reached down, held his face with her two hands, and kissed him. As he returned her lush kiss, his left hand moved slowly up her leg to the limits of her thigh. She did not resist as his probing fingers finally found its mark. They fell down onto the carpeted cabin floor.

Vincent returned to Monte-Carlo a few days later. He sensed immediately that something was wrong. Eva did not hug and kiss him warmly, as she usually did at the airport in Nice. Their conversation was different. It seemed tense. She refused to look at him directly in the eye when they spoke. He confronted her. "What's wrong? Why are you behaving like I'm some kind of stranger?"

Eva astonished him. She confessed her infidelity. "Vincent, I'm really *very sorry.* I had a foolish affair with this Greek Captain. He is much too young for me. It was only a kind of passing fling."

"How could you do such a thing, while I was away trying to build a future for us? How could you betray our love so easily?"

She began crying. "It was during a moment of weakness. The separation from you was too much for me to handle. When you go away, some part of me goes away with you. It was also the enormous pressure of the fashion show. What do you want with me, anyway? You have a wife and children ... I do not demand anything. I am now over thirty-five. What do you want with me?"

Vincent was depressed and sickened by her affair. At the same time, he appreciated her truthfulness, her honesty.

She's right, what kind of future can I really offer her? After all, she is a *free individual.* There is no real commitment between us.

Eva could not sleep that night. She kept thinking about their relationship. She was afraid that he must want someone else; that he wanted a *different* Eva—more than the real person. That fear kept her from giving herself fully. She was *trapped* in a vicious cycle. She could not derive complete joy from Vincent because she was afraid of losing him. As a Madam, she heard all kinds of sordid stories from "her girls." That made her believe that *all men are deceitful.*

On his next flight back to the States, Vincent kept blaming himself. Am I too vulnerable to the seductiveness of a younger, sexier woman? Eva did not know where she stood with me. What kind of future could she have being a *part-time mistress?* She wanted something more permanent from our relationship. He was sinking in *Quicksand,* and did not know how to save himself. The real reason for this affair, which he did not understand at the time, was her *extreme insecurity.* He was determined to make the right decision, to resolve her sense of uncertainty and his situation, one way or the other.

* * *

Vincent and Susan knew that the cause of their languishing marriage really began years ago. It did not just suddenly happen. They avoided the obvious signs earlier because both saw how broken marriages deeply affect young children. Now that excuse did not exist anymore. The children were away in college. They were alone together for the first time in twenty-one years. Vince could not stop thinking about his dilemma. There was no easy answer. He could not continue to live a dual life—a life of lies. (Psychologically, he wanted to justify his own deep guilty feelings since he betrayed his vows of marriage).

When Vincent returned, Susan sensed that something was very wrong. Conversation together was only be about her medical career, the children, the house and his business. There was no intimate discourse; no sensitivity to each other's emotional needs—*no passion.* Was he experiencing a mid-life crisis? Was he beginning to doubt himself, and his ability to perform sexually?

Vincent knew the real cause of their dispassionate life together. It was that unexpected dreadful thing happened two years ago. It continued to eat at his gut. That event kept him from Susan's bed.

He had to change his life. He needed to find some purpose, some meaning to his empty existence. The more Vincent tried to soften the blow to Susan, the more he hurt her. He could not tell her the *dark secret,* the real reason for their marriage predicament. (Eva did not insist that he divorce Susan, although she knew they could not continue to live like this anymore).

First, he told his wife "Susan we should have a trial separation, for a few months, so that I can think more clearly about our future together."

"Is there another woman?"

"Of course there's no other woman! How could you think such a thing?"

Vincent had to stop lying to such a good person who deserved better treatment from him. Susan's doctor cautiously advised him to face reality. Yet, he could not possibly tell Susan the truth. That might seriously affect her vulnerable psychological condition. Because of her past *terrible incident,* he just could not give himself to her anymore. Their emotional and sexual life together was *finished.*

Months later, after he moved to an apartment nearby. He could not face Susan directly and honestly. He sent the divorce papers by special delivery. He did not realize how badly she would take this cold stupid way to end a marriage. Later that evening Vincent went to see her. Even in the dim light, the glistening of tears spilled from her despondent eyes. He could not explain his rationale for the divorce. It was *too disheartening* to talk about the "real reason" (which was unrelated to Eva). It would really destroy her if she knew the truth. Vincent held her in his arms as the tears ran down her cheeks. How could I hurt this good person so terribly?

I felt like a heel, but I was "past the point-of-no-return." There could not be any turning back now. To prolong the divorce would only hurt her more. The children could not understand how I could be so callous. They thought their father was a bastard. *They were right!* I told her it was not necessary to hire a lawyer. I agreed to give her the house and furniture, and pay reasonable alimony, without any legal hassles. Susan hired a lawyer anyway. She ended up with nearly the same alimony that I had promised. As if this were sufficient compensation for the terrible hurt that I caused this gentle, loving human being. *Will God ever forgive me?*

***

DISILLUSIONED

"We can only know what we can truly imagine.
Finally what we see comes from ourselves."

—Marge Piercy

Vincent was very disillusioned by what was happening to American society. The radical left "progressive movement," which began decades earlier, postulated total liberty and equality, *without* individual responsibility. Extreme liberal groups called for abortion-on-demand for teenagers, without parental consent. There were quotas for minorities, even when they were not qualified for the job. There was the banning of prayers in schools, although the dollar still says, "In God We Trust." Everyone demanded the right to free speech, without restraint, such as pornography, and defacing the American flag.

Certain issues resurface during election cycles. Issues like welfare, education, the environment ("climate change" remained an unchallengeable doctrine for the left. What if there was a future freeze? Which would be worse?). Then there was taxes and spending. In this age of envy, greed and entitlements, minorities find it increasingly difficult to be self-reliant, when the federal government acts like a giant ATM. Just because one disagrees about issues, doesn't mean we have to be disagreeable.

President Obama represented all these progressive principles—*in the extreme.* The Democratic Party controlled the senate, and Senator Harry Reid was acting like an arrogant ass. In addition, 47 Inspector Generals, the official nonpartisan watchdogs of the federal government, signed a letter to Congress pleading for help. In their letter, the Inspectors reported that the Obama Administration has been restricting, blocking or delaying access to important information—making it virtually impossible for them to do their job, to investigate possible fraud, waste or abuse inside federal government agencies. According to these official watchdogs, the Administration has been blocking access to information and it is leaving the agencies "vulnerable to mismanagement and misconduct."

The Obama Administration had a long list of scandals and transparency failures, such as Operation "Fast and Furious," gunrunning into Mexico; false narratives on what actually happened in Benghazi; "lost IRS emails" concerning the targeting of conservatives; and deleted HHS emails, on the botched rollout of Obamacare. Progressive liberals were "brainwashing" a generation of Americans. In preparation for the 40th anniversary of Woodstock, they were rolling out the *old lie* that free sex, drugs, and rock 'n' roll defined the '60s. Now they were brainwashing yet another generation of Americans. Radical factions hijacked feminism, the civil rights movement, and academia, replacing conservative ideologies—based on traditional values of Faith and Family—with more extreme left philosophies of materialism and socialism.

America was becoming a socialistic welfare state. Obama's administration encouraged redistribution of wealth, and "transformation" of America from its *imaginary* colonial past. He emphasized political correctness, and government dependency, especially for voting minorities. He ruined the medical care sector, representing nearly 20% of the economy, with Obamacare and EPA rules. There were countless corrupt officials. As result, children lacked suitable role models, and moral values. Standards of excellence no longer existed. Bribes and "golden parachutes" seemed to be the order of the day. Scandals had run rampant in the IRS, in Benghazi, in the VA, in enforcing immigration laws, and dishonesty became the "new normal" in the business world.

Vincent became extremely disillusioned. He decided to move to Monte-Carlo. Maybe it would be better there. He converted part of Eva's apartment living room into an impressive office, a large, elegant area to receive clients. However, it still was not practical to run his business thousands of miles from California and New York, where most of his client offices were. He had to factor in time zone differences. Reluctantly, he had to keep one leg in the States, and one leg in Monaco, since important clients were in Europe as well.

La Jolla is a charming village by the sea. Most of the residents there are wealthy, the weather is fantastic, and there are many exclusive shops and restaurants. "The ambiance is similar to the French Rivera," he told Eva. We were able to rent a small charming house with a fireplace, with a great view of the Pacific Ocean, and a small garden for her dog to do his thing. It was only a short walk to the main village, where one could have a coffee outdoors; take a walk in the park by the sea, or lunch in many delightful sidewalk restaurants.

Whenever possible, usually on weekends, they drove down to Mexico, to a place called Rosetta, to indulge in fresh lobsters and margaritas. Vince wanted to show Eva a different part of his world. The trip down the Baja peninsula took three hours. This part of Mexico is so very different from the States or Europe. People live in small shacks by the sea and children run barefooted in the streets. Yet these humble people seem to have discovered something that has eluded much of the rest of the world: They have found how to be *truly jubilant.*

* * *

Rosetta, Mexico. As they rounded a curve and emerged on the top of a hill, there stood Villa Rosetta. Rough waves washed against huge gray and brown rocks on the beach producing enormous sprays of salt water in the air, near the terrace of the restaurant. The mist created a romantic atmosphere as the bright orange sun shined through the clouds, and slowly set beneath the sea. Mexicans played exquisite songs of love. We were the only "gringos" in the village. It was a very different environment from the States or Monaco. Eva knew a little Spanish, enabling us to communicate with the locals. The waiters catered to our every need, as if we were visiting royalty.

On the way back to the States, we stopped near the border to buy some bottles of liquor and gifts. Unlike the small villages, most of the big towns and cities were *absolute disasters.* The squalor was appalling! People in this city were packed together in shanty shacks. "They are worse off than herds of animals," Eva observed.

At the United States border, our car was stopped for a *thorough* inspection. The border guards wondered what a sexy French woman was doing in Mexico, and why she was entering the States. The delay exceeded one hour, as they searched our vehicle for drugs or illegal contraband.

When returning from such poverty, misery and squalor, to California, it was like returning to a clean fresh New World. "You really have to leave the United States for a few days, to fully appreciate what a remarkable country we have, in spite of all that liberalism crap, and other warts," Vincent told Eva.

Trips back to Monte Carlo became more difficult and expensive. The shop there became an *obsession* with Eva. Vincent realized that the only way to change her attachment and to keep her with him in La Jolla was to open another shop. They located a place between a sidewalk restaurant and coiffeur boutique. She called her new shop in La Jolla, *"Lady De Monte Carlo."* Since Paris and Milan are generally about one year ahead of the United States fashion world, Eva would buy yesterday's fashions from Europe, and sell them as the latest fashions in California. This technique allowed them to reduce some of the unsold stock in Monaco, and turn her inventory faster. She would save money on import duties, by legally claiming they were second-hand clothes.

There is a *big difference* in establishing a small business in the United States, as compared to France and most of Europe. In the States, you can start a new business in a few days, with only a few hundred dollars for a license, rent, and other relatively minor costs. Opening a small business in France takes many months to get the necessary governmental authorization, and thousands of Euros. In addition, in France and Monaco you cannot easily hire or fire anyone, for any reasonable cause. The only difficulty Vincent encountered in the States was getting Eva a "Green Card," so that she could legally work, and ultimately become a United States citizen. That Green Card required frequent trips to the immigration office, many interviews and paperwork.

We traveled to and from California and Monaco about five times a year. Eva's dog, *Zizou,* became a kind of substitute for a real child. He was her "security blanket." While I was fond of her dog, I did not appreciate waking up in the middle of the night to take a piss, and suddenly step on sharp bones her dog often left near the bed. Eva refused to correct Zizou's little habits, as if it might affect his doggie persona. "Leave him be," she would say, scornfully, "Let him put his bones where he wants."

Eva insisted on taking the dog everywhere we went. It created *significant* problems. Wherever we traveled, she took Zizou on board the flight in her small *Louis Vuitton* handbag. He only weighed about ten pounds. In France and Monaco, everyone accepted dogs. The hotels, restaurants and beaches in the States did not allow any animals. We once stayed at the Hyatt Hotel in San Francisco, and asked to leave because the dog naturally barked, when the Hotel housekeeper came to fix the room. The police gave us a ticket whenever the dog was scene on the beach. "People produce *more shit* than this small dog. Human germs are certainly more contagious than dog diseases." We still had to pay these silly fines.

Eva left me alone to take care of "her shop," while she visited her girlfriend in LA. It was a quiet peaceful morning. Very few customers interrupted me. I decided to catch up with all the shop paper work: state tax forms, bill payments and inventory control, which Eva hated to handle. I was too busy running my own business to pay much attention to her finances, until now. After updating the books, for the first six months of her operation, I finally realized that the shop losses were much, much bigger than anticipated, and the future did not look any brighter. Eva bought more and more fashions based on her personal preferences, before selling part of the current stock. If something looked good on her, she bought more. That's a sure formula for financial disaster.

Eva returned two days later. It did not take long to get back on the subject of "my" limited finances, and "her shops." "What do you know about fashions?" she said. "Why don't you stick to your technology business and keep your nose out of *my* affair."

"One thing I know for sure, you should never buy anything based on your personal taste alone. You have to select what your customers' want—not what *you* want," I responded. "This is commonsense." How could I have been so dumb to establish this business for her? It was a pending catastrophic. Both shops became a financial burden and cause for arguments, as we blamed each other for the business problems.

"You're always telling me how to run my business," she said scornfully. "This shop is really your way to keep me *trapped* in America."

We decided that maybe a public fashion show might stimulate business, and help reduce our inventories. We agreed to plan a fashion show in La Jolla, jointly with the beautician salon next door. Both parties agreed to share all expenses for the show.

As we began to plan for the show, Jonathan, the manager of the hairdresser Salon, *La Fem*, turned out to be an uptight, highly sensitive jerk, who insisted on doing things *his way,* which was the only right way. We fought with him over his contemptuous manner and egotistical temperament. During one practice session for the show, Jonathan played the stereo music so loud that the talk-show moderator could not be heard describing the fashions. Vincent went over and turned the volume down.

"How *dare you* touch my stereo," Jonathan barked, as he ran over and turned the volume up again.

Since both shops share all the costs equally, we insisted that he respect our desires and ideas for the program. "How the hell can anyone hear the speaker?" Vincent shouted.

"Right now these ladies need to improve their movement to my music," Jonathan insisted.

Gorgeous models from all over California competed to be in the fashion show. Some younger models came from the local university. The timing for changing clothes had to be just right. Movement to the music had to be perfect. Jonathan tried to show the professional models how to walk to his music. He looked ridiculous!

On the evening of the show, the house was packed to the rafters, with some of the richest people from La Jolla, LA, and San Diego, and the fashion press was there as well. While the audience adored the Lady de Monte-Carlo fashions, they objected to Jonathan's *outlandish* hairstyles. The fashion show turned out to be a huge success. Lady de Monte-Carlo netted about $22,000.

After the show, Vincent and Eva met with Jonathan to review the accounting. He was pissed-off. "Some of the girls changed my beautiful hair styles," he cried. "You put them up to it. That's why they didn't like my fantastic creations," he screamed.

"Look, only one or two models didn't like your hair style, and they asked me to change it," Vince responded. "Your shop will *never* make it in this town!" he threatened.

I was not going to take any more of his crap. "Listen, asshole, if you can't accept that they didn't like your ridiculous hair styles, get screwed."

We started roughing it up on the show room runway, of all places. He was a big guy, over six feet tall and at least two-hundred-fifty pounds. Nevertheless, Jonathan had a sensitive abdomen. My fist hit him in the gut. As he doubled over, I followed with a left hook to his mouth. Jonathan's lip started bleeding.

"I'll get you for that!" he shouted, as Eva handed him some tissues.

Shoplifters became another serious problem. Eva could not accept losses of her precious fashions, although they were covered by insurance. Some of the shoplifters were real professionals. They would appear to be serious buyers. One of the partners in crime would try on lots of clothes in the private change room. They would stuff some goods under their extra-large dress, while the other created a diversion. Pilfers would escape out the door with three or four of the Eva's best fashions, hidden under their clothes. There were also a few bad checks which could not be verified in advance because the credit check system was either too slow in responding, or didn't work. With only one helper in the shop, Eva couldn't keep an eye on all the customers. She became *very frustrated* when some of her finest fashions were gone. She took it personally.

On Halloween evening, about two weeks later, they received an unexpected phone call from the police. The cops said the shop window was smashed. Expensive Italian leather coats and jackets were stolen. Vincent knew who the thief might be, but he had no proof. It was clearly the work of Jonathan, their former partner next door. The conniving cagey smile on his face convinced them that he must have hired someone to do his dirty work.

Eva was completely turned-off on America. She wanted to return to her *safe and secure* Monaco. Vincent grew up in one of the toughest sections of Brooklyn, yet he had never been robbed or experienced such craziness. How is it possible for a peaceful little village like La Jolla to have such crime he thought? (The real answer is that thieves don't pick poor neighborhoods to rob).

After selling the remaining inventory, and fixtures to another shop in the area, at a significant loss, they closed Lady de Monte-Carlo, *permanently.* Whatever couldn't be sold was put in storage, including furniture. What a disaster! Someone once said, "Love is blind." Vincent was living proof of that expression—he was *deaf, dumb and blind.*

They established new roots up north, in beautiful San Francisco. After a long search, they found a nice apartment on Vallejo, near Union Street, the Pacific Heights section of the city, overlooking the picturesque Golden Gate Bridge. Union Street is one of the most exclusive shopping and dining areas of the city. It has numerous boutiques and fabulous restaurants, like Boz Scagg's, the Blue Note Café, and sumptuous Italian cuisine, known as Prego. San Francisco has a far more cosmopolitan lifestyle than La Jolla and San Diego. People seemed to be more interesting, there were fine ethnic restaurants, good theaters, and clean beaches. The commute for Vincent was an easy hour against the traffic, from San Fran to San Jose, where his clients were located.

That Christmas they took a long overdue vacation near a ski resort in California. Vincent hoped Eva might enjoy beautiful snow-covered Lake Tahoe. They rented a charming cabin, right on the lake. "It's too cold, light a fire," Eva demanded, as he arrived with the bags. "These mountains are not as pretty as Switzerland." Later she again complained: "This casino is certainly inferior to Monte-Carlo."

During lunch the following day, Eva suddenly said, "I've been everywhere and seen everything." Her eyes flashed around in a defiant manner. As soon as her voice broke off, she looked at him with a big smirk on her face, and asked, "Vincent, how come you never asked me to marry you?"

"I didn't believe you actually wanted to get married, so I gave up thinking about it? If you're really serious, we might be able to do it in Las Vegas."

"Dearest, I think you should know something first."

"What's that?"

"It's a secret. I *must* tell you now. In the past, I was in jail ... in Italy. That was almost ten years before we met. I was falsely accused of stealing. I was locked up in this 'Italian institution.' The jail was a real education for me, a sort of college education. That's how I became proficient in the language. Later, my girlfriend finally confessed that she had found her fur coat, which she earlier said I stole. When I finally got out of prison, with nothing except the clothes on my back, I met a Mafia character, Tony, who took a fancy to me. However, when I learned he trafficked in drugs, I *immediately* dropped him. I saw how drugs destroyed many lives in Monaco, and observed lots of tragic examples of addicts, in the Italian jails," she explained.

Eva was *totally* against this kind of deadly poison. Years earlier, Vincent remembered that Monaco police used her to entrap big drug dealers. She played her clandestine role willingly. Now Vincent understood why the police chief protected her. She performed important services for the Principality. Her confession did not change anything, except it might screw up her Green Card status, if her past record became known to immigration. Vincent admired her for telling him her deep secret, *before* they made a long-term commitment to each other.

He arranged for a car to take them to be married in Carson City. Then, *the unbelievable happened!* Our limousine broke down in the middle of the highway. The driver claimed this had never happened before. Eva, like her gypsy friends, who believed in astrologers and fortunetellers, had determined *"This must be our destiny!"*

Vincent refused to let a simple vehicle malfunction stop them from getting married. "Every human being has his or her own free will and destiny. The only imperative is to follow it, to accept it, *no matter where it may lead."* Besides, he assumed, getting married would make everything legal, and would bring them closer together.

The marriage was unnatural—*synthetic in every way.* The small chapel had plastic flowers. The taped music sounded like "elevator music." A minister, with a red beard, performed the simple ceremony. *Everything was counterfeit!* (Vincent remembered his beautiful church wedding in New York City, some twenty-plus years ago. It was so real, so meaningful, so full of sentiment—but that didn't make it last).

* * *

They returned to Monaco as man and wife. Back to Eva's "safe and secure paradise," where everyone spoke *her* language. Friends warmly greeted her. The problem was Vincent did not understand much French and had few friends there. In addition, only a handful of clients used his consulting services in that part of Europe.

Fig 4. Monaco Port

Eva introduced Vincent to the high-society of Monaco, and arranged for his official residency and legal business papers, with her "special connections." It is extremely difficult to obtain residence status and approval to do business in Monaco. The administration demands proof of everything: Your banking records must show you are financially well off; police records must prove you are not a criminal; three good references were required; finally, verification from a doctor is required to prove that you don't have AIDS or any other serious medical problem.

Vincent woke at daybreak most mornings, and went to the open marketplace where they sold fresh flowers, fruits from private groves, varieties of vegetables, olive oil pressed by human hands, and of course, that special French bread and croissants. The tent-covered market was charming. It was like something out of the past, where people greet you by your first name. They haggle over prices, and gossiped about politics, taxes, and the weather. In America, with its highly efficient, *impersonal* malls and supermarkets, we have lost that charming atmosphere and opportunity for human communication. You learn more about what is *really* happening from the marketplace; more than any local newspaper might report.

On Sunday morning, church bells rang, calling Vincent to St. Charles for Mass. He went alone. Eva claimed she did not believe in God. He was a sinner who prayed for forgiveness, and then continued to sin again, soon thereafter. After he had sex with Eva, Vince prayed quietly. He made an act of contrition, knowing that he had just sinned. He felt trapped. He was sinking in the *quicksand of sin*, and could not escape, without help from a power beyond his reach. Nevertheless, he never stopped praying.

*****

Bonnie was a wealthy, charming old woman, of about eighty-five. Eva groomed her white poodle, and often took some food to her penthouse, since she lived alone. Bonnie would open a bottle of Champagne, and Eva and Vincent would keep her company a few hours after dinner. This delightful elderly person really appreciated their companionship. Her husband had died a few years earlier. Her only son rarely visited his lonely old mother.

One evening, as they arrived, they found ribbons across her door, with an official seal imprinted in wax. "What's this all about? Did she sell her apartment and move?" Vincent asked.

Eva started to cry, uncontrollably. "That seal means she's … she's dead."

"How is it possible? We saw this beautiful woman only yesterday. She seemed to be healthy and in good spirits."

They learned that Bonnie jumped off her terrace—with her white poodle in her arms—the night before. She was deeply despondent because her son had not visited her for Mother's day. In fact, he rarely visited her during any holiday.

Her asshole son did not even show up for his mother's funeral. He was afraid that Bonnie's friends might gang up on him. He was right, they would have kicked his butt out of Monaco. A few days later an agent of the son arrived to sell his mother's apartment, jewels and valuable paintings. Her suicide was not reported in the press. That kind of news would not be good for the tourist business. There are many other Bonnie types in Monaco—*it is a village of very rich and very lonely souls.*

Vincent spent most of his quality time on the terrace, awaking early each morning, to enjoy the fantastic sunrise with his coffee, *alone.* He usually ended the day watching the sunset, with a few glasses of wine.

During hot August nights, he would sleep alone on a lounge chair, under the bright stars, and wonder, *what's it all about?* He gazed at the stars and pondered how his crazy, confused life fit into God's plan? That quiet terrace was a refuge from the bewildering world inside, below and beyond.

During the time of the *Grand Prix,* in mid-May, Monte Carlo came alive with fascinating people from all over Europe—Dukes, Barons, Princesses, actors and other well-known personalities. It was a frequent hangout (in earlier decades) for Frank Sinatra and his clique. The influx of tourists more than doubled the population. The rich and famous attended the races and grand balls. Glamour was everywhere—at the theaters.

Fig 5. The Grand Prix

The deafening noise from the racing cars in the Grand Prix reverberated throughout the village during that week. Eva sold tickets for the races, at inflated prices, and handed out flyers advertising her shop, *Troc Affaire.* Vincent and Eva watched the races from the top of the Hotel De Paris, while drinking champagne with elite guests. Eva introduced Vincent to charming, mostly wealthy people, whom she met during the ten years she lived there. He was certainly impressed.

In the summer, especially July and August, the beaches became crowded with tourists. Vincent and Eva often escaped to a more private remote beach, a few minutes outside of Monaco. It was a small rocky beach, where they could be naked together, without prying eyes. Eva would prepare a picnic lunch basket with wine, cheese and French bread. Her dog seemed to know instantly when they planned to go to there. He jumped with excitement and fetched his special beach blanket in his mouth. Zizou fetched small rocks, and then he would dig deep holes in the sand and bury them. When Vincent and Eva had a disagreement, Zizou would come over and sit on his lap, look directly at his eyes, as if to say, "What's wrong? Why not make peace?" That creature was incredibly intelligent—almost human.

On Sunday afternoon, they had brunch at the Beach Hotel, where Vincent first met Eva. They served brunch on the terrace under pastel-colored umbrellas, at the end of the dock, where smaller motorboats carried guests from their yachts would anchor. It was an exclusive gathering place for the rich and powerful of Monaco. Eva liked to be scene there. She enjoyed mingling with the upper class and all the illustrious public figures. Vincent found the constant parade of unusual characters amusing, especially when some tycoon arrived, with a stylish bikini clad woman on his arm. It was a sort of midday fashion show.

Food of every variety was laid out in the center of the terrace, buffet style, served by cooks and waiters dressed in crisp white uniforms. Now and then Eva would point out an illustrious or princely person, who happened to use her dog grooming or "other services." By one o'clock, a steel band arrived and played tropical Jamaican music.

In due time, Vincent and Eva began to argue about her remaining shop, *Troc Affaire,* located in the French marketplace, adjacent to Monaco's border. Earlier problems that existed in the States began to surface in this store as well. There were too few paying customers, excessive inventory, missing or stolen goods, and lots of red ink. It was a becoming a financial disaster!

***

Out of nowhere, this *extraordinary person* appeared. Her clothes were plain; her demeanor unpretentious, her appearance was modest. She seemed to be familiar. Vincent had seen her somewhere before, but could not remember where. She smiled at him with her deep blue eyes. It was a radiant smile; a look that seemed to say, *I know everything about you.*

"Hello, I'm Anne," she said. After the brief introductions, Eva immediately took control of the conversation and asked if she needed anything in particular?

"You have some delightful fashions," she said, while rapidly going through the racks, selecting dresses, shirts, suits, and several accessories to match.

Eva showed her the latest fashions, which she accepted without much discussion. She took particular interest in dressing up this client, who seemed to understand fashions, although she dressed modestly.

"Why don't you try on this suit with this blouse?" Eva asked. "And for the evening out, I have this fantastic light-blue dress. *It is perfect for you,* with your golden hair.

"Yes, you're right, that looks great!"

"Now try on these matching shoes," Eva instructed.

When Anne finished, two hours later, the total came to 18,000 Eros. "Please deliver these things to my friend's apartment at this address, in Monaco," she requested, while handing Vincent a huge bundle of cash, and directions written on a card.

"May we offer you a coffee ... or something?" Eva asked, as she made out a receipt. "Will you be in Monaco long?"

"Only a few days or so."

"Why don't we get together for cocktails before you leave," Eva suggested. "You shouldn't miss the big charity gala while you're here. It is the most glamorous event of the year."

"You're very kind. Let me check with my friend to see if he's willing," she said. "How can I reach you?"

A few nights later, Vincent and Eva met Anne and her friend Hanz, at the Sporting Club, for the annual *Gala of the Roses* charity ball. The "who's who" of Europe attended, including the Sovereign Prince of Monaco and his family.

Eva loved to dress up and be seen at these gala dances. She took pride in seeing Anne wearing beautiful fashions from her shop. "That cream color gown looks remarkable on you. It compliments your eyes, golden blond hair and personality."

"Why thank you. It's because of your excellent taste and sense of style that I look so nice tonight. Hanz told me that you 'completely changed my image.' Didn't you darling?"

"That's right! It is true. You look like a different woman."

Vincent told Anne about his computer consulting business and electronics import-export trade, as they danced. That seemed to fascinate her. She asked many questions about software applications of computers in business, *and the military.*

"Vincent, I have a client who is interested in buying very *specialized* computers," she whispered. "Maybe you can help me close the deal?"

"Great! Who is he? What does he actually require?"

"He needs rugged, light weight computer modules that must be able to handle high-gravity forces. I think they call it, G-forces."

Vincent probed her for more specifics. "They usually use that type of equipment for aircraft or rockets. What else can you tell me? How about the software needed, and their specific applications?"

"I'll have to contact him and get more details. It is a bit premature. When I get more facts, I will work through you. Why don't you and Eva ... maybe ... spend a few days with us in Gstaad, Switzerland, during Christmas or New Year's holidays? I should know more about their requirements by then. What do you think?"

***

STORM AFTERMATH

"When you come out of the storm, you won't be the same person who walked in. That's what this storm's all about."

—Haruki Murakami

After operation *Desert Storm,* President Saddam of Iraq was ready to sign any agreement, on any terms, at any cost. General Schwarzkopf had full authority to handle the peace talks without much interference from Washington. Surprisingly, Iraq got much more than it expected. Schwarzkopf *foolishly* allowed Iraq to continue to use armed helicopters to police the countryside.

Margaret Thatcher of the UK, later said: "They [United States] should have forced them [Iraq] to turn over all military equipment and should have insisted that Saddam himself go to the peace treaty meeting, to demonstrate that *he* [personally] lost the war."

President Bush said, more than once, "The Iraqi military and people should take matters in their own hands." However, he failed to support the people when they pleaded for his help. Secretary Baker later acknowledged, "We didn't think Saddam would remain in power."

The White House completely miscalculated events. The return of prisoners of war and reconstruction of Kuwait became the main concern of the allies after the war. The retreating Iraqis set 700 oil wells on fire, which covered all life forms in toxic fluids and gases. It took seven months to extinguish the raging fires. Iraq's Shiite population in the southern town of al-Subayr rebelled against the Iraqi forces there. The skirmish quickly spread throughout Southern Iraq.

General Powell advised Bush *against* helping the uprising. As a result, tens-of-thousands of Shiites were killed within two weeks.

A rebellion of Iraqi Kurds in March, in the north followed. After Iraqi Sunni Republican Guards savagely suppressed the Shiites, they then turned their forces northward. The attack against the Kurds caused a deluge of refugees, estimated at two million (nearly half the population), who fled to Iraqi mountaintops, and into neighboring Turkey and Iran. Washington ignored the crisis. "Why isn't Bush helping us?" asked the Kurds.

General Powell said, "What purpose would be achieved?"

The individuals who planned the war were afraid of another quagmire, another Vietnam. They were completely surprised when things really got out of control. Meanwhile huge victory festivities took place in Bush's Texas retreat, while parties in Washington celebrated the returning victorious vets. Bush told the cheering Congress: "... *aggression is defeated,*" while the blood of innocent Shiite and Kurdish men, women and children continued to flow in Iraq.

To stop the flood of refugees the United Nations finally created a *security zone* above the 36th parallel, in northern Iraq. Secretary Baker flew to northern Iraq and took a personal look at the situation. He told Bush that he had better do something before the press saw what was *really* happening; otherwise, his victory might turn into a defeat in the coming election.

Coalition forces began providing humanitarian assistance under an operation designated *"Provide Comfort,"* and later *"Safe Haven."* Iraqi military units were not allowed to cross the 36th parallel by land or air, under the terms of the cease-fire. They were forbidden to fly fixed-wing military aircraft anywhere in the country. In turn, Saddam imposed a total administrative and economic blockade of the northern region, in order to starve the people there.

The Shiite Muslim and Sunni Kurdish rebellions showed how widespread the opposition to Saddam's rule had become. That these rebellions failed was due partly to the force Saddam was able to deploy, but was also caused by the fear of Iraq's minority Sunni. They might face a Shiite majority effort to take over the Sunni-led country, if Saddam Hussein was overthrown.

Overt Iranian assistance to the Shiites, after they had started their rebellion in the south, allowed Saddam to play on this great fear.

Iraqi political and tribal opposition of many leaders, who had been in exile for more than twenty years, had only limited success after the war. They agreed on a common political platform. They continued to look to foreign patrons to help unify them. The Kurdish community living north of the 36th parallel, held free elections, a step that could ultimately assist the process of Iraqi democratization. However, it invariably unnerved both the Turkish and Iranian governments. Both countries have sizable Kurdish tribal minorities, whose desire for independence from ruling majorities was well known.

Coalition partners agreed, after the war, that UN sanctions including a complete economic embargo of Iraq would continue, until its inventories of weapons of mass destruction (mostly chemical weapons) were eliminated. Left unspoken was the coalition's expectation that these sanctions would help to unseat Iraqi leadership.

Saddam initially refused to accept the UN offer of a limited sale of Iraqi oil to buy food and medicines for his population. Their distribution would have involved a highly visible and ubiquitous UN presence. Instead, he blamed the United States for trying to starve the Iraqi people and causing the deaths of many children. This propaganda had some effect in the Arab world. It also posed a policy dilemma for the United States and the United Nations, which assumed that Hussein would not survive the war, or at least be overthrown by his own military shortly thereafter.

President Bush and his administration *did not* learn anything from history: You cannot leave a country and its people *totally vanquished.* The conqueror has humanitarian responsibility to help rebuild the infrastructure and feed the masses of the conquered. Bush, Baker, Powell, and their inner circle, had no Desert Storm *aftermath blueprint.* They never considered a kind of small-scale "Marshal Plan" for Iraq. Accordingly, they repeated the serious blunders of the past, *again.* "Let the people rise up and throw out Saddam *first,*" was their foolish policy. While Bush publicly encouraged the overthrow of Saddam by the people, he did not give the insurrectionists weapons or material support to accomplish this otherwise *impossible objective.*

Bush and Baker *secretly* wanted Saddam to stay in power in order to prevent the country from disintegrating. They thought this dictator was the only one *strong enough* to prevent tribal civil war, which might change the balance in the region. (They were right; tribal and sectarian battles increased). Consequently, Saddam's Republican Guards slaughtered countless helpless Kurds in the North, and tens-of-thousands of poorly armed peasants in the South.

If anyone questions that United States hands were *not clean,* they need only to remember that America supplied much of the arms and money for the Iraq-Iran War, during and after the fall of the shah. The unwritten Reagan and Bush policies were, "Let them bleed each other, as long as neither side wins, so long as the balance of power is not disturbed."

Former President Bush *still claims* that he ended Desert Storm after 100 hours of battle, for *humane* reasons: He did not want to slaughter the Iraqi Republican Guards, on the so-called "highway of death." Nonetheless, the result was the *reverse.* Saddam's armies using equipment that the Bush administration failed to eliminate, and slaughtered tens-of-thousands of innocent Shiite and Kurds. In addition, nearly a million faultless Kurds were forced to seek sanctuary in the mountains, following the *supposed* end of the war. As a result, many innocent men, women and children died.

Today, from Morocco, the Sudan, Egypt, Syria, and Iraq, there is a chain of Muslim *tribal* nations that are united by their Islamic faith and traditions, and by the Arabic language, history, and most importantly, by their common tribal culture. While Iran is Persian, many are *unquestionably* Islamic fundamentalists. Accordingly, whatever happens in the Islamic world is enormously significant for the economy, for the balance of power, and for peace prospects throughout the world. President Obama also did not encourage nor support in any meaningful way for the Iranian people to overthrow their evil dictators, as they rioted in the streets over Iran's fraudulent election in 2009.

***

Iran. The inner circle of the Iranian leadership opened their clandestine strategy meeting with this commentary: "Our terrorist actions have not produced any major advantages for Iran," the speaker of Parliament said. "Our support for our PLO brothers, through numerous terrorist activities, has not gained much for them or for us either. Palestine is worst off today. My brothers, our original objectives cannot be achieved with our current strategy. We need a new strategy to restore our economy, which is in shambles, and to spread the might of Islam throughout the world. Our new distinguished General of the Iranian Revolutionary Guards has a strategic plan, he calls: ***"The Sword of Allah."*** (Khalid bin Al-Waleed, *known as the Sword of Allah,* was the supreme general, about whom the Prophet of Islam said, ***"What an excellent slave of Allah: One of the swords of Allah, once unleashed."***)

The General of the Revolutionary Guards rose to speak to the hushed group. "The U.S. and Israeli Air Forces could do serious damage to our nuclear facilities. As you know, it took us many years of delaying tactics to reach this point. We will soon have enough fissionable material for three nuclear bombs. We now also have far more advanced Scuds from our friends in North Korea, to deliver our destructive power to Israeli and American dogs. Therefore, we must establish a new alliance, a new *Islamic brotherhood* between Iran, Syria, and Hezbollah, if we hope to accomplish our objectives. This alliance will enable us to decentralize our nuclear capability and Islamic fundamentalism, throughout the region and beyond. It will make us less vulnerable to attack. It will restore our greatness.

***

Assisi, Italy: Eva and Vincent drove to Italy to buy leather jackets, coats and silk sweaters for her shop. The quality of the Italian goods is much better there, and prices are significantly lower compared to France. The wholesale factory was about a ten-hour drive to a town just outside of Assisi. Saint Francis of Assisi established the Franciscan order there, and built a little church. Today there is a huge cathedral and shrine in his honor on a hill overlooking the village below. It seemed as though time had stopped, centuries ago in this lovely village.

Vincent became extremely sick from mushrooms he ate the day before. He could not drive any further. They checked into a small hotel. His fever became much worse. Eva thought he was exaggerating. She left him alone and went down to have dinner. After she left, Vincent vomited all over the bathroom walls and floor. When Eva finally came back to the room an hour later, she knew he was not bullshitting her. She found him passed out on the floor. The local doctor confirmed that he had been food poisoned.

Vincent could not sleep that night. As he lay awake in bed, he thought about how Eva abandoned him, at the very moment he needed her most. Why didn't she believe him? How can she claim to love me, and be so insensitive, at the very moment of my crisis? Vincent dragged himself from the bed and quietly slipped into the bathroom. Although very weak, he took the shower hose and washed the walls and floor. He did not want the house cleaner to see and smell the mess he made.

Alone in the bathroom, he stared into the mirror at the man who allowed himself to be seduced—like a fool, or something worse than a fool, a vain lonely middle-aged man, who was looking for something, someone seeking real love. So desperate to be loved, he hurt so many in his foolish journey—his good wife, his children and close friends of so many years. He was seeking love in the wrong places.

A few days later Vincent fully recovered. He lost seven pounds of weight from his terrible affliction. He stopped to pray alone at the shrine of St. Francis, to thank God for saving him; to ask for guidance; to ask the Lord make some sense out of his bizarre, wandering existence. "Have mercy, help me, my Lord. I'm caught in *quicksand,* a bottomless pit of sin and despair. Please save me with your divine grace, so that I may find my way," he prayed. As he closed his eyes in deep prayer, in his mind's eye he saw a vision of the golden blond angel, with her dazzling blue crystal rosary beads in her hands, which he had seen in his dream, years ago.

Again, he remembered her soft words: *"Remember these three words: We I you. I'll be with you soon."*

That extraordinary spiritual experience left him confused and at the same time enraptured. Eva noticed the strange expression on his face as if he was in some kind of trance or something. He could not talk to her about it. She would not believe or understand him anyway.

Fig 6. Florence, Italy

They drove on to Florence a few hours further south in the Tuscany region. Florence is probably the second most beautiful city in Italy, after Rome. The Medici family established the art and architecture of the region in the 15th century. Their room on the top floor of the Excelsior Hotel, overlooked the river and famous covered bridge, Ponte Vecchio, where all the artists come together to sell their arts and crafts.

They visited most of the historical museums, like the *Uffizi Gallery,* and old churches, such as the Basilica San Lorenzo, and of course, Michelangelo's famous huge statue of David. Eva admired David. "That's what I call *a really sexy body,"* she said, looking up at the huge penis of the statue. "Something like that could satisfy any woman."

"Really Eva! Is that all you notice from this beautiful work of art?"

"Well, he has a nice butt too. What else should I admire?"

Later that afternoon they had coffee served in the shade of a big old oak tree. A little girl was helping her mama in the restaurant on one of those lovely cobbled stone side streets. Multi-colored flowers hung from every window. Local musicians played familiar Italian songs. That "old world" charm that Florence perfectly epitomized was truly unforgettable.

A few days later they headed back to Monaco, stopping at *Portofino,* to sample the special pasta at a seaside restaurant, called *Café Portofino.* Sailing and fishing ships were everywhere. It seemed like a perfect picture post card, as the sun turned different shades of orange and set slowly into the sea on the horizon. Both dreamed that someday it would be fantastic to have a little villa retreat in picturesque Portofino.

At the French border, customs waved them through without checking the dozens of clothes they had bought in Italy. The Monaco license plate probably indicated that they were welcomed tourists. The shopping venture was a fantastic bargain. Life together ran "hot and cold," but it was *never dull.* It became a wild roller coaster ride. Fights continued over the three M's—Money, Manners and Marriage.

Gradually Vincent began to build his business relationships, included his import-export trade, management services, and technology consulting. He finally earned about $150,000 tax-free, that year. Eva was not impressed with his income and frequently spent more—*a lot more*—than he earned. She had never been married before. She had no awareness of her responsibilities to anyone, except her dog, or any concept of the need for mutual sharing and giving. She was a wild carefree, uninhibited free spirit, who would not, *could not be restricted.*

Upon returning from food shopping one morning, Vincent found Eva sunbathing on the terrace—*completely nude.* He quickly grabbed a towel and covered her. "What are you doing?" she demanded, as she threw the towel aside.

"How can you ... take the sun like that?"

"Don't be silly, I always sun nude; otherwise, you get all those ugly white lines on your body ... from the suit," she answered, irritated, by the question.

"Don't you see those men across the street ... hanging marble on that new building? You can cause a serious accident you know."

"They're not looking at me," she insisted.

"Right ... They're blind! With your boobs, they can see you a mile away. At least wear a bikini."

She thought he was being stupid, but put one on to avoid any further argument.

The next day, Vincent found Eva ironing shirts on the terrace. Again, she was *naked*. He picked her up, carried her into the bedroom, and threw her on the bed. She protested ... about *her rights*. "You're really uptight Vincent."

"Maybe, but as long as you are my wife, you're not exposing yourself." It became a constant battle to get this woman to keep her clothes on. During the long hot summer months, French people liked to sunbath topless, but this was too much.

Vincent found a solution. He planted two-foot-high evergreen bushes in pots, around part of the terrace wall, which blocked anyone from seeing Eva in her natural state. Eventually, even he took it all off, in this very private corner of their terrace.

During the long hot summer, throngs of tourists arrived, mostly in July and August. In late August, Vincent and Eva decided to take a few days' holiday in *St. Tropez*. This extraordinary seaside village, discovered by seductive Brigitte Bardot, is something unique. They arrived at Hotel Byblos after a sizzling six-hour drive. Byblos looked like a Greek villa with its white stucco walls, tan tiled floors, statues, terraces, turquoise pools and gushing fountains.

"Let's go to the Voile d' Or beach" Eva proposed.

"We left beaches in Monaco ... I would rather jump in that nice pool."

"It's a nude beach, darling"

"I'm not going anywhere in ... in my 'birthday suit.'"

"You can keep your shorts on, if you like. *Let's go!*" "First, I must have coffee." They stopped by the *Senequier Cafe* where artists gathered. Flowering trees were in full bloom in the courtyard. In the cafe, French locals were all speaking *at the same time*. No one seemed to be listening as artists competed with each other for attention. They were conversing mostly about local politics, while older men played bocce ball in the center of the Village square.

Every square foot of the Voile D'Or Beach was covered with naked bodies basking in the sun, when they arrived. All shapes and sizes of bodies came into view—it was a *human zoo*. Some women wore G-strings, leaving their fat asses exposed, while others were very naked. Vincent eventually overcame his embarrassment. Yet, he was determined to keep his shorts on.

Eva was not the least bit shy and promptly took it all off. Her shapely body was superior to most of the "bloated goddesses" lying on the sand. Some shapes Vince had never seen before, and didn't care to see again. There were men with muscles, and potbellied middle-aged men, with testicles that did not match their physical bodies. Many of the wrinkled asses were over-baked in the scorching sun.

At 11 o'clock, they went to the *Caves Du Roy* disco in the hotel. Youthful dancers packed the place wall-to-wall. Vincent just wanted to rest, but not Eva. She started dancing by herself until she met some friends. The ear blasting rock music paused briefly, allowing Eva to introduced Vincent to the group. Jill, a shapely red head said she lived in Paris. Tina was a natural blond Dane from Copenhagen. Michael, a youthful Frenchman, said his father had a big yacht docked at St. Tropez. He invited everyone to a party on his father's ship, the Jessica, the following evening.

Tina, the Dane, was probably in her middle-thirties, slightly stout with wide hips, but she carried her extra baggage well. There was a perceptible vitality about her, as if her nervous system was continually active. She tried to tempt Vincent with her eyes, and sly smile. He ignored her.

As they arrived back at the hotel, Eva voiced what she had keenly observed. "That Dane was trying to charm you, with those big eyes and boobs, wasn't she?"

"Really, I didn't give her a second look. All Scandinavian women do that. That's normal and typical in Sweden, Finland and Denmark, the land of the mid-night sun. Years ago, before we met, I remember spending a weekend in Stockholm. Women give warm and inviting smiles to *any man*. It is natural. It's like saying hello to a stranger."

"Really!" Eva answered. "We'll see about that."

The following late afternoon they awoke to a beautiful clear blue sky. All was quiet, except for the sound of the sea surf and birds singing in the fruit trees outside their window.

Late lunch was on the terrace. Small birds came directly up to them and ate breadcrumbs from Vincent's hand. Eva reminded him that they are invited to Michael's party on his father's yacht. "Let's get ready. It's almost sunset."

The *Jessica* was an impressive yacht. Michael welcomed us on-board and introduced the group to his father and guests. The afternoon excursion was to celebrate the start of the famous *Nioulargue* sailboat races, which take place every year in *St. Tropez,* in early September. Hundreds of boats came from all over the world. Champagne flowed by the bucket as if it were bottled water. The crew was dressed in sharp white uniforms. A combo played typical American, French and Italian music.

Eva waved to someone. They greeted her with kisses and embraces. They all started chatting in French. She forgot her manners and did not bother to introduce Vince, so he decided to explore the ship by himself. Tina spotted him. "May I join you?"

"I'm just going below to check-out the state rooms."

Tina reminded him of the tall Dane he met in Copenhagen five years earlier. He had stayed at the historic *Kon Frederick* hotel during a business trip. The *Queens Pub* was downstairs from this charming old European hotel, with its natural dark wood, glazed frosted windows and immense bar. It was one of the friendliest meeting places in the city. Olga or whatever her name was, walked into the packed bar and tried to find space at the crowded bar. He offered her his stool. "You must be American," she said.

"Does it show that much? How did you know?"

"Most European men don't offer a lady a chair anymore."

"Hi, I'm from New York. Are you Danish?"

"Half Danish and part German."

"Which part of you belongs to which country?" He slyly remarked.

"It's a military secret. That's for you to find out!"

"Do you like jazz?" she asked.

"Absolutely!'

"There's a great jazz place a few streets from here. Would you like me to show you?"

"Sure. Be my guide."

Olga brought me to *Bonaparte*. This pub seemed a bit cryptic, with only a few candles in a dark cave-like club. The excellent jazz music made it inviting. After a while, they finally played slow dance music. Olga's German side suddenly showed itself, as she took me *by force* to the dance floor. Both arms embraced me. She started to grind ever so slowly and sensuously against my body. Our mouths met. He experienced his very first "French kiss," *from a Danish-German.* "Let's go!" Olga commanded.

Something about her aggressive behavior repelled him. That unexplainable *chemistry* that should exist between male and female was not there. He could not simply jump in the sack with this stranger, merely to satisfy his basic cravings. If attacked by a beautiful woman he might surrender without much resistance, but he expected, he needed something more from a relationship. He felt relieved when the hotel clerk said, "Madame has to register ... You have to pay extra charges for your guest."

"Dear I must be at my best for a very important meeting tomorrow. Let us meet when I have less pressure. How about Friday evening?" (He left Thursday morning).

Tina looked something like Olga. She was probably about thirty-five. Her skin was milky white, with a delicate pink flush on her cheeks. Her shapely legs matched the stout body, but her breasts were extreme for her frame, which took something away from her otherwise classy look.

The ship's cabins were much larger than expected, first class in every detail. Vincent and Tina politely knocked on each door before inspecting the staterooms. "Let me show you the captain's quarters," Tina said, as she opened the door without knocking. Vince's face flushed from embarrassment. Two naked bodies were on the floor. Jill and her partner were having sex.

"Come in and join the party," Jill said without the slightest astonishment.

"No thanks! Please excuse us," Vincent replied as he closed door quickly.

"I didn't know you would be so embarrassed. This is St. Tropez you know."

"Sure I know. I really do not care for group sex. I think sex should be something very private and intimate, between one man and one woman."

The sun started setting in the dark blue sea as they reached topside.

Vincent wondered if Eva planned this sexual encounter with Tina, to test him. He remembered a similar situation about a year ago. She invited two sexy French girls to have coffee at the apartment in Monte-Carlo. She left him alone with them, while she went to buy food. The girls, probably part of her escort cadre, tried their best to tease and tempt him. He totally ignored their advances. Later he learned that Eva told them, "try to seduce Vince. I want to test his faithfulness."

Harbor lights came on. The village looked like a Christmas tree with the reflection of multi-colored lights off the sea. Artists busily showed their works to the passing tourists, along narrow old stone covered streets. The group wanted to sample *bouillabaisse,* the specialty of the nearby *Chez Fifine* restaurant.

It turned out to be a real feast, more fish stew than soup. It was the best they had ever tasted. Everyone wanted to go dancing except Vincent. He was in no shape for any further activities. *They insisted!*

After stopping by the hotel to change clothes, Eva and Vince caught-up with their newfound friends at *Papagayo's,* a delightful nightspot with fresh flowers on each table. After three or four glasses of Moet, Vincent's dancing feet came to life. There seemed to be competition between the dames to outshine each other, with their glamorous clothes and dance movements. Later, they moved on to *L'Istaria,* then to *Bain De Minuit,* with its younger lively jet-set crowd. Vincent tried his best to avoid Tina's seductive eyes, and half-exposed boobs.

***

On the way back from St. Tropez the next morning, they crossed mountains that resembled a miniature version of the Grand Canyon. *Unexpectedly,* as they approached another hill, dark clouds appeared on the other side of the bluff. The entire valley below was on fire, with thousands of acres of forest burning on every side. Fiery trees began falling. Vincent raced over a bridge down to the highway, beating the wind driven flames behind them. It looked as if an atomic bomb had dropped. Huge areas, all the way to Cannes and Nice were still burning, as they made their way back to Monaco. The long hot dry summer made southern France and the Rivera a tinderbox.

Fig 7. Mistral fire in southern France

That night the sky had a mysterious red glow, as ashes fell even as far away as Monte-Carlo. Nothing could control the flames once the hot winds, the *Mistral* from the south began blowing unceasingly. Was this a sign of worldwide events to come, Vincent wondered?

Troc Affaire was two blocks from the mainstream of Monaco. It became a gathering place for Eva's friends, a place for her "clients" and girls to meet and discuss bookings, while they gossiped over coffee. It was a front for her other more profitable activities, which Vince did not realize at that time. All were welcomed, but few bought anything, except her "services." Her clientele included the famous aristocrats and nobles, common folks and high society, as well as businesspeople. Some of the women would need a special dress or gown for the evening. Eva gladly rented them whatever was required to satisfy the needs of clients and safeguard her share of the "action." All of these activities were conducted in fast-talking French. Vincent did not understand what was going on, until much later, as his command of the language gradually improved.

After many strange episodes, Vince again concluded that Eva had a serious Pre-Menstrual Syndrome (PMS) problem. She would act strange a few days before her period. She would become extremely irritable and emotional, and argued with others. During one PMS bout, she lost her expensive silk scarf in the hotel room, and told him to call the manager. "The chambermaid must have stolen my Christian Dior scarf," she insisted. "Tell him to interrogate the maids."

"We cannot accuse anyone of stealing without proof," he replied. Later the expensive silk scarf was found in her luggage.

If something were missing from her shop, during other incidents, she would accuse the help of stealing. This naturally upset relations with the workers. The fashions in the shop were very precious to her, as if they were her own private collection.

As they were getting ready to travel by air to California, for his very important computer consulting business meeting, Eva *intentionally* took too much time packing her bags for the trip. "We will miss our flight if you don't hurry." As Vincent put the bags in the car, Eva insisted that she must stop for coffee before they went on to the airport. She knew that this meeting was extremely important for his business, and they were *very late*. "You can have a coffee at the airport," he told her *firmly*.

"No! I want a coffee now!" she insisted.

"If I don't catch this flight I'll lose the business deal," he shouted. She ignored him. Without warning, he threw her luggage out of the car on to the street near the apartment. Vincent drove off to catch his flight, *alone*.

***

THE COVENANT

"We can easily forgive a child who is afraid of the dark; the real tragedy of life is when men are afraid of the light."

—Plato

The unknown, the unpredictable, the uncontrollable drive fear in people and many nations. The HIV/AIDS and Ebola virus epidemics of recent times, the terrorist attack on 9/11, the Boston bombing, and the spread of Weapons of Mass Destruction at the beginning of the century, all had, still have, these characteristics: They create a sense of fear and chaos, a feeling of helplessness and insecurity. International terrorism includes all of these elements. It strikes at the core of our existence. It shocks and paralyzes leaders, as they become powerless to act. Individuals and their sponsors dictate events that governments do not fully understand, with unpredictable frequency.

The extraordinary wave of terrorism sweeping across Europe, the Middle East and America in modern times, created exactly that kind of paralysis in leaders. Many nations gave in to the demands of terrorists, such as President Obama's exchange of five extremely dangerous terrorists for one American soldier, who was captured while AWOL, was an example of government overreaction (Those freed terrorists later re-entered the battle field, to kill more American soldiers). The demands of terrorist militants would increase the next time around. When political leaders over-reacted in order to counter the threats, they gave the culprits greater worldwide attention, which encouraged them to perform acts that are far more daring in the future. Terrorists have a cause. Most of us think their cause is irrational. They do not think so. They will die for it! *They will kill for it!*

The economic situation in Iran became *appalling,* after the voting fraud, and another revolution was brewing.

It left Iran in a crisis. About 70% of Iran's population was below the age of thirty, and was worse off than Iraq. There was a serious recession with no end in sight. Inflation was running out of control. Unemployment reached over 40%. The price of oil, which reached a peak of about $140, during the earlier Iraq crisis, declined to $60 per barrel. OPEC production increased significantly, even *without* Iraqi oil, thus driving the price down even lower. Iran proven oil reserves were about equal to that of Iraq, Kuwait and the UAE, or nearly 100 billion barrels. The only hope for Iran's future was to force the price of oil up. The only way to accomplish this was to get the Saudi's to *decrease* production.

After many OPEC meetings, it was clear that the Saudis' would continue to control the world price of oil. All of the developed industrialized countries were still *highly dependent* on Middle East for oil. The most significant dependent countries included China, Japan, and Western Europe. The United States, according to the best scientific estimates, should be self-sufficient, due to their "fracturing" technology, by the year 2022. Thus, the window for exploiting Iran's oil advantage was maybe 5-10 years.

A select group of Muslim radical leaders held a private meeting in Iran. Those attending were General Ahmad, head of the Iranian army; the speaker of the Parliament and President, and Defense Minister, and Syrian representatives were also present. They further defined the details of the secret covenant between them, code-named, *"Sword of Allah."* General Ahmad explained the overall strategy: "The plan involves the destruction and contamination of Saudi oil fields in Hasa, which generates about one billion dollars a day in revenue, with *highly radioactive* nukes (plutonium bombs), and destroy the heart of Israel at the same time. Since over 90% of the Saudi oil fields are in the northeastern section of the Kingdom near Dhahran, AlKhobar and Jubail, the target area is highly concentrated.

The Iranian leader finally spoke: "We received most of the essential technology and nuclear materials from North Korea. That will enable us to produce three atomic weapons. North Korea has also agreed to supply Iran with their improved missile technology, which we will use to mass-produce as the Shahab-3, which covers a range of over a thousand miles.

Iran's proxy Syria, and Yemen Houthi's agreed to participate ... in order to teach the *American dogs* a lesson. "The third nuclear tipped missile could be launched from the remote regions of Iran. The international inspection team never discovered one of our concealed deep underground sites, and we only need a few kilos of plutonium to complete our bomb," Amn-al-Khass stated.

All agreed that the destruction of Israel was one of the *key* parts of the *Sword of Allah* strategy. One issue remained, How to obtain the essential microcomputers to improve their Scud guidance systems? Worried that the missiles were not very accurate, Hashemi was afraid that "a stray missile might hit the third most holy Moslem site, the Dome of the Rock, in Jerusalem."

General Ahmad agreed: "The Dome of the Rock, Al Agra, in Jerusalem and the Great Mosque, *can never* be sacrificed. In addition, our Russian friends have holy Greek Orthodox sites there. The Jews and American embassy *intentionally* moved their government to the holy city, so we cannot destroy them totally."

All resolved that limited tests must be conducted in the desert, a few weeks before the actual launch. The missiles shall be assembled in deep underground bunkers in Iran and Syria, to avoid satellite detection. General Ahmad proposed that his chief of staff, Captain Omar Kamil be appointed to direct the **Sword of Allah** project. "He's very intelligent, has excellent leadership qualities, and *he hates all Jews.*"

The clandestine group determined that the target date for the launching of the *deadly radioactive* atomic tipped missiles would be, one year during the next September 11th celebration.

General Ahmad informed Captain Omar of his new appointment, and promoted him to Colonel. Top priority is importing the special microcomputers for their guidance systems. They decided to use their bogus French company as the proposed buyer of these *highly restricted* computer modules.

***

North Korea. Foreign Minister Kim Yong Nam, of North Korea, invited representatives from Iran to a series of secret meetings in Pyongyang. Iran had previously agreed to become an active partner in the North Korean plan to proliferate their weapons of mass destruction in the Middle East. In return, Iran promised to provide North Korea with badly needed hard currency and oil.

Kim Yong Nam opened the proceedings in Pyongyang: "Comrades we have diverted enough enriched plutonium so that we will have about 5-7 atomic bombs. That is ninety pounds of pure plutonium. Each bomb requires about 18 pounds of this stuff." He went on to say, "The IAEA (International Atomic Energy Agency), and their *American dogs* are fools. They think we only have enough fissionable material for a few bombs."

A North Korean nuclear expert then presented a summary of the expected effects of a one-mega ton nuclear blast on the planned targets: "The bomb dropped on Hiroshima, Japan, in 1945, had *only* an explosive yield of about 12 kilotons (equivalent to 24,000 pounds of TNT). It killed over 100,000 people. A one-megaton (2,000,000 pounds of TNT) nuclear explosion, over a city would kill several times this number from direct effects of the blast alone. Iranian Scuds should each have about one megaton of explosive power. Destruction caused by nuclear weapons results from thermal blast and radiation. Effects vary depending on the yield of the weapon, and whether exploded at ground level or above, so that the fireball does not touch the ground, and depends on the weather, topography, and the concentration of combustible materials on the ground. Your weapon *must* hit the fields *below ground level,* to penetrate the extensive oil pool.

Fallout is reduced by 99%, two days after an attack and 99.9%, two weeks thereafter. Nevertheless, it would take about five years for 500 rem of radiation to decay to safe levels, in a 'clean bomb.' The most significant components of fallout are strontium-90 (half-life of 28 years), cesium-137 (half-life of 30 years); and plutonium (half-life of 24,000 years), which causes serious lung cancer. Our "dirty" nuclear weapon would include a *much higher* percentage of plutonium fallout. Thus, the area will remain highly radioactive for thousands of years."

The General of the Iranian Army asked about the threats from the President Obama of the United States. "I assure you that Obama and his lackey, Secretary of State Hillary Clinton, are *completely in the dark* about our progress. They are dealing from a very foolish position. America is *too weak* and afraid. Obama will never allow his forces or Israel to attack us first. In addition, our new and far more powerful reactor will soon be operational. Those fools, Obama, Clinton and Gates accepted our peace talks *on face value.* We will make a deal to eliminate our plutonium production capabilities, *after* our bombs are built, and billions in United States financial aid is provided. That agreement will take years for them to implement. Seoul and Tokyo will be destroyed if the Americans attack us. They can't afford to take such a foolish risk."

"What about your delivery capability?" the Iranian General asked. "What kind of response can you expect from China?"

"Our new, more advanced Scuds can deliver a payload of about one thousand pounds. Next year we plan to triple that payload distance to over 2,000 miles. We are also testing out new inter-continental missile. Our missiles frighten the Americans. *They cannot stop us!* They cannot stop you either, as long as you keep our plans secret. Our friends and former allies from China have become too fat and rich from their Western trade. We have assured Beijing that we will never invade Korea or hurt their trade with any other country, unless we are first attacked." (The meeting ended, after each of the representatives signed the secret pact).

***

Amman, Jordan - (Source AP): U.S. Defense Secretary Robert Gates says the United States will seek much tougher United Nations sanctions on Iran if that nation spurns the offer of talks on its disputed nuclear program. Gates says President Barack Obama hopes Iran will come to the table. The United States and several nations want Iran to come clean about what the West suspects is a bomb-making program, and have offered economic and political incentives to get talks started.

President Obama has set a rough deadline by the end of this year for an answer. Gates says the next step would be harsher and might include a number of punitive measures simultaneously. That would be a departure from the current international policy of gradual sanctions with punishments getting tougher each time Iran falls short.

Israel. When the media stories broke, especially from *The New York Times* story about the North Korean nuclear developments, the Israelis became *very troubled.* The CIA and Mossad knew that Iranians and Syrians made recent secret trips to North Korea. The AP release suggested to them that Mrs. Clinton and DOD Gates were naïve: "She [Clinton] also said that the U.S. and the world's major powers were united in preventing Iran from getting its hands on a nuclear weapon.

Your (Iran's) pursuit is futile," she said, adding that Iran did not have the right to develop a nuclear weapon. At the same time, she says that Washington remains ready for *dialogue with Iran* on its nuclear program. On another front, Clinton [and Gates] is implicitly urging Israel to give U.S. policy on Iran's nuclear ambitions a chance to work.

There are increasing concerns that Israel —seen as a primary target of any Iranian weapons program —might launch a first strike to destroy Tehran's nuclear sites before the Islamic regime is able to build a bomb. Hillary Clinton says, "Washington hopes the Jewish state understands American attempts to talk to Iran is a better approach." Meir Dagan, head of the Mossad, wrote a private memo, at the request of the Prime Minister, Netanyahu. The conclusion of which stated: "... our analysis which is partly supported by Langley (CIA), confirms the following:

- North Korea will soon have enough fissionable material for five or six bombs of about one mega ton each, and could have sufficient resources for up to ten bombs, some months thereafter.
- Iran representatives have made at least eight secret trips to North Korea in the past two years.
- North Korea badly needs oil for their industry and people, which they cannot afford, without some kind of trade deal with Iran. We think that a "nukes-for-oil and cash" agreement may have been clandestinely created.
- North Korea has sold Iran a number of *very advanced* Scud missiles, and technology, which have a range of over 2,000 miles, with a payload of about one thousand pounds.
- Iran is currently experiencing a very serious depression, unemployment and their inflation of 35%, is totally out of control. Another riot by the educated students is likely to happen in the near future.

"Therefore, all the elements exist for a probable (likely) future menace from our historic enemies, especially Iran and Syria," Meir Dagan stated.

A select group from the Knesset, Israel's Parliament, included Prime Minister Benjamin Netanyahu, and former Deputy Foreign

Minister; General Dror, of the Combatants Division, as well as Meir Dagan, head of Mossad, convened a high-level council in the Prime Minister's office. They opened the meeting by reading the Mossad Chief's memo.

Benjamin Netanyahu then asked that the objectives of the meeting be limited to three key areas: (1) Discussions about the degree of accuracy of the memo; (2) Review of all the implications of the situation; (3) Consideration of the political, diplomatic and covert action, which is essential, and *reasonable,* to neutralize the threat to Israeli security.

After two hours of open discussion, the Prime Minister reported that, "The Middle East Peace Conference has reached agreement with the PLO regarding interim self-government for the West Bank and Gaza which will likely be signed soon. We must be alert to the probability that Iran and Syria will disrupt those plans."

"The Deputy Foreign Minister proposes that, "Israel should approach the North Korea leaders, through our Arab friends, with a proposal to help their economy by investing in their huge gold mining project. In return, the Koreans might agree to stop exporting nuclear technology and Scuds, to the Middle East."

Meir Dagan *disagreed,* and banged his fist on the table to make his point: "How can we make deals with—*a real devil?* They will not honor international agreements. Those bastards will take our money and then screw us behind our backs."

"Sure that's possible, even likely," Benjamin responded. "But at least we might establish some kind of trade relationship and 'good will' at the highest levels. This strategy will get us a foothold in the country. Right now, we cannot even visit North Korea. They need our oil *very badly,* and they have no cash to pay for it. When you corner a rat, what does it do?"

After glancing at his boss, for a sign of approval to speak, the Mossad Chief spoke: "We need a way to covertly penetrate the regime. Right now, we have no human 'moles' there. Our Arab friends might be able to open a channel, though I really doubt it can happen in a timely manner."

The Prime Minister ended the session by approving the plan. "As I see it, there are no major down-side risks. At the very least, we can get some of our friends into the country, and perhaps hire locals to work for us. We need human intelligence.

We need to open up communication links with the government. Our American friends tried the 'stick' approach and that did not work. Let us try some 'carrots' for a change. If they don't honor agreements we can quickly pull out of the deal, before any significant investments take place."

The head of Mossad, Meir Dagan added, "You're right! Our agents have established firm roots in Syria, Iran and the Sudan. However, we have no human intelligence assets in North Korea. Our friends at Langley are too dependent on electronic intelligence, and don't always share it with us anyway."

The Prime Minister gave each of those attending specific follow up *highly confidential* assignments as the meeting ended.

***

Winter Holidays

The Christmas season in Monaco is not very traditional, and it rarely snows. Most residents head to northern ski resorts in France, Italy or Switzerland during the winter holidays. "Let us go to *Gstaad* for Christmas and New Year's," Eva demanded. "I'll show you *'la difference'* between Lake Tahoe, and *our* Swiss Alps," she added.

"But ... I haven't skied in ten years," Vince replied.

"Silly, we are not going there to ski. It is to see the rich and famous. If you're worried about the cost, our host will probably pick up the hotel bill."

He was not worried about the cost. His consulting and research business was finally successful, and the financial situation improved, significantly. All the bills were paid, and the tax benefits from being a resident of Monaco started to payoff. He often told Eva: "What good is zero tax, if there is zero profits?"

It was a long seven-hour drive to *Gstaad*. His small Mini handled well in the snow with its front wheel drive, as long as they were not going downhill. Eva drove too recklessly for Vincent's comfort. "You're a dangerous driver. Either be more careful, or let me drive."

"I am careful."

"No, you're not."

"Most people are," she replied.
"What's that got to do with you?"
"They'll keep out of my way," she laughed.

Fig 8. Palace Hotel in Gtaad, Switzerland

Champagne and flowers were in their suite. The note read, "Welcome. Please join us for dinner Sunday, at 8 o'clock. Affectionately, Anne and Hanz."

Eva checked with the concierge, who informed her there was a formal black tie gala, in the main dining room. "See, you didn't want to bring your tuxedo. Lucky I don't always listen to you," she said scornfully.

After that very long and tiring trip, Vincent needed fresh air, and some exercise. The ski slopes looked inviting. The surroundings reminded him of *Aspen* in the States. It was crowded. He had to share a lift with a young boy, of about six years old, dressed in the latest ski fashion, goggles and all. "How long have you been skiing?" Vince asked.

"Almost five years," the boy replied.

Incredible, children here ski almost before they learn to walk. This little boy had absolutely no fear of the steep slopes. I am not about to be humbled by a baby, Vincent thought. If he has no fear, why should I be afraid? The kid jumped off the lift like a professional. Vincent fell on his ass. About five falls later, he made it partly down the mountain without hurting anything, except his pride.

It was late afternoon, when Vincent arrived at the *Eagle Club*. Everyone was dressed in the latest ski outfits, except him. Guests came from all over Europe to ski there, basking themselves on the terrace.

They drank a special local hot mixture, which he ordered. It gave him renewed energy and courage for the final trip down the steep mountain. He now understood why Eva was disappointed with Tahoe. Gstaad is 'The top of the world,' for the rich and famous. Vince was feeling a bit intimidated by the crowd, until someone said, "You must be American?"

"Does it show that much?" He replied to the imposing woman. She reminded him of Greta Garbo, with her light brown hair, and strong nose. Her skin-tight ski outfit did not leave anything to the imagination.

"I'm from Dallas, Texas," she answered, with an obvious Southwestern accent. "Where are you from?"

"I'm from California and New York. I also spend time in Monte-Carlo."

"How nice to meet someone from the West and Monaco, my favorite casino city. I'm Sandra," she responded with a foxy smile.

"I'm Vincent ... pleased to meet a fellow American, especially from the great state of Texas. How about some coffee?"

"Thanks, darling, you're sweet. Are you coming to the Gala, Sunday? All the big stars will be there you know."

"I'm with someone."

"Don't worry, darling. We Texans know how to conduct ourselves. Is she European?"

"She's sort of a French mixture."

"See you then. Don't break anything on the way down, dear. I'm looking forward that dance with you on Sunday."

Speaking to a fellow American invigorated Vincent, after months of hearing mostly French and Italian in Monaco. He was exhausted from the long trip. His muscles ached from skiing. Champagne in the room eased all the pain. He slept like a baby.

Eva insisted on going to the hairdressers the next morning, so he took advantage of the clear skies and bright sun, to improve his tan on the Palace terrace. The sun was strong at these elevations. He became relaxed and began falling asleep.

"Hi, you remember me ... don't you?"

"What a pleasant surprise! How could I forget a good-looking Texan, like you? What are you doing here?"

"Darling, I need to develop my tan too, you know."

"Let's have some drinks and lunch, later at my chalet," she suggested.

"Sure. Why not?"

Sandra's blue *Audi Quattro* picked Vincent up an hour later. The drive was only ten minutes from the Palace to her fabulous chalet, which had one of the best views of the valley.

It began snowing. She asked Vincent to start a fire in the fireplace. It was a warm and romantic contrasted with the white snow falling outside, against the full-length French windows. "Sweetie, what can I offer you?" she asked, as she emerged from the bathroom, dressed in a long white silky robe, which did not hide much.

"Some wine will do. You look like one of those 'Dallas Cowgirls,' from the football team." She may have been fifty plus, but this woman knew how to keep her assets in perfect condition.

The red wine affected him more than he anticipated due to the high altitude. She sensed his affliction and tried to get him smashed. Vincent knew he had to stay in shape for the gala. Otherwise, there would be hell to pay with Eva.

The weather changed abruptly. Snow started coming down in buckets. He became anxious about getting back to the hotel. Sandra arrived from the kitchen with some goodies. They sat by the fireplace eating and drinking, while Vince started thinking about how to escape from her "Texan sex trap." While she was seductive and provocative, something about her voice, her manner bothered him. Her style, her chemistry just did not fit his temperament. Anyway, he did not want to "get it on" with Sandra. He was just feeling melancholy. He enjoyed chatting with a fellow American.

After about an hour, Vincent became more and more nervous. He felt like a confined animal, trying to escape from a snare that kept closing in on him. It was an alluring trap. She wanted his sex and something more. Saved by the doorbell! Some of Sandra's friends arrived. After the greetings and small talk, he asked if the driver could take him back to the Palace. Sandra was disappointed, but knew that an intimate afternoon was not in the cards.

"Darling, don't forget to save a dance for me," she yelled as he left. Five minutes more, and he would be trapped at her chalet, Vincent thought, as he made his hasty escape.

He took a well-earned late afternoon nap at the hotel suite, content in the thought that Eva was probably stuck in the snow at the coiffure, and knew nothing of his frivolous entanglement.

Lights from the hotel and surrounding chalets reflecting off the new snow gave a dreamlike atmosphere to the evening. Vincent awoke and took in some fresh air on the terrace. Eva looked elegant in her purple dress, woven with real mink in the fabric. It clung to her stunning curves. The elegant dress flattered her short blond hair, which the coiffure styled perfectly to match with her unique personality.

What an exotic restaurant! Huge silver crystal chandlers hung everywhere with real gold trimmed plates and fresh flowers on every table. The waiters were dressed better than some of the guests were.

Anne and Hanz turned out to be remarkably charming hosts. They were from "old money" families. Hanz looked every bit German-Swiss, with his long blond hair and blue eyes.

Cultural differences between the States and Europe became the hot subject for discussion during dinner. Vincent responded to negative remarks about Americans. He reminded them that most of their music, TV programs, jeans, computers and movies come from the "colonies," as well as the *almighty American dollar.* He also suggested that socialism in Europe, especially in Germany, France and Italy, makes people lazy.

"Then why are you living in Europe," Eva asked. "America claims to be the most powerful economic and military power on earth. *So what!* The Roman Empire had that distinction for a thousand years, and it declined. I find society in the States to be callous; lacking in social graces. They also dress shabby in comparison to Europeans. Everyone in America 'thinks they are equal.' They believe they are 'just as good as anybody else.'"

Anne jumped into the discussion: "In reality, *none* of us are born equal. Some are stronger, more intelligent, and better looking. Should those who are more beautiful wear masks? Should we repress smarter people by denying them higher education? A millionaire's wealth is not necessarily the cause of a destitute person's poverty. Surely fundamental goodness and decency is parceled out *unequally* at birth."

"You're right," Vincent agreed. "Great and intelligent men and women are no longer admired unless they disguise their greatness. Otherwise, they are snobs. No one is jealous of the superior athlete or entertainer. Must we bring everyone down to the lowest level and social condition, down to the lowest common denominator? There are individual differences between all of us. Thank God, we are not the same. It would be very boring otherwise. *Diversity in nature is good, not evil!"*

Eva began to talk about her experiences in the States. "It's ironic that teenagers under the legal age must have parental approval before a doctor can give them an aspirin, yet they need *no parental permission* to get an abortion. Crime and divorce rates are the highest of any society."

Vincent had to agree with much of what she said. "I certainly don't like what's happening in the States. Most of our media and TV talk shows emphasize sex, corruption, and violence because this garbage appeals to the *lowest common dominator,* the ignorant masses, and their producers say it improves ratings. It certainly does sell more things, things that most of us *don't* need."

The food was terrific. The band played old fashion waltzes and fox trots. Everyone danced to show off his or her latest fashions from Paris or Milan, and their fabulous jewels. Anne turned out to be not as good a dancer as Eva was, although she was more graceful and feminine, in her long flowing, strapless gown. Something inexplicable about her face, her countenance, really captivated him. He did not know what it could be.

Later, Eva and Vince bumped into Sandra. She introduced herself and her escort, an older Italian tycoon from Rome, Georgie. Eva wondered how Vincent made contact so fast, with such a provocative person as Sandra.

"We Americans don't need formal introduction—*we're naturally friendly,"* Vincent told her.

"French women can be *very friendly* too!" Eva invited them to join our table. She started talking fluently in Italian to Sandra's escort, to make her jealous. Sandra asked Vince to dance. Eva gave an approving gesture.

"Your French lady is pretty. They sure do talk a lot. What are they discussing?"

"I never learned Italian ... I think it's about fashions from Italy," although he had no definite idea.

The music seemed too "high society" for our taste. Eva suggested that the group move to *Greengo's,* a disco downstairs.

Anne and Hanz excused themselves. We expressed our sincere thanks for their gracious hospitality, and agreed to join them for brunch the following morning.

The disco at 2 AM was crowded. A few Euros placed in the palm of the manager's hand worked wonders. He found a cozy spot for the foursome in the corner.

Georgie spoke some English, although it was difficult to understand because of his strong accent. Surprise, they *actually* talked about the fashions of Italy. Georgie could supply Eva with the finest, latest fashions for her shop. She was dreaming that her shop was on Fifth Avenue, New York, instead of a secondary street, off the main section of Monaco. Her imagination exceeded my pocketbook—a thousand times over. Vince now knew it was a very bad idea to come there. Georgie made an *offer she could not refuse;* a 75% discount from the list prices of Milan and Rome.

Sandra and her escort left after an hour, but Eva wanted to dance and show off her new hairstyle and designer mink dress. We almost closed the place at 4 AM, and went upstairs to the suite *exhausted.* Eva was not tired; she demanded sex. Vincent broke the rule he made to himself, many years ago, after his first awful sexual encounter in Mexico. He treated Eva as a "sex object." She seemed satisfied but he was not. Vince laid awake in bed thinking about the absurdity of fornication, *without real love.*

The meeting started at 10 AM. Vincent was in no shape to contradict the "great business opportunities," Georgio offered Eva. "Sweetie, what an opportunity! Georgio will also accept payments spread over one year," she pleaded, with her sad green eyes and a desperate expression.

"But Eva, how do you know it will sell in France, or anywhere else?"

"Vincent, you stick to computers and technology. What do you know about woman's fashions anyway?"

They presented pictures of the clothes, which always seem to look better on professional fashion models, and the contract must be signed, "You must have trust and confidence in my business *immediately.* judgment," Eva told him.

Brunch with Anne and Hanz, and their *nouveau* friends, was a drag. They talked on and on about their last holiday trips, the yacht they bought recently, and who they saw at their frequent parties.

Anne sensed Vincent's lack of patience with such shallow people. She asked to see him alone.

"Vincent, about our discussions in Monaco. I am sorry, but I do not have any more specifics about the computer deal we talked about, just general facts. All I know is that my client badly wants some kind of special microcomputer modules."

She gave him a copy of the letter-of-credit for his review. The client name was blocked out and the specifications seemed much too general: miniature ruggedized computers (which must accept 10-G forces), compatible with Intel's microprocessor, 15,000 MHz, and 64 giga-bytes of memory or larger. There was no request for any input or output equipment, sensors, and software, or other essential technical details. Vincent gave Anne a list of key questions to communicate to her client so that he could better understand their requirements and obtain a realistic price quote. "Who is this for anyway?" he asked.

"I'm sorry. I cannot reveal the name at this time. All I know is that they have a French trading company in Paris, which will handle the transaction," she explained. "They say they will order about two-hundred computers, after they test samples. When I see you in Monaco I should have more specifics." She kissed and hugged him tenderly as they said good-bye. Her soft skin and perfume was intoxicating. Anne's enchanting smile gave him goose bumps up and down his spine. It was as if she could read his mind, or see inside his soul. Something about this person with the golden hair and blue eyes intrigued him. He knew that somehow, somewhere their stars had crossed before.

＊＊＊

TRUST & BETRAYAL

"For there to be betrayal, there would have to have been trust first."

—Suzanne Collins

Advertisements were placed in the *International Herald Tribune,* to sell hi-tech equipment: personal computers, microcomputer modules, copiers, supplies and services for Vincent Renaldo's import-export business. He received responses from all over the world. One of the first to respond with a request was a man named Victor Cruz, from Portugal. "I need to buy a thousand fax machines for my government," he said.

His new prospect from Portugal seemed to have impressive knowledge of international trading. Mr. Cruz called from Portugal to provide more details about the fax machines and communications specifications that were particular to Portugal.

Vincent sent him two samples to test. He responded with a pre-advice letter-of-credit. The initial order involved only ten machines. However, Cruz indicated that they needed over a thousand units, after the Portuguese government completed their evaluation. At approximately $500 each, it potentially represented half-million dollars. Vincent needed to handle an important client in California that represented a bigger deal. He left Eva to take care of this initial small order. "Be sure to call me if Cruz asks any technical or pricing questions," he told her. His remark suggested that she did not know much about how to sell it. The fact is she was not technically inclined.

Eva was pissed. "You think I don't know how to sell, don't you."

"You always told me to not meddle in your woman's fashion business. Well, the same thing goes for my technology business," he argued.

"I can sell *anything,*" she responded. *"I'll show you!* Just leave me brochures, supplier phone numbers, and some contract forms. *You'll see!"*

I am glad he left for America, Eva thought to herself. At last, I have the freedom to do *what I really want.* What future does Vincent really offer me anyway? He stops me from buying the newest fashions I need for my shop. He thinks I don't know how to run a business. He is constantly restricting me. *I'll show him!'*

Days later after typical verbal clashes on the phone, Eva decided to fly to Lisbon to close the business deal with Victor Cruz. Vincent knew it was not necessary to take such a trip, since most trade deals are easily be transacted by phone and email. Why is she going to Lisbon? Will she blow this business deal? Have they already agreed to meet?

Eva met Victor Cruz at the airport. He picked her up in his silver Mercedes. Victor spoke Portuguese, French and English fluently, but the *real* communication between them was their eye contact and body language. Eva often told Vincent, "eye contact is a *much more* meaningful way to send a message between the sexes than any other form of interaction. *It is the oldest form of communication!*

"How large is you're trading business? She inquired."

"Well my partners and I have only a modest office in this city, but we have representative offices and agents, throughout Europe and the Americas."

"Do you have family here?"

"Yes I do. My family has been in Portugal for centuries. Mother has a huge farm in the country and some apartment buildings in the city. My late father owned one of the largest banks in this country. He taught me everything I know about international trade and banking. Would you like to see Lisbon ... perhaps this evening?"

Eva knew instinctively that this big strong man would be putty in her hands. He will buy *whatever* she was selling. "Sure, I'd like that, if it doesn't take you away from your important business activities," Eva replied.

She checked into the Hilton Hotel and got ready for her host to arrive for dinner at 9 o'clock. (Portuguese and Spanish usually dine very late, typically at 10 o'clock). Eva selected one of her best black with red trim *Valentino* dresses to wear that evening.

After a long full course dinner, they danced all night at the local disco. Eva's low-cut dress was guaranteed to get him hooked. There was a kind of wholesome solidity about Victor. His dignified "executive" look also gave her a sense of security. Subconsciously, she wanted her life to be more certain, more financially stable—and much more emotionally secure.

"Eva, did you know that I have the room next to yours," Victor teased.

"Really! Why would you do that?"

"To be near you, of course."

"Such a waste of money. Why don't you cancel your reservation? We do not need two rooms. Do we?"

"I thought it might be discrete. Besides the door opens between our rooms."

They arrived at her hotel room at 3 o'clock. She unzipped her dress, picked up the gown from the floor, and walked suggestively toward the bathroom. She went inside, while glancing back over her shoulder. Her eyes were telling him things that probably were not true, but exciting for that evening. She put on her tantalizing black negligee with silk stockings, and garters to match, which augmented her spectacular feminine curves. She admired herself in the mirror. This should drive him a little crazy!

Victor could not restrain himself as Eva came out of the bathroom and joined him on the bed.

Vincent called from San Francisco, multiple times that evening. "Darling, I was with a big group of businesspeople *and their spouses,*" was her story, the following day.

"Why did you have to be out till about 3 AM?" He asked. "Don't you think that's a bit late?"

"It's not my fault. They eat dinner very late in Lisbon. Don't you want me to close some business deals? I'm really doing this for you, to help *your business, you know.*"

The second night they stayed out until 5 AM. Victor certainly would buy anything she was offering. She was captivated by his business expertise, his huge fortune, among other "huge assets."

Vincent's instincts told him something was wrong. *She is a liar!* A phone call to the hotel manager corroborated his suspicions.

"Yes, Mr. Cruz is staying here. He has the adjoining room next to Mrs. Renaldo," he confirmed. "Would you like me to ring?"

"No. I'll call later." *She is in the sack humping my client,* Vincent surmised. *Unfaithful again!* He thought about flying to Lisbon and surprising them, but resolved that would not change anything. It would blow both his California business deal, and probably their marriage.

Eva began telling Victor sad tales about her *difficult life,* married to Vincent. "He's always trying to control me. Can you imagine that I cannot even sun bathe nude on my own terrace? Can you believe that? He sends his former wife and children thousands of dollars, every month, before he even asks if I need money. Every time I want to spend a little extra on clothes for my shop, he cries like a baby."

The following evening, Vincent's uncontrollable imagination began to get the best of him. Instinctively he knew she must have been getting it on with Victor Cruz. Images of her in the sack with Victor drained him emotionally. After consuming a half-bottle of scotch, he finally fell asleep from mental, physical and emotional exhaustion.

Abruptly the phone began ringing. It startled him from a very deep sleep. It was midnight, San Francisco time. The distinctive accent and voice of Victor Cruz came on the other end of the phone, from Lisbon. "Don't you know what time it is here?" Vince shouted.

"Sorry, but Eva is emotionally upset. She's been crying all night."

"How is it that you know that? What's her problem?"

"She's unhappy living with you, she says."

"Why doesn't she tell me herself? Who made *you* her spokesperson?"

"She's too emotional to tell you directly. She asked me to call you."

"Sure, Eva is too guilt-ridden. She's been screwing your brains out every evening, that's why."

"Your wife doesn't love you. She's never really loved you."

"You're crazy!" Vincent blurted out, as he slammed down the phone.

Vincent was utterly, completely depressed—*devastated!* His worst suspicions were confirmed. He could not work, eat, or do anything, except drink himself to sleep that week.

All that he sacrificed, all that anyone could possibly give for what he thought was love—everything was wasted. He felt *totally betrayed.*

How could he possibly anticipate that the money he sent to her, to pay the bills were used for the trip to meet this stranger in Portugal? If only he was there, maybe he could reason with her, and save their marriage. In his heart, in his soul, he knew his love for her had been, destroyed—*shattered forever!*

Finally, an *"awakening"* took place within him. Somehow, his intellect, his reasoning won over his earlier crazy, fanatical emotions. *Eva never really loved me!* Love requires trust and fidelity. Love means sharing and concern for each other's needs. It requires continual nurturing. *She's incapable of love!* He had one thought, one thing that consoled him; it was the knowledge that he had been faithful to her in spite of a few trivial flirtations, which really did not mean anything. She betrayed our marriage vows. *She is the guilty one!*

The local jazz club around the corner from his flat, in San Francisco, became Vincent's hangout. The sad soul music and great jazz singers gave him a new sense, a new perspective about life. The music provided nourishment for his spirit, along with liquid spirits. Drinking could not wash away the pain, the anger, the sense of total betrayal. He felt a sinking in his heart when he heard happy voices at the bar, and laughter from unheard jokes. He was once jovial, and shared such intimate stories. His heightened depression became much worse after the effects of the booze faded away.

Vincent's relationship with Eva was *finished.* All that he did for her and for their future life together had been shattered, squandered: His divorce from Susan; the separation from his children, and the loss of his home; all the investments made in her shops; his United States business relationships—*everything was wasted.* He was a burnt-out, empty shell of his former self.

He thought about them. They deserve each other, *a perfect match,* he concluded. They will ultimately destroy themselves. He did not need to help them with their self-destruction. Why should I dirty my shoes by treading on shit?

Eva had to renew her "green card," otherwise; it would automatically expire in thirty days. Vincent's initial thought was to let it lapse; then she could never become a permanent resident or a United States citizen, now or in the future. He remembered the hassles they went through to get her that card. He finally decided not to screw her out of that significant advantage. Revenge is not satisfying—not to him anyway.

Vincent called her in Monaco. "You better get to the United States embassy as soon as possible. You have to file papers, or else you'll lose your green card."

"Is that really true? Why are you so suddenly interested in my welfare?"

"I really don't give a shit. If you don't appreciate the benefits of United States residency status, then the hell with it."

Eva left that important official obligation, until the *very last day*. Again, the unbelievable happened! Her car broke down on the way to the United States embassy, in France. Vincent remembered vividly how the limousine broke down on their way to be married. Destiny was against them then—fate was against her now. She lost all rights to United States residency, *forever*. People pay lawyers thousands of dollars to get that precious green card. She threw it away as if it was yesterday's old fashion.

***

San Francisco. Without warning, a moderate quake shook the bar. White wine ended up on Vincent's shirt. "I've been baptized already," he said with a smile, as the redhead woman next to him held more firmly on to him.

"So sorry, what a way to meet a man in this town," she said.

They met at one of those pubs, in Vallejo on Union Street, the Pacific Heights section of the city. After the bizarre way of meeting and brief introductions, they agreed to share a candle lit dinner. The restaurant lights went out again for about an hour.

Diane explained that she was an Irish nurse specializing in trauma cases. With her affectionate smile, phenomenal body, and her deep cleavage, Vince began to experience a little trauma in the lower vicinity of his body. "What brings you all the way from Ireland?"

"A nurse here makes about three times the wages here, compared to Ireland."

"What about the cost of living. It must be higher in the Bay area?"

"Well, money is not the *only* reason. Your medical technology is more advanced, and promotion is much faster.

Anyway, San Francisco is more exciting than Dublin."

Diane explained that in the recent past, she was a captain in the Irish army. She recounted interesting experiences she had nursing, in many different countries around the world. Destiny had brought them together—in an extraordinary way—and who were they to go against such universal forces? They agreed to have a picnic at *Muir Beach,* Sunday morning.

Vincent usually arrived on time for any date, be it business or pleasure. Diane was not fully dressed, as she welcomed him into her small, charming flat. "I'll take my bathing suit with me," she said, as Vincent helped her with the zipper on her tight-fitting dress, which was at least one size too small for such a full-figured woman. Diane was impressed with Vincent's raspberry color Jag. He was impressed with her stunning curves, which made it difficult to concentrate on the bridge traffic.

At ten in the morning, the beach was nearly empty. They found a private place between sand dunes and large rocks, to make their niche. As Vincent took off his jeans, Diane took out her swimsuit, and wiggled into it with a not too modest smile. Her feminine "flaming red bush" came into full view, directly in front of his startled eyes.

A few dips in the cold water of the Pacific left them seeking the warmth of each other's body. "You're well endowed," she said, as her gentle hand began moving slowly down his chest, to the much more sensitive region.

"Really? You think so. You have a marvelous body yourself."

She did not waste any time, and Vincent surrendered to her impassioned onslaught. The picnic basket was not touched.

The next few nights they spent together at Diane's flat. They exchanged "war stories" about their crazy mixed-up lives that both had led. He was not in love with Diane, but felt sort of tender feelings and curiosity about her. Her face concealed something—most conceal something, even though we don't know it in the beginning.

Some nights later, he found out what it was. Years ago, she fell in love with an Irishman in Dublin. They made plans to get married. Diane explained that a few weeks before the marriage, she suddenly realized he was *extremely possessive*—a very brutal man. The battle of words between them came to physical blows. That terrified her.

Diane knew that she had to move to another country to get away from him, and try to forget her bitter experience.

That week Diane came to see Vincent's flat, which occupied almost half of the top floor of an eleven-story building on Vallejo Street, facing the Golden Gate Bridge. Most of his furniture remained in storage. He only had a new bed, two chairs, a phone and a computer. On the other hand, the view was extraordinary. "Let's have some champagne on the terrace," he said.

The sun began setting behind the bridge as clouds began twisting, like the curls of a woman's braided hair, that beautiful October evening. Without warning, the entire apartment started *shaking abruptly*. Agitated, jolting movements occurred in every direction. They tossed about the terrace, stumbled and fell, as if intoxicated. The half-empty champagne bottle toppled off the balcony, as Diane and Vince held onto the railings, and each other, *in absolute terror*. They were not yet aware that they were experiencing the biggest earthquake in San Francisco, since the big one in 1906.

From Vincent's apartment, they could see the Marina district on fire, a few streets directly below them. A gas main must have burst, and the whole area beneath them erupted in flames, lighting up the evening sky.

Fig 9. San Francisco earthquake and gas main fire

The quake lasted some minutes, leaving Diane and Vincent entirely stunned and disordered.

Sirens blasted all over the city, as they walked down the stairs, not trusting the elevators in case of further after-shocks or electrical failure. They headed for the safety of the park nearby. Some older, early 1900 period buildings toppled, while others were leaning at all sorts of odd angles.

"I must go to the hospital. My nursing skills will be needed."

Vincent insisted on taking her there. After arriving at the clinic, which was over crowded with the seriously injured, they quickly kissed farewell. Diane suggested that he give a pint of his blood. He became very weak after a donation of his precious fluids. The orange juice did not help much. Anyone who received his blood that night would experience a tipsy feeling, since a high percentage of that red fluid was booze.

Few streetlights remained operational as he drove back to the apartment. Total confusion existed everywhere. Vincent was amazed to see how this natural disaster pulled people together. Citizens of this otherwise crazy, extremely liberal city, helped each other during the crisis. He saw restaurants giving out free sandwiches and coffee, department stores offered blankets, and taxis gave free rides. When the dust settled, there were 167 dead; over 5,000 were homeless, and there were thousands of damaged buildings.

Diane continued to be very busy at the hospital, considering the large number of casualties. They saw each other a few hours over the next few days. It was obvious that their personalities did not click. The best way to determine if a new relationship might endure is what Vincent called, "the morning after test." After all the enchantment, all the sweet talk, foreplay and sex, how do you feel about her (or him), the morning after? Is she still good looking, without her makeup? Can you communicate with each other effortlessly? Do you still like each other's silly little habits? Most importantly, *does* she give more than she takes? Otherwise, *it's just good sex.*

A man and woman must judge their relationship in the "naked light of day." How you fight with each other is also important. You really don't know your partner, until you have your third or fourth fight together. If he or she still maintains all those good qualities, in the heat of the argument, then there could be a basis for a long-term relationship. *Or else, forget it!*

Diane said she wanted someone serious and steady. Vincent was not ready for another commitment—not at this stage of his screwed-up life. Diane at least helped him regain some confidence in himself as a person.

That weekend Vincent had made a decision. He would go back to Monte-Carlo, close the office, get a quick divorce, and somehow pick up the shattered pieces of his messed-up life. It would be the last stop in his odyssey, the place where he could put to rest all the thoughts of this tragic chapter of his life that was finally over.

*****

Monaco. Upon returning to his office in Monte-Carlo, Vincent Renaldo planned to get a quick divorce and close his office. Surprisingly, Victor Cruz had arrived a few days earlier. He looked exactly as Eva had described him: six feet tall and perhaps, thirty pounds over-weigh. Dark brown wavy hair covered his large head, and his arms and chest were very hairy. His deep dark-brown eyes, topped with bushy eyebrows, had sleepless shadows beneath them. He reminded Vincent of an over-weight version of Placido Domingo, the Spanish opera singer, except his voice was much deeper and throaty. Eva needed security. He was big, strong and presumably wealthy. They deserved each other—*a perfect match!*

Victor and Eva seemed nervous at this first meeting. They looked *guilty* and a bit afraid, as if they deceived or cheated someone. *They did!* Vincent lost all respect and feelings for Eva, weeks ago in San Francisco. Greetings were cold and somewhat nonchalant. She packed her bags and left with Victor to stay at a friend's apartment nearby. "Listen Mr. Renaldo, I started excellent import-export activities. I think it would be good for both of us not to disrupt this business. I hope we can maintain a business relationship," Victor suggested.

"I have no problem with that, during normal work hours. I'm not going to disrupt anything that makes business sense," Vince responded.

"After all, it is officially my apartment. He has no legal right to throw us out of *my place*," Eva stressed.

She was right; the apartment lease was in her name. We would all have to stay here and put up with this bullshit, until the divorce can be arranged, and then I'll head back to the States, he supposed.

Over the next weeks, Victor Cruz, during business hours, began to take over the office, the secretary, the phones, and the dog—and of course, Eva. Vincent was too despondent, too burnt-out to assert his rights, or confront their crude, vulgar behavior.

Victor and Eva lived in another apartment for a while, until the friend came back to reclaim it. Then she said, "We can all do good business together. You know this is legally my apartment and office. I lived here for ten years before you arrived. You have no right to restrict me."

Eva had great connections in Monte-Carlo, since she provided "certain services" for the rich and powerful, like the police chief. If anyone was going to be thrown-out—it would be Vincent. He wanted a divorce as fast as possible, and figured it was probably better not fight too much if he hoped to get her to sign the legal papers. He knew how her devious mind worked: The trick is to get Eva to think she won the battle, and got the best of the deal. I must not be impulsive. I must be extremely tolerant, for now, Vincent concluded.

During the next few months, the expenses of the office, which they previously agreed would be shared equally, rocketed to about four times prior costs. The phones were continually busy, the car was not available for Vincent's personal use, and there was no peace. "Look at all these bills," Vincent told Victor. "I only agreed to hire a part-time secretary. Last month she worked thirty hours, and now that you increased it by ten hours, we have to pay insurance, extra taxes, and her benefits."

"We needed her to handle these pending business deals. Would you care to do all that typing yourself?" Victor replied.

"What about this crazy phone bill? It's enormous!"

Victor quickly replied, "I had to order another line. We can't afford to miss business calls, when Eva or you are on the phone."

"Why do we need the maid every day? Why don't you pick up your own shit, like I do, and she could come once a week?"

It became a constant battle—a classic triangle between two men and one woman. Never did Vincent expect educated people to be so vulgar and crude in their behavior. He was merely the visitor who happened to pay half the expenses, who is permitted to sleep in the apartment, when the daily office business ended.

A week later, at about midnight, Vincent could not sleep because of the noise in the adjoining bedroom. The walls were thin and the bed was banging against the wall as Eva started moaning in ecstasy. Even though he was completely finished with her; had no feelings left for her, the sound of them humping next door perturbed him. How could they both be so insensitive, so tacky? What a crazy scene. Here is an individual who moves into my home, dominates office resources, and ends the day screwing my wife.

One evening, while both were drinking, Victor began ripping some office files. "What the hell do you think you are doing?" Vincent demanded to know.

"Just throwing out some old documents," he replied.

"You have no right to do that ... without consulting me first," Vince insisted, while reaching for a bundle of files.

Victor's big mass and height, about three inches taller, started rising to attack. Vincent's Brooklyn "street-smart" experience trained him for such an unequal situation. He struck first, with a hard left to Victor's mouth. They attacked each other brutally.

Eva got in the middle of it, screaming while trying to separate them. Victor suddenly grabbed Vincent's hair, and tried to knock his big forehead against his. He quickly ducked under his arm just in time to avoid the blow. Big clumps of his hair were left in Victor's closed fist. This bastard is fighting like a woman, he thought, as his knee abruptly thrust upward and struck Victor's balls. That slowed him down and set him up for the finale.

As Vincent pushed Eva to one side, to keep her from being hurt in the struggle, Victor's right fist unexpectedly caught Vince's left eye. The throbbing pain made him light-headed, weak and dizzy. He fell to the floor. Victor slammed his heavy body on top of him. He started banging his head on the hard floor. Vincent thrust his knee up into Victor's ass, and pulled his arms, causing Victor to flip over and off him.

Eva came between them once again. They both tried to catch their second wind. She began shouting. "This is *my apartment!* If you don't stop I'll call the police and have you both thrown out of Monaco."

***

Letters-of-credit. They came from all over Europe, as well as Canada, Australia, and Africa.

Leading business executives came to them to get financing for projects, or to obtain letters-of-credit to buy and sell commodities like sugar, oil, copper, and sulfur. One client was a black man from Nigeria, named Mr. Butto. His commodities trading headquarters consisted of fifty employees, operating out of London. "He's finally coming to Monaco to discuss a significant venture with us, in Africa," Victor said.

They picked Butto up at the Nice airport, and took their African guest to the ultra-modern Lowe's hotel, in the heart of Monte-Carlo. Mr. Butto was always smiling. He was naturally congenial. He seemed to be a very perceptive executive for his relative youth—about the mid-thirties. After he checked into the hotel, Vincent drove him to the apartment-office for lunch on the terrace.

Eva had many serious faults, but cooking was not one of them. She seasoned huge fresh sardines grilled on the terrace. One of the side dishes included yellow rice with chicken. Her fresh salad contained a mixture of all kinds of fresh French vegetables. Bottles of Beaujolais red wine were served. The green and white striped awning was rolled down to shade the entire terrace, without blocking the fantastic view of the green-blue sea below.

Mr. Butto's cheerful and sociable personality helped to neutralize some of the tensions that often occurred between Eva, Victor and Vincent. Butto explained that he would set up a temporary office here, for just a few days. He expected us to support and accommodate all his needs, such as telephones, telex, email and secretarial services.

After a two-hour feast, Butto finally focused on the business. His attaché was loaded with all kinds of business papers, and project information for review and study. The project involved funding and joint venture plans for the operation of an iron ore mining facility, in Nigeria. Butto claimed he had a personal relationship with the dictator, who was apparently being swindled by the current Swedish managers of the mining operation. They were caught padding the invoices for services never rendered.

The project represented hundreds-of-millions of dollars of potential revenue per year for the dictator. Mr. Butto and Victor wanted an equity stake in the venture, not merely a one-time commission, for putting the deal together. A tremendous amount of paper work would be required. A proposal had to be delivered in seven days. Contracts would have to be drafted and negotiated between the parties, and agreements created for the funding bank. It represented a huge business venture, and potentially, a very profitable enterprise.

Vincent knew nothing about iron ore or mining, or the complexities of such deals, but everything would be transacted in English, and they needed his contractual expertise and computer capabilities, to create all the essential documents.

The next night, after a long hard day, they rewarded themselves with a steak dinner at the *Argentine Gaucho* restaurant. Afterward the party went to the *Living Room,* a high-class disco club, a short walk from the hotel. Mr. Butto was the only black person in the club—probably the only African in all of Monaco.

The manager greeted everyone by name, and seated them at the best table in the house. That was one of the little, but important nice things about Monaco, that "special personal touch." The Living Room Club was like a real living room, with soft light gray couches and chairs that divided the large red room into private intimate sections, surrounding the dance floor. Bottles of scotch, gin with soda were placed on the table with buckets of ice. The candle lit table contrasted with the multi-colored lights that bounced off the mirrored globe, rotating over the center of the dance floor.

By midnight, the club filled to capacity with the "jet set" of Monaco. Well-dressed women arrived with their equally elegant male escorts for a night of dancing—and whatever else may come later. Bouncers were strategically placed at the club bar and entrance. They observed everything. If a customer was not properly dressed or appeared to be drunk, or was a known troublemaker, they did not get in the door. Exceptions were made for certain famous local personalities; they added spice and gossip to the nightclub atmosphere, which was good for business.

The manager offered us a cordial on the house. Live piano music created a nice warm feeling as the crowd settled in their chairs, ordered drinks and exchanged the latest gossip. Two pretty woman friends of Eva came over to the table and kissed her on both cheeks. They're probably involved in her escort service, Vincent assumed.

She introduced them. Helga was a tall brown-haired person with a strong German accent. Natalie was a smaller French brown-haired babe, with ample curves. Both dressed to show off their voluptuous endowments.

Eva suggested that they sit between Mr. Butto and Vincent.

Butto turned-out to be a fantastic dancer. No one could compete with his natural African movements, unique tempo and rhythm. His remarkable style was like some kind of jungle native dancing to the disco beat.

The second bottle of scotch was soon empty. Victor danced with Natalie. He was very tipsy and awkward. Eva's exceptional dance style and grace suggested she was a real pro, among her other professional qualifications.

Except for Mr. Butto, the group was exhausted and ready for bed. "I'm just warming up," he said. Every woman in the place wanted to dance with this astonishing *Watsui dancer.* He maintained a certain captivating, natural charm with all the women.

A muscular Arab came over and asked Eva to dance. She refused politely. *He insisted!* Victor became annoyed and began to rise from his chair. Bouncers arrived at just the right moment and escorted the irate Arab to the door. Management would not allow anything to spoil their thriving business.

By 2 AM Victor, Eva and Vincent arrived back at the apartment. Butto went on to the Lowe's with the tall German woman. Evidently, she wanted to see if he had equally great movements in bed.

Butto did not show up for the business meeting the following morning. Vincent offered to get him at the Lowe's. He left a message with the hotel operator: "I don't want to be disturbed!" Vince went up to his room anyway. The knock on the door was answered. "Good morning, my man," he said, with a big smile. "Come on in man ... have a coffee."

Helga continued to finish her breakfast in his bed. She was not embarrassed by the interruption, but Vince was flustered and uncomfortable by her presence. "Hello Vince. What time is it anyway?" she asked. Her tall frame rose from the bed, with the white sheet wrapped around her naked body, as she headed for the bathroom. "It's about eleven. Did you have a good time last night, Mr. Butto?"

"You bet man. It was one of my best evenings."

"What's all those drugs on the table ... are you sick?"

"No! That's my 'preventive drugs and vitamins,'" he bellowed.

"To prevent what?"

"To prevent VD man! Those are *anti-bodies.* Special pills to keep me fit," he answered. "You should try some. They will help you perform better."

No wonder this person could dance all night, and then screw until morning, Vincent assumed.

Butto shouted to Helga, "Get the hell out of the bathroom!"

"Yes, honey, I'm almost finished." She began to press his shirt, while Butto shaved. Helga seemed to obey him like a "white slave."

Vincent certainly enjoyed the company of women, especially dancing. He had sexual needs like most normal males. All the women that he dated were physically attractive and some had interesting personalities, but something was lacking in them—*or in him.* Eva managed to destroy his sexuality, his spirit; he could not give himself completely, to any woman.

They arrived at the office just before noon. Several messages awaited Butto. He began placing calls all over Europe. "Shit, my phone bill will be crazy this month," Vincent fumed.

"The mining proposal is approved by the President," Butto shouted, as he hugged Eva and shook hands with everyone with wild excitement. "Now we have to develop detailed contracts and get funding commitments from those damn bankers." Only ten days remains to accomplish these considerable tasks. Otherwise that *agreement in principle* could be canceled," he explained.

Days later, to their astonishment, they discovered that the Swedes somehow knew about their deal. There must have been a leak somewhere. They knew it did not come from their end. Butto immediately called his London office (only one executive on his staff knew about the project, besides his secretary). He was furious. "Where's Mr. Jorgenson?" he demanded.

"He is not here," the secretary replied.

"Where is that bastard?" shouted Butto.

"He said that he's going to visit his family in Sweden."

"If he calls tell him he's fired!"

Jorgensen had double-crossed Butto. He made a sweeter deal between the Swedish company and the President of Nigeria, to hold onto their contract. They knew everything about our plans and profit margins. They appealed to the President: Please accept their apologies for attempting to swindle him. They agreed to make a more profitable arrangement with the dictator.

They also *guaranteed* a percentage of their profits would go directly to his secret account in Switzerland.

Mr. Butto caught the next plane to London. We were left with nearly $5,000 in expenses, including phone calls, telexes, and administrative and huge entertainment costs. *Screwed again!* Vincent concluded.

***

Washington: The CIA and the Israel Mossad are *the best* intelligence organizations in the world. All communications traffic between North Korea, Iran, the Sudan, and Syria were monitored. The National Security Agency (NSA) intercepts all voice and data traffic using the VORTEX satellite, over many different frequencies. Their secret messages were encrypted (scrambled), but the CIA had powerful supercomputers that could unscramble any message in a manner of minutes. The new top-secret La Crosse satellite, which recently became operational, can see through thick clouds with its day and night vision sensors and advanced technology image enhancement capability.

The Deputy Director of Intelligence for the CIA stated, "We are closing in on them. We have their coded names and covert relationships. Information from NSA, in Fort Meade, indicates that Muslim extremists are directly involved." He added, "Our electronic intelligence alone can't provide anything regarding their real objectives, or their plans for the *Sword of Allah*. We only have a few important fragments of the total picture. Human intelligence on the ground will be required to fill in these gaps."

"Yeah, we know they have enough plutonium to make at least three, one mega ton bombs. They have already received advanced Scud technology from North Korea. These Scuds have a range of over 1,000 miles, with a payload of one thousand pounds," Peter Mandy, assistant to the Mossad chief reported. "But we don't know shit about their intended targets, nor the timeframe for launch. Also, we are not sure where some of the underground assembly and launch sites are located."

"What human assets do our organizations have that can be used in a covert operation?" The State Department Intelligence Branch head inquired.

CIA Deputy Director of Operations answered, "I understand that Mossad has some deep cover assets. I know we have Syria covered nicely, but we do not have anyone deep inside Iran. How can we penetrate the Speaker and inner circle of the President's office? If someone could get into those offices, we could plant a few of our new bugs there. It is about the size of a big needle. It will pick up any conversation from up to about two hundred feet. The external bug controller then transmits the Intel to the remote controller, and then to our satellites."

"Perhaps we might use a German company to arrange a high-level trade meeting to get into those offices?"

"Yeah, that's possible but also very *dangerous*. If they are caught with those bugs, it means torture and execution. What is in it for them, anyway? Why would they take such a risk?" The CIA officer replied.

The CIA Director stated, "We must take some risks. This nuclear threat is much too real, *it's too serious!* We must fill in the gaps in our Intel. I would like to propose an alternative. I know a reporter for *The New York Times* who has good contacts, at the highest levels in Iran. Her name is Sue Taylor. It is perfectly natural for a woman to have a few large needles in her hair or hat. She could stick one in a chair, anywhere, when no one is looking."

"Why would she take such a risk?" Someone asked.

"Miss Taylor is *very hungry* for a news scoop. She is extremely aggressive and competitive. That woman would screw anyone for an exclusive story like this. We can control the actual flow of information. We'll only feed her some selective, interesting stuff, now and then."

"That's a great idea! Let us contact her and see if she is willing. Remember, we can't reveal what this is all about in the event she's captured," NSA directed, as the meeting concluded.

***

Vincent Renaldo should have trusted his *basic instincts,* his common sense about Victor Cruz, especially when he began bragging about all his "past accomplishments." He seemed to be extremely tense and on-guard. He was alert that one might probe his inner thoughts, and reveal what he was *really thinking.*

Victor was logical and shrewd. He had an answer for *everything*. His knowledge about finance and the intricate complexities of import-export transactions was impressive, however.

Vince remembered meeting people like Victor before, in his corporate environment in the States. Perfect people can *never* be wrong; that is a terrible burden to carry. All of us have some of the truth, but none of us has all the truth. It is an amazing experience to tell someone, we were wrong. Especially someone who is used to you making excuses, by blaming others. When we say, "we were wrong," they look at you, as if you were speaking a foreign language. In the past, I thought I had all the right answers. Today I'm pleased if I can just ask the right questions. Any successful business executive is usually unassuming, and knows his own limitations. The more you know, the more you realize, how little you really know. It is not *who* is right that matters, but *what* is right that is imperative. Vincent's instincts sent him enough signals, but he did not follow the warning signs.

The trust that existed in their business relationship quickly faded away when Eva began opening Vincent's personal mail. He caught her searching his attaché case one afternoon. "How could you open my mail," he protested, snatching the package of envelopes and papers from her hands.

"I thought it was related to our business," she claimed. "You really don't have to be so cynical."

"What are you doing with documents from my briefcase then?"

"Really Vincent, why do you have to hide anything from us? We are all in this business together."

I assumed you were trustworthy, in business anyway, until now."

She became very indignant. "Of course I'm trustworthy. I never deceived you."

"You never deceived me! What about that Greek Captain? What about Victor? Don't you think they were deceptions?" It really hurt to think that the person he once cared for was depending on and trusting an individual, that she only recently met. How can anyone switch loyalties so quickly?

Victor Cruz was always secretive about his past. However, after a few drinks among comrades, he could not control his enormous ego and big mouth. During one bout of drinking, he started boasting that he worked for the United States Drug Enforcement Agency (DEA), and the State Department.

Since Victor had lied to him before, Vince decided to check out his background, and those fantastic stories. He hired an international law firm to do the checking, and gave them a copy of Victor's passport and other known facts about his life. After weeks of research, the firm came up with *absolutely nothing.* Victor did not have any history in data banks, nor in legal files. He had no criminal record, no credit ratings—nothing at all. *Victor Cruz did not exist!*

John Murphy III was the senior partner of a distinguished Law firm that had offices throughout the world, including Monaco. At last, Vincent found a highly intelligent professional lawyer who also happened to be American. He might understand all our complex financial deals and protect him from the craziness of Victor and Eva— and most importantly, he spoke English.

Murphy agreed to a free hour of consultation before deciding whether to take on the case. When they met again, they discussed the nature of the business transactions, including the contracts required, and the separation agreement. He asked many probing and intelligent questions. At the end of our third meeting, Vincent stated, "Mr. Murphy, I want to be straightforward with you, *up-front.* I have a limited budget. About ten thousand dollars has been budgeted for your legal services. Please inform me, *in writing,* when we reach about half that amount. Once a project is completed and some cash begins to flow in, your fees could be extended if necessary."

"That seems reasonable. Let us first try to scope the tasks so that I can give you an estimate of the time involved. That is, if I decide to take on your case." He seemed to be playing the role of the distinguished lawyer, whose services are not available by just anyone. Mr. Murphy's habit of lecturing him during the first thirty minutes or so, at *every meeting,* made him nervous. His "legal meter" was probably ticking away. Since they were fellow Americans, Vince supposed he is just trying to give fatherly advice to a novice—a "babe in the woods."

Lawyers, with few exceptions, are "business prevention" people. That had been his experience in the past. They give you a dozen reasons why something *cannot* be done, but rarely tell you *how to get it done.*

Business contracts were drafted, and the separation agreement was finally concluded. This took perhaps eight trips to Murphy's Law office, over a period of about two months. Vincent received no notice that he had exceeded the five thousand limit, so he reminded the lawyer of their arrangement, at the next meeting.

A few days later, this seemingly endless twenty-five page invoice came over the fax machine. Naturally, Victor Cruz, who has eyes *everywhere,* saw this invoice. "What's this? Who is he investigating?"

"Oh that. He is simply checking the names of the companies in the draft contracts to make sure they are legal corporations. That's all."

The bottom-line was a colossal $12,500, excluding required Value Added Tax (VAT), which is another 19 percent. Murphy's secretary must have made a mistake. A quick phone call would resolve this a ridiculous mistake.

"The invoice is accurate," said John Murphy III. "Actually that's only an *estimated* invoice. The full amount will be forthcoming after I check with my office in NYC, to see how much time they spent investigating Cruz."

Murphy was insulted that Vincent *dared* challenge his "professionalism" and standard fees. "Don't you remember our initial agreement?" I asked. "Didn't I ask you to terminate the investigation of Cruz, when your firm discovered *absolutely nothing?"*

"I had to continue for your own protection," Murphy replied. "Characters like that can cause you very serious legal problems. If Cruz is breaking any international laws, like dealing in illegal financial arbitrage, you need to know that. *It's my professional duty to protect you!"*

"Why did you send it by fax? You must have known that this investigation of Cruz was *confidential,*" I reminded him. "Don't you have any respect for confidentiality?" The phone line went dead.

A week later, the *final* invoice arrived. It was nearly double the initial charges. Vincent was *outraged* and phoned Murphy, immediately. "Are you forgetting my letter to you, some months ago, that clearly *confirmed* our agreement regarding the upper limits of my budget? You *agreed* to inform me when it reached $5,000."

"That's how little you know of the law. You *didn't* send that letter *registered mail* and request a signed returned receipt," he replied.

"I thought I was dealing with a 'fellow American,' a professional law firm," Vince answered. "If you're going to screw me, based on that bullshit invoice, *you can kiss my ass*. I have a personal witness to our verbal agreements."

"In Monaco and France, for your information, verbal agreements are *not binding,* like they can be in some of the States. I will sue you. *You will be kicked out of Monaco!"* he shouted, as the conversation abruptly terminated.

After a few more threatening letters from John Murphy III, Vincent went to see the Minister of Justice, whom Eva knew *personally.* He hated to use her contacts at this stage of their precarious relationship, but he was being badly shafted, and Murphy didn't provide any lubricant.

The Financial Minister of Monaco was too busy. He was kind enough to introduce them to his assistant, however, who told them how to fight this facture (French for invoice). "Insist on more details," the Assistant Minister explained. "Ask him to show a breakdown of services performed by professionals, paralegals and clerks. Monaco has *fixed* hourly limits for all such services, and United States expenses are *not taxable*."

Far more interesting was the fact that Murphy's partners recently merged with another law firm in New York. "He has no official approval to do any business in Monaco. He must issue a new invoice, when his new law firm receives official approval to do business here. Until that happens, all his threats are *completely moot,"* the assistant minister explained.

After learning these interesting facts, Vincent wrote to Murphy and asked for a more detailed invoice, by registered mail. *He refused!* As a result, Vince never paid that son-of-a-bitch anything, beyond the initial check for 2,000 Euros.

Vincent decided that he had better attempt to check Victor out himself. Secret agents, by definition, are supposed to be secret. Victor's passport was probably just one of many that such agents might use. Either Victor Cruz is a real secret agent, or he is the greatest actor and bullshit artist that ever existed in Vincent's world. Whichever was the case, he had to find the truth.

Vincent knew some of Victor's past business associates and alliances. He decided to contact them by phone, while the office was empty. Surprisingly, some of his earlier sidekicks agreed to talk, *confidentially.* Some of them were angry by Victor's past dealings with them, and spoke candidly. A sort of profile on Victor Cruz's legend began to materialize: He grew up in Lisbon, the only child of a Romanian Jewish father and Portuguese Catholic mother. His mother spoiled him, although his father was extremely strict. Victor was married and had two daughters, but was divorced about five years ago.

His former friend, Thor, in Switzerland, further enlightened him. "Victor has one significant asset—an *elephant memory.* His photographic memory made him a 'quick study expert,' on almost any subject. It is uncanny. This guy could remember names, dates, places, and vivid details on anything that happened, decades ago."

Thor continued. "Victor has one *crucial sickness.* He is a *pathological liar,* who really believes he is telling the truth. If you tell enough lies, when you finally tell the truth, it is hard for anyone to believe you. He worked in Switzerland. From Geneva where I met him. He exploited his financial skills and made millions from all kinds of import-export trades, mostly oil. He was a very good high-stakes trader: if there were questions—he had the answers; if there were problems—they would be solved. It would take nerve—*he had plenty.* He lost millions at the casinos. Mr. Cruz finally skipped out of Switzerland to avoid arrest for unpaid income taxes."

Pieces of the Victor Cruz puzzle began to fit together. Victor and his childhood Portuguese friend, Paulo Gershon, whom he met in Monaco sometime earlier, were former secret agents. They were still on the payroll of the State Department, and British MI-6, respectively, on a part-time consulting basis. Now and then, they received "consultant's fees." No names, no records were needed.

Victor was the financial brains and had maintained influence with the State Department and DEA. Paulo had the banking contacts and well connected with MI-6, the British Secret Intelligence Service (SIS), and *Mossad,* the Israeli intelligence organization. They both took early retirement for *unknown* reasons. However, they did not intend to live on the petty retirement sums their respective organizations provided.

After years of tracking down and catching terrorists, drug czars, and business criminals, at some personal risk to themselves, they became experts on "sources and methods," used by crooks for laundering money, and how they invested it in legitimate enterprises, for even greater profits. Why shouldn't they profit from their unique knowledge, experience and contacts, as long as they did not cross the line. They had immediate access through their former colleagues, to huge government networks and computer databases, which the State Department, Interpol and the British maintained on individuals and companies. They could easily obtain the latest profiles on anyone, anywhere, anytime. They also remained useful to their former employers, should their services be required in any international emergency.

Someone at a very high-level, in one of the secret agencies, knew that Victor Cruz *knew too much* about various covert operations given his photographic memory. They must have assumed he had hidden files somewhere. They would not do anything that might cause such sordid secrets to fall into the wrong hands, like the media. That was Victor's "insurance policy." Paulo established his financial consulting operations in London, the center for most international banking and trading activities. Victor setup his consulting business in Monaco, also a very significant financial center, second only to Switzerland, for *hidden* banking transactions.

This team only needed a few personal computers, telex machines, telephones and a small office. They had copies of all kinds of contracts, letters-of-credit (LC's), and various complex agreements in their computers that could be used as prototypes, for almost any kind of business activity. They knew many of the leading banking executives and private investors *personally,* which gave them the all-important *creditability factor*, and excellent references. They could get detailed facts on any company, institution or individual, whenever needed. Moreover, their various aliases were not "black listed" in any of the international databases.

Vincent had become unwittingly, the *naive* consultant who provided the office facilities—and had approval from the government to do business in Monaco—who might be sucked into their international business schemes. There is one *significant* problem that Vincent recalled Thor telling him. "Remember, both of these characters have *huge egos*.

They constantly compete to see who is the greatest con artist. Both were Jews by birth and grew-up together in Portugal. They were comrades in tracking down terrorists and drug suppliers—but, *they didn't trust each other."*

Even though Victor Cruz was (is) an *arrogant asshole,* Vincent was impressed with his financial and business knowledge. Top executives and banking officials called or fax him, from around the world, seeking his expertise. As a technology specialist with little knowledge of international financing, or import/export transactions, how could Vince question such an *illustrious* financier of the rich and powerful?

One of the new venture projects they were working on required standby letters-of-credit from one of the top world banks. Victor and Eva scheduled a luncheon meeting with an executive from one of these ten international banks. Vincent and Pierre, the former Minister of Finance of Monaco, also attended the meeting. Ex-minister Pierre was a gentle old man of about seventy-five, who had two weaknesses—*beautiful women and wine.* He was responsible for much of the success of Monaco, in earlier times.

Pierre lost that important role in the government, one fateful evening, because of his two vices. Princess Grace was attending one of those important high society charity galas, when the old man tried to introduce her to one of his women—who happened to be a well-known escort—"a lady of the night." You *never* embarrass the Prince or Princess of Monaco, if you plan to work or live in the Principality. The Sovereign Princess of Monaco, who helped to clean out many of the Mafia drug lords and prostitutes in the Principality, had him *promptly retired.* Ministers of the realm, however, get to keep their title for life. He was a charming and honest person, whose only major weakness,—was he was a romantic—*with the wrong women.*

Pierre admired Victor's inventive financial plans, when he was not pickled from drinking. They had to catch the Minister before lunch if they hoped to have an intelligent conversation with him. Near the end of the private luncheon meeting, the banking executive, Michael, came directly to the point: "You know, I saw this interesting villa with a pool, which I would love to buy, if only the price was more affordable," he said. That not too subtle hint suggested that if his bank (meaning he) approved the project, he would appreciate the villa as a "gift."

The banking executive would, of course, pay a fraction of the actual price, to keep the transaction "clean."

These particular international banking executives were some of the biggest crooks in the world. They had official licenses to steal. Greed and corruption are the customary way of doing banking business in the international arena. Victor and Vincent discovered that bankers would attempt to steal the financial transaction from them, if they were stupid enough to give the bank executive all the details. High-level bank managers would attempt to circumvent the agents or brokers, and go directly to the buyer and/or seller, thereby keeping the sizable commissions for themselves.

Victor became involved in all kinds of import-export transactions: oil, sugar, copper and chemicals, aircraft—even shoes. Whenever a client requested anything to do with military equipment, however, he always checked with his friends in the State Department first. Though it seemed imbecilic that selling agents would possibly attempt to peddle thousands of tons of commodities, which they *did not really have*—they did. They tried to sell "virtual products," and Victor always caught them. He would insist on contract numbers, lifting schedules and complete warehouse vouchers, before he issued letters-of-credit. They could not deliver some of those essential documents. On another occasion, a "respectable" representative of an oil supplier tried to sell the same shipment of the product to multiple buyers, *at the same time*. Again, Victor knew that, after carefully checking the documents. The import-export business can be, often is, a *very dirty business,* where the uninformed are badly burnt.

***

MEDIA POWER

"Whoever controls the media controls the mind"

—Jim

Sue Taylor lived by her belief that, *"The pen is mightier than the sword!"* As a reporter for *The New York Times,* she saw many examples of how the power of the news media, and influential television networks, actually controlled world events—*for better or worse.* She covered *Desert Storm,* in the past, and saw how that war abruptly ended in only one hundred hours, because of media headline stories concerning the "highway of death." At that time, President Bush was fearful that he might lose reelection if the incessant media reports about the slaughter of the retreating Iraqi armies continued. Bush terminated the war prematurely, and lost the election anyway. Ironically, Iraqi President Saddam remained in power after Presidents Bush and Clinton were out of office.

News appetites are insatiable, and their methods can be brutal. Miss Taylor was a gutsy woman with an abrasive style, who would do anything to get an exclusive story. The petite brown-haired woman had a reputation as an aggressive probing, investigative reporter, who would turn over any stone to get at the *real facts.*

After many hours of soul searching she finally agreed with her editor to cooperate and work with "The Company," for *exclusive news scoops,* which they promised her. Sue arranged to setup an interview with the Iranian Speaker of Parliament, at the request of her CIA controller. During that meeting, when the Iranian leader was distracted, she stealthily planted two long needles from her hair— miniaturized electronic bugs—in his office. Over the next few months, "The Company" fed Sue Taylor lots of fascinating news scoops, mostly about the political infighting that was going on in Iran.

She beat all of her more experienced colleagues at *The New York Times, Washington Post and Newsweek,* with exclusive front-page headlines.

Without verification, Miss Taylor's boss said that he could not publish her latest *sensational* story about the inconceivable secret agreement, code named "Sword of Allah," between Iran and Syria to become allies, with Sudan, in a plot to attack the Saudi oil fields and Israel. "It came from the same CIA source as other stories," she argued.

"Yeah, well remember, the CIA has their own agenda. Running this sort of story is going to require hard-source quotes; otherwise, we just can't use it. Get some corroboration!"

After weeks of probing for anything that might support her story, Sue met her CIA controller for cocktails at her hotel. "Great news, I finally got approval to meet with Iran's Deputy Prime Minister," she said excitedly to her lover, Abu Amir.

"You're dealing with some *very sensitive* information you know. Do not ask him any sensitive or probing questions. That might suggest that you know too much about their clandestine alliance," Abu strongly advised her.

"Really Abu, *I'm not stupid!* I am not some naive writer just out of school. I'm an experienced, seasoned reporter for *The New York Times.*"

"Please listen to me! Just stick to the questions we discussed. Otherwise, you could blow your cover and jeopardize my situation as well. They might deduce that there are spies or bugs in the inner circle of Iran."

"This is the *greatest* scoop of my life. I'm not about to blow it!"

Abu Amir had to catch his flight. He kissed her warmly. "Happy hunting, I hope your interview is successful. We need to get that implausible story out to the public, as soon as possible."

Miss Taylor would interview Ibrahim, Deputy Prime Minster of Iran. She reluctantly accepted to meet the deputy after the Iranian media representative agreed not to limit the scope of her subject matter. However, *only* if the interview could be one-on-one, in a private session.

That evening the representative from the Deputy picked Sue up at the hotel in a chauffeur driven limousine and escorted her to a private home in a village about ten miles outside of Tehran. Everyone was respectful and polite. Coffee and cakes were served immediately after she arrived. It was about 11 PM and she was visibly tired. The strong coffee should keep me alert, she hoped.

The coffee was very strong indeed! Sometime later, after its drug effects wore off, Sue woke up in the basement of the house, hanging by her arms. Her bound feet barely touched the floor. She was in a state of bewilderment. The small dark room smelled of excrement, smoke and vomit.

"Did she tell anyone where she was going?" Khatib, chief of the secret police, the much-feared *Amn-al-Amm,* asked.

"No, just her CIA contact. Only Abu Amir knows about this meeting. He's on his way back to his office," the captain answered. "They have been instructed to follow him to locate all his comrades, before picking him up."

"Have you found *all* her notes?" Khatib demanded to know.

"Yes, we found a draft of her story and took her Laptop from the hotel."

"Good work! Now the fly has come into the spiders' web," he laughed. "Now we will do a little interviewing."

Sue eventually came out of her initial state of bewilderment. She tried to think logically, in the cold damp room. Could they possibly know that I knew about their secret deal? Maybe they don't know that. I had better invent something believable. Shit, why didn't I tell someone where I was going? My chief warned me not to travel alone. Yet, if I told my colleagues, they might try to scoop me. They wouldn't dare do anything to an influential reporter from the NY Times—*would they?*

Her worst fears were confirmed, as the heavy wooden door swung open. "I trust that you had a good sleep, my dear," Khatib (also known as "the tormentor") said, with a big grin as he entered the room. "Now it's my turn to do a little interviewing."

"My office knows I'm here," she said nervously. "I'm a very well-known international reporter, you know. If … if I'm not back soon ... my boss, my chief will alert my government, *immediately."*

"Sure he will. We happen to know you only told your CIA controller about this meeting," Khatib boomed, as he approached with a bright lamp. "We know what a *big-shot* reporter you are—and big spy you are too. I have your notes and computer. You think we are dumb Arabs. We're educated Persians, not brainless nomads."

The fat massive body of General Khatib came up to her, so close that she could smell his disgusting breath. With both hands, he ripped off her dress in one powerful downward thrust. "Let's see what you have hidden on your petite body," he said, as he took out a huge knife and cut away her bra. "What are these wires? Why do you need the miniature recorder taped to your backside? Are they tools of your trade? Too bad it's not a transmitter."

"I'm not a spy. I am only ... a reporter ... trying to do my job. That recorder is only used to get the facts accurately from my interviews—*nothing more,*" she insisted. Sue tried to control her trembling body. "What do you want from me?"

"Bullshit! Tell me all your contacts? How did you get those fascinating news stories? Who is your sources? Names, I want their names," he growled. "Don't worry my dear, we will let you go as soon as you tell me everything. You're right we certainly cannot harm such an influential *New York Times* reporter. No one will believe your fairy tales anyway."

She tried to be brave, but tears of fear welled up and trickled down her face. Her frightened eyes revealed that whatever courage she once had, was gone. Omar Khatib sensed panic beginning to overwhelm her. It was now, in these first instants of fear and hysteria that the advantages were with the inquisitor. Break her, the general's instincts told him, break her quickly, before she starts to reassemble her shattered psyche.

"He doesn't work here. His name is Abu Amir," she cried. "Really, I didn't have any idea ... I didn't know he's connected with the CIA. I met him at an embassy party. Abu and I were lovers. *That's all!"* Sue was not a courageous person. She was not about to be tortured for a news story that might never be published.

The general's long-honed instincts knew where the trembling, nearly naked woman, hanging by her arms would be most vulnerable. "I see you're a little cold. I'll warm you up a bit so that you remember a bit more," he joked, as he dropped his pants.

"What are you doing? No! No! Please don't ..."

Sue finally told him *everything,* including the concealed bugs she planted in the president's office in Iran.

They buried her corpse in the vast Iranian desert. No one would ever find her remains.

The Iranian secret police followed Abu Amir from the airport. Some of his comrades were picked up, hours later. After two days of barbaric torture, which few humans could endure, they learned all they needed to know.

Abu knew very little about their covert *Sword of Allah* plans. Nevertheless, he compromised his network of agents working in Iran, by revealing sources and methods.

After this disastrous calamity, the Company (CIA) and Defense Intelligence Agency (DIA) became *extremely* alarmed. They would have to change strategies; whole networks would have to be restructured. Confusion would be the order of the day. The President's National Security Advisor directed the DIA to provide around-the-clock interception and decoding of all scrambled communications, between Iran and Syria. Monitors at Fort Meade (NSA) constantly scanned all foreign phone calls, telexes, and supercomputers sifted them for any nuggets of information.

In spite of President Obama's new "Axis of Engagement" verses President Bush's "Axis of Evil" strategy, the CIA knew that Bashar Assad of Syria turned his country into a safe haven and major transit corridor for radical Iranian Shia jihadists, in route to fight in Iraq. He also supported Hezbollah and Hamas against Israel.

Diplomacy does not work when one of the parties, the jihadists, firmly believes that *all* non-Muslims should be killed, *especially Jews. The Koran says that agreements with infidels do not have to be honored!* In addition, numerous Lebanese anti-Syrian politicians were murdered, such as Lebanese Prime Minister Rafik Hariri. Still, Obama's "experts" decided to restore diplomatic relations with Syria and Iran, even in the face of such outrageous assassinations.

Finally, as result of this intensive effort and the earlier bugs planted by Sue Taylor, the CIA obtained a few fragments of intelligence about the clandestine *Sword of Allah* plans that puzzled them for many months. They learned that Iran and Syria would soon have enough fissionable material for at least two and possibly three one-megaton weapons. They understood that the Iranians were seeking sources for specialized microcomputers for their missiles, which were not very accurate without them.

They were confused about the strategic purposes for this treacherous and perilous scheme. Why would they plan such foolishness, when they knew the United States, NATO, and Israel had the power to destroy them? No one had any idea where all the missile sites were located. They assumed that Israel was probably the major target, although the senior CIA analyst for the region did not accept that assumption. They wondered if Iran would really sacrifice their religious icons for the pursuit of world power. Many Muslim shrines, such as Jerusalem's Mosque of Omar, among other historical sites were located there.

***

Monaco: The French Revolution is celebrated on July 14. At midnight, rockets streaked up into the night sky and exploded, producing an immense shower of red, blue and white streamers. The bright rockets lasted a few moments, before fading and swallowed up in the blackness of the moonless night. It seemed that Vincent Renaldo's life was no different: A moment of bright light—that burning hope that his life would change for the better—which would just as quickly fade into the darkness, once again.

Fig 10. French Revolution fireworks on July 14

She appeared the following morning. He had not seen her for nearly a year. They had last met in Switzerland during the winter holidays. She thought that Vincent and Eva were the "perfect couple," so in love and happy, which was partly true when they last met her in Gstaad.

Anne arrived at the office unannounced. She came to seek Vincent's expertise regarding her Iranian client's microcomputer requirements. Eva greeted her warmly and introduced her to Victor Cruz, her "new paramour." Victor was sitting at Vincent's desk, deeply involved in paperwork. Anne quickly sensed Vince's precarious situation. She asked if he would care to have a coffee with her, *privately.*

They went to a little café across the street from the office. Anne's face was a little sad but remarkably attractive, with bright deep blue eyes, a passionate mouth, with excitement in her voice. She was wearing an eggshell-white silk blouse that clung voraciously to every indentation of her breasts, partly opened at the top showing the deep chasm within. She began to ask questions in her low delightful voice; it's a voice that the ear tunes into, as if each utterance was a special musical note. He told her about his bizarre entanglements with Eva and Victor, and events that led up to their current predicament. She understood and sympathized with everything he said.

This was a very secretive woman, who would not reveal anything important. She was always polite, yet she would not lay bare her innermost feelings. (He thought she would make an excellent secret agent, one that would never betray a confidence by idle chatter).

Anne surprised Vincent by sharing with him some of her own deep secrets in regards to her past: "I met a man named Armin an Iranian alien, at the philharmonic in Paris. He desperately wanted to stay in France. Armin was extremely handsome in his mid-twenties, with dark hair, impressionable black eyes and a light-brown complexion. Armin needed my support and contacts in the government to get his residence card and a French passport. I arranged everything: An apartment in Paris; residency status and passport; spending money and a job. We became lovers during the next months."

Her mother and father totally disapproved of Armin but that was not going to affect her love for him. Armin dominated her life and she was devoted to him. They traveled to Iran to meet his mother and father. While in Iran during those weeks, Anne studied their traditions, history, language and customs of the country. Her loyalty and devotion to her lover was *absolute!* Anything he wanted she granted (except sex).

Later both went to San Diego, California, where one of her biggest clients was. They rented an apartment for the season near the beach. She completed her business much earlier than expected. To celebrate her good fortune she bought him a special gift and some champagne. Strange sounds came from the living room, as she entered the apartment. It sounded as if he was in pain. He was screwing the housekeeper on the living room couch. The shock was too much for her to handle. How could the person she so adored, destroy everything? She caught the next flight back to Paris, *without him.* Her first romance came to a bitter end.

With each gesture, Anne's lips spread wonderfully apart, causing her cheeks to form neat transient hollow dimples. Her expression appeared confident and mysterious. Her deep blue eyes radiated a soft fury, were fixed and unblinking as she talked. She had an intelligent face—enchanting and extremely attractive. Vincent tried to ignore her eyes, but could not. When their eyes met—*they knew immediately* that something special existed between them. She appreciated his crazy situation, although her experiences seemed to be far more outrageous than his were.

She continued her story: "About two years later, in Paris, I found an attaché case in the back seat of a taxi, which someone lost. The case contained an American passport, some cash, diamonds, and important business papers."

"What's so bad about that? What did you do?"

"I contacted the man's family in New York. "The owner of the case arrived at my apartment. I turned over the attaché to him, after he identified himself."

The next day, a manager from *Cartier* arrived at my apartment. He had a fantastic diamond necklace for me. It was "small token gift from Robert Mellon," he said.

"I agreed to meet Robert for dinner that night at *Maxim's.* Over the next six months or so, our relationship blossomed. We became lovers, and made plans to be married. Wedding invitations went out everywhere.

"During my shower party in Paris, two weeks before the wedding, I received a phone call from Robert's father.

They said I collapsed on the floor. Robert hit a parked truck. That terrible experience caused me to lose my voice, for many months."

Anne explained that she met her third boyfriend, one year after her fiancé, Robert Mellon died. It was at a cocktail party in Paris. "A French banking executive introduced me to Hanz, the son of a German industrialist from the Krump Federation. The six-foot-three, man with long blond curly hair and light blue eyes, completely captivated me. Don't you remember him from the Gala of the Roses with us?"

"I remember him. In fact, I thought you two were really in love."

"Hanz had a chalet in Switzerland, overlooking Lake Geneva. We spent a few winters skiing and the summers sailing. He loved boating. In fact, I bought him a small yacht, which he named after me. Our romance blossomed over the next two years.

"Then, one fateful day, Hanz's ex-girlfriend falsely accused me of fraud. She claimed I did not live up to the terms of our business contract. I tried to explain that my wire transfer was delayed due to a mistake made by the bank, but they did not believe me. That's when I discovered that Hanz *'had no balls.'* Can you believe that he was afraid to become involved in my legal battle? His family's 'good name' might be tainted by the scandal, he said. He left me all alone to handle the court fight and went off on *his yacht,* to ... to forget me. He deserted me when I needed him most."

"He's a *real bastard!* What was the outcome of the trial?"

"Oh, I'd rather forget the past." Anne was not ready to tell Vincent how that trial changed her life. It was too personal, too distressing to talk about.

They had dinner together that evening. Anne was a *real* French woman, with Swedish blue eyes from her grandfather's side. Her ancestors date back to a thousand years of French history. She had pale skin, but it was a healthy skin. There was not a trace of makeup anywhere on her face; none was needed. Wavy golden blond hair fell perfectly on top of and below her shoulders. This educated elegant woman was remarkably humble, the complete opposite of Eva. Her angelic face and demeanor revealed an honest gentle, extremely feminine woman, with her own particular style and elegance. She was a person with lots of that old European charm—and presumably lots of old money. There was something wonderful about her heightened sensitivity to the promises of life—it was an extraordinary gift of hope; a romantic spirit that Vincent rarely found in any other woman.

Each time they met over the next days and nights, she wore a different splendid outfit, and always a special hat. Hats were her hallmark, her symbol of refinement and elegance. They loved classical music, and often took in the ballet, near the Casino.

Vincent finally moved to a small but charming apartment with a kitchenette, bathroom and terrace overlooking the sea. Their romance grew stronger and stronger at each meeting—without sex. Anne, with a cunning smile, always declined to see him alone at the apartment. They held each other's hand in the street and restaurants, like young innocent lovers. Finally, they kissed. As their lips touched, she opened her mouth for him, like a budding flower, whose blossoming was complete. "You know I love you," she murmured.

Her devotion to the Catholic faith was unquestionable. All kinds of religious medals hung around her neck, as if they could protect her from the evils of this world. When they traveled on the train together, she always carried a small book of prayers or the story about some saint. One evening she insisted that they stop to rescue a bird that was hurt in the street. On another occasion, a column of ants took up residence in the kitchen. Vincent started to kill them. Anne stopped him *immediately*. "Don't hurt them," she said quickly. "They are part of God's creation." She made a trail of breadcrumbs to the outside garden, and they followed the crumbs away from the kitchen.

"Vincent, don't you know we exist in *dependence* of each other, to complete each other, in the service of each other," she said. See those trees; they are dependent on the atmosphere, the birds and bugs to exist. Birds make homes there, consume its fruit and transport its seeds. Bugs produce fungus, nourishment for the roots of the tree. You see, a web of *interdependency* exists in all of nature—one with the other, and all collectively."

They would talk for hours and hours about many things. Their way of thinking and philosophy about life were uniquely compatible. Anne really surprised Vincent by revealing that she also visited Iran, at about the same time his CTS team made their quick escape by way of Turkey. "Why were you there?"

"I met this General in Paris. He asked me to come," she said, with the curve of a smile on her lips that hinted at some puzzling past encounter.

"The revolution was happening. Why did you risk going at that time?"

"The Green Revolution didn't start until later. The General had a sort of fondness for me. I took advantage of that to do a small service for some friends."

"What do you mean by that? What kind of service?"

"I was in the import-export business, selling jeans in Iran. During the crisis some of my business associates and young friends became trapped there."

"What could you do about that?" A mysterious, puzzling expression began to show on her radiant face.

"Well, it's sort of *secret,*" she said, thoughtfully.

"Come on Anne we don't need any secrets between us, do we?"

Anne explained that she went to Iran to smuggle counterfeit passports and exit visas, to help families who were former anti-government supporters escape. "They were all trapped there and marked for death. The General met me at the airport. I was able to avoid normal customs checks. The passports were delivered to those helpless people."

"You really took a big chance," Vince responded, staring at her in disbelief.

"Not really! I was in God's good hands. He gave me this 'mission of mercy.' It was a chance to help others. *I was the Lord's secret agent.*"

Then Vincent then told her about his business adventures in Iran. How they escaped the day before the rioting in the streets over the election fraud.

Anne asked, "Why didn't we meet before you were married?"

"If we met then, your mother might think that I was some kind of dirty old man, trying to seduce her daughter. You were very young then. Maybe you wouldn't have been attracted to me anyway."

She laughed, as if I said something very witty, and held my hand for a moment, looked up into my face, promising that there was no one in the world she so much wanted to be with. "I've always been attracted to mature men, you know."

"Our time wasn't right then. Otherwise, our stars would have somehow met," he told her. Is it not strange how people *seemly* meet by accident? The orbits of our two stars intersected in Iran, almost came together in La Jolla, and *finally converged* in Monaco.

Many months of platonic friendship suddenly came to an abrupt end. Rosy, Anne's roommate, a rich snob from New York, became extremely possessive and jealous of their relationship: "Vincent is the wrong person for you. You can do *much better* than that! Look, there are many handsome men in this city. You are too beautiful to waste your time with that *oddball.* I can introduce you to more cultured, much smarter, and very affluent men."

Their arguments concerning Vincent became extreme, until Anne had enough. Rosie's insulting remarks about her new lover caused the opposite to happen. Anne immediately packed her bags. She had made up her mind to move in with Vincent, at his small apartment in Monaco.

"I really shouldn't sleep with you, you know. In the eyes of God you are still married to your first wife," she said. "The Church doesn't accept your divorce."

Vincent could not tell her the *real reason* for his divorce. It was too personal to discuss with her at this stage of their relationship. "Of course you're right from a Catholic viewpoint. Anne, you must understand that there are different kinds of love. I will always love Susan, as the wonderful person that she is, as the mother of my children. I have been through *absolute hell* because of my foolishness. God punished me for what I did. I deserved that punishment. What else can I say? I only know *I love you.* You are the answer to my prayers. I know that I'm at peace, really happy, when you're in my arms."

Anne completely understood what he needed—what she needed. His passionate kisses were so sensitive, gentle. "Vincent, please touch me here," she pleaded. She then proceeded to unbutton her dress from the top. The swelling of her breasts was alluring. They kissed, her lips parting; the soft swollen flesh and moisture of her mouth aroused him. She pressed her body against his, pulling his right hand to the breast beneath her half-open dress. She leaned back, breathing deeply.

He began very gently, fearing that he might harm the unspoiled delicate flower in his arms. To his amazement, this conservative, modest woman, became a *passionate volcano* that suddenly erupted. "Vince, do you realize what you're doing to me?"

"Yes, Anne. I am exploring every crevice of your body. The smell of your perfume is intoxicating. I want to smell, feel, and taste every part of your femininity."

Two mighty forces finally came together, and the cosmic energy that burst forth was *burning love*. They never experienced such beautiful lovemaking. He now realized that sex—*with real love*—had incredible significance. They did not have to measure who gave more than the other did. They willingly gave to each other, *in full measure.* They did whatever came naturally, without any inhibitions.

She fell asleep, on her front, her face against his chest. He placed one hand on the nape of her neck, as she murmured something. Finally, they experienced *real* peace and contentment. Nothing else was important—*not anymore.*

***

Office expenses began to exceed "the partners" limited income. Victor Cruz had lots big ideas, many starts, but zero finishes. "Victor had a little bad luck. Look at all the possibilities for our future, Eva said. "You're too negative, Vince!"

"Yeah, well when is his luck going to change? Anyway, I think we need a more formal business relationship."

The new lawyer drew up a contract. The separation agreement was accepted, after many fights over the fine print; especially the clause that said, *"Eva had to "vacate the premises immediately."* She insisted he delete from the final version. Nevertheless, Eva agreed to pay Vince alimony, whenever Victor made his millions, and she got her share. He insisted on alimony because he gave his first wife most of his estate and alimony, since he broke their vows, and Eva certainly did not keep her vows with him.

Everyone seemed content with the agreements, which were signed and notarized. Henceforth, all office expenses and profits were to be shared on an equal basis. There was only one problem—Victor did not have *any money.* Victor Cruz lied to everyone about his apartment buildings in Portugal, and his mother's huge estates, among fabricated stories.

Eva came up with a new solution: "Victor should charge all clients for his consulting time, like many lawyers do. Invoices were sent out. To our surprise, two weeks later, about $15 thousand dollars flowed in, to keep the ship afloat—*a ship of fools*—and Vincent was the jerk who went for the ride, a very expensive voyage over rough seas, with no port in sight—and Victor was the self-appointed captain.

Meanwhile, back in Vincent's apartment, the fax machine came alive. Details for the Iranian computer contract finally arrived for Anne. She scanned the pages. "You remember that deal we discussed in Switzerland, don't you?"

"Sure. Let's see the list of equipment they want," Vincent answered, as she passed the document to him. "Who's the client?"

"It's that Iranian general I told you about earlier, General Ahmad."

"I wonder why they want *ruggedized* computer modules. We better check with Victor's connections, in case there are export restrictions on this stuff." He did not want to get Cruz involved in her private business; however, the client was buying the electronics through a French trading company, and they knew the goods were destined for Iran.

Victor did not know shit about computer technology, though he pretended to understand everything. "Let me call Paulo in London, and maybe the State Department," he suggested. "You can get your ass in a sling if you don't clear this transaction through official channels, you know."

"Why do you think I'm here? Don't you think we know something about export restrictions?"

Paulo got the message, and returned the call two hours later. "Call me back on a public phone, *immediately!*" he said, with trepidation in his voice.

The call was made from the pay phone downstairs. "The State Department wants to meet you ASAP, about those microcomputers," he said.

The State department came through that night, with a fax message: *We are sending "special consultants" to meet with you and your organization tomorrow. Do not make any further contact before this meeting! REPEAT: Do nothing further until this meeting!*

Sylvia from Mossad, and the top agent, Mr. Hanson, met Victor and Vincent at the Hotel de Paris lobby, the following evening. Hanson was a straw-haired man of about forty, with rather a hard mouth. His dark black eyes dominated his face. He spoke with a husky voice, which added to his arrogant manner.

After the polite B.S. introductions, Hanson got right to the point. "We want to know about *all* your contacts and communications with the Iranians."

"Before I consider that, I must know what this is all about?" Vincent insisted. "There's nothing that's unique about this transaction."

"You're right about the basic specifications. But they requested compact, ruggedized versions, which are highly restricted— *especially for Iran*," Hanson explained. "Whom have you been dealing with?"

"Some general, called Ahmad, who contacted me through a third party."

"Who's the third party?"

"Sorry, I cannot reveal her name at this time."

Sylvia, the blond representative from Mossad, was more graceful and diplomatic. She interrupted. "I think it's wise to go ahead with this transaction. Don't you agree?"

Hanson seemed to understand what she meant but Victor and Vincent did not. "If it's restricted equipment, why do you want me to go ahead with the deal?"

"That's *not your concern*," she said firmly, while glancing at Hanson.

"I'm a United States citizen. I do not take instructions from Israel. If you don't trust me or tell me what's happening, you can forget this *bullshit* business." Vincent stood up to leave. "We don't need this kind of crazy business anyway. The profits certainly don't compensate for the potential risks."

"Sit down! You will only take advice from *your* State Department," Hanson ordered. "You're right they might be able to buy these special computers from other sources. We want them to buy it from *you,* so that we can track the shipment to its destination. A tiny transmitter device will be shipped with the goods, so that our satellites can track where it goes," he explained.

"What if something goes wrong? Suppose they find the transmitter."

"Don't concern yourself about that. We always use two transmitters. One will be in the special suitcase handle, and one in the computer module itself. It's the latest state-of-the-art device. It's undetectable."

"What do they want this stuff for anyway?" Vincent asked.

"That's not your concern! Just do your part to help your country and insure peace and security in the world," Hanson said.

"I insist that the State Department send me an official letter approving the shipment to Iran to protect our asses," Vincent responded. *"Otherwise, no deal!"*

***

Clients from Russia's computer industry asked for Vincent Renaldo's services. Three key Russian executives were coming to France. They invited him to meet them in Paris for a consulting project. Considering his growing office expenses, Vince badly needed some additional income. The fax message said: "IBM is developing an advanced computer series, code named 'Summit,' which is about a year away from introduction and we would appreciate your views on its technology."

They agreed to pay him $2,000 per day plus expenses to assist them as a consultant. Vincent was pleased to get away from the squabbles and pressures of Monaco for a few days.

Fig 11. Paris at dusk

Paris is too good for the French! The locals take this beautiful city for granted. They do not appreciate its unequaled charm and matchless beauty. The Eiffel Tower is unique. There is also the fantastic Tuileries Gardens and the Arc De Triumph at one end of the Champs-Elysees.

No city has that romantic feeling, that certain *old world charm*, as Paris. Artists along the Seine try to scrape out a paltry living. The 18th and 19th century architecture is extremely charming. The Louvre is one of the finest museums in the world. The extraordinary churches and quaint sidewalk cafes are a wonder. Wide cobblestone streets shine when it rains. It is beyond doubt the *"Queen of Cities."*

The Paris Vincent had come to visit, was not the same city he remembered. Chaos was everywhere due to frequent strikes. The volatile French, especially young unemployed Muslims, erupted on almost every street and in the parks. Taxis were scarce—practically nonexistent—and restaurants were closed because of lack of deliveries. His Russian clients stayed at the flamboyant *George V.*

As Vincent approached the hotel, a plainclothes police officer, from the *Direction de la Surveillance du Territoire,* asked to see his identification card or passport. "What's going on? Why all this security?"

"There were a few bombings this week by radical Muslims," the hotel clerk answered. "It's only an extra security check; nothing to worry about." (Nearly 10% of all French citizens are now Muslims. This caused serious economic and ethnic problems). If there is nothing to worry about, why is the city an armed camp? Police with machine guns were at the airport, train stations, and office and government buildings.

His host met Vincent at the front desk. He explained that worker strikers were responsible for the series of bombings this week. They had thrown bombs into shops and one sidewalk café, near rue St. Germaine, had been severely damaged. Dozens of people were wounded. Vincent remembered having coffee at that same cafe with Anne, when she was visiting her parents in Paris. It was such a lively place, where people from all over Europe stop for coffee, to observe the procession of high-fashioned Parisians passing by, or to watch young lovers kissing on the church steps, across the street. Why would anyone want to trash such a friendly place? What political cause could warrant such horrendous acts?

The Muslim population of France reached an estimated 6.5 million, or about ten percent of the population. France has one of the largest Muslim population in the European Union. Not surprisingly, Islam and the question of Muslim immigration were ever-present topics in newspaper headlines. The debate over Islam in France centered mainly on questions about French identity, secularism and security-related issues.

Car burnings were increasingly commonplace in all French cities, and were attributed to shiftless young Muslims, who reside in suburban slums known as *banlieues*. French authorities are especially eager to avoid a repetition of earlier riots, when the deaths of two Muslim teenagers in the *banlieue* of Clichy, near Paris, sparked weeks of looting and car burning, and led to the imposition of a state of emergency.

The female hostess play an important basic role in Russian culture. They are part of the executive compensation package. These charming women, light your cigarette, pour the booze, make small talk, and otherwise serve their *masters*. Every city in the world has these talented women available, on-call at a moment's notice for visiting guests and their clients. Paris was no exception, except that they happened to be the most beautiful, feminine, and well-endowed women imaginable.

These are no ordinary executives. Vincent was amazed by this strange tradition. There was a checklist, where one may choose the type of host you wanted. The result of my selection was impressive. She was called, *Hirime,* an Oriental name, which when translated into English, means *Spring Beauty.* She was tall with ample breasts (a rarity for Asian women); a music lover; excellent dancer; and extremely feminine and pretty. A hostess is not necessarily a sex partner; she is simply part of the Russian business tradition. You *insult* your host, if you refuse her. Even your spouse *must* accept the woman that is offered (Japan has a similar social tradition).

The Russians are *extremely* team oriented and competitive. Vincent recalled an incident during a past meeting, when they were bidding on a big project to replace a Bank computer system. One of the insiders at the bank slept with the key manager. She reported everything she could learn about their private project meetings, especially the bid price from their competitor, Siemens. Because the *paternal* relationship in most companies is so strong with its employees, this shy woman believed it was her *solemn duty* to do all she could to help them get that information. She played her role perfectly.

In Paris, they had no such computerized system, but the selection seemed better than I remembered in Moscow.

After the private dinner with lots of wine, at a restaurant near the George V, they all went up to the suite and got smashed on expensive Johnny Walker Black Scotch. When the Russians get drunk, they each take turns singing old sad songs. They tried to get me to sing-along but that was not one of my consulting talents. Later that evening, Hirime, who was a mixture of French and Oriental lineage, tucked me into bed. I was in no mood or condition to do anything except sleep next to her warm, milky-white body. After she finished the professional massage, I slept like a baby.

Mr. Katskowski, the key Russian executive in charge, arrived the following morning, promptly at 9 o'clock, for our breakfast meeting. He had high cheekbones, generous lips, and clear eyes that shone behind his horn-rimmed glasses. His eyes were full of intelligence—cold at first glance, yet somehow warmer the longer one looked at them. He whipped out a bulky document labeled: "IBM Summit Series: Technology and Business Plan." Its top heading also read: "IBM CONFIDENTIAL," in big red letters.

"Where did you get this gem?" was my tactless remark.

"Mutual teamwork and collaboration," he replied with a smirk.

"What do you mean by that?"

"That hostess you slept with last night is *very proficient*. She received this document as 'a gift' from an IBM development engineer," he said as he passed over the bulky report to me. After some further discreet probing, the Russian executive revealed that she seduced the IBM engineer, and a hidden camera showed their great performance. "That motivated him to 'offer to share' this material with their good friends from Russia, as a gesture of his sincere gratitude," so he claimed.

The technical experts back in Moscow were very confused by all the IBM technical terms and code names, thus the reason for Vincent's services. "Your key assignment is to translate all the code names and make some sense out of this material," he directed.

"Sure, but that will take some time to read and digest."

What a gem! The IBM report contained all the details on the new computer processor chips, the fiber optic protocols, technology changes, circuit packaging, and plans for improvements. Marketing details and anticipated shipments for the systems were presented in chart form. Financial projections and profit margins for the next five years was also part of the planning document. *It was a gold mine!*

Then I thought why should I help these bastards with their industrial espionage, especially for a mere $2,000 per day? I had enough of this kind of crap, back in Monaco. Being the good United States citizen that I am, and admirer of IBM, I could not allow this to happen—*not at these prices anyway.* I went for a walk, and called IBM from a pay phone. After switched to three different departments, I finally reached the right manager in charge of security.

"What specifically is this all about?" he asked. "Why don't you send us a copy?"

"I don't have time to copy this document right now." Vince read a few paragraphs and gave him the coded reference numbers from the report.

"That sounds like one of our highly-confidential reports. I'll contact you soon."

"Look, I don't want to blow my cover. These people happen to be good clients…. I cannot afford to screw-up that relationship. I hope you'll be discreet."

"Don't worry we've had a few other cases like this before. We have our own professional team who know how to handle it," he responded. "In case they bug your room we'll call you at the hotel and say: 'your tickets for the concert are ready.' That will mean that you should see us as soon as possible at this local address ..."

IBM treated Vincent as if he was the Prince of Monaco, when he arrived the following morning at the private address they had given him. They did not want to meet at IBM Paris headquarters, just in case he was followed. The top executive in charge of *all European* operations greeted him warmly—*without* any French kisses. Mr. Jones, the executive in charge, led him into an inner office, where several serious looking men were deep in conversation. "This is Vincent Renaldo, the gentleman who has agreed to take care of our little problem."

The executive's predictable statement, after all the introductions were over, was, "Headquarters in New York *really appreciates* your professionalism in this matter."

Mr. Jones went over their plans to trap the Russian executives. A special communications squad would be busy that afternoon bugging his suite with electronic gear, including hidden TV cameras.

Erroneous translations of the secret IBM product code names were provided in case they faxed some of the material to Moscow, before IBM could close the trap.

At the afternoon meeting with the Russians, the man in charge was particularly demanding. Vince listened politely. He wondered how they expected him to digest all this technical shit, about 750 pages, in only 48 hours, and give them a written report. "A written report would take too long. I'd rather give you a *verbal summary.*"

They instantly understood Vincent's concerns about *written reports.* A meeting was arranged the following day to review his understanding of the key parts of the document. "It's better if you come to our suite," he said. "We have a much bigger room and plenty of the best wine and food for your enjoyment."

It seemed as if the plans he made with IBM were being sabotaged. Did they have someone follow him? Are they just being cautious? Vincent went down to the lobby to buy a newspaper. He called IBM from a phone booth.

"Don't worry, we thought of these possibilities," Mr. Jones, the executive in charge said. "Do exactly what they want you to do. Go to the meeting in their suite."

After about ten minutes into the meeting, there was a knock on the door. "It must be our food and drinks," someone said. Sure enough, the waiter came in with lots of goodies on a cart with wheels. Another hour passed. Still no IBM action. Maybe they did not know the room number, I thought as the meeting ended, about three hours later.

That evening, Vincent received a call from his IBM contact. "They have all been caught as they went through passport control at the airport," he boldly stated. *"Great job!* Please come and see us tomorrow morning at 9 o'clock."

"Why didn't you catch them during the meeting?" I asked.

"We didn't want to blow your cover. Besides your relationship with the Russians might be useful to you—and to IBM—in the future."

The next morning the IBM team briefed him. The cart that brought the food and drinks included a bug concealed underneath it. In addition, they found the camera and tapes the Russians used to record the *entire meeting.* The bastards got him on camera as well. They could have used this in the future to *bribe him,* in case his loyalties changed.

IBM presented Vincent with a $10,000 check, a new personal computer, and a nice letter from the European President. IBM is having a tough time making its goals this year, the executive claimed. "I know you will appreciate that during these hard times, this is a 'substantial and extraordinary.' Congratulations, you helped IBM—*and America*—maintain its competitive advantage."

On the flight back to Nice, I thought about this crazy adventure in Paris. Many United States companies are *naive* about industrial espionage. It is happening everywhere: in Germany, in Japan, and especially by the Chinese. When the culprits are caught, what does the United States administration do? They turn the other cheek. Then the crooks get even more daring. That's because international laws are inadequate and the penalties are relatively minor. Many companies are also too embarrassed to report espionage activities. That's because they do not want their peers to know how stupid they were. Tiny computer chips and software are easily smuggled out of the country, and reverse engineered by the competition. It might also become a big patent infringement battle, which can take many years to settle.

Vincent was relieved when the IBM check was cashed. He sold the personal computer for $2,500 and went back to Monte-Carlo feeling a bit richer and satisfied. A few weeks later, the Wall Street Journal reported that the Russian company agreed to pay IBM sixty million dollars for certain "technology rights." The sting operation did not seem to change anything. Vincent's meager award was *insignificant,* just a small rounding error on what IBM collected from the Russians. The IBM engineer lost his job, but more significantly, he also caught *syphilis* and passed it on to his wife, from the Oriental-French host. Shit, that could have been my fate, Vincent thought, if he had not been so tired and drunk that night. *It was a blessing in disguise!*

***

MYSTERIOUS

"*It's the unknown that draws people.*"

—E.A.

Colonel Omar responded by telex with the order for computer modules. It required an immediate reply:

"My Darling Anne: We would like to receive a few samples of the computer modules, before our people will accept the full shipment and your payment terms. Please try to see that the goods are available for inspection by our French trading company. I will personally be arriving in Paris next month, and will be pleased to see you then. I hope we can 'continue that delightful experience' we had together in Iran. Faithfully Yours," Omar.

Anne came home later that evening. Vincent showed her the fax. "What's this *'My Darling Anne'* business?" What does he mean by *'continue that delightful experience?'"*

She laughed. "Oh it's nothing. I met him before we met, you know."

"Were you romantically involved with him?"

"Just a little fling," she replied, with a mischievous smile. "He's extremely handsome, like my former Iranian boyfriend. He's so tall, dark ... and very strong too."

She came over and kissed him tenderly. "You're not jealous of him, are you?" she asked, as her body pressed against his.

Pulling away abruptly, he looked at her directly, impatiently. "He happens to be *very dangerous!* Did you two sleep together?"

Anne paused, before answering. She came over and wrapped her arms around his neck, and whispered "darling, if you really must know, the truth is we had *phenomenal sex*. It was only one night. That delightful evening ended much too quickly."

Anne knew that after Vincent's traumatic experience with Eva, he had difficulty having an erection. She eventually learned how to provide the necessary 'remedial treatment' to solve his psychological problem. The solution that always seemed to work, was to tell him fantasies about her past erotic experiences, even though they were actually a product of her imagination.

"What *really* happened? Vincent looked directly into her eyes, searching for the truth. "Tell me the truth, *the whole story!*"

"I don't think I should tell you. *You can't handle the truth!*"

"Just tell me what actually happened, and, don't leave *anything out.*"

"Well, if you really insist. Promise that you will not be angry. *Promise!*"

"Okay. I promise. But don't bullshit me!"

"Well, after I finished dinner with the General, I invited Omar up for coffee in my hotel suite. It was very hot and humid that evening, so I changed into my light blue dress. You remember the one, don't you darling? It's that *très sexy* dress you said I should never wear in public, because it's too short and clings to my body."

"Sure I remember. *That dress scarcely covers anything!* How could you wear that skimpy outfit with him?"

"It was extremely hot and humid that night in Iran, dearest. I had only one cool dress. Anyway, I powdered my body all over and let down my hair to my waist. The powder did not help much; that thin cotton fabric kept sticking to my hot moist body. Anyhow, I sat directly across from him on the couch, as I'm doing now. Well, as I went to get my coffee from the table I bent down. See like this. All of a sudden, my tits flopped out of that low-cut dress."

"How could you expose yourself to a stranger like that?"

"It wasn't intentional," she said, with a seductive cunning smile. "It was an innocent accident. In any case, I did not consider him a stranger, since we became very *intimate friends.*

Anyway, I quickly pushed my tits back into my dress."

"What was his reaction?"

"Well, he wasn't blind you know. I noticed his eyes *suddenly* move down and focused on my thighs. I blushed all over when I realized that I forgot to put on panties."

"I can't believe that a classy lady like you could forget her underwear."

"It was too hot and humid for underwear, dear. In any event, I sensed that my thighs got him excited. So I crossed my legs again, see ... like this ... to give him a better view."

"Better view of what?"

"Let me demonstrate." She pulled up her dress a little, crossed her stunning legs in front of him, exposing her private area. *"Now you know what it means!* Doesn't that turn-you-on?"

"You sure know how to get a guy excited. What was his reaction?"

"He instantly dropped his coffee."

"He spilled the coffee on the floor?" "No on his pants. I had to wash them with cold soda water."

"He took them off?"

"No silly! I came over and rubbed the soda on them. As I started rubbing the stain, he reached into my low-cut dress and grasped my breasts with his big strong hands. I became extremely *excited* ... Je suis devenu extrêmement a excité. My nipples hardened at once to his touch. Je ne peux pas commander mon de même. I just could not control myself.

"I don't believe you," Vincent said, laughingly. "You have a very vivid imagination."

"If you don't believe me, then I won't tell you what happened next."

"Okay, okay. I believe you teased him *a little,* but you're exaggerating the rest. Go on with your fairy tale."

"The cold water and my gentle rubbing caused his thing to become enormous."

"What thing? Vincent asked, as if he didn't know."

"His masculinity of course. I looked up at him with a sly smile, and then he abruptly pulled up my dress, and …"

Vincent could not take her excruciating teasing anymore. "Come over here and get your punishment, you shameless woman." He grabbed her, put her over his knee, pulled up her dress, and began gently spanking her firm bare ass. He then pulled the dress over her hips and removed it. She pushed Vincent onto the carpet, to mount him. He penetrated her fully. This shy demure woman became a passionate live wire on top of him. Intense orgasmic eruptions consumed her. Vincent reached his climax in multiple bursts. Exhausted they collapsed into each other's arms.

After about an hour, Anne took a soft wet cloth and washed him. "I'm not through with you," she whispered. She started massaging him with baby oil on his backside. Slowly and firmly moving up to his shoulders. "Turn over!" she ordered. The rubdown continued from his legs, up to the top of his thighs, while she remained seated. She teased him again, and again, with her delicate rubbing. Her stroking movements and kisses tormented Vince, and soon revitalized his feeble member. Tantalizing *electric sizzles* ran all the way up and down his body, to the tips of his toes.

"Oui. See how it came back to its original vigor. *Très sexy.* Now, I want you to *really give it to me!* Show me how much stronger you are my darling."

Exhausted they finally collapsed into each other's arms. Anne turned over and faced him. "You know I was only kidding to get you excited. You know how my imagination, my fantasies turn both of us on, darling. Don't you?"

"Yeah, you sure have a fascinating imagination. What would you do if Omar *actually* attacked you?"

"I would kick him right there."

Vincent thought about her tall-tales. She enjoyed teasing him with her incredible flight of fantasy to make him jealous. It got them both excited. "Talking a little dirty was an innocent way to add spice, a little *hot sauce* to love making," she would say. It achieved its objective, *perfectly.* He fell into a deep sleep.

Anne could not sleep. She knew how to play her role well, as that actor, Audrey Hepburn did in Paris, to make Gary Cooper jealous, in that movie she saw years ago. It was *Fascination.* Her sexual therapy solved Vincent's psychological problem, for the time being. However, she could not get out of her mind what he said: "What would you do if Omar actually attacked you?" Anne knew that she would be far too terrified to protect herself.

The following morning, Vincent was determined that Anne would not jeopardize herself with this risky situation. "Omar is a very dangerous character. I don't want you to have anything to do with him."

"Really, Vince you're being silly. You're just acting jealous again."

"Jealous? If not jealous, you would know that I really didn't care. I refuse to expose you to this dangerous situation. I am going to call that Mossad agent, Sylvia. She can handle it. It's her job, anyway."

Sylvia agreed to take over the delivery of the computer modules. She knew that Anne was too inexperienced for this risky business. "Tell Anne to call Colonel Omar. She should tell him that her father is critically ill, and she has to go to Nice to be near him. Say that her girlfriend Sylvia, who shares an apartment with her in Paris, is agreeable to receive him for dinner tomorrow, and would give him the package."

The call finally got through to Iran. Omar appreciated Anne's concern for her dying father. "I completely understand. In my country, the father of the family is highly esteemed," he said.

***

Paris, France. Colonel Omar arrived two hours earlier than they had agreed. Sylvia answered the doorbell. "Bon soir, Madam Sylvia, I presume. Anne suggested that we meet."

"Bon soir. You're Captain Omar?" Anne was so right, she thought. This guy is extremely handsome.

"Well I'm now a Colonel, but just call me Omar. Please excuse me for coming early. I forgot to set my watch for French time."

"No problem, except I just finished my bath. As you can see, I'm not fully dressed yet," she answered with a warm smile. "Please have a seat and pour yourself a drink. I'll be back in a few minutes."

Omar *intentionally* came early to surprise her. It was part of his intelligence training. He quietly checked out the apartment for possible hidden bugs or anything unusual. He flipped through her personal phone book on the dining table. He checked all the photos on the wall and table. He found nothing of concern. He was pleased that Sylvia had Nordic-like, European features, similar to Anne. Her gray eyes, fair complexion, and natural honey blond hair, were not the characteristics of any Mid-East woman, and *certainly not a Jew.* He thought she seemed less inhibited than Anne did.

Anne warned Sylvia that Omar was the type that could easily seduce any woman if given a chance. Sylvia determined that sexual distraction would be *exactly* the best way to disguise her real role. That is what made her a good agent. (Remember this guy is turned on by *boobs,* Anne had stressed).

Sylvia finally appeared in a full-length, multi-colored, silk dress that showed ample cleavage. She pinned up her long hair, exposing her long pale neck and shoulders, which gave her the look of an exotic dancer. "Omar, before I forget, Anne left this package for you."

"Thank you. I will remember to take it. How long have you known her?"

"Not very long, we only moved in together about three months ago. Anne is very modest, you know. I have been trying to get her to be a little less conservative."

"Yes, you're right. Women in Iran are also very conservative. It's refreshing to come to Paris, where everyone is less conventional," he added.

Sylvia served him another glass of red wine. "I must be cautious. I am not used to your French wine. In my country drinking is forbidden you know."

"Well, Omar, as they say, 'when in Rome, do as the Romans do.' Enjoy the Parisian way of life."

Her gentle teasing began to work on him. She could tell by his quickening eye movements, to all the right places. She handled herself well by putting a proper distance between herself and Colonel. The radio was playing romantic French music. The candle lit dinner consisted of fresh poached salmon, sprinkled with black caviar, on a bed of lettuce. He told her that it was "almost as good as Iranian caviar."

"Do you like to dance in your country," she asked.

"Certainly! We love dancing."

"Well, how about this music. It's perfect for dancing, don't you agree?"

"Sure! May I have this dance, Madam?"

Her perfume reminded Omar of Anne. Her slow sensual body movements caused blood to rush to his face, among other places. Then faster and more exotic dance music began.

"Please excuse me. I must sit this one out," he insisted. "The wine must have affected me. Have you ever been to the Middle-East?"

"No! Never! Perhaps you might invite me some day?" Sylvia's instincts and training told her to be careful not to over-play her role. Do not seduce him too hastily. That opportunity might come later. (He left with the "package," just before midnight).

Omar sent a dozen red roses the following day. The note read, "Dear Sylvia, Thanks for a wonderful evening. I will call you at 6 PM. I hope that you will be able to join me for an evening in Paris."

Something about that man fascinated her. It was not just his good looks or sexuality. He was gentle, yet very strong. He was extremely knowledgeable, and at the same time seemed to be humble. Omar was a master, who intentionally allowed her to enslave him. Sylvia could not put him out of her mind.

After calling ahead as promised, Omar arrived promptly at eight that evening, with some perfume. It was the same brand that Anne wore in Iran, called *Samsara*.

"Omar, *you're too sweet!"*

They went to an old charming hotel that Sylvia recommended. It was on the left bank of Paris. It is called *Le Hotel,* with its unique white spiral marble staircase that reached up all five floors, to a magnificent frosted glass dome ceiling above. The famous playwright Oscar Wilde used to live and work there. They ate in its secluded underground cave restaurant. Exotic birds hanging in cages seemed to chirp to the piano music that played in the background. The *Steak Oscar* was fantastic, as was the exclusive selection of wines, and dessert of tropical fruits, with sauce made from liquor.

After dinner, they headed for the *Follies.* The extravagant performances included the popular Can-Can dancers. Later they walked arm-in-arm along the Seine, which reflected the lights from antique gas street lamps near the river. Sylvia pointed to all the museums, churches and other famous historical places.

By 2 AM, they arrived back at Sylvia's apartment. Seduction was part of his job. Omar was normally coldly businesslike. However, there was not a way to be coldly intimate—at least not if he wanted to achieve the goals of his mission. You adapt your approach to the individual and idiosyncrasy of your subject. In this case, it was a mid-thirties woman with surprising good looks. It was not his first subject, and there was always something unique about all of them, as well as something pathetic.

He could not know that his target *this time* was a highly skilled Mossad agent, who had similar training—and was *very good* at her game. All she had to do was press the right buttons—create the right feeling. There was a flush of warmth from her touch. It was a feeling that no normal male could resist. Unlike Omar, she never thought of him as a mere target. How could she accomplish her mission, without authentic feelings? She was proud of her abilities, and gave her best performance.

When her warm sensitive body pressed against his, the seduction was complete. Her strength surprised him. He was barely able to take his next breath, so amorous and powerful was her sexual performance. Part of what had once been her conscience, told her that she ought to be ashamed; but *it was her duty!* It was for a higher-purpose.

She offered everything for her country. Sylvia then gave him a mischievous smile.

"Why do you look at me that way?"

"I gave myself to you. Yet, I hardly know who you are!"

"What do you want to know?"

She shrugged. "Nothing important—I mean what could be more important than body language?" She kissed him again passionately. "When will I see you again?"

"Soon, I hope. Maybe you can visit me in Iran?"

"I'd like that very much. Call me when you get back, will you."

"Of course," he said as he again took her in his arms.

Sylvia previously coated his glass with the special drug, *before* pouring his last glass of wine. It quickly made him very sleepy. She could feel his body muscles becoming slack as the drug began to take its effect. She relaxed quietly in his embrace, and she also had difficulty staying awake. Some of the drug residue must have remained on his lips, when he last kissed her.

The urgency of her mission was very much on her mind. Would I fail in my duty? The Colonel was a master on how to win over and control *any woman.* This bastard was an expert at exploiting feminine emotions and vulnerabilities. Thoughts about possible betrayal, or how she might jeopardize the mission, consumed her, as she laid awake next to him. Her Mossad comrades might perceive her weakness, from recordings of their conversation, and during their moments of rapture. Somehow, she *must* regain composure and complete her mission.

Sylvia took out the special equipment provided for her assignment. No person, no matter how strong, could withstand the injection of the newly improved, faster acting *Scopolamine*, the highly effective "truth drug." Secret information could not be inhibited or fabricated, once the gates of recall are chemically ripped open. He started to talk, although his eyes remained foggy. He began mumbling something. Sylvia started with the preplanned questions:

"Are you Colonel Omar?"

"Yes, I'm Colonel Omar Kamil."

"Do you live in Iran?"

"Tell me about the *Sword of Allah?* What does it mean?"

"The *sword* ... it shall destroy our enemies," he responded.

"Who are your enemies?"

"American dogs, the Jewish state ... *those infidel pigs!"* he shouted.

"Which infidels? Tell me who they are?"

"The Saudis, with their black gold."

"Aren't they your Arab brothers," she asked.

"No! *Sunni bastards!* They control the price of black gold, but no longer. *Allah* shall send missiles from the sky ... and their earth shall be contaminated, *forever."*

"Where and when will the *Sword of Allah strike?"* She inquired.

"From the deserts. The deserts of Iran and Syria." He said, as his speech became more and more garbled.

"Exactly where? ... When?"

It was too late. The drug began losing its effect. He might awaken in a few minutes. If the CIA is right about their new drug, he should not remember a damn thing. After phoning the details to her contact, Sylvia finally relaxed and fell asleep next to him, physically and emotionally drained.

The Colonel woke up a few hours later. He immediately thought he had some kind of unpleasant dream. He quickly checked his second precious package. He was relieved to find that it is still there and its contents were not disturbed. Sylvia remained sound asleep next to him.

Sylvia's contact Aaron became alarmed, when she did not keep her scheduled rendezvous with him at the park, the following morning. He called for instructions. A backup team arrived. They reached her apartment minutes later. (They did not see the Colonel leave but it was much too quiet inside). The duplicate key opened the door without making a sound. They lunged inside, crouching, listening, and leveling their guns in front of them, prepared to fire in an instant. The sound of running water came from the bathroom. The bloodied bath water completely covered her naked body. Both wrists were slashed.

The Colonel must have departed by way of the back window and fire escape.

Aaron called for instructions. "Omar escaped with the computer modules, and our agent is dead," Aaron informed them, with his *frantic* voice.

"Do not stop him! Repeat: Do not stop him!"

He acknowledged the unequivocal order given by his superior on his cellphone, which scrambled all private conversations between them.

"We are activating the transmitter concealed in the package."

They rolled her body inside the living room carpet. The apartment was thoroughly inspected. Minutes later, he heard his chief's voice. "Good! It is working. We are receiving signals from two locations. He's heading for Charles De Gaulle airport."

Colonel Omar had no reason to believe his secret mission was compromised. Still, being a highly experienced agent, he could not leave anything to chance. Something about Sylvia's manner, her style, made him uneasy. Why didn't she ask him personal questions during two evenings together; that is *not normal for any woman?* Maybe their sex together was too easy. He remembered some vague, obscure dream, which bothered him. Did he speak in his sleep, as his wife said he often did?

He thought of how he left her very satisfied last night—*her final sleep!* She had such a peaceful expression on her pretty face. She did not feel anything, when he gave her that fatal injection, before placing her in the bathtub, and slashing her wrists. It will appear to be a typical suicide.

He pulled his blue Mercedes into the airport parking area. He parked and checked his watch. The flight would leave in about an hour. Omar retrieved the suitcase that contained the vital computer modules. As he walked to the departure terminal, speakers announced his flight: "Mesdames et messieurs, s'il vous plait, flight to Tehran, via Athens, departure..."

***

Monaco. Even before Vincent could speak, her voice came through the receiver. "Thank God you're there. You must help me..."

"Christ, what's wrong?" Vincent said, cutting through her hysteria, "Tell me where you are? What's happened?"

The sobs overtook her again. "I'm in Monaco."

He cut in. There was not time to worry about getting the whole picture crystal clear. Whatever words he might have expected, whatever revelations might have come, nothing prepared him for what he heard.

Her voice was a *shrieking cry of pain, of torment. "It's horrible, what he did to her,"* Anne cried.

"Get control of yourself. Listen to me! What is it?"

"Sylvia is dead! They found her ... with her wrists slashed. He made it look like a suicide," she explained in her broken voice.

"Now maybe you understand why I was so determined to stop you from being involved in this risky business. She is a professional, an experienced Mossad agent. I am so, so sorry for her. It could have been you, my darling."

The newspapers the following day called it a *suicide.* The cover-up by the French DST authorities was perfect: "The young former professional dancer had a 'history of depression,' and had been under the care of her psychologist." This was the key part of the fake press story about Sylvia's tragic death. Bogus medical records were put into the doctor's files in case Iran agents attempted to check out that phony story.

That Sunday, Vincent met with Hanson and Aaron, the special Paris agent for Mossad covert operations.

"Was her death worth it?" Vincent asked. "She was so young and attractive."

"Who are you to speak about my colleague, *asshole?* What do you know about her? I worked with her for more than five years. She is one of our best agents—she was *my dearest friend.* It is deplorable. I will miss her ... She died in duty to her country. What she did could save thousands," Aaron *shouted.*

Hanson interrupted him, before he inadvertently revealed anything more about their covert operations and methods.

"Well, we can't tell you any specifics. *It is classified!* I can inform you that Iran was planning an international situation, which could affect the region. We have some pieces of their scheme, thanks to Sylvia. You *must not* reveal this to anyone. *Do you understand? Do you hear what I'm saying?"*

"Of course, I understand. I'm not as stupid as you think," Vincent replied.

"Any further contact by phone, telex or whatever means must be reported to me *immediately,"* Hanson demanded.

"Sure! *Absolutely!* However, you must assure me that Anne does not get involved with those bastards. Besides, you probably have a bug on our phones."

"Okay! But, if the Colonel calls Anne, she *must* continue to play her role. Otherwise, she could be in serious danger. This thing is not over yet. She must send the final shipment, when the order comes in," Hanson insisted.

"As long as she doesn't have to meet him or his associates, we will play along. *Otherwise, you can forget it!* I want you to cover our asses in case something goes wrong."

"Fine. Then we have your *word of honor* that Anne will play this thing out? I'll provide two of my best agents to shadow both of you, day and night."

"Yeah, sure. What choice do we have?" Vincent remarked, as he stood up to leave.

"By the way, there's some *good news.* Our tests show that the Colonel has SIDA, if that's any consolation," Aaron casually remarked, as they started leaving.

"What's SIDA?" Vince asked.

"That's French for AIDS. He had sex with Sylvia before he murdered her. His secretions tested positive. *He's going to die soon!"*

That off-handed, casual remark, *stunned him.* If the Colonel has AIDS, then Anne might have it too. If she has it, he probably caught this virulent disease from her. What a bloody mess! He must see her right away.

Vincent could not wait to contact Anne. He called a local doctor. "I need a blood test for HIV."

"That would take about 72 hours before we would know the results," the doctor informed him.

Weeks later, Anne was busy with the morning mail when she received a call from the Colonel at her apartment. "Bon jour, how are you, my dear?

"Well, I'm not feeling so good."

"What's wrong? Is it your father again?"

"No. It's my girlfriend Sylvia. You met her a few weeks ago?"

"Sure. She is such a lovely person. We had a great evening together."

"She ... she was very depressed ... and took her own life. She cut her wrists. *She's dead!"* Anne said, as her voice choked with emotion.

"My God! I cannot believe that lovely young woman did such a thing. Please accept my sincere condolences. She seemed so normal, so full of life."

"Her housekeeper found her," Anne added. "Did she seem depressed to you? Did you see her take her pills?"

"No! What pills?"

"Her Anti-depression pills. Her doctor told her that they are *vital.* She ... she had to take them every night." Anne tried to gain some control over her emotions but her voice betrayed her.

"I called to tell you some news. But this is the wrong time to discuss business," Omar said. "Perhaps I should call you back in a few days?"

"Thank you for your concern, Omar. You are right. I am in no mood to handle any business. Perhaps you could call ... or send me a fax, in a few days?"

"I completely understand, my dear. If you need me for anything, you know how to reach me. Please take care. I'll call you in a few days."

"*You're so sweet!* Thanks for your sincere concern. I am sure I'll get over this shock in a few days. Why don't you call me Thursday evening?"

"Until Thursday then. Good-bye."

When Anne finally arrived at the apartment, Vincent told her about the meeting with the area chief from CIA and the Mossad agent. Anne related the details of the phone call she received from the Colonel.

"Listen dear. I have to ask you a *very serious* question."

"What about?" "Did you really have intercourse with that bastard? *Tell me the truth!"*

"How can you ask me such an *absurd question?* Why are you on that subject again? Really, Vincent, do you actually think I am the kind of person who jumps in the sack with *anyone?* Don't you trust me? Do you think I am like Eva, *who sells her ass for money?* Did you *really* believe my fantasy story?"

"Sorry, honey. You do not know how relieved I am. Colonel Omar has AIDS. I mean, what you French call SIDA."

"I thought that bastard was a 'womanizer.' *He's a killer of women, isn't he?"*

Days later, Sylvia's doctor office was broken into. The fake records were photographed. Iranian agents had to check out the press reports, and Anne's story. The Mossad put a special dust in the file, which verified that someone tampered with them, exposing them to flashes of light from a camera.

Vincent received the results from his doctor that evening. The HIV blood test was *negative.* It is not that he did not believe Anne. He thought that he might have gotten AIDS earlier from Eva, considering her many sexual adventures before and after they met. It was the logical thing to do.

On Thursday, a fax arrived authorizing the order for additional computer modules. A French bank, PNB, confirmed the letters- of-credit. The shipment was to be sent to the bogus French Company. Then the CIA traced the package on its final destination to Tehran via Air France, that following Monday. Hanson carefully eliminated all fingerprints from the internal packaging. The tiny transmitter hidden among the complex circuits would be turned on, a few minutes each day, when the United States spy satellite was directly over the region;

only then would the signal generator become activated, and then it would send location coordinates.

Weeks later, two of the computers were still in Tehran. Three modules had been located in the remote Western region of Syria. However, the remaining two computer modules could not be located. Were they in a highly shielded environment? Did the transmitters fail to operate? Could they be in deep underground bunkers, somewhere in the desert? The CIA and Mossad had to locate the other computer modules.

***

Washington: The CIA received the full news report at Langley, which was passed on to the Mossad in Israel. They learned that North Korea shipped some of their more advanced missiles to Syria. As a result, Israel saw itself threatened from all sides, with a far more menacing force then it had ever faced before.

A high-level meeting commenced in Washington D. C. The State Department hosted the conference. Members of Mossad, the CIA, NSA, DOD and the Chiefs of the United States military, all participated.

Israel wanted to launch a *preemptive* strike against Iran's atomic facilities and all the Iranian supported missile sites, *at once.*

Secretary of State Hillary Clinton forcefully argued: "Such action without substantial proof would precipitate an Islamic fundamentalist uprising against Israel and our strategic interests of the West.

"They did not have any direct proof that Iran was the brains behind the impending crisis. Direct action might be the right thing to do later, if and when, they have conclusive evidence.

"If one challenges *directly* the power of a nation-state, you also risk a direct response from them. Right versus wrong assumed different meanings at this level. What were the rules? What was the law? Were there any of either?"

Secretary of Defense, Robert Gates, assured Israel: "Everything is under control:

The computers in the missiles have an electronic device that can be activated instantly, crippling them by remote control, *whenever it's necessary*. If that should somehow fail, our Cruise missiles could *easily* take out all the launching sites, as soon as we have established their exact locations, if we concluded that they represented an *immediate threat*. Our more advanced anti-missile missiles were installed near Tel Aviv. Iron Dome could easily knock out incoming enemy missiles."

The Israeli representatives were *not impressed*. "If the target was Washington or New York, *would you feel so secure?* The Mossad chief, Meir Dagan told Gates. "Don't try to sell us your bullshit anti-missile missiles—they didn't do shit for us during Operation Desert Storm. Besides, there are two computer modules whose locations are unknown."

Secretary of State Hillary Clinton took charge of the debate. "President Obama and I *personally assure you,* this crisis has our 'highest priority.' Our strategic interests in the area are also extremely vital. Let us focus our combined resources on what we must do to obtain additional intelligence."

All agreed to make an extra effort to locate the other computer modules. None of the existing intelligence reports expected Iran to be ready for at least another six months.

Some weeks later, leading Saudi Princes began moving their families and their fortunes to the United States, Europe and other regions. Did someone leak *top-secret* intelligence reports to the Saudis'? In addition, about $500 billion was electronically transferred to American and Japanese banks. This kind of activity, if it became publicly known, might tip-off the press that something big was about to happen. Iran and the other culprits would then change their plans. *Absolute secrecy was imperative!*

By June, Mossad discovered through their local Iranian informants and intercepted phone conversations, that the Iranian engineers had analyzed two of the missing computer modules. "Urgent that you immediately inhibit any signal transmissions to and from computer modules X164 and X168," Mossad advised the CIA in Washington. (The CIA could turn the transmission circuits on or off within each of the modules, by remote control. They also planted a self-destruct mechanism in the computers, in case anyone tried to probe or tamper with the complex electronic circuits inside the highly-integrated package. The key integrated circuits would then experience a power overload, causing the computers to become useless. (A week later, Mossad learned that two of the Iranian engineers who worked on the computers were shot by a firing squad, for espionage. Agents in the field learned that the two missing computers were ruined by tampering).

Dubai: Iran's former President claims the United States is attempting to thwart the return of mankind's savior, according to reports from *Al Arabiya,* a television news station based in Dubai. Ahmadinejad reportedly claims he has documented evidence that the U.S. is blocking the return of Mahdi, the Imam believed by [some Shiite] Muslims to be their savior. "We have documented proof that they believe that a descendant of the prophet of Islam will rise in these parts and he will dry the roots of all injustice in the world," he said during a speech, according to *Al Arabiya.*

"They have devised all these plans to prevent the coming of the 'Hidden Imam' because they know that the Iranian nation is the one that will prepare the grounds for his coming and will be the supporters of his rule," Ahmadinejad was quoted as saying. Ahmadinejad continued his ranting by claiming there have been plots by both the West as well as countries in the East to wipe out his country, according to Iranian news Web site *Tabak.* "They have planned to annihilate Iran. This is why all policymakers and analysts believe Iran is the true winner in the Middle East."

He also alleged that foreign nations seek to control Iran's oil and natural resources. "In Afghanistan, they are caught like an animal in a quagmire. Instead of pulling their troops out to save themselves, they are deploying more soldiers. Even if they stay in Afghanistan for another 50 years they will be forced to leave with disgrace—because this is a historical experience," Ahmadinejad reportedly said. "They know themselves that they need Iran in the Middle East, but because of their arrogance they do not want to accept this reality.

They are nothing without the Iranian nation and all their rhetoric is because they don't want to appear weak."

***

ODD PARTNERS

***"You don't get explanations in real life. You just get moments
that are absolutely, utterly, inexplicably odd."***

—Neil Gaiman

Samoset Enterprises was bankrupt. Eva was convinced it was an opportunity to pick-up some furniture and equipment, on the cheap. Victor Cruz, being the great financial whiz, decided to go for the whole thing—*the entire syndicated company*—not just a few chairs, desks and office machines. The president of the corporation, that was rapidly sinking, saw Victor as his "savior," and opened the books for his review and financial wizardry. Sam forgot to mention that he borrowed 350,000 Euros from dubious partners, *the Mafia,* to keep his business alive. They promised to break his legs if he did not pay, yesterday.

A few days later, two big goons showed up at the office. They had been shadowing Sam, the ex-president of bankrupt Samoset Enterprises. Victor did not intend to be intimidated or bullied by these two characters. "You're dealing with a financial professional. It will be resolved in about 48 hours," he said.

"Are you taking responsibility for his debt to us?" they asked.

"But of course!" Victor said, in his typical arrogant style.

When Vincent arrived at the office two days later, these characters were having coffee with Victor and Eva. Everyone spokes French, *in a very nervous fashion.* Vince did not have enthusiasm to learn the language, after Eva's affair. Nonetheless, he could tell that the *goon squad* was not there for a social call. "What's going on?"

"Everything's Okay. Victor has the situation under control." Eva said. "He just needed a little extra time."

Fast-talking Victor, who could sell the Eskimos ice, or the Saudi's oil, saved the day.

The Mafia agreed to pick up their past due payment next month—*or else!*

Surprise! Victor and Eva had an invitation to meet with Chinese investor, Mr. Wong. "In Hong Kong the bankers are more intelligent. They would understand and quickly approve my financial plans," Victor Cruz claimed.

The loan sharks would simply have to wait until they returned, with the millions that he expected to bring back. Victor and "his woman," would stay at a five star hotel, the Hong Kong Hilton, in order to impress all the investors and bankers. Victor refused to travel, without *his love,* and she did not want to leave him alone with all that anticipated loot, which he might put into a secret bank account.

Vincent was trapped! His consulting contract in the States had only one month left, and cash was quickly running out. Meanwhile, office expenses reached new highs. Being nearly broke, Vince took this *last gamble* with part of the remaining ten thousand dollars in his account, and sent them on their way. He hoped that this "final bet" might payoff for all their past nonsense; then he could get on with his life, *without them.* Besides, he badly needed a few weeks of peace and tranquility.

***

Hong Kong. The first few weeks proved to be very promising. Victor formed a Hong Kong company, together with Chinese investor, Mr. Wong, who had deep pockets. Private stock certificates were printed and distributed to the investors and founders, including Vincent Renaldo. Drafts of the agreements were prepared and ready for execution, with fancy letterhead for the new joint venture company.

Vincent remembered meeting Mr. Wong when he visited the office in Monaco, some six months ago. He looked like a kid just out of college. Mr. Wong happened to be responsible for hundreds-of-millions of dollars of investments. Nevertheless, Vince did not like his shit-eating smile, which seemed to hint that Wong knew something that they didn't know. Both Victor and Wong also had enormous egos. There seemed to be competition between them to see who would be screwed first.

The joint venture was *a total disaster!* Victor argued with Mr. Wong, the investor who supposedly had the $200 million to invest in their joint projects. They allowed personal arrogance to get in the way of the business deal. Eva also claimed Victor was often drunk and "tried to screw the hotel secretary," whom he hired to type those "creative contracts." Eva was pissed. He was frequently inebriated, as was determined from his phone conversations, but she gave him too much credit for his sexual talents.

"I'm the only one *being screwed!*" Vince concluded.

Eva was a three months pregnant with Victor's bastard. She was sick much of the time and could not keep her eye on all his business activities. Who knows what really happened? The hotel bill totaled nearly $15,000. (Sometime later, Vincent learned that Victor forged a "friend's" signature on a credit card, to escape from Hong Kong).

Back in beautiful, sunny, affluent Monte Carlo, Vincent was *impoverished.* He managed to borrow ten thousand dollars from Anne, to eat and to feed the dog, as well as to pay the critical bills, and keep the office afloat.

The pair of lying, cheating world travelers arrived back in Nice, just in time for Christmas, with gifts for the jerk that helped to send them there. "I don't want those ugly shirts and ties, or that leather attaché case. All I want for Christmas is an attaché full of money," he told them.

They were all in the same boat; and it was sinking fast. All they could do was bailout the water together. Victor came up with a new "super plan" to complete the financing *without* the Chinese investment. Since last year was definitely not a successful year for business, or their crazy relationship, a simple New Year's party might be a good idea—to wash away the old and welcome in the new—hopefully rewarding New Year.

Anne went away to visit her family in Paris for the holidays. Vince became *very depressed* and lonely, especially during Christmas. The music in particular made him moody. It reminded Vince of his deep sense of loss. It is the season to be with the family, whom he loved and missed *enormously.* For more than twenty years, he was rarely away from them during the holidays. They would usually attend Christmas midnight mass, together. Then they would sit around the Christmas tree and fireplace, opening gifts. Susan would be busy cooking a big turkey, with all the special trimmings.

Vincent was friendly with a tall blond beauty from Norway, Mia. She sang at the Monte-Carlo Casino club. He met her at Eva's shop months earlier. They enjoyed each other's company. Vince gave her "fatherly advice," now and then, since he was twenty years her senior. They were simply good friends. Mia was in love with a boyfriend who had to stay in Norway during the holidays. They were both very lonely.

At the Casino where Mia was singing, this playboy was trying to seduce Mia. Vince knew he was married. He discussed his philandering reputation with Mia, privately. "He's simply taking advantage of your vulnerable situation," Vince told her.

Mia followed his advice and broke off the relationship before it became too serious. Vince took Mia to the New Year's party at the office. When they arrived at the office at 11 PM, Victor was already a few drinks ahead of everyone. He had cases of champagne, locked away in the small storage shed on the roof, which he opened and shared. After toasts to bring in the New Year, Victor began talking to Mia. He wanted to show off his knowledge of the Norwegian language, which he learned years ago. Eva did not understand any Norwegian and became very jealous and angry over their private little chat. (Mia had no interest in Victor).

Mia told Vince, "Victor Cruz is a big hairy ape with no moral fiber. How can you work with this *repulsive oddball?*"

Powerful charges were building up in the atmosphere. Eva started screaming at Victor. *"You bastard!* I'm pregnant with your kid and you're making a play for this woman." Her outrage became harsher in French. All of a sudden, without warning, a half-full bottle of champagne went flying across the room towards Victor's head. Eva's aim was not too good. It smashed into a big mirror, missing his big head by inches.

"Some New Year's celebration," Vince said. Monaco fireworks were bursting outside, at the stroke of midnight, while emotional fireworks began exploding inside the apartment. He took Mia by the arm. *"Let's get the hell out of here!"*

They escaped from the emotional tirade that had erupted and went to the Casino club where Mia would be performing that night. The club was packed. Everyone was dressed in classic gowns and tuxedos. Mia's style and voice was reminiscent of Judy Collins.

Fig 12. Monte Carlo Casino

During the break, Mia joined Vincent at the bar and introduced him to a few dancers from the show. Nancy was the only American in the dance group. Nancy and Vince hit it off, swapping stories about the States and Monaco, over pink champagne. Her long dancing legs and incredible curves went well with her long black silky hair. Nancy's skimpy gold-laced outfit barely covered her bosom, which drove him crazy.

"Could you drive us home after the show?" Mia asked.

"Certainly! It would be my pleasure." Mia whispered something to Nancy before he dropped her at the flat. It was only a short ride to Nancy's place, a nice penthouse on the top of a building, off boulevard de Moulin.

"How about a nightcap?" One should never mix scotch with champagne, he thought, after it was too late. She sensed that He was mentally and physically exhausted.

"Why don't you take a nice cool shower, honey?"

He took her up on the idea. She handed him a white robe. Less than five minutes into his shower, the door suddenly opened. "I forgot the towels." She smiled at his erection and embarrassment. "May I join you?"

"Sorry, Nancy. Normally I would love to, but I happen to be in love with someone *very special.*" (Vince was not going to let his penis control his brain anymore).

At sunrise, Vince arrived back at the office to see if any blood was spilled on their nice Persian carpet. They had a big fight.

Eva threw Victor out of the apartment. "I'm tired of him making charms to other women in front of my eyes, when I'm five months pregnant with his baby," she cried.

"Be calm Eva, he really wasn't making a pass with Mia. He's only showing-off his language skills, and his big fat ego."

"I've decided. I'm getting an abortion!"

"That's crazy. That is no way to act!

He was drunk. You know how he gets after a few drinks. Look, the baby is a way to give both of you a sense of responsibility. It can be the 'glue' to hold both of you together. You know how much he wants that baby."

Vincent Renaldo was against abortions. He believed there was no such thing as a "safe" abortion. Abortion-on-demand was morally repugnant to him. Abortion cheapens human life, tears apart families, and contributes to the violence that plagues society. Whether legal or not, abortion is lethal for the unborn child, destructive of the mother, and society. Many feel it is really a *private* decision for the woman. She has a "right" to control her body. Nevertheless, where there is a *victim*, there is a "voiceless person," and it becomes a moral issue.

Victor slept on the roof. He looked like an unshaven bum when he arrived hours later. He apologized. Eva somehow accepted Vincent's reasoning. Harmony again existed—for a while anyway. It was *ironic* finding himself acting as the "peace maker" between his soon-to-be ex-wife, and her new lover. Vince finally understood that Eva has serious psychological problems. She became emotional and fought with him before. Now she was fighting with Victor, the shop workers, the housekeeper, *everyone*.

***

Weeks later came the Chinese New Year— *"the year of the tiger."* Vincent was riding that tiger, but could not dismount—without being devoured. The Mafia henchmen wanted their promised cash, *with interest.* Victor did his magic and got someone from London to send him money, based on future "standby letters-of-credit." The two blockheads went away contented at least until the next payment was due, the following month.

Some projects from London were desperate for investor funding. The president of the firm sent his trusted representative,

Cathy Collins, to keep an eye on the progress. Vincent met the shy conservative, British woman, who appeared to be about fifty-years old, at the airport. She told him that her boss sent her to "oversee operations."

Cathy, ate, drank and practically slept at the office. She knew nothing of Victor's fancy financing, except that the crap was getting a little heavy for her to handle. She could not understand why it took so long to find collaterals, and obtain standby letters-of-credit from the banks. Vince agreed that something seemed fishy; he kept pushing Victor to keep his promises.

Eva found a male escort for Cathy. A much younger "Italian Stallion," to keep her busy at night, so she would be in no condition in the morning to oversee *anything.*

Some nights later, Vincent was in a deep sleep at the apartment, after working all night on the contracts at the office. Suddenly the lights went on in his bedroom. Victor stood in the doorway, swaying and smelling of whiskey. "Good evening sweetie. Were you sleeping?"

Vincent became *furious* over this crude invasion of his privacy and sleep. He jumped out of bed, put on his jogging, and went into the office, where Victor started pouring himself another drink. Carlos, a friend of Victor from London and Eva, were having some kind of discussion.

"How dare you wake me you ugly guerrilla. *You're an asshole.*" Vince shouted.

Victor was stunned by this insult, in front of Carlos, his old drinking buddy. His mouth dropped as he looked at Eva and then back at Vince. Eva looked at Victor to respond to this insult. His eyes bulged with anger as he started to speak, but not before Vincent turned and faced him directly.

There was a pause, and then Victor reached out to grab Vincent's hair. He quickly ducked under Victor's arm. Vince connected with a solid left to Victor's nose. He tumbled against the sharp edge of the table, cut his arm and fell to the floor. The booze slowed his reaction. Victor then managed to grab him from behind. Instantly his elbow crashed into a soft spot just above the center of Victor's stomach. The wind was knocked out of him. A final right blow to his left eye finished him off. Finally, he beat this huge jerk.

Seeing him on the floor bleeding gave Vince *great satisfaction*. All his pent-up frustrations were finally released.

Victor then got up and started to pack his bags. "I'm finished with you. I'll take my business elsewhere," he shouted.

"Go ahead—I had enough of your crap anyway. There's the door, no one's stopping you," Vince yelled as he went back to bed, after locking the bedroom door.

Victor could not leave. Where could he go, *without money, without his love,* Eva? Now it was her turn to play peacemaker.

The following night it was uncomfortably hot. Vincent slept on the terrace. He awoke from sleep by moaning and cries. Eva was standing next to him in obvious pain. "What's wrong now?"

"Maybe you should drive me to the hospital. I think it's the baby."

"Did your water break?"

"No. The pain comes and goes," she explained with flowing tears.

Vincent was already dressed in his jogging suit. He searched frantically for the car keys. Eva then changed her mind. She began sobbing uncontrollably. He could tell it was emotional stress, probably caused by Victor's drunkenness.

Minutes later Victor came staggering into the living room. "What's going on here?" he moaned. "Why is she crying? What did you do to her?"

Vince glanced at Eva, who stood *terrified* between him and Victor. Then he turned back to answer Victor. He was startled by Victor's threatening expression. Booze brought out his paranoid personality and vicious nature. He looked like he was about to get physical again.

"Eva was experiencing some pain from her pregnancy—which could be life threatening you know."

"Why didn't she wake me?" He began talking excitedly in French to Eva. He was denying he was intoxicated, and began defending his "good name" against accusations that had been made against him.

In his current state, anything was possible. Vincent decided to humor him, to play on his ego. "You were sound asleep, silly. I was reading and she saw my light. Eva did not want to bother you. She knew you needed sleep, to be alert for that important meeting tomorrow. Anyway, her pains went away. *Let's all get some damn sleep!"*

"Yeah, you're right. I need be fresh to think of something for those people who are coming in the morning. He took Eva's hand and went back to bed.

The following morning, the Mafia loan sharks arrived for another installment. Eva began to get very nervous, since they were not very friendly personalities. She put to good use her "special" Monaco contacts, and *secretly* contacted her police chief friend earlier, so that he would keep an eye on the two goons.

In general, the French are not known for keeping their appointments on time. These bad people were exceptions to that axiom—and they were *very pissed.* As they arrived at the office, Vince made some excuse to leave. This was not his affair. Besides, he would be pleased to have those characters bust Victor's ass or some other vital part. (He became concerned that Eva might get hurt in the process). He still had some innate feelings for the bitch, especially in her pregnant condition. She might get hurt, *or worse.* He called Victor from a hotel phone next door. "Should I call the police?"

His simple reply was, *"right on!"*

No sooner did Vince hang-up the phone, after speaking with the police captain, when the commandos arrived. The Monaco police had been tracking the bastards and arrived with guns drawn, in a well-coordinated professional raid. Vince helped them quietly enter the office with his key. In a manner of seconds, the goons had guns stuck in their faces, and cuffed.

Now Vincent's ass was in trouble, since the Mafia knew he called the cops. One of the cuffed characters said to him, "Put away your complaint, *before it's too late.* We have no quarrel with you."

The police began wondering what two men and a pregnant woman were doing *together,* in the same apartment. They thought they were really "odd partners."

At the police station, Eva started crying. She shook her head and covered her eyes. "What in hell are you crying about?"

She continued crying. As she spoke, her voice cracked with emotion. "I took one of your checks and gave it to the Mafia for security," she said, while wiping her face. She began sobbing loudly, and again buried her face in her hands.

"When did you do that? How much?" She raised her head and spoke haltingly, fighting back the tears. "It was last November, before we left for Hong Kong. It was 50,000 Euros. I was so afraid," she whimpered.

Why didn't I stay in peaceful San Francisco, Vincent thought, where the city only quakes now and then and everyone is gay? The bad guys were also caught with stolen bonds in their car. They probably thought that Victor could cash the bonds for them, given his gift for financing. Otherwise, it was stupid to keep booty in their trunk.

Ultimately, one of the two Mafia characters was charged with extortion, possession of guns, stolen bonds, drug trafficking and kidnapping. They took Sam from Samoset Enterprises, as a hostage to assure their final payment. (Vincent later learned that Sam's mother paid the goons *in full,* but they were greedy bastards. They figured they could make additional profits by squeezing Victor and Eva for a little more).

The shit was getting *deeper* now. Vince was sinking in it, along with his *"partners."* They were all pleased with the efficiency of the Monaco police, but they knew that the Mafia *never forgets.* Someday these thugs would get out of jail and probably snatch their collective asses. (One of the shady characters was freed, after only a few weeks. He was a *"model Monaco citizen,"* with a good prior record, according to the judge. Monaco *rarely* jails one of its own citizens).

Spring arrived and Victor was busy trying to close on something to get them out of this insane mess; at least enough dough to buy a ticket to some faraway place. Everything Victor did *turned to crap.* He was jinxed. He had his fingers in lots of business deals, like oil and various commodities trades. Nothing significant developed. It was always the same bullshit story: *"Wait until next week, you'll see!"*

Although Vincent's two-room apartment gave them limited space, Anne and he were like-minded and compatible. Anne kept busy with her import-export activities, while he went to the office, which was only a few blocks away. When he came home, he often found Anne busy cleaning, ironing his shirts and putting things in place. She would often fix a bubble bath, and they would soak in it together. Anne could not cook, he did not mind. Vince enjoyed making a special new dish; they could not afford to go out for dinner. They would throw a few cushions on the floor, light a candle, and eat on a small coffee table.

The single bed was small, so they put the mattresses on the floor, and actually slept conformably.

Vincent often became despondent. Anne tried to console him, but at times, even she could not help. "I'm a middle-aged man, who once had a good wife, two wonderful children, good friends, a million-dollar estate, and a budding business—that's now nearly bankrupt." He also worried over how to pay for the apartment and office expenses, which were mounting and due soon. Worst of all, there was no prospect, no hope of the situation improving. Life is just like the stock market, he thought; just when you hit bottom—*it gets worse.* Then, when the market begins to turn up, you lack the funds to ride the upside curve.

Never in Vincent Renaldo's entire life did he depend on anyone to make a living—*until now.* He had always been independent and self-sufficient. He was now depending on Anne, for everything. Although she did not care, it really bothered him. When you are young, there's always hope in the future. In spite of the many challenges of life, you can handle most of the difficult situations, somehow. At age fifty, it is a different story; it was a feeling of *total insecurity,* during the prime of his life.

*****

"Every limit is a beginning as well as an ending."

—George Eliot

President George W. Bush selected the "Best and the Brightest" for his cabinet. History has taught us, especially during President Kennedy's administration, in 1962 and beyond, that the 'Best and the Brightest,' often make *momentous blunders,* such as the "Bay of Pigs" fiasco that led to the Cuban Missile Crisis. Robert McNamara, the brilliant Secretary of Defense, who dragged us into the long and tragic Vietnam War.

President Bill Clinton cut the defense and intelligence budgets to the bone, to pay for "progressive" social programs, and left Bush with festering difficulties around the world. These hotspots included North Korea, which was selling missiles to terrorists; India and Pakistan nuclear threats against each other; the Northern Ireland predicament; the revolutionist wars in Africa; China's challenges against Taiwan; the Mexican border turmoil; and the never-ending Middle East chaos. Clinton also failed to give the order to kill Osama Bin Laden, when he was an easy target for the CIA.

Senator John McCain lost the election mostly due to the weak economy, which Democrats and liberal media analysts blamed on the GOP and Bush administration. The historical *facts* show that the economy and jobs grew *significantly,* in seven out of the eight years George W. Bush was in office. The economy also grew in spite of terrorist attacks on 9/11, and the great impact this disaster had on the economy. It is *a historical fact* that Bush failed to control government spending, during his second term in office. In addition, Senator McCain was pathetic and weak candidate for president.

What *actually* caused the economic collapse? There were multiple causes. It was due to appalling mismanagement of Fannie and Freddie, and lack of proper oversight of banks by Congress, especially Barney Frank and his flunkies. There was obvious greed by financial institutions, mortgage companies, and Wall Street firms.

The Democratic congress was "in charge," under the leadership of Senator Reid. Both Barney Frank and Senator Dodd finance committees *insisted* that Fannie and Freddie (who financially supported their reelection campaigns), take over "toxic loans" from the banks. The banks, in turn, offered home buying opportunities to minorities, even though they had *poor credit ratings*, and really could not afford them, especially after the "teaser" rates expired and ballooned, two years later on their mortgages.

President Obama's administration did not learn much from history, so they repeated dumb blunders that happened in the past. Obama begins by surrounding himself with *"progressive czars,"* including some socialist characters, such as Valeri Jarrett (an Iranian), and most of his team lacked actual management experience. Obama starts out with a serious recession; a crisis in Afghanistan and Pakistan; a mess in the Congo; weak Russian relations; more missile tests by North Korea; Hamas terrorist threats against Israel; Iran missile tests, and the spread of nuclear arms. What can he do? What does he do?

President Obama makes lots of promises and many speeches. He knows that the rhetorician's art is to persuade. (John Locke had a darker view; rhetoric, said Locke, **"is an instrument of error and deceit").** Obama is making public speech the "central act" of his presidency. He feeds the American public, almost daily on TV networks, on all kinds of crap. He is very good at his game! He *reinterprets* Cold War history, and claims that America was "too belligerent" in the past. He gives a major speech on Islam's *essential* place in American history (which is utterly false), and its important future relationship to the [Christian] world. Obama speaks at Normandy, where he *fails to emphasize* that America actually saved Europe, with her youth's blood and fortune. In fact, Obama *apologizes* to the world for America's past "conceit and arrogance."

Inspiration matters, but the office of President requires acts of leadership. What does Obama actually do? He cuts the defense forces to the bone (from about 566K troops in 2010, to 420K troops), and the military budget is cut (from $250 in 2008, to $185 billion by 2013). He spends, way beyond his budget for Obamacare. He doubles the U.S. debt to $20 trillion. He gives foreign terrorists a worldwide platform in NY federal court, to spread their propaganda. He fails to create jobs with the $790 billion stimulus bill. One might reasonably ask, *What good is stimulus without security?*

***

Washington. President Obama's special task group met to review the pending crisis in the Middle East. Hillary Clinton of State, Adm. Dennis Blair, Director of National Intelligence, Robert Gates of DOD, and the Operations Chiefs attended the conference. They now had intelligence from the bugs planted by Sue Taylor in Iran, and the Mossad transcripts from Colonel Omar in Paris. These revelations allowed them to piece together fragments of the puzzle, known by the code name, ***Sword of Allah.***

The missing pieces were the missile locations and the likely date of the pending attack. They believed from the interrogation of Omar, that the targets were Tel Aviv and key Saudi oil fields. The range of the Iranian new missiles was about 1,200 miles. (Newer Scuds have a range of about 2,000 miles). The secret recordings made of Colonel Omar, revealed that the launching could be from known underground facilities in Iran, and remote regions of Syria. Spy satellites focused on these regions. They could track the computer modules if their GPS transmitters continued to function.

Major Scott, an analyst with the National Security Council reviewed the history of the region for the task force. "Here's an overall chart of the PLO, Hamas, Hezbollah and its splinter groups, as well as its leaders and sponsors: The Arabs and Jews are not fighting over land—they are fighting over *Holy Land,"* the analyst said. "Jerusalem is only a patch of land less than a mile square, but they believe it's been *touched by God."*

The National Security Advisor reviewed recent events in Iran: "The nation possesses abundant petroleum resources, but the price of their 'black gold' has declined to about $65 per barrel, from a high of $120-135 in recent years. About two-thirds of the population is under thirty years old, and inflation has climbed to over 30%, because of American import/export restrictions. Iran is important because of its strategic location. It oversees navigation on the Persian Gulf, the Strait of Hormuz, and the Gulf of Oman in the south, where about 60% of the oil goes to the world. Iran also shares borders with Turkey and Iraq on the west, and Afghanistan and Pakistan."

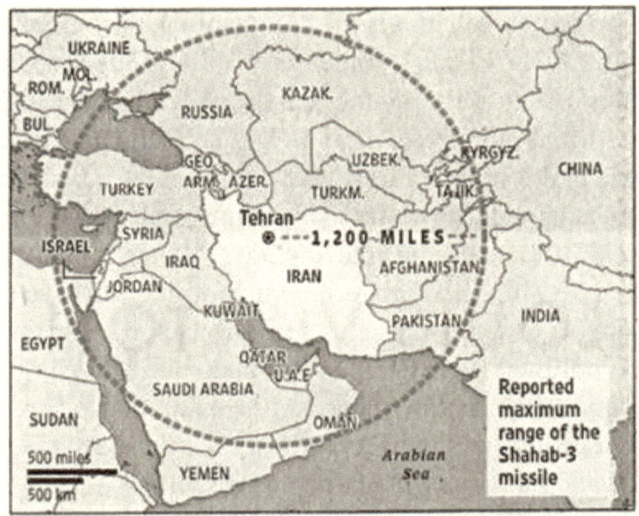

Fig 13. Map of Iran's missile range.

While the task group looked at a map of the region, the NSA analysis continued: "We must assume that missiles, which we have labeled *alpha and beta,* could also be launched from the Northeastern region of the Sudan in order to be within range of the Saudi oil fields. Missiles labeled *gamma* will probably be located near the Western section of Iran, if its target is Israel."

"How sure are we that the target is Israel?" President Obama asked.

"Colonel Omar himself said it was targeted at Israel. However, one or two megaton atomic tipped missiles could not destroy the entire state. Moreover, the Iranians must know that Israel would certainly retaliate against them with their far more numerous nukes," the NSA expert responded.

He continued with the history lesson for the group: "Iran is the sixth-largest producer of oil in the world, with an average output of 700 million barrels per year. Most of their oil fields are located in the Southwest, in Khuzestan province. Some are under the waters of the Persian Gulf. They do not have refineries and *must import* gasoline and diesel fuel. With limited gas supplies, they cannot run their military equipment more than a few months.

Venezuela agreed to sell them all the gasoline they need, however.

"About 93% of all Iranians are Shiite Muslims. Iran is the world's center of Shiite Islam, and it is the official state religion. Most of the ethnic tribal minorities include Kurds, Baluchi, Turks, and the Arab minorities are members of the Sunni sect of Islam. Leadership of the Shiites rests with a priestly class of mullahs, whose leaders have great political influence, and that includes 400 Ayatollahs, or 'Holy Ones.' "Iran's revolutionary government continues to have significant domestic support despite shortages of food, lack of foreign exchange and extreme political repression. It has become increasingly isolated in the international community, partly due to its links to Hezbollah and other terrorist groups and their activities. President Obama asked him to define *Islamic fundamentalism* objectives.

"About 85% of Moslems in the world are of the *orthodox* Sunni group, who strictly follow the written doctrines of Mohammed. The minorities, about 10-15%, are of the Shi'a sect, who support and affirm divine infallibility to whoever is their current tribal chieftain, or Imam. Of the Middle East *Shiite* population, Iran is the largest with about 90%. Most Shiites minorities in Saudi Arabia are underground because the *Sunni majority* persecutes them. Extreme Sunni fundamentalism also exists in Afghanistan, Pakistan and Saudi Arabia.

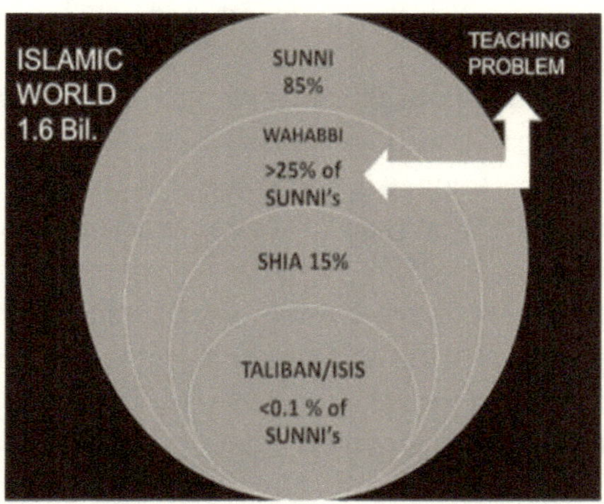

Fig 14. Different Islamic Groups

"The Party of God, 'Hezbollah,' is an army of fanatics in Iran and Lebanon. The basic goal of Hezbollah is the submission of the world to the 'will of Allah.' They believe that many Moslem governments are illegitimate because they are not based on *unconditional submission to Allah.* The divine duty of Hezbollah is to punish with death wrongdoers against Islam, especially heretics within Islam. This so-called *Holy Terror* does not permit forgiveness, compassion, leniency or any restraints. If the Hezbollah and their army of fanatics in Iran, gain control over most of the world's oil sources, it could send waves of panic throughout all developed nations."

After the high-level briefing, President Obama ordered that top priority be established for NSA, DIA, and the CIA, in cooperation with Mossad, to locate *all* of their Scud missile sites. The State Department will get additional computer modules for their Monaco agent, and will make sure delivery happens without any hitches. If she is unwilling to cooperate, ask our French DST friends to *"do whatever is required."*

President Obama ordered a specially trained, rapid response strike force into staging areas in the Red Sea and Persian Gulf. All United States war ships in the region are to be put alert, without causing undue alarm. The code name for the United States mission to neutralize this threat would be *"Golden Fleece."* The Special Forces team was to pinpoint the exact locations of the Scud sites in *a top-secret* clandestine mission.

***

INJUSTICE

"Injustice anywhere is a threat to justice everywhere."

—Martin Luther King, Jr.

Monaco. It was early summer in Monaco. It was a beautiful time of the year. Vincent would take his time and walk to the office through the magnificent park in the center of Monte-Carlo. Birds were singing. Children played with their dogs. Bright sunshine and bursts of flowers were in full bloom everywhere. Young lovers held hands, while some kissed in the long shadows created by tall, majestic trees. He had a certain conviction that his life might have a new beginning with the bright summer season.

Just when Vincent thought, his life was back on track—*the shit hit the fan!* Cathy, the shy representative from the London projects got angry and bold. She filed a complaint with the police. Her "Italian Stallion" encouraged her to take action. She was pissed by the delays; however, no one was involved in any fraud. What could she really do, anyway? Vincent tried to be the peacemaker. He arranged a meeting with Cathy. Unfortunately, hours before the meeting, Cathy made some insulting remark about Victor. Eva then slapped her across the face, and threw her out of the office.

Men can get physical with each other, share a beer, and be friends the next day. It is not the same for *some* women. They seem to hate much longer. Vincent realized that trouble was brewing. He suggested that they store non-essential critical files away from the office and prepare for the worst. Victor and Eva ignored his advice. "The bitch has *nothing* to charge us with," he stated arrogantly. He explained how carefully he covered our asses with contractual legal clauses, which effectively meant that they were not responsible for anything. "See for yourself. That dumb broad signed this document, *blindly*. It legally releases us from any and all responsibility."

Vincent arrived at the office, the next morning. He realized he had forgotten his keys and rang the doorbell. The door *suddenly* thrust open. A big gun was stuck in Vincent's face. The tall man dressed in jeans looked like *Clint Eastwood,* with his huge 357-Magnum pistol. Vince did not move a muscle. The same cops, who arrested the Mafia characters a few months ago, were now just as efficiently cuffing him. The police were like American cowboys, and they were the bandits. "Shut your mouth and sit here," the detective commanded in reply to his many questions.

Victor was cuffed in the next room, and an eight-month pregnant Eva looked as if she was about to give birth in the middle of the office. The police finally called a doctor. "I'm an American citizen and official resident of Monaco," Vince proclaimed. "You have *no right* to treat me like this."

"I told you to shut up, didn't I," the police officer replied. "You can tell the judge about your *American rights.*"

They were all treated as gangsters, accused of some crime against a nice old woman. Vincent had one of the starring roles in this very bad movie. Eva's frightened dog took cover under the bed. Then the doorbell rang. It was an Arab client from Morocco, who just happened to be visiting. The cops attacked and cuffed him. They were all shocked and extremely embarrassed as the police eventually pushed all of them into the waiting van, like common criminals. Crowds of neighbors gathered outside the apartment, wondering what sort of criminals they were.

It was a *very traumatic* experience. How is this be happening to me, Vincent thought, while looking out the van window on the way to the police station. He never had more than a speeding ticket, in his years of life on this earth. This must be a bad dream. They took all their private files, the secretary and even the housekeeper to jail for interrogation. Vincent warned Victor about hiding the sensitive files, but no—he was too smart, too confident in his own cleverness to take anyone's advice. Maybe the jerk will heed his counsel in the future— *if they have any future*.

***

Monaco. Anyone charged with a crime is *presumed guilty,* until proven innocent.

One can be held in jail three months without a court hearing, and wait longer if it takes time to complete the investigation. With frequent coffee breaks and two-hour lunches, the Monaco police are accustomed to, that timeline might become much longer.

The French and Monaco legal systems are still in the "dark ages." Judges have vast powers. A prisoner has no right to a phone call or a lawyer, until the "Instruction Judge" approves. Unlike the States, you are dependent on his personal judgment. They do not have anything like a grand jury—it is the personal decision of the "Instruction Judge" to review all the charges.

Vincent's interrogation was a jarring and exhausting experience. Two experienced officers took turns asking many rapid questions, while a third took everything down on the typewriter. "Monsieur Renaldo, you knew Victor Cruz was a crook. You can get five years in jail if you don't tell us the truth," the detective barked.

"I thought that a judge and jury make that determination," he answered. "What's Victor accused of anyway?"

"He's accused of fraud! He was selling financial services and *not performing,* among other illegal things, yet to be determined."

"Oh, is there a Monaco law against *'not performing?'"*

"What about this wire transfer of thousands of dollars?" the detective asked. "That's a place well-known for drug money."

"Look, I don't know shit about that transaction. All I know is that the funds were transferred from a major New York bank and they *must certify* that the funds are *'good, clean and clear.'"*

There was not even a hint of sympathy. The professional interrogators' search for the revealing flicker of the eyes, the subtle shift in vocal tone that would expose their quarry. "That's dirty money!" the officer insisted.

"Those finances were based on one of our projects. A contract exists. Ask Victor about that. He's the financial expert, not me."

"You used your office as a *cover* for these illegal activities, didn't you," the second cop insisted.

"Victor was a guest of my wife. He did his type of work, and I did my consulting. It's the same thing as if someone visited a Monaco hotel and did his business using the phone, fax machine and secretary from the hotel," Vincent argued forcefully. "Would you arrest all the hotel staff that helped the guest? What are you claiming that's *specifically illegal?"*

The officer started again: "How much money did you receive from him?"

"Clearly it was not enough to cover all my office expenses."

"Aren't these bogus companies?" the first officer demanded to know.

"They are legal corporations. See the stamp from the State of Delaware, signed by the Secretary of State."

There were many personal questions, which were arbitrary but they kept probing for something to pin on Victor. If he is guilty of something, like some sort of fraud, Vincent was by definition *his accomplice.* They were interrogated separately for hours, before compelled to sign a statement *in French.* "I do not intend to sign *anything* that I can't understand," Vincent argued.

A police officer translated the statement. Vincent signed the official statement, after writing: *"I don't understand French or anything on this paper,"* next to his signature.

Hours after their arrest Anne arrived back from visiting her family in Paris. No one answered the phones. She dropped by the office to see what was wrong, and was promptly arrested and sent to jail for interrogation.

"You must be watching American police stories on TV and got carried away. We're not gangsters," Vincent quipped. They did not appreciate this wise-ass remark. They tightened his cuffs to make their point.

Much later Vince learned he is accused of *"complicity in escroquerie."* Victor was clearly the *real crook* according to them. They acted as if they were the judge, jury and executioners. That did not make anything clearer. "Could you be a little more specific? What did we do? Whom did we do it to?"

"Victor was selling the wind," the officer replied.

Vincent joked: "Is there a Monaco law against hot air?"

They let frightened Anne go after many hours of stupid and personal questions. As Anne was leaving, she suddenly reached in and tenderly kissed Vincent's hand through the jail bars.

He gave her a phone number to memorize. He told her, "Call Paulo in London. With his connections, something might be done to get us out of this mess."

It was a wasted phone call. Paulo did not bother to lift a finger to help his friend.

They could not tell the police that they were involved with the French DST, the Mossad, and U.S. State Department. *That was secret and it had to stay that way.*

During the first 48 hours in the holding cell, they kept the lights on all night. Vincent could not sleep. He watched moths circling the light in his cell. He wondered how he became stuck in this quagmire, this *Quicksand.* It was pulling him down deeper and deeper into a seemingly bottomless abyss.

Two days later they were individually introduced to the *juge d' instruction.* He was the same adjudicator who handled the Mafia. He was a macho Italian character, unusually tall, with a very fancy elegant mustache. From his contemptuous manner, Vincent determined that the judge must be one of those *Fascist,* left over from the last war. He was pleased that he had listened to Anne a few months earlier, when she insisted that he modify his police report. "Vince, please put away your complaint against those two mafia mobsters; *it's really not your affair,"* she insisted.

Vincent later revised his report: "I merely called the cops at the request of Victor and had nothing to do with these gentlemen." He wanted to correct his original statement, which was the truth. Vince did not know if the cops hated revisions but they appeared to be very annoyed about his complaint withdrawal.

Eva's sad story, with tears running down her face, and her very pregnant condition, swayed the judge. He let her go. Victor and Vincent were promptly sent to the Prince's dungeon, to keep company with the Mafia tough guys. The judge fortunately ordered the guards to keep them separate from each other, and away from the Mafia goons. For that small act, they were thankful.

Before they were placed in separate cells, the guards strip-searched them, including looking up asses to see if anything was concealed there. They were placed in isolation in ten-by-fifteen-foot cells, in an *old dungeon* cut out of solid rock.

Vincent had *never* spent a day of his life in jail. The first few days were *traumatic.* He could not eat, sleep, or think clearly. He felt like a caged wild animal. Each night added to the pattern of his fantasy, his imagination until sleep finally closed down upon some vivid scenes. For a while these reveries, these daydreams provided an outlet for his imagination. They were a hint of the *"unreality of reality,"* a promise that the bedrock of the world was really founded on fantasy.

None of the guards spoke English. He had no lawyer, no visitors, no mail, and no right to make a phone call. How can beautiful, affluent, modern Monaco have such a *primitive system?* Was he dreaming? Is this really happening to me? At least Anne is outside and knows I am completely innocent. She believes in me. She loves me and would do all that is humanly possible to get me out of this hellhole.

***

Special Visitor. Anne sent Vincent a visitor. "Finally, a lawyer has arrived," he assumed. He was a Catholic priest. Nevertheless, the priest was of great comfort. He was also a direct communication link with the outside world. Anne also sent him a small Bible, with a private letter carefully hidden inside. The priest heard his confession and administered Holy Communion. His parting message was, "We cannot overcome evil by ourselves alone, *without* the grace from God. Remember, you cannot be angry with God, *without also believing in Him."* Since he was on a *forced holiday* with nothing to do, he began to read this little Bible. To his amazement, he enjoyed much of the Good Book. He prayed occasionally. Now Vince had something very significant to pray for—*justice and freedom.*

Vincent experienced a kind of rebirth, a *spiritual conversion.* He now understood that The Lord uses evil people to accomplish good ends. God freely willed to create a world "in a state of journeying" toward its ultimate perfection. Surrender is acceptance. One must accept what happens, *not* because they like it, but because of faith that *God is truly with you.* The love that is within makes this possible. *"Be it done unto me according to Thy will."* Life is a process of surrendering. The priest suggested that Vincent write his thoughts down. "It will be a good way to find peace," he said.

Vincent's life had been confused and disordered, but if he could return to a certain starting point, and go over it all slowly, he might find out what life is all about. One of the hardest lessons he learned is that, "one does *not* have the power to make anyone happy, or to save them spiritually." While there may be someone who can offer words of comfort and friendship, that person cannot rescue you. No matter how much we love or care for another, we cannot do it for them.

We have to find the strength and courage to navigate our own way through rough seas, and trust that God will guide us on our journey. The amazing thing about his journey is the events for which he is grateful now, were most painful then. It is progress, not perfection.

Both constructive and destructive forces exist in nature. With good, there also exists evil, as long as creation has not reached its ultimate perfection. Angels and men as intelligent free spirits and creatures have to journey toward their ultimate destiny, by their God-given *free choice* and preferential love. They can go astray. Thus, moral evil entered the world. The Lord is not the cause of moral evil. He allows it because He respects the freedom given to His creatures, and mysteriously knows how to derive what is good from it. Everyone is on a *journey towards wholeness!*

We experience bliss when we are in love because we feel complete. Men crave freedom and independence; women crave intimacy and cooperation. The challenge for men is to develop their *feminine side.* In order to become whole, a man must learn to listen with his heart, share his feelings, and express his emotions. The challenge for women is to develop their *masculine side,* to develop assertiveness as women, and assertiveness comes from self-esteem.

Many problems center on the emotions of the woman versus man's need for greater freedom. Until a man understands the importance of his own emotions, he cannot appreciate it in the lives of others. A woman will never appreciate a man's need for freedom or a personal life, until she develops one herself. We are much more than the sum of the parts of our bodies. The love that is inside each of us, is a vital part of us, though one cannot see it, cannot feel it, nor sense it, unless we are willing to share it with someone else. Yet it is *more real* than anything you can see, hear or touch in God's fantastic universe.

He remembered what Anne told him: We exist in dependence of each other, to complete each other, in the service of each other. A complex web of *interdependency* exists in nature—one with the other and all collectively. Within every human being, there is a kind of balance between beauty and ugliness, good and evil. People, many with innocent faces, in the name of God or Allah, do so much evil, and good in the world.

All life is like a *magnificent play* and we are the actors. Each of us has an important role to play. We cannot play that role alone.

We are dependent on the interaction of others, *especially* on the grace of God. Each moment of each day is important—not next week, or next month. What is a day? It's a collection of moments! We should live each moment, *as if it is our last.* We wait for all the tomorrows. It will be better later, we think. We anticipate the future with hope, while squandering today. Anxiety takes control of our lives. We are wishing for, expecting some grand new thing or event, while ignoring the present opportunity to do what is good, *at this very moment.*

Vincent became more tranquil and creative in jail. He wrote letters and poems, made drawings, and read at least a dozen books, besides the "Good News." He finally understood the reason for his years of discontent. We shall always be discontent as *Homo sapiens.* Our aspirations pushes us from behind, and pulls us in front—to do more, to be more, to know more, because the seed of our Divine Creator, the remembrance of earlier times, was received from our predecessor, and the Adam and Eve within us, cannot be rejected.

The Lord's angel repeatedly sent Vincent messages, with signs or clues to guide him in life —If only he would open his eyes, ears and mind to see, to hear, to comprehend, and follow those signals. Most of us do not appreciate such faint images and ignore their message *until it is too late.* The future, year by year receded before him. It eluded him then, but no matter—tomorrow, soon he will find truth and love, and will arrive there.

In the morning, a young lawyer arrived at the jail. He looked as though he had just graduated from law school. He had a big asinine grin on his face. Since the Mafia selected the best lawyers in Monaco, Vincent only had this inexperienced novice. He happened to be the only lawyer available in Monaco who spoke English. The first word out of his mouth, after the phony greeting, was about "his required minimum fees."

"Don't worry about that. Why don't you perform some services first? How long have you been practicing law in Monaco?"

"Two years," he replied.

"Okay. Get me the hell out of here. I do not have access to my checkbook. The police took everything. I'm sure Anne will guarantee your fee."

The following morning, they sent Vincent to see the "Lord of the Dungeon," the Judge, who did not understand a damn word of English.

The scoundrel of a lawyer did not show up for this important session. His cryptic note indicated that he would not lift a damn finger, without his initial fee.

A pretty police officer finally arrived to handle the translation. After a while, it was clear that she liked him, but more importantly, she believed his pathetic story. The judge knew less about financial transactions than Vince did. He was confused by Victor's fancy contracts and business deals—as were many of his sucker clients. Vince attempted to demonstrate his knowledge of Finance-101. The judge was not impressed. Protests about specifics of the charges, due process of law, and his rights, got nowhere.

"You are not in liberal America," was his response, in French. "You think there's a big difference between our systems of justice, compared to America?"

"Absolutely!" he replied. *"You bet there's a big difference!"*

"Explain the difference!" he demanded in a boisterous manner, using the *stunned* translator to respond.

Vincent was to write to the judge and explain the differences. His letter was as follows: On Independence Day, we celebrate the birth of the United States of America and the Constitution. One of the important parts of that excellent document is the "Bill Of Rights." These human rights are 'natural', and are 'international rights.' As a citizen of the USA and resident of your country, I demand my human rights. I am a victim of injustice and abuse of my fundamental human rights.

Here is a summary of the injustices and abuses, you requested. I realize that I am subject to the laws of Monaco. Nevertheless, "human rights" are international. In the United States of America, "due process of law" is enforced. Police cannot arrest anyone, or search and confiscate private property, without probable cause of a crime and approval by a Judge. The accused has a right to know the specifications of the charges, immediately. Every citizen has the right to have his or her lawyer present during interrogation and may refuse to sign any statement, which may cause self-incrimination. Citizens may not be jailed for more than a few days, without a hearing before a Judge and usually have a right to post bail. My defense lawyer should have a right to receive all copies of documents and evidence against me and obtain any relevant information for my defense. False arrest and imprisonment is a very serious act. The victim may claim damages from the accusers, or the state. Prisoners have a right to practice their religion, receive mail and visitors.

These are some of the differences between our justice systems versus Monaco. Since the French and Monaco Constitution are partly based on the American Constitution, I cannot understand how fundamental human rights can be *totally violated*. After all, Monaco is not a third world country. I hope that the above summary of the differences between our systems of Justice answers your request. Respectfully Yours, Vincent Renaldo.

***

The hours seemed like days, the days like weeks, in solitary confinement. It was a terrible waste of precious human time. Children were playing outside his small window in the lush green park below; their happy voices were without a care in the world. Pleasure yachts passed back and forth, while he remained trapped. *What a tormenting agonizing contrast!* The worst thing was not knowing what's really happening outside and not speaking their language. Vincent had no indication of how long he might remain there; it could be weeks, months or years. Anne's letters were his only comfort—*his only joy.*

Another week passed before the judge sent for Vince again. This time he was more specific regarding the *charges.* The *good news* was that the prosecutor had checked with Cathy and her boss in London. They acknowledged that he had *nothing* directly to do with the alleged fraud. In fact, they agreed that Vincent had tried to help them, many times. The *bad news* was that the prosecutor has established *additional* charges. "You acted as a 'cover' for these illegal activities of Victor Cruz and Eva," the Judge said, through the enchanting police officer interpreter.

"How is that possible? I did not invite Victor to Monaco. Eva invited him."

"Why didn't you throw them out of your apartment?" the judge asked.

"Because it was not my apartment. She lived there many years before we were married. In your pile of documents there must be a copy of her lease agreement."

The judge found it and examined the document. "You knew that your spouse never filed *obligatory* papers with the police, to become a legal resident," didn't you?

"Sure, I knew that! The police also knew she was living in Monaco for about ten years, *without* the required residence card. Why didn't they take some legal action?"

The Judge was simply reading what the prosecutor asserted. He had no definitive rebuttal against his *statements of fact.* He knew that Eva could never rent an apartment in the Principality *without* the approval of someone in a top position within the administration. She clearly had a "guardian angel." The old Minister of Finance was her longtime friend. She had the Police Chief in her pocket as well. They all used her "services."

The Judge wondered aloud: "How could you put up with Eva's lover sharing the same apartment with you? Why did you allow this kind of eccentricity to continue?"

"I was caught in a sort of *Quicksand.* There was no escape. The more I struggled to get free, the deeper it ensnared me. By the time I woke up to the reality of the situation, I was broke and trapped. These business deals were my only ticket out of here."

He sent him back to jail. The case would be considered at a later date.

The guards finally let him mix with the other prisoners, *except Victor.* Vincent met a young man in prison named Jacques, who spoke English fairly well. He said he was a Foreign Legionnaire. "Why are you here?"

"The Monaco police think I robbed some jewels from a local shop. Someone about my size with a similar motorcycle helmet held-up a store," he explained.

"What proof did they have? How could the shop owner identify you if you had that helmet on, which completely covers your face?"

"During the line-up I was the only one without shoe laces, so she picked me out. She claimed that the diamonds I had were hers. Naturally, the bitch wanted to take my stuff."

"Where did you get those diamonds?"

"In Africa. I bought them while I was a Foreign Legionnaire."
"Tell me, how were you arrested?

"I was shopping for my wife, in France near the border. The Monaco police grabbed me and took me over the border," he alleged.

"Isn't that illegal? That's not their territory."

"Sure, but they did it anyway."

This young man of about twenty-five years was recently married. His wife was nine months pregnant. They had limited money and could not hire a lawyer. Unlike the United States, in Monaco (and in France, at this time) court-appointed legal counsel was not provided. If you cannot afford a lawyer, you rot in jail until your case comes up. Then you have to defend yourself, *without* proper legal advice.

Vincent thought about some way to escape. This was a *maximum-security* prison. There were two sets of iron bars in his small window, and some kind of electric fence beyond the window. The doors are made of heavy steel, with only a small slot to pass food. Cameras are everywhere, observing the prisoners every move. Guards often search cells, without any forewarning. It seemed impossible to escape.

One day, while taking his daily one-hour walk in the courtyard, he noticed that the cell windows on the second level were less secure. There was only one set of bars and no electric screens. The bars were rusted from seawater spray. Outside the windows, a roof walkway appeared to lead to the garden below and some convenient pipes that could be a ladder. How can he be transferred to the upper cells?

The guards admired Vincent's artwork. His drawings included pictures of famous performers and important people. He offered one to the chief guard, Tony, a big portly Italian, who only knew a few words of English. "Here's a gift for your wife, Tony. It's a picture of *Greta Garbo.*"

"Multa bella! Bellisima!" Thank you very much.

"Tony, I want to make a drawing of the sea for your family, Bene?"

"Si, si. Okay?"

"But I can't see most of the park or sea from my window."

"What you want from me? Vince"

"Porfavore, can you move me to the upper cell, with a better view?"

"Si, if you give me your nice watch, maybe it's possible."

Vincent gladly gave the guard his imitation gold watch.

Then he remembered that his solid gold *Rolex* that Eva got him to buy, from a casino gambler, was still in a safe deposit box. He could use that Rolex to get some cash to help pay for the lawyer, and support himself, if he ever got out.

A few hours later, Tony came with the guards to move him to one of the upper cells with the better view on the second level. It was a crazy idea, but he had to try something. He had no idea how long it would be before he saw his lawyer again; never mind getting out of this *deep abyss.* Sure enough, not only were the cell bars badly rusted, the cement was also deteriorating.

Vincent worked a few hours each night digging away at the bar foundation, using a butter knife, being careful to paste the loose cement fragments back in place before morning. With his growing gray beard and confinement in this *ancient dungeon,* he felt like the *"Count of Monte Christo,"* the main character in a novel by Dumas; except in his case, there was no hidden treasure on the outside, except his Rolex.

Isolation from the other prisoners and lack of communication, at times became too *much.* Nevertheless, it was probably better to have a private cell than to be stuck with a criminal who might have AIDS or something worse. He needed privacy and valued his peace, especially when reading the Bible.

The prisoner next door turned out to be *crazy.* In the middle of the night, he screamed and banged on the door demanding attention from the guards. One evening they gave him the attention he demanded; they opened the door to his cell and gave him a bath, with a high-pressure fire hose. He was very quiet thereafter.

The Judge gave explicit instructions that Victor and Vincent are *forbidden to communicate.* I did not accept such restrictions on my freedom of speech. I sent a written message to Victor hidden in a re-sealed pack of cigarettes. An hour later, the door to my cell suddenly swung open. Tony, the big fat guard had an expression on his face that was easy to translate, in any language. It indicated that the guards were smarter than I thought.

"What's ... this crazy message about?" he demanded to know.

"Nothing important," I said as Tony banged a large threatening stick on the small table.

"What ... does this mean?"

I used American slang words and abbreviations in case they found the paper. They were very confused. It did not translate into anything that made sense to them.

My fresh air privileges were eliminated for three days. Thereafter, I was strip-searched before taking my daily one-hour walk in the yard. The guards were afraid that I might leave a message in the yard for Victor Cruz. I refused to be stripped in front of cameras and demanded to see the warden. He arrived minutes later. The warden seemed to appreciate my concern regarding privacy. I threatened to go on a hunger strike if they strip-searched me again. They never did.

I was reading my Bible, while walking from one end of the courtyard to another, when I heard a voice from above saying: "How are you, my brother?" I thought it must be a voice from a guardian angel. It was actually from the *devil.* The showers were on the second level cell area, above the courtyard. Victor was taking his bath there.

"Do not look up! The cameras will see you," Victor shouted.

"I'm hanging in there. How about you?"

"Fine, fine. My lawyer says they don't have a case against you."

"Then why am I still here?"

"They want to use you against me."

"I never said anything against you. Did Eva have your baby?"

"It's due any day now."

"Why didn't Eva call her friend, that Finance Minister, to help us?"

"*He's dead!* He died from excessive drinking, days after we were arrested," Victor explained.

Suddenly the guards came to fetch me. Our conversation ended. (We were never intimate friends; we were "comrades" who happened to experience similar trials together—the craziness of Eva and the Monaco dungeon).

Finally, a batch of letters came from Eva and Anne. The judge's staff translated and reviewed them in advance. The contrast in content and tone was interesting: Eva complained about bills and how difficult it is to survive without cash. "You and Victor have a free room, good food and nothing to worry about," she wrote.

Right, my ten by fifteen-foot cell, with its pint-sized window was a hotel suite. The cuisine was five stars, and we did not have a care in the world. How can this woman send such a bitchy letter?

She only cares about herself. She also sent a legal form for me to sign so that she could take out her jewels and my Rolex from the safe deposit box, and "sell them to pay for lawyers," so she claimed.

In contrast, the letters from Anne were supportive: "Darling, I pray for you in the church everyday ... You can be sure that I'm doing everything possible with the lawyer to get you free.... *I shall never be happy,* until you are in my arms once again."

***

THE SWORD OF ALLAH

"A small body of determined spirits fired by an unquenchable faith in their mission can alter the course of history."

—Mahatma Gandhi

What we "think" is true about adversaries does not make it true. Everybody lies—the question is what do our enemies think? A simmering dispute between the U.S. and Israel over Iran's nuclear program burst into the open as U.S. Defense Secretary Robert Gates, on a visit to Israel, called for continued "diplomatic engagement with Tehran," while Israeli officials repeatedly warned of a possible military strike against Iran's nuclear facilities. Mr. Gates indicated the Obama administration might support stronger measures against Iran, if progress is not made. If the engagement process is not sufficient the U. S. is prepared to press for significant additional sanctions," he said.

Tehran, Iran: A meeting took place, which included a very select group of planners for the *Sword of Allah,* which excluded certain earlier partners. They now had only five Scud missile guidance computers. The engineers who tried to probe their complex inner circuits accidentally destroyed the other modules. One computer was for a test launch, and the other was available for backup. Three remaining computer modules were installed in missile guidance systems.

"The strategy for the *Sword of Allah* must be changed," General Ahmad insisted. "We must assume that the bugs planted by Sue Taylor in Iran, gave away our prime target, Israel.

We must modify our plans: two missiles should now be launched from the Syrian mine complex, aimed at key Saudi oil fields and refineries The other should be launched from Western Iran and its target *must* be changed to Kuwait, instead of Israel.

"We need to realize that one or two megaton atomic bombs will never be sufficient to destroy any major part of Israel," the General argued. "Besides, Israel moved much of its government to Jerusalem. We cannot possibly destroy that city. It is our holy city as well. We that Israel knows that we targeted them. Obviously, *must assume* they have many more nuclear weapons to retaliate against us."

The Iranian President then stated, "The easier destruction of Kuwait would not only drive oil prices *much higher,* but it would also give us an opportunity to kill thousands of United States troops that will be concentrated there."

The newly proposed strategy called for Iran to move its divisions near the Kuwait border, which would certainly cause the United States to send a large military counterforce to the region. Then the *trap* would be set for the complete destruction of the area, *immediately after* they move Iranian troops north, out of the range of the initial blast. "When thousands of body bags are sent back to the States, the American public will have no stomach for any warfare in the region," the General argued.

"President Obama will be greatly humiliated. Iran and Syria would then become the *most powerful* Islamic economic and military countries in the region, united against Israel. Turkey, Egypt and our other Muslim brothers will then certainly join us in our common cause, *in the name of Allah."*

The inner circle reasoned that Iran would not be blamed for invading southern Iraq, since their *principal purpose* would be to protect thousands of Shiites and Kurds living near the northwestern Iranian border. Besides, the Iraqis are Shiite brothers.

Planners for the *Sword of Allah* reviewed the details of the recent Gulf War, to be sure that every possible contingency was considered, and that their plans were both logical and achievable. The Iran Foreign Minister began: "This time China and Russia will be on our side, and they will prevent the UN from passing any resolutions against us, with their veto power."

"NATO and the United States are now extremely limited in military reserves. They can't possibly afford another trillion-dollar war like Iraq and Afghanistan," General Ahmad added. "Obama plans deal with us: He said he would 'engage' our leaders by offering talks *without preconditions.* He says that Bush's policy was unsuccessful because of his 'axis of evil' charges against us."

The General continued: "We kept the U.S. and Europeans talking while building our nuclear plants and Scud systems. Ultimately, Obama and the EU reduced trade restrictions, and gave us a plane loaded with billions in cash. *They were real fools!"*

Ayatollah Ali Khamenei reminded them: "During Mr. Obama's recent Cairo speech, he *actually apologized* for the CIA overthrow of Iran's Prime Minister, Mohammed Mosaddeq. He publically admitted: "the U.S. played a role in the overthrow of a democratically elected Iranian government."

Ayatollah Ali Khamenei added: "This time they will not have time or the military resources. President Obama foolishly cut the military forces and intelligence budget to the bone, in order to provide money for his domestic programs. Therefore, they cannot reinforce their capability in the region. They will not know who the aggressors are," Ali Khamenei stressed. "It will be all over in a matter of a few hours."

"Could they intercept our Scuds before they actually arrive on target?" the Iranian President asked.

General Ahmad quickly responded: "*absolutely not!* They will have very little warning since our Scuds will be much closer to their targets. *The Patriot is highly overrated!* It really was not effective against Iraq's mobile Scuds. Our new rockets are more advanced, especially if we install the computer modules, which will significantly increase their accuracy. Besides, our Shia Houthi brothers have agreed to send a few missiles to our Saudi enemies from Yemen, to distract them from the main attack."

"We must remember that in the past, President Bush's decision to conclude the Iraq ground war at the very moment of pending Iraqi defeat *was absurd.* He had Saddam and his Republican Guards 'by their balls,' yet he allowed Baghdad to save a large amounts of military equipment, including 800 tanks and 1400 armored vehicles and his elite Guards, who were totally surrounded near Basra. Bush and his advisers were *fools.* They worried about the worldwide media tarnishing their 'good image' instead of destroying the enemy. Americans foolishly allow the media to control their strategy."

General Ahmad responded: "The end result was *far worst* for the population. Iraq's Shiite population in the southern town of al-Subayr rebelled against the Iraqi Sunni forces there. The skirmish quickly spread throughout the South of Iraq. This was followed by a rebellion of the Kurds in the North. Saddam Republican Guards then turned northward to wipe out the Kurds, and savagely suppressed our Shiite brothers with poison gas bombs.

"Our Muslim brothers were poorly organized; they didn't have any significant fire power. We will make sure this does not happen this time," the Iranian president stated. "We will give them a taste of poison gas, from our Syria brothers.

"In conclusion my brothers, here are the keys to our future success," General Ahmad said, "The Saudis and the United States will believe that the Scud attacks came from Yemen. Iran and Syria involvement cannot be proven. The Saudis should lose at least 60% of their total oil production, for a very long time, from the radioactive fall-out and deadly contamination. Iran will more than double its oil production capacity, when we move into Southern Iraq to protect our Shiite brothers. Iran and Russia will then control the world price for oil. Out of this chaos, Iran and Syria will emerge as the Islamic leaders of the world. Islamic nations will then join *our just cause for Allah.*"

Supreme Ayatollah Ali Khamenei and the group then agreed that Colonel Omar should immediately try to get another three or four computer modules. Iranian leaders *insisted* that each rocket should have two computers in case one failed during launching. It took them many years to get enough fissionable material to make three nuclear weapons; they did not want *anything* to disrupt their final plans.

***

Monaco. Hanson of the CIA contacted General Henri Bertrand, head of the French equivalent of the CIA, known as *La Piscine,* and requested their assistance. Even during the most difficult times of Israel's relations with the U.S., the bonds between the CIA and the Mossad intelligence had deep-rooted respect for each other. Whatever Israel learned they passed on to Washington; the reverse was not always the case.

Anne did not want to do any business with the Iranians, since Vincent insisted that she avoid *all contact,* especially because he was in jail and could not help her. The French DST *demanded* that she help them. (The DST knew Vincent Renaldo was innocent, but they kept him in jail longer, so that they could force her to do whatever was required, based on instructions from the U.S.). Director of National Intelligence, Dennis Blair said, *"Do whatever is required to get her to cooperate!"*

"If I help you and the American State Department will you promise to get Vincent released from the Monaco jail?" Anne asked.

"Absolutely! He will be free when you accomplish this *little mission for us,"* the representative of France's intelligence service promised her.

"I want a full pardon for him. He did not do anything wrong," she insisted. *"I also want your promise in writing!"*

"Well, we cannot put something sensitive like that in a memo. You can be sure that we always keep all our bargains. I'll send a private message to my colleague, Marcel Piqueton, commander of the Gendarmerie National, right now."

The Mossad and French secret service met privately with Anne, after she received another fax message from Colonel Omar. They tapped her phone lines and knew everything. They read the message from the colonel together:

"Dearest Anne, I urgently request that you immediately order six additional computer modules, and personally deliver them to Iran. We have much business here for you, my dear. We also need at least 100,000 jeans and other fashions. Why don't you come, so that we can complete this significant business together?"

Anne weighted the considerable risks involved. She could not bear to think of Vincent locked in that dungeon, *without hope.* She knew that everything depended on her.

"Don't worry, dear," the Mossad representative, told her. "We will send our best agents to protect you from harm. Your country needs your support in this *vital mission."*

***

Tehran, Iran. Colonel Omar greeted Anne graciously at the airport in Tehran. If she's working for the Mossad or CIA, he would certainly find the truth during her stay. After all, why would Anne risk such a trip after her girlfriend Sylvia was found dead, a few weeks after he left Paris? She is either "clean," or she's a *very foolish agent.*

"The General sends his greetings," Omar said, with a big smile. "He arranged for you to stay at that same beautiful hotel."

"Wonderful! How is the General and his charming son?" Anne asked.

"Both are very well. He has finally retired from the army."

Anne handed the package containing additional computer modules to Colonel Omar. "I'm sorry but I could only obtain three modules, on such short notice," she explained.

"That's fine. We can get more at later date; there is no rush. I really wanted to see you again. You know I missed you so very much. You are such a lovely person. Frankly, I must confess that I used this business as an excuse to get you to come again. How about dinner together tonight at 8 PM?"

"Sure. That will give me a few hours to get some rest," Anne replied, as she kissed him on the cheek.

Not only was Anne's hotel suite bugged, TV cameras were installed in almost every room, behind the mirrors. Anne began to strip to take her bath. Omar sent his aides away. This was *too private* for them to see – *it is for his eyes only.*

As her clothes fell to the floor, the soft pink skin of her nakedness came into full view. She's so different from the Arab women Omar frequently slept with. Anne took a razor and began to shave under her arms. She lay there enjoying the bath, relaxing and caressing her skin with bath oil, rubbing it through the passageways of her body and massaging her breasts. She lifted one leg from the bath water and rubbed the foam along her thighs and inner legs. She gave herself a final glance in the mirror. She had a taut flat stomach, firm buttocks, and the upward thrust of her breasts was awesome.

Omar could not control his excitement as the camera zoomed in on her delicate moves. As she bent over to check her handiwork in the mirror, he could not restraint himself. He suddenly felt wetness in his pants. He let the VCR record the rest of her performance, while he changed his uniform.

It was like a small oasis she thought, as Anne arrived in the garden of Omar's villa, with its palm trees and exotic flowers. She wore a long white linen dress, which complimented her long golden blond hair and deep blue eyes. The large pearl necklace accented the deep valley between her breasts. The gold chain belt gave form to her small waist and striking feminine curves.

They sat on cushions under a tent in the garden, and ate from a collection of bowls on a round table, Persian style. The spiced food was strange to her taste but delicious. Two servants dressed in Persian fashion served them tea and fresh fruits.

"How is your father?" Omar asked.

"His condition changes from time to time. He's much better lately, thank God."

"Tell me, how did you get into your import/export business?"

"Well, I really wanted to be a fashion designer, but guess I had limited talent. The competition in Paris was too great for me to earn a living in this type of work. Then, I learned that I could make more money by selling fashions, instead of creating them. My first big order came from Bloomingdales, in New York, about ten years ago."

"What's ... Bloomingdale?" he asked. "It sounds *Jewish?*"

"It's a large chain of high fashion department stores. They are very popular in America," Anne explained.

It was a pleasant dinner. Omar was totally relaxed and captivated, not only by Anne's alluring look and manner, but by her intelligence as well. Her answers to all his questions appeared to be logical, natural, and believable. She also acted like *most women;* she asked questions about his personal life, without any discussion of military activities, *whatsoever.* She did not know how to act as a spy, or how to probe for secrets, and did not care anyway. Her innocence was her best shield. Her natural beauty had already intoxicated him.

Anne remembered how Sylvia was found in her apartment, in Paris, in the bloody bathtub, with her wrists slashed after the Colonel met her, but she was not afraid. This character is like *putty in my hands,* she thought. Her goal was to deliver the goods and get the hell out—*that is all!*

Omar drove her back to the hotel at one in the morning. "I'm very exhausted and need to get some sleep tonight. Please excuse me darling, you understand, don't you," she said as they kissed. Omar did really mind.

He remembered the exclusive taped showing of her intimate moments, and he was eager to see what new spectacles might delight his senses.

The Parisian beauty sat back on the bed and put on her white laced bikini undergarment, the one that Vincent found so fascinating, so alluring. She could not know how Omar felt, watching her from the hidden camera. She could not hear *distressing groans* from him in the room above hers. She remembered her last passionate night of love making with Vince, and emitted a low cry, as vivid mental images of their amorous lovemaking consumed her. Her thoughts shifted to getting back to Monaco, to be in Vincent's arms once again.

The next morning, Omar came to the hotel, at 10 AM. "My dear you are so lovely this morning. Did you have a nice sleep?"

"Yes, and I dreamed of living here dearest, in this fantastic oasis," she said, kissing him tenderly on his cheek. Her intoxicating perfume made him think about the images seen last night. He had to have her! No other conquest mattered. Nothing else was more important. *She had conquered him completely!*

"As I promised, here is your letter-of-credit for 100,000 jeans, and that's just a beginning of the fantastic business we can do together," he told her with a sly smile that betrayed his eagerness.

"Thank you, my darling. You kept your promise! This is a great beginning for our new relationship. Now, I must get back to Paris. I have to persuade my suppliers to respond to your additional computer module requirements," she said. "I hope you will come and visit me. You can be my special guest in my new apartment. Then we can get to know each other *much more intimately.* Okay?"

"Why must you leave so soon? You have only been here a few days, and I have made plans for us," he said, with discernible distress on his face.

"Well ... my sources have informed me that they have more modules for your business. I know how important this is for your future success. Besides, I must find the jeans that you requested, as soon as possible. Don't you agree that our business should be finished first, before our pleasure?"

"You're right. We must finish our important business. However, you *must* at least spend the day with me. Okay?"

"Sure, where will you take me, my darling?"

"To the beautiful blue Caspian Sea, which is like the color of your eyes?"

They took Omar's official vehicle, with two of his personal guards sitting in front. It was a long trip, directly north from Tehran to the Caspian Sea.

The agent in Monaco coached Anne perfectly. "Act natural. Ask lots of typical woman's questions about his personal life," she advised her. "Keep him off-guard." She followed that advice, *flawlessly*.

It was extremely hot over the desert roads before they reached Chalus, the southernmost part of the Caspian Sea. "Why don't we take a swim to cool off," he suggested.

"I didn't bring any swim suit," Anne explained.

"We can find a private area behind those rocks and swim in our underwear. I assure you that my private guards can be trusted; they will see that no one bothers us."

A *strange tingle* ran through Anne's body. Here I am, completely alone, with a powerful, dangerous, and seductive man, who could easily attack me at any moment, and I am helpless to defend myself. (Images of him mercilessly attacking her rushed through her imagination, causing *immense fear*).

She stripped down to her white laced bikini underwear, behind some boulders, as Omar organized the blanket and basket of food on the beach. She finally appeared with a blushing smile. Omar took her in his arms and kissed her. He took her by the hand, and they ran into the inviting cool sea. As they came out of the water, their scanty wet underwear could not conceal the nakedness of their bodies. They moved to the warm blanket. The cold seawater stiffened her ruby nipples, causing them to protrude through her wet white bra. They kissed. His hands began to explore her, *everywhere.*

Suddenly she became tense and frightened. She remembered what happened to Sylvia in Paris ... and most alarming, that he has SIDA (AIDS). *"Omar please. Stop!* I must tell you that it is that time of the month. You know what I mean ... don't you?"

"Of course, my dear, I understand. It's against our religion to take any woman during her menstrual period." *He was really pissed!*

While she was getting dressed, Omar reached for the very large bulky towel. He approached her with the opened towel to dry her. Instantaneously, abruptly, there was a deafening blast. His body became a *mass of blood* as he fell to the ground.

Omar's two bodyguards came running. They could not see nor hear Anne through the sounds of the breaking surf. She was running frantically and screaming hysterically. Two soundless shots followed. One of the bodyguards arched backward, as the first bullet penetrated the base of his spine. Other shots then came separately, with finality. They entered the other guard's skull, propelling him forward over the rocks. A final spasm and all life movements stopped.

Anne thought for a moment that she would vomit. She had passed over the edge of hysteria. She had to pull herself back and get hold of herself.

Minutes later, two men dressed as Persians arrived in a fast jeep. "We have been following you since you left Monaco and Tehran," Josh, the Mossad leader said. "We are the agents sent to protect you."

"*You fools!* I did not need protection. Now you ruined everything."

"Why don't you look inside that towel?" the Mossad leader suggested.

Anne picked up the towel. A long lethal knife dropped to the sand. Her face turned white in *absolute horror.* She remembered him coming towards her, the look of alarm on his face as he approached, and the explosive sound of gunfire, the frightful scream as he fell backward. It all happened in seconds.

"We saw him put that knife in the towel while you were dressing. He was about to *finish you off,* as he did to our agent in Paris. He had his fun and got what he needed. He did not need you anymore. This *bastard* doesn't leave anything to chance."

On the ride back to the Turkish border, the two agents talked about the future crisis expected in Iranian politics, and the extreme Islamic movement. Anne did not inquire about anything to do with politics or the military. She did not give a damn anymore. She just wanted to be in Vincent's loving arms, once more.

The agents planted sufficient evidence so that the General and his investigators would believe that insurrectionists, the Kurdish rebels attacked the colonel and took his escort hostage. They will believe the Kurds kidnapped Anne. They will think she is in mountain camps, near the border with Turkey.

"Your mission was accomplished," Josh said with a big smile.

Anne colored her hair dark-brown and put-on glasses, so that no one would recognize her at the Turkish airport. She left on the first direct flight to Paris.

***

Monaco. Vincent could not understand why after two weeks, he had not received letters or any word from Anne. His imagination wandered endlessly. He remembered the strange dream he had the night following his decision to accept the job offer from Charley. Someone warned him about his future, but he had not listened. Eva could have been that devil, with sad green eyes. He was stuck in *Quicksand,* in Monaco. That sword battle in the dream, could it have been the *Sword of Allah?* That angel with the golden hair, might that be Anne? Incredible as it seemed now, much of his dream had come true.

His thoughts shifted to his innocent childhood years. Vincent Renaldo grew-up in Brooklyn, one of the toughest cities in the world. It was a troublesome city to grow-up in, but it had lots of personality. As the Frank Sinatra song goes: *"If you can make it there, you can make it anywhere."* In the early years, Brooklyn was still a relatively clean and decent place to live. You could walk or take your bicycle anywhere. Everything was local. It was short walk to school. It was just a few blocks to the grocery store. Prospect Park was twenty minutes away. His friends and relatives were close by. The local corner ice cream soda store was a hangout for all the kids on the block.

Vincent grew up in a "blended family." His biological mother abandoned her four children (he was less than one year old at the time). Father placed them in a foster home, until he remarried. His new wife had three children from a prior marriage. Their new stepmother naturally favored her children. There were many arguments and drunken fights over money, marriage, and manners. This was clearly an extremely dysfunctional family of seven children.

What saved me from this family crisis? I think it was my cousin, Marietta Gehring, who took a special interest in me. She was the art teacher at St. John's. Marietta took me to her home after school, taught me about art, and told stories about her brother, Reverend Frederic Gehring, called by the Marines, the *"Padre of Guadalcanal,"* during the War in the Pacific. Capt. Rev. Gehring was the first navy chaplain to receive the Legion of Merit Medal from the President.

He also authored a book, A *Child of Miracles,* the story of Patsy Li, during the war in the Far East. These stories really inspired me, deepened my faith and trust in the Lord, and gave me a very positive attitude about life, at the age of seven and eight.

As a young boy, how implausible it now seems that I was once in love with my Italian classmate named, Grace Monaco. She was my childhood idol—*my first love.* Grace was a top student at St. John's school, in the Williamsburg section of Brooklyn. She was a gifted concert pianist at the tender age of ten. She had blond hair and a remarkable classical voice. Grace's Italian mother and father believed in the fundamental traditions and customs of the "old country." They taught their children three essentials: Faith, Family, and Friends, and the value of a good education.

Vincent was a student at that same school. He was a young artist with latent talents, who was in love with God, the arts, and "overflowing with Grace." Young Vince was a faithful Catholic and altar boy, who helped the priest serve Mass almost every morning. He was *so innocent* back then. During those childhood years, his life was filled with adventures and excitement. There was *always hope* and anticipation of what the future might bring. When he became twenty-one, he remembered thinking, as a grown-up, everything would be different. He would have a car, a house and all those "things" that many adults have, and that would be real happiness—so he thought.

The Renaldo family was relatively poor in terms of money, but very rich in everyday life experiences. His hard-working father died at the age of forty-four from lung cancer. His dad supported seven children and his aged father. Although he was poor, there was real joy in the daily challenges of Vincent's life. Unexpected encounters and frequent adventures always seemed to happen in Brooklyn. Each day represented a new challenge, an opportunity, and adventure for this child with a vivid imagination.

Street gangs existed back then, but they were merely groups of teenagers who stuck together and played stickball, and organized block parties on weekends. Some fights happened between rival gangs, but they did not kill each other, as they do today in NY, LA, and especially in Chicago. Just a few heads were bashed. Somehow, those street gangs never influenced Vince, although peer pressures, antagonists, and macho behavior affected his older brothers. Vince was a sort of *egghead,* who was always thinking and reading.

His friends made fun of that, but they also respected his knowledge. He ultimately became the gang's advisor and strategist.

He would never forget his first big date with Grace, at the age of nine. She finally received approval from her parents to go to the movies with him. When he arrived to pick her up, he was flabbergasted: Her mother and little brother were going to *chaperone them*. Vince earned a few dollars after school, running errands, like buying coffee for the factory workers on Broadway. He barely saved enough cash to pay for the four tickets at the RKO Theater. Grace's mother sat between them to prevent any handholding or anything else.

Some evenings Vince would climb over Grace's backyard fence and knock on her window. She would come out on to the back porch. They would talk for hours. Rarely did they kiss. When they kissed, it was merely a friendly peck on the cheek. Their childhood love was pure, without thoughts of anything else. He was *enchanted* with her persona, her goodness, and lively spirit.

The family moved away from Brooklyn to "greener," Long Island. He was *devastated*. Sadly, Grace also moved somewhere, at the same time. They lost contact with each other for seven years. (Everything in life seems to run in seven-year cycles). By then, at the age of eighteen, Vincent had joined the military to escape his suburban life, the artificial, bullshit life of Long Island, where everyone tried to "keep up with the Jones'."

He was determined to find his long lost first love. However, her father was trying to get away probably from the Mafia. He had covered all of his tracks and had an unlisted phone. After much effort, Grace and Vince finally met again. Nevertheless, they were *not* the same childhood sweethearts of years past. They went on a date to Radio City, to see the Christmas show in Manhattan. She took his arm and played her part as "the perfect date." Yet, he could sense that her earlier deep feelings were not there. *The only constant in life is change*. They had both changed.

Vincent was now in the U.S. Air Force, and had to return to his duties in Greenland. They corresponded often. His letters were passionate and filled with thoughts about life. Her messages were warm and friendly, but she soon sent him a "Dear John" letter. Vince knew he had no chance of competing with her new lover. *If only I had searched for her harder, I might have found her sooner*, he thought.

Our early childhood romance might have ripened as we grew up together. Nevertheless, she rejected him for another character.

Grace would eventually drop her boyfriend for Bill, whom she married. Vincent went to their wedding. He was hurting inside but at the same *time truly happy* for her. He only wanted whatever was *good* for her, even if it was not him. Many years later, he learned that Grace and Bill divorced, when she learned the truth about his *hidden sordid nature*.

Since his first taste of *innocent love*—Vincent was searching for another *"angel."* Decades later he found himself in a place ruled by a different Grace—the late Princess Grace of Monaco, and he finally found his new angel—Anne—but not before the devil had his way with him.

***

After many months of confinement, Vincent's faith slowly began to fail him. Late one Friday evening he fell to his knees and prayed to the Lord: "Jesus, you know I'm a sinner who is lost. I am stuck in this *Quicksand of Sin.* Finally, I found you here, in this dark prison. The Holy Spirit finally pierced my pride, my hardened heart, my soul— and I will never be the same again. You know that I have no hatred towards my enemies, only forgiveness. I even pray for Eva, for Victor, for my jailers, and those who have wronged me in the past.

Now I finally understand what life is really about. All life is self-maintaining, self-renewing. Life is interdependent with all other life forms on earth. *Love is that vital force that governs all life.* Through freedom of choice, we must align our will with your will. Lord, please hear my plea and set me free. Why do you continue to ignore my prayers? (Above all, Vince believed that prayer must be sincere. You must *totally* believe that the Lord understands all your prayers, even before you think and speak of them).

An hour later, guards came with an order from the Judge. *Unbelievable!* After months in "purgatory," Vincent was free— *provisionally.* No ride downtown was available. He gladly walked the few miles down the hill to the village of Monte-Carlo. Once again, he marveled at the beautiful view of Monaco—*from the outside.* It was amazing how much one appreciates the simple things of life—trees, grass, flowers, birds, everything.

When one sees something beautiful—a lovely child, a great snow covered mountain, a special seascape, or a fantastic sunset—think about how much greater must be the Creator of such beauty, such intelligence. When one hears majestic music, such as Mozart, or wondrous human voices singing, they must marvel about the God that created such genius and vocal instruments, that so invigorate the mind and spirit.

Saint Charles Church would be his first stop, to thank the Lord. To his surprise, a Mass was just beginning—*just for me,* he assumed. The priest nearly dropped Holy Communion when he looked up and saw Vincent waiting to receive Christ. He must have escaped from prison was his first thought. Vince had called Anne and asked her to meet him outside the church. As the congregation began leaving they emotionally embraced and kissed in front of the church "Darling, finally I can hold you in my arms," she said as tears of joy ran down her face.

"It's a miracle," he told her. "I prayed to Jesus Christ to be set free, and an hour later it happened." (She had a certain puzzling smile on her face that suggested she knew something about that miracle).

"That's wonderful darling. Let's go home."

They dropped by the office nearby, to get clothes and pick up his car. Eva was *shocked* to see him, when she answered the door. She gave him a big hug and kisses, and then started to cry. "How did you get out? Where is Victor? Did you escape?

"They finally realized that I was not guilty. How's your baby?"

Eva had given birth to a baby girl, Emily. Unfortunately, the illegitimate child looked too much like Victor. Perhaps she would not inherit his craziness and character. Vince had a special interest in this innocent infant, since he saved its life when Eva wanted to get an abortion. He could not support her aborting a five-month-old embryo. Vince argued passionately from common sense: science has *not* been able to refute that an embryo is a living person with a soul. This moral law has existed for thousands of years. You (we) cannot reject God's fundamental laws, as if one is shopping for things in the marketplace. You have to accept the "whole package" of moral laws, if you claim to be a true Jew. Somehow, he had persuaded her to keep the baby.

Here was an unwed mother, without any money, with countless bill collectors hounding her. Vincent wanted no part of this insane relationship anymore; especially a crying baby and a bitching mother, who thought he is "part of the family"—and would naturally take responsibility for bills which she and Victor ran up so easily in the past.

Vincent went to see the lawyer. He took the file from the young arrogant attorney and paid him part of his outrageous fees. As he was about to leave, the lawyer stated: "Monaco jails are certainly nicer compared to French prisons. Right?"

"Why don't you try it sometime, asshole? *You're fired!*"

Victor was still enjoying his sabbatical in his jail cell. *Interpol* had a special interest in his international financial dealings *from the past*. Vince felt sorry for the poor scoundrel. He gave him 550 Euros, about one-third of his total fortune to keep him supplied with cigarettes and coffee. After living together closely for over one year—somehow they had established a kind of "compatriot" relationship, which was hard to cut completely. He also remembered the Bible passage he read in jail, "… *forgive and pray for your enemies.*" This was one of the most difficult teachings of Christ to follow. Nevertheless, God sent His only begotten Son, into this world to save *all sinners*. Vince felt compelled to abide by Christ's perfect example, in spite of everything that happened, to finally forgive Victor and Eva.

The new lawyer was *phenomenal*. He insisted that Vincent get Eva to sign an "official" document acknowledging that the baby was not his. There is an old Napoleon law, established during the wars with Russia and England, which still exists. It says, the ex-husband remains responsible for the child, even if conceived by someone else. Later, the illegitimate child can claim a share of his estate, assuming that he had any assets.

The lawyer drafted the legal document. Vince wondered how he could get Eva to sign it. She was not going to give up any "rights" for the child without a fight. He caught her in a good mood sipping coffee in bed one morning, and presented the papers. He gave her *"an offer she couldn't refuse!"* If you don't sign this paper—after all it's a true statement isn't it—then I will have legal rights to 50% of all current and future profits that you and Victor make on any, on all future business transactions."

"How can you make such a claim?" she said, scornfully.

"In United States law, which you are still governed by, as my legal spouse, I have *property rights* on any and all transactions that have been started *before* our divorce. Keep in mind that this divorce may not be recognized in the States (which was not true but she didn't know shit about American divorce laws)."

Eva *promptly* signed the document.

Weeks later, when they finally went to the court to complete the divorce settlement, Eva had the *chutzpah* to ask the three judges, 3,000 Euros per month in alimony, for herself and child support for her bastard child. When the judges saw the "legally notarized" document she had earlier signed, they regarded her as nothing more than an *unfaithful prostitute*. The divorce received prompt approval. In fact, it was the second fastest divorce on record, after the famous Borg case, the celebrated tennis champion of Sweden. The court justices must have understood what a blood-sucking person she really was. As she came out of the private meeting with the judges, she was in tears. The judges ruled: "She didn't deserve a single Euro in alimony!"

Anne and Vince moved to a small French village known as *Cap Ferrat* by the sea. Astonishingly, the townhouse sign read, "Villa Anne Marie." That evening moonbeams streaked down from the warm night sky, glancing off the breaking surf, which scattered into sprays of white foam, smashing against the rocks on the shore. Vincent's head was on Anne's lap. She sat on the sand, her back against the smooth boulder. She stroked his hair. Her fingers circled his face gently, outlining his eyes and lips. The moon rays shown through with extravagant soft light upon her glowing face. Her voice enthralled him as he listened. A burning passion flowed from her as if her heart was trying to come out to him. "Dearest, I missed you so much. You are a vital part of me. I was completely lost without you, during these endless days and nights."

Anne did not know how to cook—Vince did not care. She could not handle his correspondence in English—he wasn't concerned. She was a good housekeeper, did his laundry, and pressed his shirts, among the other everyday duties, but that was not what he needed. Her real talents were not any of those domestic chores. She was an accomplished lover—and that is what he wanted; that's what he needed most of all. (Anne never told Vincent about her clandestine, dangerous trip to Iran. Nor did she tell him about the deal she made with the State Department and French DST to free him).

The situation, on a more practical level, became more and more arduous. He was almost broke.

He lost his only business clients and office. He had no contact with his first wife Susan and his two children in the States, for many months. Eva refused to give him back his car. Freedom, without money is another kind of prison, he thought. The jailhouse is bigger, and the windows are larger, there is a kitchen for cooking, if there was food. He could travel a little further—*it's a deluxe cage.* People occupy their "cells"—some are smaller or bigger; some are more exclusive than others are—but they are still in a kind of cage, totally restricted without the "currency of freedom."

That slap Eva gave Cathy proved to be costly, for everyone. All they hoped to accomplish; all the relations they had established; all the potential millions they thought would soon flow, were now *lost forever.* Vincent's main concerns were how to clear his good name? Where to earn money? How to pick-up the pieces of his shattered life, with the help of Anne? Love—*without money*—is like that wonderful French cooking, but without the sauce or meat.

Anne came up with an idea! "Why not take back your car from Eva, which after all is in *your* name, and we can sell it for some cash?"

Vincent's first attempt failed. Someone saw him and called Eva. Her neighbors told her the car is being towed. She came running like a crazy woman with no shoes or bra. She stopped the tow truck.

"What are you doing? Who gave you permission to take my car?"

"Mr. Renaldo told us to take it. He said it's his automobile," the confused tow driver explained.

"Bullshit! It's my car," she shouted, as she ran up to Vincent and slapped him. He was stunned. The police soon arrived and were confused by this bizarre craziness. Vince remembered his Bible, turned the other cheek—the raving maniac hit him again!

Since Vincent did not speak much French and the police seemed to sympathize with her version of the story, he decided to avoid any hassles with the police. He simply walked away from this insane street scene.

The following night, the car was *quietly* recovered. It was much easier this time, since Eva left the keys in the ignition. Of course, the local British Mini dealer gave Vincent practically nothing for the car. He received nearly 5,000 Euros. Still, it gave them time to think of something else to do to earn a living.

Always a resourceful person, Eva had taken Vincent's Rolex out of the bank and sold it while he was in jail. Vince took their diamond engagement ring out of the same bank and traded it for cash. The engagement ring was a symbol of their love—the love she had betrayed. The cash did not last too long. He paid for his small apartment in Monaco, which was essential to keep his resident status. Unfortunately, Vince was legally partly responsible for the bills that Victor and Eva ran up. They had to be paid; otherwise, he might go back to the dungeon.

***

HIDDEN SCARS

*"Out of suffering have emerged the strongest souls;
the most massive characters are seared with scars."*

—Khalil Gibran

Something was bothering Vincent Renaldo. He was uneasy about asking Anne, but not this time. "Anne, you gave me the impression that you were well-off financially—if not loaded. You bought a yacht for Hanz, your former fiancée. You said you had lots of jewels and paintings. What about that expensive apartment in Paris? If that is true, why are we living like we are destitute. Why are we so hard up?"

"Well it's a long complicated story. I should have told you about my situation in Switzerland, some time ago. I thought you had enough problems to handle, without adding my personal problems to your difficulties."

"What situation in Switzerland?" Anne took her face in her hands as if feeling its shape. Her eyes seemed to move gradually out into some far away void. "Some years ago, as you know, I lived with my former sweetheart, Hanz in Switzerland. One day we received a summons to appear at police headquarters in Geneva. Hanz was away for a few days, visiting his mother in Germany. I decided to take care of the court summons. He had a habit of collecting many overdue parking tickets. He parked anywhere, mostly in the wrong places. So I went to pay his tickets."

"Bon Jour. I'm here to pay for my friend's parking tickets," I told the police officer at the desk as I handed him the summons notice.

"Are you Anne Marson?" he inquired. "Your identification, please."

"Yes, that's me," she answered with a smile, while presenting the passport to the officer.

"Would you please come with me, Madam," he politely requested.

"Where are you taking me? I'm sorry he did not take care of those tickets sooner. I told him to..."

"Just wait in here. The inspector just wants to ask a few questions."

About ten minutes later two plainclothes police officers entered the private room. "Madam, empty your purse on the desk," one of the officers ordered.

"What's this all about?" I asked, dumping the contents of my purse on the table.

"Madame, just sit down. Is that your signature on this document?"

"Sure, that's my signature ... but I don't understand. Why? ..."

The inspector cut Anne off. "We will ask the questions. You failed to pay for goods that were shipped for your import/export trading business."

"Well ... I can explain that. I was only about a month late ..."

"According to the official complaint, you are forty-four days late and the amount overdue is *considerable,*" he replied, as he pulled the document from her hands.

"It's not my fault... The bank screwed up! They sent the money transfer incorrectly. They had to send the funds again. That delay caused ..."

He interrupted her again. "So you admit that you failed to perform on this $228,000 contract?"

"Yes, but it's *not my fault!* You see ..."

"Save your excuses for the Judge. Our job is to interrogate you and get your *confession,*" the other inspector bluntly replied.

Anne has never been arrested and was *completely shocked* by such accusations and harsh treatment. "There must be some mistake. My girlfriend, my business associate, will verify everything," she tried to explain.

A stout police officer then came in to the interrogation room carrying some clothes. "Madame, take off *all* your clothes and put this on," she commanded *firmly.*

"What for? There ... must be some misunderstanding."

"Just do as I say. Put this on *immediately.*"

"I can't be expected to strip *in front of these men,*" Anne protested.

"Do you want me to *forcefully* undress you?" the heavy-set woman replied, with an insidious smirk.

Anne struggled to take her dress off and put on the drab gray uniform, while trying to conceal her partially naked body.

"Off with your bra and panties as well," the stout officer ordered. "And bend over so that I can see if you're hiding anything up there."

Anne could not control the tears that welled up in her eyes, as the police officer put plastic gloves on, and tossed her coat and dress to the inspector to search. Tears streamed down her face. "I know my rights! I refuse to do what you ask, in front of these men."

The two police officers were asked to leave the room. Anne then removed her underwear and put on the ugly gray prisoner's dress.

"Now bend over more, and spread your cheeks apart," the overbearing female police officer commanded.

The utter embarrassment of being forced to disrobe and roughly searched, was too much for her to endure. "You're hurting me," she cried, as fat rough fingers of the police officer brutally examined her private area.

Anne was in a holding cell until the Judge could see her the following morning. As moths and flies circled the small light in the cell ceiling, thoughts about her unbelievable situation kept her awake all night. She thought about Kate. *She is a good friend. She is my business partner; and would certainly resolve this terrible, absurd mistake, in the morning. They will realize what a big blunder they made, tomorrow. I will sue them for false arrest and brutal treatment.*

The following day, she appeared before the Judge. Superior Justice Frienstein emerged in his formal black robe and hat. *Fantastic! He is the sweetheart of my friend Kate, my business partner. Now those bastards will really pay for my false arrest.*

"Madame, you are accused of grand fraud—of conspiring to cheat your business partners out of $228,000. How do you plea?" he coldly demanded.

"What do you mean? Who accuses me of this crime?" Anne inquired, in a *loud, agitated voice.*

"Your business partners accuse you, Madame. I have a formal complaint from four *respectable* Swiss citizens. They claim you swindled them out of $228,000, after they delivered the merchandise for your business enterprise."

Anne's court appointed lawyer advised her to plead guilty. "I'm sure it's just a *'technicality'* between your partners and the Swiss legal system. They will surely let you free. At most, the judge will give you a suspended sentence. Just confess that 'you simply didn't fully understand your financial responsibilities under this complex contract,'" he recommended.

"That's not true! I fully understood my financial responsibilities. I always planned to pay them for the merchandise they shipped. A confession would be *false,* a fabrication. I shall plead innocent! I am totally innocent of these charges!"

They sent Anne to the main Geneva prison to await her trial. They placed her in a cell with five other woman prisoners. Some of her cellmates were the *most notorious* members of any decrepit society, including drug addicts, professional prostitutes, common thieves and a few more hardened criminals.

I must maintain my sanity somehow. I have to cope with this insane situation. Where is Hanz? He should be back by now. Why hasn't he rescued me from this hellhole? Maybe he does not know I'm here. My money transfer from the bank should arrive in a few days. They will see that I never intended to commit any fraud. I know the *real facts* will prove my innocence.

The hours and days dragged on. Each day seemed to get longer in the overcrowded prison cell. Finally, they sent for her. Finally, I will be freed she knew, as the guards escorted her from the cell. Hanz must have arranged bail money and a more competent lawyer. Thank God, he has arrived on time to rescue me from this insanity.

They escorted her to a room with no windows. There were only three chairs and a single light in the center of the ceiling, in an otherwise empty room. Two guards emerged from the barred steel door. "We're here to get your confession," the small guard announced as they sat down. "Just sign here and you can leave this place in a few days, after some formalities are taken care of," he stated.

Anne carefully examined the "confession" document, written in French. She was appalled by its contents. "I'm *never* going to sign such a pack of lies, such fabrications," she said loudly, defiantly.

"I think you may change your mind, Madame, after we give you a little sample of our special physical therapy."

The guard came up behind her, and abruptly hit Anne across her head with a hard rubber truncheon. The bigger guard then quickly put cuffs on her hands, and bracelets on her legs, connecting them to the chair. *"You will confess!* You will sign this paper, if you know what's good for you."

"Bullshit!" she replied. "I'll never sign such a pack of lies ... that's a *sham. "*

They took turns beating her legs, back and head with the truncheon, being careful not to leave any permanent marks on her body, until she lost consciousness. She awoke in her cell, hours later. Black and blue marks covered much of her torso.

Her cellmates implored her to sign the statement. "We have all been through this before. They will not let up on you until you sign a confession. Do not try to resist! *It's hopeless!"*

Anne was *strong*—mentally, physically and spiritually. She was a woman of substance and strong character. Anne would *never* give in to demands by her torturers. (She was not afraid during her perilous mission to Iran to deliver visas and passports for her friends). She would remain diffident no matter what they did to her.

Beatings continued over the next three days, growing more vicious with each occurrence. Anne grew more and more obstinate with each brutal beating. She would not break despite such physical torture.

Her day in court finally arrived. Her lawyer still maintained that she would get off *easy,* if she "only pleaded guilty." The judge indicated in his private chambers that he would have mercy on her, considering your special situation, if only she showed some remorse and confessed.

"You're supposed to defend me? She said to the attorney. *I am not guilty!* I will never, never confess to such false accusations," Anne answered *scornfully.*

Witness after witness took the stand, with contrived testimony about how Madame Marson hurt their businesses and families by not paying them for the goods that they delivered. "She's a crook who cheated us out of our life-long savings. She caused significant harm to us personally and to our company's image and reputation." That was the essence of the witness statements.

Anne listened carefully. Her demeanor remained courteous and respectful. Finally, her friend Kate took the stand. She revealed, in explicit detail how her former business partner and "good friend "... *deliberately* cheated her and others out of their hard-earned profits by not living up to the contract terms.

Anne became *livid, furious,* as she stood up and confronted her so-called "friend," and the other witnesses. *"You are all liars!* If you don't tell the truth, God will *damn* all of you, and ... *and your families."*

The judge interrupted. "Madam you're a Christian... isn't that true? How can you threaten these *reputable* witnesses this way? Such behavior is not at all Christian-like, is it?"

She did not answer him.

"I will give you another opportunity to apologize to these highly-respectable witnesses," the judge said.

Anne then shocked everyone by kneeling down in front of the judge. She prayed silently.

"What are you doing? Go back to your lawyer's table and take your chair Madam," the judge ordered sternly.

Minutes later, she stood up proudly and spoke in perfect French, in a loud clear voice. "I tell all ... *especially you,* Judge Frienstein, God's angels shall punish *all of you and your families.* My prayers have been answered: Some of you will suffer from cancer, from SIDA and other diseases. *You will all die,* because of such false accusations against me."

They forcefully removed Anne from the court as she continued to repeat her denunciation to everyone, included the shocked spectators in the courtroom and bewildered members of the local press.

The following Monday, the court continued with the case against her. Surprisingly, the Judge arrived with his arm in a brace, with a sling around his shoulder. He explained that he fell and broke his arm last night. The high-class, powerful witnesses looked with *astonishment* at the judge, at each other, and then at Anne. The case against her seemed *flawless.* Nothing she did or said could possibly change the outcome.

Judge Frienstein then pronounced sentence: "Two to five years in jail. Your bank accounts and assets shall be frozen until all the parties have received full compensation plus damages.

All court costs must also be paid by you."

Anne was led away from the court *screaming her curse.* Her eighty-year-old feeble mother and father were completely heartbroken. They cried in each other's arms as they saw their only daughter dragged away. Anne's mother collapsed in her seat.

Two months later, one of the witnesses died of cancer. Soon thereafter, another accuser's teenage child died of SIDA (French for AIDS). A third witness then became so afraid from the news reports of the others that he sent Anne a certified letter confessing that he had lied. A copy was sent to the judge. The terrified witness begged Anne's forgiveness. He *pleaded with her* to remove the curse on him and his family. She then prayed. His request was granted on Christmas day.

Vincent Renaldo sat motionless for nearly a minute, while studying her eyes. They revealed sufficient truth. Anne had not been lying. She clearly had spoken the truth, as she believed it to be.

Anne continued: "While in jail, I met a beautiful young Polish woman, Christina, who was placed in my cell. Christina and I became close friends almost immediately. The young woman of twenty-two, had been a translator for the Polish embassy."

Christina finally told her tragic story to Anne: "I became engaged to be married to Martin, a handsome young man whom I loved for many years. I had good reason to believe that Martin was having an affair with my Italian girlfriend, Maria, who worked with me and shared the apartment with me. Maria frequently spoke in her sleep. One night she spoke passionately about Martin. I became extremely jealous. I had to learn more about her affair with Martin, before we were to be married. I contrived a plan to give Maria chloroform to make her sleep deeply so that I might learn the *whole truth.*

"Tragically, Maria had a heart attack or something, which must have been caused by the chloroform. *I panicked.* I became shocked and afraid by Maria's death that I foolishly hid her body in a plastic bag and covered it in a woodshed. A few days later, the police using specially trained dogs found her body. The coroner determined that Maria *didn't die* from the chloroform; she died from suffocation, sometime later."

Anne interrupted her. "That's terrible, horrible! The *fact* is you did not really intend to kill her. It's clearly a dreadful accident."

"Of course, I never wanted nor expected her to die. I only wanted Maria to *sleep,* so that I might learn the truth about her affair with Martin," she cried.

"During the trial my lawyer informed me that, that ... Maria was the only daughter of the chief of the Italian Mafia, in Milan Italy." Christina then began crying uncontrollably in Anne's arms. Her situation seemed hopeless, *catastrophic.* Even if she could somehow prove it was an accident, the Mafia would ultimately kill her anyway.

Anne tried to comfort her, prayed with her, and thought about her pitiful situation, day and night. Christina's dreadful predicament helped Anne take her mind off her own serious problem, which seemed insignificant in comparison. After many deep prayers, Anne finally conceived of an idea that might help. She told Christina to write a passionate letter to the father of the dead girl, the Mafia leader. Tell him how aggrieved you are at his loss. Anne helped compose the letter. The closing sentence said: *"If I could take the place of your daughter in her grave, I would do so willingly. Please forgive me for this terrible accident caused by my insane jealousy. I will never be able to erase the memory of Maria from my mind. I live in torment of my terrible deed, day and night."*

The other female prisoners were angry with Anne for her sympathy and "misplaced compassion" towards Christina, whom they believed was a heartless murderer of their Mafia friend's only child. One morning they cornered her in the bathroom. They all ganged up on Anne and beat her *ruthlessly.* She spent three weeks in the hospital from broken ribs and a concussion.

Vincent was not beaten in prison. How could the Swiss and others could treat anyone so cruelly, especially gentle women like her? He wondered. "Did Christina get any answer from the letter?" Yes!

The Mafia leader, about two weeks later, wrote a response to Christina: *"You touched a very sensitive nerve,"* he told her. At the end of his letter, he wrote, *"I understand how jealousy can cause someone to do foolish things. I have also done some very irrational things in my life. I forgive you! I hope that you will visit me when you get out of prison. If you need anything at all, please call my private number."*

When the other women learned about the letter from the Mafia chief, they came to my cell and *pleaded* with me to pardon them for their foolish attack. I forgave all of them.

"Why couldn't you use your money or jewels to get a decent lawyer?"

"The Judge and his lover Kate secretly conspired, with my court appointed lawyer, to steal my valuables—all my jewels, furs, and paintings. The lawyer had the keys to my Swiss Condo. They took everything of value. It amounted to about $150,000." Anne explained. "My bank account, which received the *late* money transfer, a total of nearly one million from my import-export business, also remained frozen. I could not use the funds until my appeal to the higher court against claims of injustice and torture was heard. That legal process would cost a small fortune and take years to resolve.

After she was released, Anne Marson was *"persona non grata"* in Switzerland. The police escorted her to the French border. Her aging mother had lost twenty pounds of weight from her many months of distress, while Anne was in jail. Her father died a few days before she was freed. Anne could not use the considerable funds, which remained frozen in her Swiss account, to clear her good name, or to sue the powerful corrupt Geneva officials. Although she was emotionally broken, Anne was not broken in spirit. She was determined to someday, somehow fight the injustices that she and others experienced in Switzerland.

***

Vincent could not believe Anne's incredible story. She must have exaggerated some of the facts. That was his feeling, until he read the front-page story in *The New York Times:* "Swiss Used Nazi Victim's Money, files Show." The report claimed that banks in Switzerland kept billions of dollars' worth of gold, jewels and cash from Jewish Holocaust victims, during the fifty years following World War II. If no one claimed the assets or had sufficient "official" proof that their relatives deposited the money, or had safe deposit boxes in the banks, they could not obtain their funds. Moreover, legal relatives of Holocaust victims were required to produce an "official death certificate," if they wanted to recover any assets from their dead relatives.

"Nazis did not provide official death certificates they pleaded. Sorry, that's our law, the bankers replied." The Swiss banks used the poor victims' money to help finance the part of the earlier Nazi war machine, and after the war, they invested much of the unclaimed funds in all kinds of very profitable international commerce.

Then Anne told Vincent about the *"Swiss chocolates case,"* which actually affected both of them, personally. The case involved a young woman, from New York City, called Rosy. Rosy stopped one day to buy some chocolates in Geneva. She then moved to another counter in the *same* shop, to buy something else. The store detective promptly arrested her. In Switzerland, there is a little-known law that essentially says, "You are not allowed to change counters in any store, without first paying for the item you selected at the first counter." Most foreign visitors do not know about this absurd law. The Swiss are very vigilant about shoplifters. (They think their chocolates are jewels. Rosy had enough money to buy the entire store).

Shocked Rosy was promptly sent to jail for "interrogation." For foreigners, cross-examination often includes physical abuse and torture, until a confession is given. Young Rosy did not want to take any of this *Swiss bullshit.* She promptly confessed, even though the charges were false, on the promise that they would let her go with a small fine. However, the judge did not like the rich foreign snob, so he sent her back to jail. Christmas arrived, which means all the lawyers, judges and the legal system closes down so that they can celebrate, *"peace on earth and good will to men."*

Miserable Rosy had to wait until after New Year's, before they would review her case. Rosy found herself sharing a cell with Anne, who dried her tears and offered her words of comfort. She gave Rosy one of her nightgowns to keep her warm. Anne and Rosy became "bosom sisters." Later when released, they shared an apartment together in Monaco. Their friendship grew stronger until that crucial day when the "sisters" had a quarrel about "Money, Manners—and Vincent." It became evident that Rosy forgot about all the loving tenderness and emotional support Anne gave her in the Swiss jail. She refused to accept the fact that Anne wanted to have her own life and share it with Vincent. Anne would not tolerate Rosie's possessiveness. (Too much affection, without freedom, can be, and often is, very destructive).

Vincent's Monaco prison experience was a "paradise," compared to Anne's experience in the Swiss jail. "They put her together with cell mates who were drug addicts, hardened criminals, lesbians, and some had SIDA," she said.

This gentle woman had been subject to vulgar abuses from some of the most reprehensible people on this earth. Who could believe that Swiss judges and lawyers could be so *Machiavellian,* and the police so brutal in their treatment of foreigners?

Vincent's image of the country was shattered. Like many Americans, he believed that Switzerland was a place of clean snow-covered mountains and hard- working watchmakers. The land of *Heidi*—that wonderful children's story which appears on TV, every Christmas. The Swiss government and banks love money—*other people's money!*

The mystique about secret numbered accounts is overrated, as the late Mrs. Marcos and Mr. Gattas found out. If they suspect that your bank deposits resulted from *possible* criminal activities, the Swiss will freeze the accounts, and the money ultimately goes to the state for its use, in the name of *justice.* Their secret banking laws are like their Swiss cheese—they have "lots of holes."

The key challenge for Vincent was how to help Anne, since she was still despondent over her past Swiss scars, and the loss of her valuables in Geneva. She wanted to "get even" with the judge and Kate, who was the business partner that betrayed her. Her terrible experiences also engendered within her, hatred for all Jews, since they were witnesses against her, and the judge was Jewish. That deep animosity and desire for revenge was *consuming her.* Vince had to find some way to release that hatred and those negative forces; otherwise, it could affect their relationship as well.

How can one *really* forgive our enemies—those who debase and hurt the ones' we love? This is one of the most difficult teachings of Christ to follow. Vincent recalled from his Bible in prison, that Christ came into the world to save all sinners—*every one of us.* Christ also forgave the Jewish leaders who tortured and killed him, with His last dying words. He remembered that Pope John Paul II personally visited the criminal that shot him, and forgave him. Sometimes it takes a long time before one can truly forgive our enemies. Nonetheless, the desire for revenge can be, actually is, *extremely destructive.*

Anne continued: "the Judge instructed his girlfriend to take everything from my Swiss apartment, just a few days before I was freed."

"Were there any witnesses?"

"Yes, there were. But I can't go to Geneva to meet them and get proof."

The judge seemed *invincible*. I had neither the power nor the funds to fight him, even if that were possible.

Couldn't Anne just forget it? Just block it out; somehow erase it from her mind, so their life can be normal again? Maybe a therapist could help her? Vincent felt totally inadequate and powerless to handle her psychological scars.

Anne continued to fill in details of how it all happened. "I met Kate, the former beau of Hanz, at a party in *St. Moritz,* where the rich and famous take their winter holidays. Kate appeared to be friendly and admired my jewels. She offered me some cocaine at her birthday party. Her offer was declined. Kate got smashed on drugs and booze. She began boasting to me about her drug business with the 'jet-set.'

"Anyway, I agreed to open an import-export operation for woman's fashions in Geneva, with Kate and her friends as partners. We later signed an agreement whereby they would provide the clothes and I would be responsible for marketing and the money end of the business. I did not read all the fine print in the contract. I did not know about a clause that stated, "Any late payment thirty days past due is considered a breach of the agreement and is subject to legal recourse, penalties, etc., etc.

"During that party, Kate told me that she travels to South America and picks up about 10 kilos of pure cocaine every winter. Since she is a Swiss citizen, customs don't check her baggage, and she has the Judge to protect her butt, if anything happens."

Marvelous! A light went on in Vincent's head. Anne knew all the details—times, places, contacts and customers. Vince decided to compose a detailed letter to *Interpol* about this sordid business, using a code name: *"Nightingale,"* for their protection.

After he composed it, they mailed the letter from another post office, some distance from Monaco. Vincent also wiped his fingerprints off the letter and avoided licking the glue on the envelope, before mailing his *bombshell*. That's something he learned from secret agent Victor Cruz. "Interpol can easily analyze and connect you by the DNA of your saliva," he once said.

Illicit drugs debase people, affects youth by clouding their mind, and ultimately ends their young lives. Narcotics generate enormous money to corrupt those who peddle it.

Drugs also degrade institutions at every level, in every way imaginable. As long as it is profitable to sell illegal drugs—*suppliers will always meet the demand*—and it is extremely profitable.

Nearly two months passed before they heard about Kate's arrest, along with other "high society," drug users. The judge could not save his girlfriend's ass this time. She was snatched in Italy, while attempting to cross the border at Lugano. Kate the big-shit drug pusher, the perjurer, received a ten-year sentence. The judge was now under investigation for his connection with Kate, the Swiss news media reported.

Anne became elated, ecstatic, thrilled, when she heard the news. Her desire for revenge was now *completely satisfied*. Her mood became positive, once more. Now, at last, they could concentrate on each other.

Vincent came to her one afternoon, not long after the media coverage of the arrest of Superior Judge Frienstein. He told her, "You must now pray to God to *forgive all* your former Jewish enemies, who were false witnesses against you. Revenge is ultimately *self-destructive.* Hate the evil within, like the disease that it is, *not* the soul of the person. Doctors treat the disease to save people. After all, Jesus Christ was (still is) the greatest Jew of them all."

"I know that. I have already put away my denunciation of them. However, I need time to think about praying for their immortal souls. Yes, Christ was a Jew. He was also tortured and killed *not* by ordinary Jewish people, but by the leaders. I cannot pray *sincerely* if I do not believe in what I am praying for. That would be hypocritical."

***

The Message. Being there, at the right time, with the right contacts, is far more important than all the expertise of the world, and best conceived plans. That is the lesson of international finance business—timing and good contacts are *everything!*

While Victor Cruz remained in prison, a message arrived for him on Vincent's office fax machine. The intriguing message came from a representative of a top Middle-East Prince, one of Victor's past clients (they did not know he was in jail). The client was an international executive who had total authority to move billions-of-dollars from United States banks for the UAE Prince. They needed

Victor's "expertise" in this *secret transfer* in order to move their U.S. dollars to greater interest bearing currency accounts in Europe and especially in Asia.

It was not clear why the Prince wanted to transfer such huge petrol dollar (black gold) sums *secretly.* Perhaps there was some concern about the falling value of the U.S. dollar vis-à-vis the Yen, or some pending Middle East crisis? It involved the exchange of billions of United States dollars for Japanese Yen, for deposit in a tax-free European bank account. The fax message read: *"URGENT" OFFICE OF THE PRINCE:* Victor Cruz, Monte Carlo, Monaco Re: YEN and United States DOLLAR EXCHANGE. We are pleased to offer to you the transaction to begin with United States $150,000,000 (one hundred fifty million United States dollars) on the first day, and on the following days, United States $300,000,000 (three hundred million United States dollars), four days a week, until United States dollar and Japanese yen are exhausted. THE DISCOUNT: Gross 2% to the yen provider. We have already an irrevocable bank pay order for half of the amount...

"NON-CIRCUMVENTION: Enclosed herewith, please sign and seal and send to us, so that we can provide the contract details with United States dollar account number with our bank. If you are successful, we will provide additional contracts for a value of United States $30 billion per week.

"We look forward to your fast reply, with complete details of the yen provider and your agreement RWA [Ready, Willing and Able] confirmation. Yours very sincerely, Prince Saud Abdullah"

The Prince had his own private numbered account in Switzerland and it was "understood" that about 5% of the profits from the deal would be sent to his account. No business is transacted in the Middle East, without providing a substantial "gift" to the key personalities involved. It did not matter if your products or services were the best and you had the lowest price—bribes are the "Standard Operating Procedure," and *essential* to complete any business deal.

Victor was released. Unlike Vincent, Cruz was overweight, pale in complexion, totally broke and *extremely bitter* from his experience. He found he had no phones, no telex, no computer or anything else to transact business. He depended *completely* on Vince and his office to be the "communications center" for this new important business opportunity.

Vincent would now become the "senior partner."

Mr. Kamal Bostan, the trusted representative of Prince Saud Abdullah arrived from Turkey, a few days after Victor's released. Bostan said he had *total* authority by the Prince to handle the financial transaction. They quickly began to draft the essential contracts and documents to handle this huge money transfer. Eva's lawyer said he could handle the legal details and would introduce them to a *private* bank in Monaco. Vincent agreed to provide office and communications services, which were vital for the business. He would get thirty-three percent of Victor and Eva's share. In private, they verbally agreed to the shared percentages. In effect, Vincent's take would be about three million dollars for just the first billions of dollars transferred.

Victor assumed responsibility for finding the closing "trustee bank" to handle the deal. He would also have to negotiate with his sources for high-quality financial instruments, known as Prime Bank Notes (PBN's), which guarantee that the funds are safe and secure. The Bank must certify that the Arab Prince would receive the agreed fixed interest rates, for the Japanese Yen, currently available for the next twenty years.

They encountered a classic "chicken and egg" situation: The PBN supplier wanted to *see proof* that the billions existed, and the funds' provider demanded a *guarantee* that high-quality PBN's were actually available at the interest rates promised. Mr. Bostan could not reveal the name of the bank and private account, where the funds were located. In that case, the PBN supplier insisted on a Performance Bond of $300,000. Bostan refused! As a result, Victor could not provide the PBNs. Victor and Eva *only* had the trustee bank as their contribution to the business transaction. With his "great" international contacts, Victor claimed he would soon find the PBNs.

Meanwhile, Victor Cruz. being the "financial whiz" that he claimed to be in the past, *conspired* with the distinguished Monaco lawyer, to create a *secret contract* between them and the bank, which gave Cruz and Eva about $33 million *additional* interest from the complex deal, over the expected twenty year period. This private agreement was hidden from Mr. Bostan.

One evening while Mr. Bostan left to copy some documents, intoxicated Victor started boasting about how he increased their profits by "his clever scheme." Vincent was shocked by this deception.

"Why do you want to cheat Bostan out of additional profits? Didn't you learn anything while you were in jail?"

"If he's stupid, why shouldn't we gain from his ignorance," was Victor's absurd reply. "What's your problem, Vince? You're going to get your share of the extra profits."

"Why screw this guy? He presents you with a fantastic opportunity, and agreed to share the commissions equally, didn't he," Vince responded angrily.

"Look, there are profits being distributed to other sources by him in the pay-orders," Victor said. "See here's the listed names for the final distribution of the funds."

"Those people are involved in the deal. He's giving them their share of the profits," Vincent argued. "Why do you want to screw-up this business just because you're greedy? A small slice of a very large cake is much better than none at all."

Bostan was not as stupid as Victor thought. He got out his pocket calculator and discovered for himself that Victor was trying to take most of the "cream" from the cake. Vincent told him nothing of their private conversation that evening, until he discovered the deception game that Victor was playing for himself. He became very angry. "You don't screw with a Turk!"

Later that evening while sharing coffee, he asked Vincent, "Why do they have to be so greedy and try to screw me?"

"I don't understand Victor's mentality. That bastard is gaining a fortune yet he wants more. And they offered me 33% of their profits," Vince explained.

"Thirty-three percent, is that what they said? They told me that they would give you about $100,000 for your services," he revealed.

Mr. Bostan did not have to cancel the financial transaction since the bank director refused to transact the deal, the next day for other reasons. Perhaps they checked with *Interpol* and discovered Victor's record. Maybe the director of the bank became apprehensive because Eva's lawyer changed the parameters of the transaction once too often. The bank canceled a critical meeting at the *very last minute.* All seemed lost.

The bills began mounting. Vincent was holding the empty bag, once again. He paid the hotel bill for Bostan, since Victor and Eva had no money. He paid for the international phone calls and telexes.

He spent many late hours developing the agreements on his personal computer. All of these checks would ultimately bounce. There was barely enough money in the bank to pay the office rent which was one-month over-due. They were living on borrowed money. Vincent lived each day and night in fear of a knock on the door. He had to try to complete something to get out of this quicksand, this abysmal pit, and he was sinking deeper and deeper each day.

Vincent suddenly remembered Myram, that influential and remarkable woman from his CTS days. She was the Iranian ambassador's spouse and knew the presidents of most of the banks in Europe *personally*. A quick call was made to her in Milan. After a brief summary, Myram thought that she could arrange a speedy meeting with a *Liechtenstein*-banking executive. Liechtenstein is a very small tax-free country similar to Monaco, she explained. Vince was *ecstatic*.

Nearly 48 hours later, Vincent arranged to fly Bostan to meet the top executives of the Liechtenstein bank. They agreed to consider the transaction that Myram, the highly respected diplomat had briefly discussed with them. There was one small problem: Victor and Eva somehow found out about this new business relationship with Mr. Bostan. They were *furious*. They saw him going to Vincent's apartment. They correctly assumed that Vince might be helping Bostan save the business.

"Are you trying to steal this deal from us?" Victor demanded to know.

"Don't be so cynical! You know I don't know shit about such complex financial transactions," Vincent replied. "You're the expert, not me."

"Why was Bostan seen visiting your apartment?"

"He just asked me to type a few memos for him, that's all."

Mr. Bostan then told them: "I'm going to Lyons, France to see a friend." That was a distraction, since he knew Victor and Eva were out for *vengeance*. With Victor's secret agent connections, he might have the French police arrest him on contrived charges. However, Bostan was on his way to Liechtenstein early the next morning.

Meanwhile, Victor Cruz planned "a welcoming committee" for him in Lyons. They were all completely surprised when he did not show up.

Bostan agreed to pay Vincent, Victor's share of the profits from the deal and his good friend Myram would *guarantee* that he kept his promise. Anne and Vincent also agreed to pay Myram one million dollars for her *special* services, out of their share of the expected commissions. Vince would have to use his checkbook to cover this gamble, *again.*

That week the hotel manager called to ask about unpaid bills. Vincent sent him a "professional memo," faxed on distinctive company letterhead, taking "*full responsibility* for all expenses." Because Myram was an ex-diplomat's wife, the manager questioned nothing further. (Sometimes in life you are presented with a once in a lifetime opportunity, and you either go for it, or miss the chance to make it big, Vincent thought).

Mr. Bostan called Vincent to inform him "all large banks in Liechtenstein are tightly controlled by the 'Jewish Mafia.' They don't allow foreigners, *especially Turkish Arabs,* to do any big deals without their participation." (They did not expect this unforeseen snag).

Later Bostan called again: "I finally found a trustworthy Jewish lawyer that I used in the past who claims he has good connections with that bank. Naturally, he expects his 'piece of the cake,' which is *not* an insignificant slice."

The most difficult problem remained. How to conceal the name of the United Arab Emirates Prince, in Abu Dhabi? Because of the new international laws, all the bankers *demanded* to know the source of the funds, *in advance.* However, if they knew the name of the owners of the funds and the sending bank, *before* they signed a contract, they could easily cut Bostan and Vincent out of their commissions by circumventing the agents. It was a "Catch- 22" situation.

Eventually, after many hours of discussion, they solved this problem by using the name of a "respected European corporation" as the *account holder* (a temporary account). Anyone can "rent" certain corporate names temporarily for a fat fee. Victor was the one who taught Vincent that ingenious bit of craftiness.

Unbelievable, the multi-billion-dollar transaction was held up because the key bank executive was literally "out to lunch." He arrived back at his office too late to close the deal that day. The additional interest lost each day on the multibillion-dollar transaction was about $350,000. This is because the funds were frozen by the sending bank.

That was an extremely expensive lunch!

After two more days of wearisome administrative delays, the board of directors of the bank finally agreed to accept the transaction. The Senior Vice President in charge of the bank invited Bostan and Myram to a private dinner that night to "celebrate the deal." During dinner, the VP discussed "special fees" that he *expected* to be deposited in his private numbered account via the Pay Orders, when the funds were transferred. "A *confidential* contract would be ready in the morning for this "extra" part of the pact."

Mr. Bostan called Vincent to seek his approval to give up additional shares of their waning commissions. "Never did they expect it to be so difficult to transfer billions-of-dollars, which are *certified* by a world class prime bank, as: "good, clean and clear," Vincent said in disgust.

"We have no choice," Bostan explained. "We have to pay 'tribute' to complete this business. Actually, these *bribes* cost us less than that stupid lunch delay and the interest lost each day from any further delays."

The following morning, the contracts were signed and sealed. The "secret payoff" agreement was also "legalized." Finally, the Key Tested Telex (KTT) was sent that afternoon to "Call the funds."

Minutes later billions-of-dollars, in trances of hundreds-of-millions, began to flow into the new account. Bostan was *elated*. He promised to immediately sent Vincent part of his commissions. That money arrived just in time to save his ass from going back to jail. Weeks of frustration and living from hand-to-mouth were finally over.

No human being could experience such emotional highs and lows without enormous stress. Mr. Bostan had to see a doctor that very day. He experienced a minor heart attack the hour that the banking business was finally completed.

Monaco. Victor and Eva were kept in the dark. Somehow, they learned the news about the new financial deal and went berserk. They called Vincent. *"You bloody bastard,* we know how you went behind our backs and stole this business from us," was the sum and substance of their deranged phone conversation.

"You lost the business. I simply found a bank to do the deal after you lost it, because of your greed," Vincent said calmly.

"However, since it was your original contact, we have agreed to give you and Eva a 'finder's fee,' to maintain goodwill."

For all his intelligence, Victor Cruz was a man ruled by childish emotions. Vincent thought about this crazy situation. Victor screwed-up a business deal due to his own greed. How is it also possible for Eva, whom he trusted and cared for, treat him so harshly? Why does money *obliterate* close relationships between people? Somehow, he felt sorry for them. People like them may never find real joy or love, since they are so cynical of others, when the real distrust and hate is *within themselves*.

***

FATE & DESTINY

*"Love is our true destiny. We do not find the meaning
of life by ourselves alone - we find it with another."*

—Thomas Merton

Monaco. A special invitation arrived from Anne's very close girlfriend. "Vincent, do you have a tuxedo? My best friend's child is getting married. Prince Albert will be there. He is the godfather of the groom. Why shouldn't we go? It will be fun. Besides, you'll have an opportunity to meet the Prince of Monaco."

The reception was at the grand old Hermitage Hotel. Antique paintings covered the ceilings and walls with nude plump Nymphs, much like Rubens paintings. Flowers and candles were everywhere. Champagne was served on the terrace overlooking the clear blue-green sea. Every member of high society came to the reception. Women were dressed in fabulous gowns with beautiful adornments. The bride and groom arrived in a horse drawn carriage. It was as if they were back in the 18th century. The classical music was mostly Mozart and Bach with a few waltzes.

Princess Caroline arrived *without* her husband. She was thinner than Anne had remembered. She seemed apprehensive. Anne later introduced them. Vincent offered to light her cigarette. Her marriage was not going very well according to the local gossip. Maybe that was the reason for her nervous condition, they thought.

Anne and Vincent danced waltzes and fox trots all night long. Vincent finally met Prince Albert near the end of the reception. The Prince was surprisingly warm and congenial. They chatted for twenty minutes about the States, sports and the arts. The prince did not know that he was talking to the same Vincent Renaldo that wrote to him from his dungeon. Vince did not bring up the subject. Instead, they talked about all the speedboats parked in the harbor below.

Prince Albert explained that Monaco has boat races every year. Princess Caroline's husband is one of the top contenders. One of the boats began smoking as it was parking in the harbor after its initial trial run. A strange sign, he thought. Vincent started to advise the Prince about how Monaco could attract more technology companies to the Principality. He introduced him to his aide who took a few notes. (He really wanted to talk to Prince Albert about the need to improve his *bullshit justice system,* but thought that subject might not be appropriate at such a celebration).

Widespread rumors suggested that Prince Albert was gay. Everyone in the Principality seemed to be concerned, since he had taken over from his late father. They thought that Albert might make Monaco the "homosexual capital" of Europe. Vincent found those fears false. The prince had dated his friend from Norway, Mia. She did not find anything strange about his *sexual preferences.* Moreover, Prince Albert was linked to one of the infamous "sex queens." His photo with her was splashed all over the world. Cynics claimed his inner circle planned it to counter his actual sexual orientation. The popular press loves to spread gossip—*it sells magazines.*

It is not how much money you have—*it's whom you know* that counts in Monaco, and elsewhere. The media is controlled by the state. Any article or book not approved will result in the author or the publisher banned. There is one police officer for every five citizens in this small country. A file exists on every stranger who stays for more than a weekend. Phones are tapped in homes, businesses and hotels.

Monaco is an *absolute monarchy,* which means officials have the power to expel anyone, for whatever reason, without any right to appeal. Individuals and companies, Europeans and Americans, can be forced to leave the Principality on very short notice. For example, if you or your firm happens to get involved in any public scandal, guilty or not, you are promptly declared: *"persona non grata."* Then you must sell all your assets and leave immediately. If you have some powerful connections in the government, you might get your residency status extended. Now that Monaco is a member of the European Economic Community, perhaps the Prince might eliminate some of his outdated totalitarian policies and change their system of justice. He might also introduce a Bill Of Rights and bring Monaco into the modern world.

They arrived back at the villa a bit weary from the wedding reception, but buoyant. Vincent took a quick shower, while Anne slipped into her white bikini, with its dainty lace around the edges. She then put on a sheer white negligee and checked herself in the mirror. Vincent came out in his bathrobe and found Anne sitting on the couch with one of her long shapely legs hanging over the armrest. His earlier psychological problem, caused by the unfaithfulness of Eva, was now mostly over. He no longer needed any fantasy stories to arouse him. The remedy: unconditional love!

"Vincent, I told you what I planned to do to you when I got you home," she said. "Didn't I? Come here!" She reached up, opened his robe and pulled him to the couch. As they kissed tenderly as his robe fell to the floor. She took complete control over his body—he willing surrendered to her onslaught. She drove him crazy with her meticulous delicate touching, before their bodies finally came together in precise rhythmic movements. They slept snuggled together in absolute bliss.

Anne and Vincent watched the boat races the following day. They had a fantastic view of the event. The Prince's aid arranged tickets for them. The speedboats raced at incredible speeds. *Suddenly* one of the boats hit a wave and began to sink. Divers jumped into the sea from the helicopter above. "It's the boat that Princess Caroline's husband was driving," someone shouted.

Hours later, they learned that he died. Was it *really* an accident? Vincent's thoughts returned to that ancient Monaco curse, by the rejected mistress of the Prince, during the 14th century. She put her curse on all future royalty of Monaco by declaring: *"... none will ever enjoy a happy marital relationship in the future."*

The historical record is amazing: Grace Kelly married prince Rainier III, and she died in 1982, in an automobile accident, after a turbulent marriage. Princess Caroline married Phillippe, which ended in divorce. Now her second husband died in a boat accident. John Gilpin died, 40 days after he married Princess Antoinette, her second marriage. Princess Charlotte, mother of Prince Rainier III, divorced the Prince de Polignac. Prince Albert's first wife, Lady Victoria Douglas Hamilton, fled from him, five months after the wedding. His second wife, Alice Heine, divorced him in the early 1900's. Grimaldi died leaving the kingdom to his elder son.

His nephew stabbed him to death, and later killed his younger brother. In 1604, the Savoyard of Savoy stabbed Hercule Grimaldi to death.

Perhaps it was just an *incredible* coincidence, but earlier news reports said, Princess Diana's lover, the wealthy playboy, Dodi Fayed, jilted another lover by breaking his engagement to her, some weeks earlier. Then Dodi bought the Princess a special antique diamond engagement ring, which was **part of the curse,** from a jeweler under the "Patronage of the Sovereign Prince of Monaco." Hours after she accepted that "Tell-Me-Yes" ring, both died tragically, in an automobile accident in Paris.

The family of the Sovereign Prince of Monaco had a very long history of rivalry, intrigue and incredible misfortune. Now *another tragic chapter* was unfolding before our very eyes. The lesson is clear: **No matter how high your station in life, it cannot protect you from your ultimate destiny.**

***

TRANSFORMATION

What you are supposed to do when you don't like a thing is change it. If you can't change it, change the way you think about it."

—Maya Angelou

The people that influenced Obama during his earlier life include his stepfather in Indonesia, where he studied the Islamic faith, until the age of ten. (His middle name is "Hussein"). Frank Marshall Davis, a well-known communist, was his teenage mentor in Hawaii, who indoctrinated him in communist ideology. At Columbia University, Obama studied under the Palestine activist, Edward Said, a fervent critic of America, who exposed him to ideas about "anti-Colonialism."

Said claimed America had replaced Britain, France and Germany as the "global imperialist power" after World War II. (As president, he later made a speech about 'American Colonialism'). Obama's teacher at Harvard was Roberto M. Unger, an *extreme leftist* revolutionary. Unger called for a coalition of countries—supported by progressives—to reduce the influence of America. Those countries were China, Russia, and Brazil; they would lead the anti-American coalition, *'transforming American Colonialists.'* Obama made speeches promoting such claims in Cairo and Europe. (See the Appendix).

Obama's later mentors in Chicago were revolutionaries, like Saul Alinsky, and Professor Bill Ayers, co-founder of the Underground Weatherman fanatics. Rev. Jeremiah Wright (who preached hatred of all white people) was Obama's neighbor and teacher for twenty years. Such radical ideologies had to have some influence on anyone's thinking. Later, President Obama surrounded himself with people in his administration who followed his *"Transformation"* policies. What has President Barack Hussein Obama *actually done* that supports such radical beliefs and ideology?

President Obama made a major speech in Cairo Egypt and Europe that discredited America's moral and superior role in the world. (See the Appendix). He gave military aide and support to the terrorist Brotherhood in Egypt, during that bloody revolution. He lied to Americans about the causes of Benghazi, two months *before* his reelection in 2012. (Including the threat of Russia, which he discounted strongly, while debating Romney). He lied about Obamacare: "You can keep your doctor," and he substantially changed that law, without approval by Congress. He failed to protect the U.S. border with Mexico.

He failed to support America's energy needs, which would have made us less dependent on Middle East oil, thus weakening America economically and strategically. He reduced the size and capability of the U. S. army, by 25 percent, and significantly cut the military budget. He made a deal with our enemies, Al Qaeda and Iran, at a time of war, and freed Al Qaeda prisoners from Guantanamo, who would later kill Americans, once again.

Finally, Obama "pre-announced," and forced the United States to pull most of its military forces from Iraq by 2011, and from Afghanistan in 2016. That decision left a "serious power vacuum" for terrorist forces to fill. It meant that eleven years of war, the shedding of American blood (4,500 dead soldiers, and tens-of-thousands wounded), and a trillion dollars of treasure, was squandered by this unquestionable irresponsible action by President Obama, and Secretary of State, Hillary Clinton.

The Obama (and Bush) administrations did not realize that they were dealing with "Tribes," not "Societies or Nations." These tribes, which consist of interrelated families, and cultures with different traditions, were not ready to become "Societies or Democratic Nations." Extremist terrorist elements, such as the Shia jihadists from Iran, and ISIS (Sunni fanatics), ultimately filled that huge vacuum. President Obama *naïvely produced* ISIS, by creating this Iraqi (and later Syrian) power vacuum. Both terrorist groups were *incompatible,* in terms of religion and culture, and hated each other for centuries, and all "infidels" from the West. Russia supported the Iranians and Syrians, while Saudi has supported the *majority* Sunni Muslims, with oil money, in this ever escalating, disastrous conflict.

Unless one dealt with *each tribe,* one would never understand their inter-relationships, traditions, fears, and objectives.

As the threat from extremist Sunni militants in western Iraq escalated, Prime Minister Nuri Kamal al-Maliki (Iranian Shia ally) asked the Obama administration to carry out airstrikes against *known* Sunni (ISIS) staging areas. Obama rebuffed Iraq's appeals for a military response. He felt that ISIS Sunni forces were 'only a small group of amateurs,' and that they might cause parliament to change the Prime Minister. Moreover, Obama was reluctant to open a new chapter in a conflict that *he insisted was over,* when he withdrew U.S. forces from Iraq (except for a 10,000-man training force).

The swift capture of Mosul by ISIS militants (Sunni extremists) has underscored how conflicts in Syria and Iraq have converged into one widening regional insurgency, with fighters coursing back and forth through porous borders between the countries, and Iran. Kurds in the north, after a hundred years of conflict, finally established Kurdistan, next door to the Turkey.

"Iraqi officials at the highest level said they had requested manned and unmanned U.S. airstrikes against ISIS camps in the Jazira desert," said Kenneth M. Pollack, a former C.I.A. analyst and National Security Council official. Experts claim that American military action could be helpful if Mr. Maliki takes steps to make his government more inclusive. "U.S. military support for Iraq could have a positive effect, *but only if it is conditioned on Maliki changing his behavior within Iraq's political system,"* Mr. Pollack said. "He has to bring the Sunni community back in, agree to limits on his executive authority, and reform Iraqi security forces to make them more professional."

In a speech, Susan E. Rice, Mr. Obama's National Security Adviser, said that the American effort to buttress Iraq's forces had been effective. "The United States has been fast to provide necessary support for the people and government of Iraq," she said, in remarks at the Center for New American Security in Washington. ***That was a totally false statement—it was clearly a lot of bullshit!***

The rapid deteriorating situation in Iraq was not what the Obama administration anticipated when it withdrew the last troops in 2011. Why not one might ask? Obama had the military "sticks" and financial "carrots" to *demand* a new "Status of Forces" (SOF) agreement" with Maliki. The truth is that Obama would not go against his "election promise," to get out of Iraq, ***no matter what the*** *consequences. His huge ego dictated strategy, and he saw this disagreement a valid justification for getting out of Iraq prematurely.*

In a March 2012 speech, Antony J. Blinken, Mr. Obama's Deputy National Security Adviser, proclaimed: "Iraq today is less violent than at any time in recent history."

***

Full Circle. After experiencing the tragic boat accident and thinking about the ancient Monaco curse, Vincent could not sleep that night. His mind concentrated on his own life, which had come **full circle,** from where he started years earlier. It is incredible and ironic how his destiny had changed. The extraordinary lesson from his experiences became clearer: Be careful what you wish or pray for—you just might get what you ask.

Vincent needed something more in his life. He wanted challenges—an adventure of some kind—and real passion in his life. He now understood that feelings are *more than moods;* it is a whole way of being; it is what you are born with; you cannot invent it. Passions incline us to act, or not to act, to that which is felt or imagined. Passions are a *natural* part of our human psyche. They ensure the connection between life of the senses and the mind. Passions are good, *only* if that which is loved, is good.

He received all that he wished for—*and much more.* He experienced incredible challenges, wild adventures, and misadventures. Vincent's bizarre experiences were more than he bargained for. What he was searching for was passion of the flesh. What he finally found was: "passion of the spirit, the soul." He was looking outside for something that was always inside.

On Saturday afternoon, Vincent and Anne went to confession at St. Charles Church. Later, during lunch Anne said, "You know you should go back to your wife, Susan. You are still married to her, 'in the eyes of God.' France and Monaco are not good for you, Vince. You are *'out of your shoes'* here. The language, the culture, the way of living and doing business is foreign to you. Please Vincent, go back to her ... and I will be happy—knowing that you are happy," she pleaded.

Vincent *finally* told Anne the *real reason* for his divorce from Susan: "Anne, I didn't get a divorce for sexual reasons, as important as that is, or for any other foolishness. The truth is that seven years ago, Susan gave birth to our third child, *prematurely.* The doctor told me, *privately,* that the drugs she took for her depression caused this untimely birth. As head nurse, she had access to drugs and started taking them for her condition, *without* any doctor's advice. The premature death of our boy *totally devastated me.*

While giving birth, the doctor discovered a growth inside her and removed her reproductive organs, without my knowledge or approval. After that dreadful experience, I just could not give myself to her anymore. Our intimate life together was finished. She was barren, and I needed, I wanted another child."

Anne completely understood. She hugged and kissed him. "Vincent, why didn't you tell me sooner?"

"It was too personal to share with anyone until now. The doctor treating her told me she was *extremely vulnerable.* She might take her own life if she knew the real reason for the death of our premature baby."

"My darling, please try to understand. All I want is what's best you."

The measure of her love was what she was willing to *do* for it, what she was willing to give up for it. Anne only wanted what was good for him—even if he would not be part of her future. Vincent finally understood that love is *not* just a feeling, or to will what is good for the person, but far more important, to do something about it. *Love requires action.* True love is unselfish, unconditional. (What was remarkable is that Anne was willing to sacrifice *everything* for "her man," even her own happiness). She fit the true meaning of love, which was his *kind of love.*

Susan somehow appreciated the craziness Vincent went through, even though he caused her great pain and suffering. She wrote to him some weeks earlier. Susan's loving words tormented his soul. Her closing words: *"…Vincent, I will always welcome you back, because I still love you so very much. The children also miss you terribly. Please come home my darling. We need you here."*

He showed the letter to Anne. After she read it, she said, "The only constant in life is *change*—we both changed.

Our temperament, our feelings, our habits changed. "Vincent darling, we cannot build our happiness on the unhappiness of others."

It was a cold winter evening, unusually chilly for *Cap Ferrat,* in February. Vincent put some logs on the fireplace in the villa. They watched the crackling fire silently wrapped in each other's arms. They had never been closer, never more tranquil, nor did they communicate more profoundly, *without* any need for words. The flickering fire in the dark room made them sleepy. Anne came into the bed next to him still dressed. "Why don't you undress?" he asked. "Are you still cold?"

Anne began to speak in a low whisper, bringing forth a meaning in each word never before revealed. "No darling, I'm not cold. It's because even though I want you so very much, my dearest, I do not want to tempt you. We both confessed our sins to The Lord in church today. We are now reconciled with Him. I want this night together for us to remain *forever,* in this state of grace."

Never did Vincent feel such peace, such contentment and serenity as Anne finally fell asleep in his arms. As he looked at the golden-hair woman that slept so peacefully in his arms, he prayed silently as the faint glow of sunrise began to appear on the horizon. Vincent thanked God for saving him, for forgiving him, for teaching him the true meaning of love.

It was dawn in *Cap Ferrat.* Birds began singing in the trees. There was a pleasant movement in the air from the sea beyond. Scarcely a wind disturbed this lovely day. They had made a decision that would change their lives *forever.*

"God is understanding and merciful," Vincent told Anne, as they kissed warmly and tenderly at the airport. Her face broke into a radiant smile. They could not control the tears of joy and sorrow that flowed down their faces. It was the great joy of discovering the *true meaning of love,* and deep sorrow, knowing that they would never be together ever again.

***

WHISTLE-BLOWERS

"Letting go means to come to the realization that some people are a part of your history, but not a part of your destiny."

—Steve Maraboli

It was not just about the preventable death of the ambassador and three other gallant Americans. It is not just about why help was not sent to save them, or where President Obama was all that time. The important issue and real scandal is, what was really going on in Benghazi? Why was Ambassador Stevens there in the first place, with very little security? Experts believe that Stevens was running guns from Libya, through Turkey, to the "good rebels" in Syria. However, many turned out to be Al Qaeda or associated terrorist rebels. Some thought that Stevens was also trying to retrieve the more serious weapons through Benghazi. Al Qaeda then, *took him out!*

Whistle-blowers claim that Ambassador Stevens was in Benghazi to buyback Stinger missiles from Al Qaeda. Stingers are capable of downing military or civilian aircraft. Not the weapons you want in the hands of terrorists. This gunrunning operation was *not* being done through the CIA, but through Hillary Clinton's State Department. CIA did *not* want to provide such weapons to the terrorists, but she authorized it. (Hillary would never do anything without Obama's specific approval, however).

The whistle-blowers asserted that CIA Director General David Petraeus' "affair" was leaked to silence him about such "clandestine" operations. There were also reports that General Carter Ham, head of AFRICOM (Africa Command) "Special Ops" team, could have been sent to Benghazi in 2-3 hours. He was ordered by someone in the White House *not* to send the troops to rescue the Ambassador.

All this happened on September 11, 2012, two short months before the presidential election. Any exposure of the "real facts" would have *clearly jeopardize Obama's reelection chances*. Former Secretary of DOD Leon Panetta, publicly stated that he had only one meeting with Obama, and did not see or hear from him again. Obama had to be as far away from this thing as possible. Nevertheless, if Hillary Clinton knew what was really happening, then *Obama certainly knew*.

These four men were sacrificed to cover-up this secret buyback of weapons operation. President Obama and Secretary of State Hillary Clinton then played their roles perfectly, as the "grief-stricken" leaders, during the nationwide media funeral of the four murdered victims, to gain further voter sympathy. *It worked perfectly!*

***

CHANGING OF THE GUARD

President Obama's second term began with many of the key players retired or replaced. Hillary Clinton got out just in time to save her exposed butt for her 2016 run for election. Her *false testimony* about the murders of the Benghazi Ambassador and his aides, and the Middle East crisis that developed did not hurt her, and she had no viable contender for the Democratic presidential race, except for extreme socialist Senator Sanders.

President Obama replaced Hillary Clinton with John Kerry, who has the ability to make Obama's crap smell good. John has that special political knack with words. John Brennan, CIA director, and one of the leading men in this new cast of characters for the next saga. He has decades of direct front-line experience, and clearly knows how to cover ones' ass. He described the Obama focus as being about "extremists," not "Islamic jihadists."

Nevertheless, America was at the threshold of a war with *Islamic jihadist,* in Afghanistan, Egypt, Iran, Iraq, Liberia, Nigeria, Sudan, and Syria, who were spreading their venom of hate throughout the region. The UN is useless in this kind of crisis since it is two-thirds of its members are Muslims. Russia and China supports Iran and Syria and have veto power in the UN.

Obama and his top advisers, most of whom lack direct military experience, decided to let the Islamic jihadists kill each other, even though hundreds-of-thousands, especially in Syria, are innocent civilians.

- President Obama fired or replaced experienced generals, mainly those who did not accept his Middle East policy of "leading from behind."
- Obama ignored Iranian cries for independence and help, during the "Green Party Revolution" and Iranian government voting fraud of 2009.

- The administration sent tanks and M16 jets to Egypt, paid for with U.S. taxpayer money (borrowed from China).
- Obama forced troop departures from Afghanistan too early, leaving a token force of about 10,000, which the Taliban easily neutralized, thus exposing nuclear-armed Pakistan to further instability.
- Finally, Obama failed to demonstrate genuine support for Israel during this critical time, leaving America's only major ally in the Middle East open to multiple enemies from all sides.

So far, the total death toll in Syria, with standard weapons, exceeded 300,000, mostly innocent civilians. If Syria's poison gas got into the wrong hands, like Hezbollah, this figure would rise many fold.

* * *

Connecticut. "Mr. Renaldo, we didn't tell you everything about our covert operation," Hanson from the CIA stated.

"What else is new? Does the CIA ever reveal the *whole truth?*"

"Let's not get into truth or consequences games. Your friend is now in Syria."

"Who's that? What friend?"

"Victor Cruz, your former partner in Monaco."

"How do you know that?"

"A Lebanon diplomat informed us." "Shit! They must be desperate to use that big asshole."

"Hold on. Mr. Cruz has become a major arms dealer in the region."

(After Victor's release from jail, the State department arranged to "clean" all Interpol criminal records pertaining to Victor Cruz. The United States government was paranoid about his elephant memory concerning illegal DEA activities in Columbia and other sordid CIA secrets).

Vincent thought about the true meaning of Victor's last name, "Cruz," which means *"Cross,"* in English. Victor tried to get him and everyone else he had contact with, nailed to his cross. It is not just winning that counts in business and human affairs—*it is how you play the game.* What good is it to win the game by stepping on others?

You then lose your family, your friends and your immortal soul.

***

Washington. Republicans were pushing the Administration to establish a "Safe Haven" for opponents inside the Syrian regime.

Senator Lindsey Graham said, "I want an action plan to ensure that the chemical weapons are secured after Assad is disposed. We should neutralize the Syrian air force, tanks and the war ends pretty quickly then."

Senator Ben Cardin, Foreign Relations (D-MD) weighed in saying, "I talked with the Syrian opposition and they are clearly looking for more leadership from the U.S. We are providing nonlethal aid. Question is whether it is getting to the right people and the right amount of support in order to accelerate the end of the Assad regime."

Here is the Foreign Relations spokesperson saying he does not know if the aide we are sending is going to the right people and in the right amount. Maybe if we had [some] boots on the ground or utilized our troops and advisers in Jordan to oversee our aide, we could discriminate who was who. Then one would be in position to extract chemical weapons for later disposal.

"It would be a major mistake to put American troops in Syria," wrote former House speaker, Newt. "No one in the region wants us invading yet another country. None of our allies' desire our strength diverted from Iran. There is no practical mission [the] American forces could accomplish without a very large commitment.

"America has three practical interests in Syria:

"[First] of the highest urgency is keeping the Syrian chemical weapons stockpile from getting into the hands of terrorists. Imagine the Boston bombing with a chemical weapon and you can see why containing the Syrian chemical weapons is a very high, practical value for the United States.

"Second, it would be helpful in containing and undermining Iranian power if the Assad dictatorship (its only major ally is Iran) were to fall.

"Third, there is significant risk in having millions of refugees destabilize Jordan and weakened Turkey.

"None of these interests justify a major American military campaign in Syria. Syria's neighbors have an even greater interest in ending the war and controlling the chemical weapons. Israel, Turkey, Jordan, and Saudi Arabia all have a stake in making sure chemical weapons do not show up in their country.

"The United States can provide intelligence, technical support, and in a worst case air power to destroy the sophisticated and massive Syrian anti-aircraft defenses (built with Russian support to stop Israel). If the [Syria's] neighbors are not sufficiently worried to act, however, the United States should not be drawn in to acting for them.

"We are in a period of retrenchment on military spending. Adding a third major war would lead to either massive increases in defense spending or a collapse of the Pentagon as an effective system. The 'red line' President Obama established about chemical weapons has to be a red line for the neighbors and for the world community. It cannot be simply a red line for the American military.

"We should ponder the lessons of Iraq and Afghanistan and think long and hard before launching our third major war in 12 years. No US troops in Syria is a pretty good place to draw the line."

***

SHIFTING RED LINES

Does anyone think that the Iranians are not watching Obama's lackluster inaction of *"leading from behind,"* and his words to Syria? This would be a profound example of how seriously they perceive Obama will handle their "red line." Will his ambivalence allow them a test, as well? Israel is also watching. They have their own "red line" boundaries, but are far more serious about carrying out promises, and their enemies know that well.

What does this mean now? Ultimately, the U.S. will need boots on the ground. American Troops are the only ones "qualified and trusted" enough to pick up, dispose of and make sure the deadly chemicals do not fall into the hands of Al Qaeda. If we do not dispose of them, then who gets them?

Syria's abundant chemical weapons is a known fact. Their arsenal contains Sarin, Mustard Gas, Cyanide and VX. Syria has at least 600 warheads capable of delivering chemical weapons. While the UN special teams removed most of the deadly chemicals, about 10% are in secret caves. Israel describes Syria's Chemical Weapons arsenal as "The largest in the world." CIA Estimates Syria produces 100 tons of chemical agents per year.

How does Obama feel about Syria's use of chemical weapons? He has repeatedly warned them it would "not be in their best interest," in speeches on: August 20, he said, "A Red line for us is seeing a bunch of chemical weapons being utilized or moved around." On Dec 3, he said, "Use of chemical weapons would change my calculus." On March 20, he announced, "The broader point is, once we establish the facts, use of chemical weapons will be a game changer. If you make the mistake of using these weapons there will be consequences. *You will be held accountable."*

***

Iran. The Iran military test-fired Shahab III, an intermediate ballistic missile in order to intimidate Israel and Iraq. President Vladimir Putin in Moscow formalized a "Strategic Alliance" with Iran's proxies (Hezbollah) and Syria, who remain the principal threats to peace in Iraq and Israel. Israel intercepted at sea a shipment of arms destined for its Hezbollah enemies.

Afghanistan, Iraq, Iran, Libya, Pakistan, and Syria are battlegrounds in an international conflict that will define America's geopolitical future. This conflict pits the West against an emerging alliance of many oil-rich dictatorships who are working together to reverse the trends of globalization. One of their prime objectives is toppling neighboring pro-Western democracies.

Russia and Iran are acting very much as Japan, Italy and Germany did in the mid-1930s, when each took advantage of each other's aggressive moves to extend their own regional powers at the expense of democracy. The chessboard of traditional competitive geopolitics is back with a vengeance. Pakistan and North Korea are the main sources for Iran's nuclear capability. China and Russia is also principal UN obstacles to international sanctions, with their ultimate veto power.

Between them, Mr. Putin and Tehran's mullahs clearly aim to control access to every major source of oil energy from the western end of the Persian Gulf to the Caspian Sea. Putin also temporally cut off gas flow to Ukraine to pressure them to come under greater control of Russia, although he does not want to take over the country since it owes about $35 billion and is effectively bankrupt. These dictatorships are recently flush with cash due to earlier rising oil prices; and they want regional domination.

All openly observe a model of government that is authoritarian in opposition to Western market-oriented economies and representative democracy. All run economies built on mafia-style capitalism. All denounced U.S. "Imperialism," and evidently hoped that the American reelection of Obama will help to bolster their geopolitical plans. *That is exactly what happened with the reelection of Obama as President.*

Despite Russia's nuclear arsenal, none of these states posed a *direct* military threat comparable to the Cold War Soviet Union especially during 1959-79. For all their bluff and bluster, Russia and Iran have a very tenuous position in the world; for all their oil wealth, their economies remain fundamentally weak and unstable. They are all highly-dependent on the price of oil remaining at $60 or greater.

A broad strategy of targeted economic sanctions and multilateral diplomacy backed by U.S. military power, together with a determined effort to push down oil prices by expanding supply and strengthening the dollar—can introduce sober realism into the strategy of this evil alliance and force them to realize how vulnerable their money and power really is. Will Obama's administration really make use of their advantages? The answer Obama will leave to the next administration to solve.

***

TRUMP'S TRIUMPH

Amazingly, in spite his numerous negatives; Donald J. Trump became the 45th President of the United States of America. Trump's first term was impressive. President Trump's accomplishments included significant economic growth, especially for minorities, women, and stock market. Preventing a North Korea war. Profitable trade deals with China, South Korea, Canada & Mexico, Japan, among others. Restrictions placed on Russian, Iranian, and Chinese trade. Significantly improved military budgets and weapons to protect the peace. Elimination of ISIS and key terrorist leaders in the Middle East. Build 400 miles of walls to keep out illegal immigrants, drugs and terrorists. Eliminated many excessive regulations to help small business thrive. Middle East peace treaties with Israel and three former adversaries. America became the leading world supplier of petroleum products. Three new Supreme Court Justices appointed and approved. That was clearly an enormous achievement in four years. However, the Covid-19 Pandemic destroyed the Trump economy.

Social Media presented endless reports on pandemic cases, when the *true measure* is death rates as a percentage of regional or country populations, not simply the number of cases (more testing means more cases). Dishonest reporting claimed that the Trump administration did *nothing* to contain the virus and solve the pandemic. *That was outrageously false!* The truth is that the Trump administration took abrupt action, stopped travel from China and Europe, and created a highly skilled task force to get equipment, a vaccine and effective treatments for this contagious virus. An effective vaccine was produced and mass distributed beginning in December 2020. ***That is amazing fast for any vaccine development and delivery!***

Trump's re-election process began with Media propaganda. More than 92% were false or misleading reports against Trump.

In the city of Philadelphia, ***birthplace of the American Constitution,*** poll watchers could not look at 600,000 ballots, which is against state law. Democratic attorneys filed hundreds of legal challenges to change State election laws and rules, before and after the election "game" began, such as: (1) Demands to eliminate voter signatures, and matching requirements. (2) To expand time limits beyond Nov. 3$^{rd.}$ (3) Limit poll watchers to observing ballots at a six feet distance. State judges overruled some state statutes and approved other changes, *after* the ballot verification and counting process began.

Democratic election officials, in general, used the pandemic as an "excuse" to keep pole watchers six feet away from seeing ballots, which is crazy, since pole watchers could not see anything at that distance. A key issue was *"chain of custody of ballots."* In some states, such as Nevada, Wisconsin, and Michigan, there was no chain of custody. A verified ballot review and recount was required in 4-5 states. This is but a few examples of apparent widespread voter fraud. (The Supreme Court needs to act quickly to fix this problem for future elections).

Nevertheless, Republicans (GOP) kept 50% control of the Senate, with Mitch sharing leadership with Schumer, and the Democrats would have difficulty get anything meaningful accomplished in the House for the next two-four-years.

Meanwhile, documented *"facts"* about Joe Biden's political influence to enrich his family with Chinese, Russia and Ukraine business connections went *unreported.* Twitter and Facebook prevented distribution of the *"truth"* on public media networks. Yet, these same news sources allowed "false stories" about the President's connections with Russia. (One may recall retired Navy officer Tony Bobulinski told Fox's Tucker Carlson that the Biden family hoped to avoid scrutiny over their web of financial ties to foreign influence peddling with two simple words: ***"Plausible Deniability."***)

Although President Trump received about 75-million votes, he lost the re-election to Joe Biden, due to illegal ballots sent to millions of unqualified voters in five states, and *unproven* voter fraud. Finally, his speech to a crowd of supporters during the counting of the State elector votes caused a riot at the Capitol in D.C. that tarnished Trump's image for the future. Then the DEMs impeached him again over this insurgence. (If truth be told, he never encouraged supporters to attack the Capitol).

The <u>second impeachment trial</u> of former President Donald J. Trump kicked off, about a month after he was <u>charged by the House</u> with ***incitement of insurrection*** for his role in allegedly egging on a violent mob that stormed the Capitol on Jan. 6 2021.

However, the Capitol Police, DHS, and the FBI *all failed to inform* the president or vice president that rioters with weapons were planning to attend the President Trump's rally on Jan 6, and they ***intentionally*** failed to send defense forces to protect the Capitol and Congress. That would seem to represent a "conspiracy" by ***multiple democratic*** leaders to ignore prior known threats, with the probable motive of letting the riots happen to damage Ex-President Trump's future election prospects. *They succeeded!*

Acting U.S. Attorney Michael Sherwin (Wall Street Journal 01/11/21) said "Inflaming emotions isn't a crime. The president didn't mention violence, much less provoke it." The WSJ on Feb. 9 headline stated, **Capitol Riot Warnings Weren't Acted On**. 'This was a systemic failure' said Frank Taylor retired Air Force general' who led DHS's intelligence branch from 2014 to 2017. Washington D.C. Mayor Bower on Jan. 5 also urged federal agencies ***not*** to send additional forces without consulting [her] local police.

Attorney Schoen offered a clear rationale for why a former president, should not stand trial, arguing, "it would *set a dangerous precedent* where any former official could be punished after leaving office for having carried out his or her duties."

If Trump does not overdo his (rightful) indignation against "Democratic Dirty Tricks" (DDT), he may have another opportunity to "rise from the ashes," and become the America's leader once again. That *assumes* he maintains his mental and physical health, and does not get involved in any legal hassles. By 2024, the country should be extremely weary of the "Sleepy Joe" administration, especially if he fails to address economic, social and international challenges.

Then again, who can really predict the future of world events?

***

Connecticut. Vincent Renaldo returned to America. Victor's student became the master; a professional not only in how to do business but what is far more important, the kind of people and business *traps to,* *avoid.* It is not just winning that counts in business and human affairs—*it's how you play the game!* What good is it to win the game by stepping on others, and lose your family, your friends, and most important, your immortal soul.

Vincent learned many painful lessons from his bizarre experiences. After years of marriage, an affair occurs in life. There are innumerable reasons; no two cases are the same. It might be a mid-life crisis that middle-aged men experience, or the lack of sensitivity to the needs and feelings of your spouse. It might be the dull routines of daily life. It is often about sexual fantasizing: "The grass always looks greener in other pastures." *It is a total illusion!* The mythical new lover makes you deaf, dumb, and blind to the actual truth about your immortal life and ultimate sanctity.

Like a modern day *"Count of Monte Cristo,"* that old story by Dumas, Vincent was at the pinnacle of his life. He had a loving family, a good home and a small fortune, many friends and social status. Then, *all came crashing down!* He found himself broken- hearted by the betrayal of his fictional lover, falsely accused and imprisoned in an ancient dungeon—isolation from the world. The broken man was deprived of all his basic human needs—fresh air and sunshine, companionship and love, *without hope.*

Then a miracle happened! The confessed sinner, the confined prisoner was given another chance, a second opportunity to rise from his deep abyss, to become reconciled again with his loving wife and the Lord. From this chaos, this disorder, he learned the true meaning of love—which was dormant within him—a love that burst forth renewing all his life forces. He finally found real peace and tranquility. Music was more melodious, food tasted better, flowers seemed far more beautiful, sunrises and sunsets were fantastic. These basic things of life are so different—when there is true love, which is always *unselfish sacrificial love.*

After more than a half a century of terror and wars, the Jews of Israel and Arabs, the Syrians and Iranians, with Russian backing, have not learned how to settle their disputes at the conference table. There was no possibility of long-term peace and coexistence between Israel and its regional neighbors. The parties to peace plans must realize that bad deals lead to future hostilities.

Final history lesson: One should not make bargains with the devil!

A SOCIALISTIC PRESIDENCY

P resident Joe Biden, and his partner, Vice President Harris, were *partly* prevented from implementing their reckless socialistic plans, like the Green New Deal, Paris Climate Change funding, increasing Taxes, imposing Pro-Choice abortions on the population, restricting private schools, compromising religious freedom, and supporting Marxist BLM. Nevertheless, as Commander in Chief, Joe Biden and VP Harris policies got America into conflicts around the world, especially in the Middle East.

During President Obama's first term, Mr. Blinken became an assistant to the president and his principal deputy national security advisor. Blinken also chaired the forum for deciding foreign policy, helping shape policies on the Iran nuclear program and Afghanistan. After he won a second term, Obama nominated Blinken to become the deputy secretary of state. As the nation's number two diplomat, he helped determine the administration's timid response to Russia's invasion of Crimea, the failed global refugee crisis. He was responsible for rise of ISIS, and the war in Syria, as well as the failed attempts to recalibrate U.S. relationship with Asia and China.

Blinken recently spoke about the "sense of responsibility he feels" about the policy in Syria, saying all those who worked on it have *"to acknowledge that we failed, not for want of trying, but we failed" to prevent "horrific loss of life" (about 500,000) and massive displacement of refugees.*

Nevertheless, President Biden promotes a man, who admits he failed under Obama, to greater responsibility, as Secretary of State.

John Kerry was also a major failure, especially his Iran Nuke deal, as Obama's Secretary of State. He becomes a Cabinet-level official in the new Biden administration, *and* sits on the National Security Council. This marks the first time that the NSC will include an *official dedicated to climate change,* reflecting the administration's commitment to addressing this as a national security issue.

Kerry is another of Obama's cronies to get a significant position under President Joe Biden. In addition, Kerry's December 2019 *denial* of having any knowledge about Hunter Biden or Burisma is total B.S. It is inconsistent with the evidence uncovered by Senate Committees. John Kerry was clearly informed about Hunter Biden, Burisma and his stepson Heinz the day after Burisma announced Hunter Biden joined its board. Secretary Kerry's senior advisor sent him press clips and articles relating to Hunter Biden's board membership. This is yet another example of high-ranking Obama administration officials blatantly ignoring Hunter Biden's association with Burisma. *John Kerry is clearly a liar!*

Susan Rice gets to head the White House Domestic Policy Council for Biden. When Rice was Mr. Obama's National Security Adviser, she said that the American effort to buttress Iraq's forces had been effective. *"The United States has been fast to provide necessary support for the people and government of Iraq,"* in remarks at the Center for New American Security in Washington. *That was a false statement!*

Ms. Rice, who also served as Obama's UN ambassador, had been in the running to be Biden's vice president before Kamala Harris. If Rice had a more critical role, she would have faced opposition from Senate Republicans for her part in foreign policy screw-ups under Obama. Rice was then under fire for characterizing the 2012 deaths of four Americans including U.S. ambassador in Benghazi, Libya, *"as part of a spontaneous protest taken over by extremists rather than a premeditated terrorist attack."* That was a huge lie, which she said on five Sunday TV shows. Biden's team said that in her new role she will "turbocharge" Biden's agenda to "Build Back Better" American.

Thanks to former President Trump, America's military is much stronger before Biden can do any damage, such as planned budget cuts. As expected, they immediately tried to restore the Iran Nuke deal, and increase Islamic immigration, but the Senate did not approve it. President Biden's administration appears to be handicapped for the next four years.

***

Stamford, Connecticut. Vincent Renaldo was now more than one year back in Connecticut, with his loving and devoted wife, Susan.

He had told her about all of his crazy experiences, and many trials and tribulations. Vince confessed how foolish he was, especially how much he must have hurt her. They repeated their marriage vows once more at St. Mary's Church. (According to the civil law, they were divorced. In the eyes of God's Church, they were never divorced). Although Susan forgave him, without hesitation, and happily accepted his return, she was apprehensive about his true feelings for her. She knew that it would take time for the deep wounds of deception and abandonment to heal. As an RN dealing with mental, emotional, and physical ailments, she knew the healing process would be difficult. However, her faith was strong. She would certainly give it prayers and time to heal.

The children were college graduates, and all were doing well in the business world. They were alone for the first time in decades. They again renewed their love for each other, by doing the little things of daily life, like serving her coffee in bed in the morning, walking in the park holding hands, and anticipating each other's little needs. Susan received therapy, and was no longer dependent on drugs. She was also very busy with her nursing job at Stamford General. Vincent was mostly idle, except for a few Information technology-consulting jobs that did not fully cover expenses. He took this time to read some good books, while also catching up with world events.

A knock on the door awakened Vincent from his short summer nap. It was CIA Assistant Director Hanson. He was the handler Vince dealt with in Monaco, nearly two years ago. "Greetings, we understand you are looking for challenging opportunities?"

"How did you know that? I suppose that's a really dumb Question?"

"We need people with your intellect and skill set." He replied.

"Look, you must also know I have no fondness for Biden and his bullshit amateurs. They have the uncanny ability to make a bad situation worse."

"We agree—*unofficially!* That's why our special group needs people like you."

"If you feel that way, how can you work under those assholes?" Vince replied.

"Our operation is independent of control from the White House."

"Yeah, but you still report to that jerk, what's his name?"

"He's now retired. Look, it is what it is!"

"Let us cut the crap. What do you need?"

"We need your help in a special covert operation."

"What kind of operation? Let's not bullshit each other."

"I can't discuss your specific role at this stage. However, the deal is $100,000, plus a million dollar policy for your wife and kids. You have 24 hours to decide."

After Renaldo learned more about the dangerous mission, he demanded twice the initial offer, with fifty percent upfront. He would be a special member of the UN Aid team to help Syrian refugees. This "humanitarian" group would have special UN status with credentials, allowing them access to the battle zones between Syria, Lebanon and Turkey. Its code name was *"Hades."* Vincent would be going into a place comparable to *hell on earth.* Hanson agreed to double his compensation since it was other people's money, and the CIA calculated that he probably would not survive this risky mission.

All combat forces, including the Jihad radicals, should welcome them as non-political providers of essential medical and food supplies to their forces, *assuming* these bad people were civilized. Assumptions are very dangerous in this part of the Muslim world, especially for Vincent with his pale white ass and poor Arabic language skills.

The Mission: locate Syrian's nuclear Scuds and hidden stockpiles of poison gas (they concealed an estimated 10% of gas shells from UN inspectors). The team would try to obtain GPS locations for NATO Blockbuster bombs to destroy. One problem was that this deadly gas was allegedly in mobile missiles ready for battle. Vincent and his team, if they were somehow exposed, could not carry antibiotics to counteract this deadly poison.

***

INDECISIVENESS

"The risk of a wrong decision is preferable to the terror of indecision."

—Maimonides

President Obama's nuclear deal with Iran is widely considered a disaster by the conservative foreign policy establishment. The Trump administration pulled out of the deal in 2018, citing its inability to deter Iran's nuclear development and failure to discourage Iran's efforts to destabilize the Middle East through supporting terror groups and militias. Besides, the John Kerry foreign Iranian agreement is really a "treaty," that was never presented to the Congress for approval.

The Trump administration has taken a hard line against Tehran, enacting a "maximum pressure" campaign aimed at isolating Iran financially so that it will come to the table under more favorable circumstances for the United States. Special envoy for Iran Elliott Abrams said that Iran is in extremely poor economic condition. "A lot of money is tied up in various ways by our sanctions." The Biden administration would enable cash-strapped and isolated Iran to regain ground, especially in its nuclear program, a major area of concern for Jerusalem. The Iran deal's logic from the Obama-Biden years was clearly mistaken. President Joe Biden has said openly, that he "will go back to the nuclear agreement." If Biden stays with that policy, there will be a violent confrontation between Israel and Iran.

***

Damascus. Victor met Vincent at a Greek restaurant for a dinner of roast lamb and imported French wine. Hanson supplied Vince with "tools of the trade."

He had the latest undetectable miniature bugging devices, sleeping pills, and a secure satellite phone.

"How's your daughter, what was her name?" Vince inquired.

"Emily is fine, last time I saw her. She is better off with her mother. I gave Eva full custody of our child."

"Time has passed so fast. It good of you to let her mother bring up Emily."

"I'm not the fatherly type. Besides my crazy life is too risky." Victor explained.

"What business is possible in this poor war-torn country?"

"Don't let that fool you, lots of money can be made here. One only needs the right contacts and my expertise. Come let's have a few drinks at my place."

They drank and exchanged stories for hours. Vincent slipped a sleeping drug into Victor's wine when he went to the bathroom. About twenty minutes later, he was out cold. Vince planted bugging devices in strategic locations throughout the apartment and in later in Victor's car. Hanson's agents would be responsible for recording everything from now on. Vince then fell asleep on the couch. The next morning they had coffee together at the local sidewalk café. Victor tried to get him involved in his weapons for cash business schemes.

Five days later, the bugging paid-off. Victor Cruz could not keep his mouth shut. He bragged about his contacts and deals. That night, he drove to the secret weapons facility in the mountains of Syria. They searched his car but the guards could not detect the new, highly advanced GPS device.

***

Washington. The Crisis Management Group met throughout the week in the Situation Room, in the basement of the White House, monitoring information flowing from COBRA. It became essential for the CIA and Mossad to confirm the exact location of the Syrian Scud launching sites. Ground inspection of the Iran facility was not necessary since the intelligence community knew its underground silo location. Heavy truck traffic in the mountain region, in the Western section of Iran could not be concealed. Sensitive night sensors from more advanced satellites could detect a mouse in that area.

Since this was the western section of Iran and closest to Israel, the CIA assumed that Tel Aviv was their probable target, although assumptions can be erroneous and dangerous. United States aircraft had complete freedom to fly over Iraq, area near Iran without interference. Intelligence from detailed photos suggested that only a few of the new sixty thousand-pound "block buster" bombs would be necessary to eliminate these underground silos.

The situation in Syria was *completely different.* A covert ground team would have to go in to confirm particulars of the site and its topographic details. The clandestine team, under the command of Major Gideon and his comrade, Joshua of the Mossad, were requested by the United States to include Vincent Renaldo as part of the three-man team. Vince protested that he was not qualified for this part of the difficult mission. They ignored his protests. The goal: "to confirm the exact location and physical layout of the Scud facilities in the Syrian, while avoiding detection—*at all cost.*"

***

Major Gideon, a seasoned operative, was in overall commander of the operation. His leadership ability was proven in the Golan Heights War. Vincent and Joshua were the junior members of the crew in terms of field experience. Joshua's physical strength and electronics knowledge would be vital to the mission. Since much of the trip would be over desert and rocky terrain, camels would be the best means of travel until they reached the mountains. They would disguise themselves as Bedouin Arabs. Gideon spoke the local dialect. Joshua was fluent in the Arabic and Farsi. The only equipment they would carry were high-powered cameras equipped with special night vision capability, infrared detectors, some lethal pills, knives, and their expert black-belt skills.

The GPS device planted in Victor's car by Vincent, pinpointed the *probable* location for the Scud site in the southeastern region of Syrian near an old mine. Intense activity and movement at the site suggested that this could be the main facility. Normal mining movements provided excellent cover for camouflaged underground activities.

The top-secret three-man mission under code name *"Golden Fleece,"* entered Syria, about 150 miles south of the mine.

As they reached the mountain area some ten hours later, they climbed up about five thousand feet on foot, under the cover of night, to approach the suspected site. For inexperienced mountain climbers it was a difficult climb, especially in the darkness of night.

They approached the summit with extreme caution, until they emerged above the valley. They had to crawl the last few yards to the edge of the rise and looked down into the valley. "It must there," said Renaldo, as he pointed with his forefinger.

"Where?" asked Gideon.

"Look at that mining village. It looks to me to be unnatural. It is a perfect replica of a mountain peasant village. But it is heavily guarded."

The small village or hamlet included a barn, grazing sheep, and typical mud-brick houses with thatch roofs. "The hills nearby are probably alive with foot patrols. We had better not go down now. Can you do a survey of the area from our vantage point on this mountain Joshua?"

"Maybe ... I think so? We must find the main entrance to the mine, which is the most likely launching point. This place is so well camouflaged; you would never suspect anything abnormal from the air at 30,000 feet."

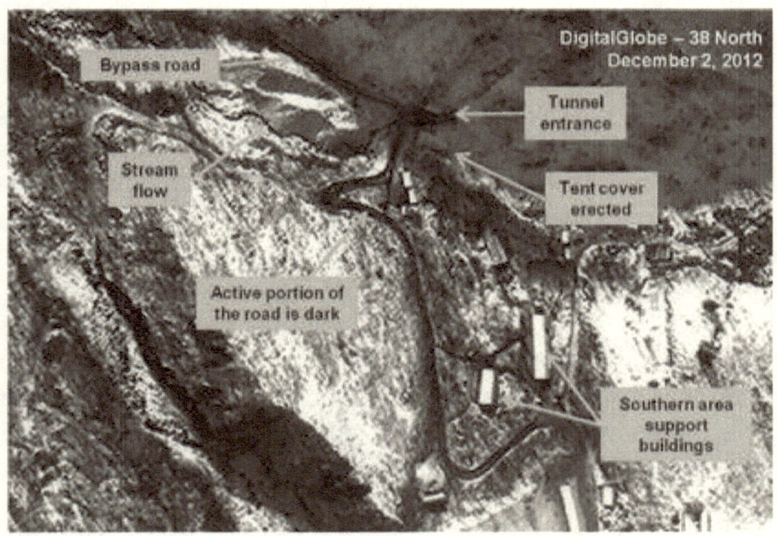

"There's the sucker! Those rail tracks lead into an underground cave. All they have to do is roll out the Scud on the tracks and launch it."

"Yeah ... that must be it! Gideon concluded. Notice how well that enormous boulder above protects the tunnel entrance. It would take a direct hit by at least a sixty thousand pounder to seal that huge cave."

Infrared scopes picked up the otherwise invisible motion sensors that encircled the area around the installation. Just then, trucks arrived loaded with liquid fuel, confirming that the enemy was *not* drilling for gold in the mines below. "Let's get a closer look and take some pictures," Gideon commanded.

Joshua found an excellent spot to set-up his gear. Dozens of telescoped close-up photos were taken. (They could not send the photos via satellite for fear of detection). An hour later, a special motor vehicle arrived with a large force of armed guards.

"Okay, we got what we want. Let's *get the hell out of here* before sunrise," Vincent insisted. "Those bastards could be ready for a launch in a matter of just a few days."

They started down the mountain using an old goat trail that was barely workable. As the team came around a cliff, *without warning* they came face-to-face with two patrol guards just a few feet apart from them. The Mossad agent reacted instinctively, instantly leaping at the surprised guards before they could ready their weapons. Gideon's fingers were on the guard's throat and squeezed. He would not let go. After a few minutes the eyes of the guard closed, his face went blue and then his tongue came out as his life ended. Joshua kicked the chest of the other guard. He fell crushing his skull and died instantly. They discarded both bodies down a deep crevice. Large rocks covered their remains making it look like an accident.

It was 4 AM. They had only two and half-hours to get down the mountain before sunrise. Patrols would be sent out at first light to search for their missing comrades. As the group rushed down the steep cliffs, Joshua lost his footing and fell about fifty feet. His right arm and leg were severely broken. He started coughing blood. Even if he could survive the accident, it would be impossible to carry him down the steep cliffs. Sunrise was only about an hour away. Joshua did not have to be reminded what each of the team members knew was *imperative.*

"Please tell Marcia that ... that I love her. Tell my children that their father gave his life for the security *and for peace ... for Israel.*" He said a short prayer in Hebrew. Then bit into his special capsule. Both said prayers over his body before they removed all traces of his gear and thoroughly covered his remains with stones and tree branches.

The sun came over the mountain as they finally reached their camels at the base of the mountain. They would take a southern route. A high-speed boat was waiting for them to cross into Saudi Arabia. They buried most of the equipment in the sand. The vital film was the only thing *indispensable.* Their UN credentials would give them passage beyond the Syrian border. A helicopter in Jidda was waiting and flew them immediately to the Saudi base. The film was quickly scanned and sent on to Israel and Washington via satellite for further analysis. Operation "Golden Fleece" had most of the proof and critical details needed to commence immediate operations.

* * *

Washington. It was ten o'clock when President Joe Biden entered the National Security Council conference room in the West Wing of the White House. All rose when he appeared in the doorway. There was a certain aura about the personage of the President; the implication of the extraordinary dimensions of the problems he bore, and of the frightening power that was his to command. These responsibilities made the holder of this office *unequaled* among men. "I thank you all for being here tonight," he said in a gentle, almost remorseful tone.

He took his place at the oval conference table. It was here that many vital decisions had taken place in the past: The Cuban Missile Crisis; the Iranian Hostage Crisis; the determination to end the Vietnam War; the decision to commence Desert Storm; and Obama's resolution to pull out of Iraq and Afghanistan.

A massive screen covered nearly an entire wall showing the map of the Middle East and the current position of all United States strategic military assets in the region. There were banks of communications consoles, which linked the room to every essential nerve center of the government: State Department embassies around the world; CIA and FBI regional offices; military leaders of the Pentagon; National Security Agency; NORAD's Command Center in,

Colorado; and the "hot lines" to many foreign leaders.

President Biden turned first to the CIA Director to ask for a report on recent developments. He reported that the "fail safe" feature, the destructive element within the computer modules *would not* work under certain conditions, such as caves. "Simulated tests were conducted and our satellite failed to trigger the circuits within the modules, when they were also shielded inside Scuds," he revealed.

"What a mess! Who's responsible for that screw-up?" demanded Israeli's chief of Field Operations.

"Let's not get into any finger pointing," insisted President Biden.

The former chief of NSC, added, "We have to re-evaluate the situation calmly without fault finding at this stage."

"That's easy for you to say. Washington is not the target for poison gas or nuclear tipped Scuds," Israel's representative promptly responded.

President Biden then called his former boss, Obama to get his assessment. Obama told him to "delay any action until he gets an update on the current situation from *all* intelligence experts."

CIA intelligence gave Biden an update. The leaders of Iran had planned this scheme, together with Syria over the past five years or so. They have hidden poison gas missiles, and three nuclear devices of about one-megaton each. They are planning to use *known* underground facilities in Iran, and a newly discovered facility in Syria. Our joint commando mission with Israel has *successfully* pinpointed this new underground facility in the mountain region of Syria.

The overall objective of this strategy we believe is to destroy a *significant* part of the Saudi oil fields and refineries. They have likely targeted parts of Israel key cities with poison gas missiles. The goal, probably in collaboration with Russia, is to control about two-thirds of the world's supply of oil, and significantly change the balance of power in the Middle East.

President Biden (with direct advice of former President Obama), decided to delay immediate action for now. John Kerry added, "This is also an opportunity to diminish oil that is polluting the world's environment."

President Biden said to the group, "America has plenty of oil for our allies to make up any temporary shortfall. Let's try bargaining with *these Iranian and Syrian devils,*" he commanded. "If they know that we know what they are up to, they will certainly not take any immediate action."

He ordered the navy fleet to be in position, just in case. The Joint Chiefs would "quietly" activate DEFCON2, one of the highest alert states for the armed forces.

***

Turning Points in History
It's not hard to do the right thing—it's much harder to know what the right thing is to do."
Russian state-owned television was urging the country's residents to stock their bunkers with water and basic foodstuffs because Moscow might go to war with Washington. Warning that the potential conflict between the two superpowers would be "catastrophic," the anchor for Russia's TV network recommended that people buy salt, oatmeal and other products that can last a long time on the shelves, during any nuke attack.

Russia's economic lifeblood was crude oil and gas. Its GDP was only $1.3 trillion, and growing at a mere 1.5 %, *before* the Trump and Biden administrations squeezed their economy with trade sanctions, reducing per capita income to $8,500. Poverty was increasing, and pensions threatened, and the escalating war with Ukraine caused significant domestic political unrest.

Russia maintained control of the Black Sea from southeastern Ukraine, thus threatening energy sources from Iraq, Kuwait, and Saudi Arabia, to Europe. Europe purchases 35% of its gas from Russia, and over 50% comes through Ukraine pipelines. More than a dozen countries, including Germany, were highly dependent on President Putin's tighter control over oil and gas. Excessive taxes on carbon use by EU progressives, and Germany's dumb plan to shut down its nuclear power, increased its need to import energy.

By 2020, the United States and Canada was expected to become "the major producers and exporters of gas and oil," from fracturing. New pipelines and shipping resources could give Europe a steady source of energy, *just in time*. Cutting off Russia and Iran from its primary source of money was the *best strategy.*

The U.S. and NATO now have to have the guts to stop Russian's aggression. Will they have the willpower to do it?

TEL AVIV, ISRAEL

"It's not hard to do the right thing—it's hard to know what the right thing to do is."

After Mossad chief, Meir Dagan provided the details of the high-level meeting in Washington to President Shimon Peres and Prime Minister Benjamin Netanyahu, they hastily called an emergency meeting of all security advisors. "Tel Aviv can't wait for the National Security Council, the Pentagon, CIA, and indecisiveness from President Biden, who wants to 'further scrutinize the situation and examine all options,' before taking any action," the Prime Minister remarked.

They debated the possible alternatives available for about two hours before coming to a unanimous decision: *"We have no choice,"* Netanyahu concluded. "We cannot live with these madmen with poison gas and nuclear weapons."

Prime Minister Netanyahu commanded Israel's defense chief, General Aviv Kochavi to take *immediate action* to destroy all Iranian and Syrian Scud facilities, and weapons depots.

"Our Iron Dome shield should protect us against most of their missiles." (Each Iron Dome battery is comprised of interceptors, radars, and command and control systems. The system shoots down incoming rockets mid-air before they hit the target. The system only intercepts rockets that would hit targets of value. This allows the system to preserve interceptors and save more resources than if it were shooting down every single rocket).

Israeli military always move quickly in any emergency. Speed of response was *a life-or-death reflex* in a country that could only count on minutes of warning of a pending attack.

At five in the morning local time, the Israeli air force executed multiple preemptive strikes on both the Iranian and Syrian launching sites simultaneously, *without* informing President Joe Biden.

In a statement later that evening, after Israeli aircraft were over their targets, Prime Minister Benjamin Netanyahu said the campaign against terror groups would continue until all rocket fire ceases, and accused Iran, Syria and Hamas of rebuffing all recent attempts at restoring peace.   .

"The State of Israel is in the middle of a campaign to bring back peace and security for our citizens," Netanyahu said in the statement. "We won't tolerate rocket fire on our cities and towns. So I have ordered operations against these terrorists." The United States AWACS failed to detect the Israeli planes, until they made an abrupt turn and arrived close to their intended targets. Wave after wave of Israeli F-16 aircraft fired their blockbuster, laser guided bombs. The entrances to all the mines and underground nuke sites were demolished. Anything inside would be sealed under huge avalanches of falling rocks.

As he made another pass over the Syrian target area, squadron commander Cohen screamed into his radio, "Shit there must have been a second entrance to that mine? Central control, *URGENT! URGENT!* We failed to destroy one of the Scud launching sites," he shouted. Suddenly, the enemy missile, with its deadly nuke payload blasted up from the mine.

No power on earth could stop it now. Within minutes, it reached its target. Major oil fields in the Saudi desert were blasted. Satellite cameras picked up the fireball soaring over the desert and sent it onto display screens at the Pentagon. The dazzling kaleidoscope of light from the exploding gases, a precursor of the tide of thermal gamma rays and beta particles, rapidly rushed towards the east.

Fig 15. Nuclear Explosion

The lethal missile was slightly off target. It hit the area known as Abu Hadriya, north of the major Persian Gulf port city of Dhahran. Nevertheless, it took-out approximately thirty-five percent of all the Saudi oil fields. Radioactive fall-out from the blast might contaminate the region for centuries. Fires raged out of control over the entire sector. The 10-megaton nuke exploded slightly below ground level, causing a dark sand cloud to block out the sun that fatal morning. Nevertheless, the nuclear blast did *not* contaminate all of the main oil fields. Those oil wells were thousands of feet below ground level.

Secretary of Defense Lloyd Austin sent experienced former commander of Desert Storm's coalition to be in overall command of *Operation Golden Fleece,* and most of the military forces in the Gulf. He immediately ordered follow-up strikes by United States bombers that were already over the target area, with their new sixty-thousand-pound "smart bombs." They wiped-out the remaining bunkers in Syria and Iran.

Iran never expected that the United States military knew most of the essential details of their scheme. They were caught off-guard. To prevent Iran from exploiting the situation, American paratroopers immediately blocked the Iraqi Southeastern border near the city of Basra. AWACS indicated that Iran's Air Force did not challenge the new more superior American F-22 aircraft or troops near Basra. The Iranians evidently learned some lessons from the Gulf War. Near the Iranian border with Iraq. The Iranian army was outflanked and annihilated.

Squadrons of American Air Force jets moved at great speed down onto the enemy units. The enemy divisions there ceased to exist. Waves of helicopters from the Carrier Strike Forces in the Southern Gulf made short work of the enemy tanks and armored motor vehicles that remained.

A few hours later United States Marine forces entered the region with little resistance. The main concern of the American General was the possibility that the *highly radioactive* cloud might change direction and move north towards their troops. Paratroopers were ordered to put on their specially designed clothes and helmets, which sealed their bodies against the dust. *Ironically,* a strong western wind that fateful day caused the deadly cloud to move over the Persian Gulf *towards Iran.* Many innocent Iranian civilians died in the cities of Bushire and Shiraz. Tens-of-thousands of survivors would live long enough to suffer a terrible agonizing death.

The United States, Russia and China called for an emergency meeting of the UN Security Council. Washington was *compelled* to support Israel's preemptive attack. Satellite photos *proved* that Iran and Syria were the primary aggressors. The UN would not pass a resolution demanding that the World Court turn over the Iranian leaders for trial, since two-thirds of those voting were representatives from Muslim nations.

NATO set up an administration force under United States command, to try to manage Syria and Iran. A new government was reestablished with representatives from the Sunni, Shiites, and Kurds. Civil war *did not* breakout as expected by Biden administration "experts." However, a strong NATO force of twenty-five thousand "boots on the ground" (mostly Americans) would have to remain to keep order.

OPEC increased significantly with Iran and Iraqi pumping capacity at full production. Its proven oil reserves made up most of the shortfall from the Saudi situation, which drove oil prices down even lower. The UN cleaned up contaminated Saudi soil, using the initial money from Iranian oil revenues. Construction crews dressed in protective gear, scooped up the entire surface of sand over a five-mile radius. The deadly sand along with the bulldozers and other equipment was buried in deep underground areas in remote parts of the desert.

The strategic objectives of the ***Sword of Allah*** failed. Most of Saudi's main oil wells were not contaminated, although full production was interrupted for two years. The price of oil which reached an initial peak of about $154 per barrel, settled down to approximately $55 per barrel. A few missiles aimed at Israel cities were intercepted by Iron Dome's counter-missiles, and did not affect Tel Aviv.

Iran was in a worse crisis. General Ahmad, the former head of the Iranian army shot himself. Most of the Islamic fundamentalist fanatics in the government, including the Ayatollah Ali Khamenei, head of the Council of Guardians, Iran's supreme leader and the President, lost control over the population of the country.

The PLO was *temporarily* cut-off from financial aid and weapon sources from Iran, Syria and Hezbollah. They had no choice but to sign a new peace compact with Israel. All the parties to the agreement kept their word (for now). Women in Iran, Syria and most Moslem countries had *nearly* equal rights with men, such as the right to sign contracts, to own land, and most importantly, the right to vote.

Russia maintained control of the Black Sea from southeastern Ukraine, and ultimately linked up with Iran, thus threatening *all* energy sources from Iraq, Kuwait, and Saudi Arabia, to Europe and the United States. Europe purchases 35% of its gas from Russia, and over 50% comes through Ukraine pipelines. More than a dozen other countries, including Germany, were even more dependent on Mr. Putin's tighter control of oil and gas. Excessive taxes on carbon use by socialist progressives, and Germany's plan to shut down all of its nuclear power production, increased its need to import more energy. In addition, Moscow signed a 30-year $400 billion energy deal with China. Thus, Russia became far less depend on European markets.

The United States and Canada would become major producers and exporters of gas and oil from fracturing. New pipelines and shipping resources gave Europe a steady source of energy, *just in time*. Cutting off radical Islam from its only source of money, "black gold" was the best strategy. NATO must somehow have the guts to stop Russian aggression. Will they have the willpower to do it?

President Joe Biden was out of office after only one term. At the age of 82, he was clearly senile and oblivious to the Middle East crisis. He had sympathies for radical Muslims, as former president Obama did, against Israel. He claimed to be Catholic, but failed to support Christian rights, especially the unborn Right to Life. He actively engaged in negotiating with our enemies, China and Iran, against United States interests. President Jo Biden's abysmal legacy would be forever tarnished in American history.

***

Crazy Presidential Choices.
Only two contenders dominated the 2024 Presidential election. No competent candidates, including Governor DeSantis of Florida, or former Vice President Mike Pence, had the financial resources or populous backing to gain sufficient elector-college votes. America's only choice, no matter what was sought after idealistically, was between President Joe Biden's *senility* and alleged corruption, and ludicrous Middle East decisions, and Donald Trump's *narcissist* governance. One must realize that it is never the President who implements U.S. policy; it is his inner circle that acts on orders from the Commander in Chief (selection of staff is thus the key to future successes or failures.)

While the final election decisions were not yet determined, and Joe Biden will probably be encouraged (forced) to resign, for the "good" of the Democratic Party elite, due to "poor health," while ignoring other key issues. Probably Governor Newsom of California will be the choice in the election in November 2024.

However, one might expect that the majority of U.S. voters will once again ignore Donald Trump's arrogance, considering that Biden was unreliable in the Middle East, which almost caused a major international nuclear war. Trump would likely be much more decisive when it comes to dealing with Russia, China and Iranian threats to U.S. and NATO.

While nearly 50% of the U.S. voting public "love to hate" Trump, he will certainly reverse all of Biden's *irrational* domestic policies. This is especially likely regarding the Dems inflationary spending, excessive taxes, fossil fuel restrictions, and dumb regulations, while at the same time cleaning up the Justice

Department, reducing out-of-control crime rates, and supporting U.S. and NATO military defense posture vis-a vis China, Russia and Iran. Moreover, if the GOP defeats the Dems Newsom's socialistic policies and regains control over the Congress, President Trump could be much more effective in implementing his policies during a second term, especially if he can overcome his many former negatives, such as:

Trump's Tragedy

President Trump failed in his anticipated reelection in 2020. A pandemic from China, the Covid-19 virus, spread throughout the world and the U.S. was vulnerable. It destroyed numerous world economies and Trumps developing American economy began to collapse during the November 2020 election. Trump claimed "the election was stolen" by the Democrats, but he could not prove his assertion on time before the final votes were tallied.

Joe Biden became the new president, even though he mostly stayed in his home basement. He had the powerful Democratic machine to support his election, and about 85% of the President Biden's administration leaders consisted of former President Obama associates. They became Biden's inner circle. One might rightfully claim this was actually "Obama's third presidency." Biden was senile and over his head as President, and VP Harris was his "dodo bird. " Obama's people wrote daily scripts for Biden to follow on TV. All he had to do is recite Obama's extreme left progressive plans, without fumbling. (Nevertheless, he stumbled many times with embarrassing public blunders.)

President Biden began his administration with dozens of "executive orders," which reversed most of what Trump had accomplished (except Supreme Court conservative appointments) including "climate change" edicts that nearly destroyed the U.S. fossil fuel industry. His open border policy enabled millions to cross the U.S. southern border *illegally.* He suddenly pulled out of Afghanistan after twenty years, leaving allies and friends *defenseless.* He spent hundreds-of-billions to support people out of work, and other domestic inflationary spending. He continued to appease Iran by allowing them to collect $6 billion in frozen assets, in a prisoner swap "pact," with the irrational hope that Iranian leaders would stop building nukes and make peace in the Middle East. They did neither. Perhaps more seriously, Biden caused the U.S. and NATO to support the Ukraine war against Russia, which threatened to use nukes against NATO. China rose to become the greatest military competitor, and seriously threatened to invade Taiwan. President Joe Bien also was allegedly involved with his son to enrich his family by his influence, both as VP and President, and now faces articles of impeachment in the House. That was Biden's more significant misadventures, during his first three years in office.

However, the GOP regained control of the House purse strings, and strong action by the independent Federal Reserve to control inflation with higher interest rates, finally reduced rates from 9% in 2022, to about 3.3% by the end of 2024.

Then again, who can really predict the future of world events?

***

Connecticut. Vincent Renaldo returned to America. Victor's student became the master; a professional not only in how to do business but what is far more important, the kind of people and business *traps to avoid*. It is not just winning that counts in business and human affairs—*it's how you play the game!* What good is it to win the game by stepping on others, and lose your family, your friends, and most important, your immortal soul.

Vincent learned many painful lessons from his bizarre experiences. After years of marriage, an affair occurs in life. There are innumerable reasons; no two cases are the same. It might be a mid-life crisis that middle-aged men experience, or the lack of sensitivity to the needs and feelings of your spouse. It might be the dull routines of daily life. It is often about sexual fantasizing: "The grass always looks greener in other pastures." It is a total illusion! The mythical new lover makes you deaf, dumb, and blind to the actual truth about your immortal life and ultimate sanctity.

Like a modern day *"Count of Monte Cristo,"* that old story by Dumas, Vincent was at the pinnacle of his life. He had a loving family, a good home and a small fortune, many friends and social status. Then, *all came crashing down!* He found himself broken- hearted by the betrayal of his fictional lover, falsely accused and imprisoned in an ancient dungeon—isolation from the world. The broken man was deprived of all his basic human needs—fresh air and sunshine, companionship and love, *without hope.*

Then a miracle happened! The confessed sinner, the confined prisoner was given another chance, a second opportunity to rise from his deep abyss, to become reconciled again with his loving wife and the Lord. From this chaos, this disorder, he learned the true meaning of love—which was dormant within him—a love that burst forth renewing all his life forces. He finally found real peace and tranquility. Music was more melodious, food tasted better, flowers seemed far more beautiful, sunrises and sunsets were fantastic. These basic things of life are so different—when there is true love, which is always *unselfish sacrificial love.*

After more than a half a century of terror and wars, the Jews of Israel and Arabs, the Syrians and Iranians, with Russian backing, have not learned how to settle their disputes at the conference table. There was no possibility of long-term peace and coexistence between Israel and its regional neighbors. The parties to peace plans must realize that bad deals lead to future hostilities.

Final history lesson: One should not make bargains with the devil!

END

APPENDIX

Whistle-blowers

Benghazi. It was not just about the preventable death of Ambassador Stevens and three other gallant Americans. It is not just, why help was not sent to save them during that time. The actual scandal is what was really going on in Benghazi? Why was Stevens there in the first place, with very little security? Experts believe that Ambassador Stevens was running guns from Libya, through Turkey, to the "rebels" in Syria. Surprisingly, many turned out to be Al Qaeda, or associated terrorist rebels. Stevens was also trying to retrieve the more deadly weapons through Benghazi, and Al Qaeda then they *took him out.*

Whistle-blowers claim that Ambassador Stevens was in Benghazi to buyback Stinger missiles from Al Qaeda. Stinger missiles are capable of downing military and civilian aircraft. They are not weapons you want in the hands of terrorists. This gunrunning operation was not approved by the CIA, but went through Hillary Clinton's State Department. CIA did not want to provide these weapons to the rebels, but she authorized it. (Nevertheless, Hillary would never do this without Obama's specific approval).

The whistle-blowers asserted that CIA director General David Petraeus' "love affair" was leaked to silence him about these "clandestine" operations. There were reports that General Carter Ham, head of AFRICOM "Special Ops" teams, could have sent rescue troops to Benghazi in 2-3 hours. He *allegedly* was ordered by the White House *not* to send the troops to rescue the Ambassador and his team.

This happened on September 11, 2012, two short months before the presidential election. Any exposure of the "real facts" would clearly jeopardize Obama's reelection chances. Former

Secretary of DOD Leon Panetta publicly stated that he had but one meeting with Obama, at that time and did not hear from him again. Obama had to be as far away from this crisis as possible. Nevertheless, if Clinton knew then *he certainly knew.*

These four men were sacrificed to cover-up this secret weapons buyback operation. President Obama and Secretary of State Hillary Clinton then played their roles perfectly, as "grief-stricken" leaders, during the nationwide media funeral for the four murdered victims, which gained lots of voter sympathy. *It worked perfectly!*

Interviews and press release on former President Obama and Robert Gates

Source Summary of Interview by: NICHOLAS D. KRISTOF Published: March 6, 2007

He [Obama] spent four years as a child in Indonesia and attended schools in the Indonesian language, which he still speaks.

"I was a little Jakarta street kid," he said in a wide-ranging interview in his office (excerpts are on my blog, www.nytimes.com/ontheground. He once got in trouble for making faces during Koran study classes in his elementary school, but a president is less likely to stereotype Muslims as fanatics—and more likely to be aware of their nationalism—if he once studied the Koran with them.

Mr. Obama recalled the opening lines of the Arabic call to prayer, reciting them with a first-rate accent. In a remark that seemed delightfully uncalculated, Mr. Obama described the call to prayer as ***"one of the prettiest sounds on Earth at sunset."*** *The following is an abbreviated transcript of an interview by Michael Gordon and Jeff Zeleny of The New York Times with Senator Barack Obama. Many questions are edited for brevity and clarity, and extraneous material was omitted. (Published November 1st 2007)*

Q. Ambassador Crocker told the Senate Foreign Relations Committee that if the United States withdrew forces on a chronological schedule, without adjustments to take account of developments, it would backfire. It would not succeed on putting pressure on the Iraqi government to achieve a political accommodation. How do you assess that argument?

A. *"I fundamentally disagree with the ambassador on this. I think Ambassador Crocker, as well as General Petraeus are trying to play a bad hand well and are trying to play out the mission that has been given to them. [However], I see no evidence, whatsoever, that our actions to date have encouraged the kinds of political reconciliation that has been the objective of the surge and our purported objective of the last several years. I believe the reverse. ..."*

Q. If you saw that the Iraqi government, under the duress of American withdrawals, was not making progress or if sectarian violence was beginning to increase in Iraq, would you call a halt to withdrawals or proceed anyway?

A. *"I think that it is important to understand that there are no good options in Iraq. There haven't been for a very long time. I've said previously that I would not be surprised to see some spikes in violence as we begin the withdrawal. It is not going to be a perfectly smooth transition. But I think there is a way of managing this that keeps this violence contained. Now, at some point the Iraqis are going to have to respond to a change in the security situation inside Iraq, one way or another, and those in the region are going to have to respond as well...."*

Q. The Bush administration has little influence on Iranian behavior in Iraq. How would you elicit cooperation from Iran and Syria that the Bush administration has failed to obtain? Would we offer assurances that we would not be engaged in a policy of regime change. What would you do?

A. *(Abbreviated) "... I've already said, I would meet directly with Iranian leaders. I would meet directly with Syrian leaders. We would engage in a level of aggressive personal diplomacy in which a whole host of issues are on the table. We're not looking at Iraq, just in isolation. Iran and Syria would start changing their behavior if they started seeing that they had some incentives to do so, but right now the only incentive that exists is our president suggesting that if you do what we tell you, we may not blow you up.*

"My belief about the regional powers in the Middle East is that they don't respond well to that kind of bluster. They haven't in the past, there's no reason to think they will in the future...."

Q. You've argued that the United States should leave behind residual force in Iraq and the region. How large would the force be and how much would be inside Iraq versus the Persian Gulf Region?

A. *"What we're not going to be doing is engaging in broad-based counter insurgency. We're not going to be providing long-term and constant embedded training operations and logistical training operations and the sort that, I think, Senator Clinton has in some cases talked about. We're certainly not going to be engaging in what I consider mission creep, where we are structuring our forces based on preventing Iranian influence in Iraq, something that Senator Clinton has talked about as a possibility in a previous interview. We're not going to be using forces there to strike at what she's called other terrorist organizations, without being clear as to whether those are just terrorist organizations inside Iraq or terrorist organizations outside Iraq. We're going to be focused very narrowly on making sure that Al Qaeda in Iraq and terrorist activities in Iraq are prevented."*

Q. If you're asking voters to consider your judgment? What kind of people would you populate your administration with? What kind of person would be a defense secretary candidate or a candidate for national security adviser?

A. *"On the issue of judgment, I absolutely think that the decision about who the next president should be has everything to do with judgment and character. I will say when it comes to the most important issues in foreign policy that we've faced over the last several years, my judgment has been better than my opponents.*

"I want somebody in the Secretary of Defense office who has enough credibility to sell our military on the idea that we're really going to be serious about making progress on those other elements of security that have been neglected under the Bush administration. I want also that Secretary of Defense to be someone who has the confidence of mid-rank officers and troops on the ground that their interests are being looked after. That they are not just being sent into missions based on ideology or based on preconceived notions, but that somebody is their advocate."

Q. So when you think this through, obviously you put a lot of effort into what is a very detailed plan which you unveiled in September, why does this lead you to the conclusion that you don't need to have conventional combat capabilities in Iraq and you can afford to take them all out and maybe not even have special operations forces in Iraq?

A. *"But the analogy with what happened in Afghanistan is somewhat different in the sense that you had the opportunity there, potentially, to dismantle the entire leadership operation of Al Qaeda international, which was the main objective of our invasion into Iraq and we failed on that central mission. With respect to Al Qaeda in Iraq, my hope is if we've done our job, they continue to be much weakened, they don't have any obvious key leadership that is a rallying point for operations there. We may not have the same kinds of broad-based requirements that we might have needed in Afghanistan or Tora Bora.*

"But listen, I am not going to set up our troops for failure and I'm going to do something half-baked. If the commanders tell me that

they need X, Y and Z, in order to accomplish the very narrow mission that I've laid out, than I will take that into consideration."

Q. Where does Senator Obama's position clearly differ from Senator Clinton's on the way forward? Obviously there are a lot of similarities. Granted there are profound differences in what happened in the past.

A. *"As you know, you don't want to look backwards, but obviously our general view about this mission as a whole has been very different. She missed the strategic interests that should have dictated whether we went to Iraq in the first place or not, but she has not been clear about the pace of withdrawal and I have.*

"Senator Clinton seems to be comfortable with this notion that somehow even though the single thing that has made Iran more formidable of a threat is our invasion of Iraq that now that becomes the pretext for us continuing down that same course. I think we have to change course—fundamentally. ..."

Q. But how do you go back into Iraq without military forces?

A. *"No, no, no, no, no. You conflated three things. The latter two that you talked about are not military missions. Let's just be clear about that."*

Q. An armed escort is not a military mission?

A. *"Look, I want to be clear about what I've said. I think it would be irresponsible for a president to suggest that there are no circumstances—ever—in which we would consider military action as a consequence of humanitarian concerns. I think we have seen great cruelty in our history, over the last 100 years. If there are ways for us to prevent wholesale slaughter, then I think that's something that we have to look at. I have not suggested that is a mission that I have set forth. ..."*

****

Robert M. Gates book, "Duty: Memoirs of a Secretary at War"

The Iraq surge by President Bush, was successfully implemented by General Petraeus, and had actually worked.

"Hillary [Clinton] told the president [Obama] that her opposition to the surge in Iraq had been political because she faced him in the Iowa Primary. The president conceded that [his] opposition to the Iraq surge had [also] been political."

***

The following is an abbreviated summary of the text of President Obama's prepared remarks to the Muslim world, delivered on June 4, 2009, as released by the White House.

The relationship between Islam and the West includes centuries of co-existence and cooperation, but also conflict and religious wars. More recently, tension has been fed by colonialism that denied rights and opportunities to many Muslims, and a Cold War in which Muslim-majority countries were too often treated as proxies without regard to their own aspirations. Moreover, the sweeping change brought by modernity and globalization led many Muslims to view the West as hostile to the traditions of Islam. ...

The attacks of September 11th, 2001 and the continued efforts of these extremists to engage in violence against civilians has led some in my country to view Islam as inevitably hostile not only to America and Western countries, but also to human rights. This has bred more fear and mistrust. ...

I have come here to seek a new beginning between the United States and Muslims around the world; one based upon mutual interest and mutual respect; and one based upon the truth that America and Islam are not exclusive, and need not be in competition. Instead, they overlap, and share common principles—principles of justice and progress; tolerance and the dignity of all human beings. ...

As the Holy Koran tells us, "Be conscious of God and speak always the truth." That is what I will try to do—to speak the truth as best I can, humbled by the task before us, and firm in my belief that the interests we share as human beings are far more powerful than the forces that drive us apart. ...

I am a Christian, but my father came from a Kenyan family that includes generations of Muslims. As a boy, I spent several years in Indonesia [until the age of ten] and heard the call of the azaan at the break of dawn and the fall of dusk. As a young man, I worked in Chicago communities where many found dignity and peace in their Muslim faith.

As a student of history, I also know civilization's debt to Islam. It was Islam—at places like Al-Azhar University—that carried the light of learning through so many centuries, paving the way for Europe's Renaissance and Enlightenment. ... And throughout history, Islam has demonstrated through words and deeds the possibilities of religious tolerance and racial equality.

I know, too, that Islam has always been a part of America's story. The first nation to recognize my country was Morocco. In signing the Treaty of Tripoli in 1796, our second President John Adams wrote, "The United States has in itself no character of enmity against the laws, religion or tranquility of Muslims." ...

Moreover, freedom in America is indivisible from the freedom to practice one's religion. That is why there is a mosque in every state of our union, and over 1,200 mosques within our borders. That is why the U.S. government has gone to court to protect the right of women and girls to wear the hijab, and to punish those who would deny it. ...

In Ankara, I made clear that America is not—and never will be—at war with Islam. We will, however, relentlessly confront violent extremists who pose a grave threat to our security. Because we reject the same thing that people of all faiths reject: the killing of innocent men, women, and children. And it is my first duty as President to protect the American people.

The situation in Afghanistan demonstrates America's goals, and our need to work together. Over seven years ago, the United States pursued al Qaeda and the Taliban with broad international support. We did not go by choice, we went because of necessity. I am aware that some question or justify the events of 9/11. But let us be clear: al Qaeda killed nearly 3,000 people on that day.

The victims were innocent men, women and children from America and many other nations who had done nothing to harm anybody. ...

That's why we're partnering with a coalition of forty-six countries. And despite the costs involved, America's commitment will not weaken. Indeed, none of us should tolerate these extremists. They have killed in many countries. They have killed people of different faiths—more than any other, they have killed Muslims. Their actions are irreconcilable with the rights of human beings, the progress of nations, and with Islam. The Holy Koran teaches that whoever kills an innocent, it is as if he has killed all mankind; and whoever saves a person, it is as if he has saved all mankind. The enduring faith of over a billion people is so much bigger than the narrow hatred of a few. Islam is not part of the problem in combating violent extremism—it is an important part of promoting peace. ...

Iraq's sovereignty is its own. That is why I ordered the removal of our combat brigades by next August. That is why we will honor our agreement with Iraq's democratically-elected government to remove combat troops from Iraqi cities by July, and to remove all our troops from Iraq by 2012. We will help Iraq train its Security Forces and develop its economy. ...

America's strong bonds with Israel are well known. This bond is unbreakable. It is based upon cultural and historical ties, and the recognition that the aspiration for a Jewish homeland is rooted in a tragic history that cannot be denied. ...

Palestinians must abandon violence. Resistance through violence and killing is wrong and does not succeed. ... Now is the time for Palestinians to focus on what they can build. The Palestinian Authority must develop its capacity to govern, with institutions that serve the needs of its people. Hamas does have support among some Palestinians, but they also have responsibilities. To play a role in fulfilling Palestinian aspirations, and to unify the Palestinian people, Hamas must put an end to violence, recognize past agreements, and recognize Israel's right to exist. ...

This issue has been a source of tension between the United States and the Islamic Republic of Iran. For many years, Iran has defined itself in part by its opposition to my country, and there is indeed a tumultuous history between us. In the middle of the Cold War, the United States played a role in the overthrow of a democratically elected Iranian government. Since the Islamic Revolution, Iran has played a role in acts of hostage taking and violence against U.S. troops and civilians. This history is well known. Rather than remain trapped in the past, I have made it clear to Iran's leaders and people that my country is prepared to move forward. The question, now, is not what Iran is against, but rather what future it wants to build. …

I understand those who protest that some countries have weapons that others do not. No single nation should pick and choose which nations hold nuclear weapons. That is why I strongly reaffirmed America's commitment to seek a world in which no nations hold nuclear weapons. And any nation—including Iran—should have the right to access peaceful nuclear power if it complies with its responsibilities under the nuclear Non-Proliferation Treaty. ...

I know there has been controversy about the promotion of democracy in recent years, and much of this controversy is connected to the war in Iraq. So let me be clear: no system of government can or should be imposed upon one nation by any other. … Islam has a proud tradition of tolerance. We see it in the history of Andalusia and Cordoba during the Inquisition. I saw it firsthand as a child in Indonesia, where devout Christians worshiped freely in an overwhelmingly Muslim country. That is the spirit we need today. People in every country should be free to choose and live their faith based upon the persuasion of the mind, heart, and soul. This tolerance is essential for religion to thrive, but it is being challenged in many different ways. …

Freedom of religion is central to the ability of peoples to live together. We must always examine the ways in which we protect it. For instance, in the United States, rules on charitable giving have made it harder for Muslims to fulfill their religious obligation. That is why I am committed to working with American Muslims to ensure that they can fulfill zakat. …

Now let me be clear: issues of women's equality are by no means simply an issue for Islam.

In Turkey, Pakistan, Bangladesh and Indonesia, we have seen Muslim-majority countries elect a woman to lead. Meanwhile, the struggle for women's equality continues in many aspects of American life, and in countries around the world. ...

We have the power to make the world we seek, but only if we have the courage to make a new beginning, keeping in mind what has been written.

The Holy Koran tells us, "O mankind! We have created you male and a female; and we have made you into nations and tribes so that you may know one another." The Talmud tells us: "The whole of the Torah is for the purpose of promoting peace." The Holy Bible tells us, "Blessed are the peacemakers, for they shall be called sons of God."

****

New Middle-East War 50-Year Later. Hamas Attacks Israel.

Vincent was not an "expert" on Palestine or Israeli history, although he studied the topic and visited the Holy Land in 2008. It is an undisputed fact that the Philistines (sea people probably from Crete) settled in Canaan, after the Bronze Age.

We all should know David killed Goliath, and the Philistines killed King Saul of Israel. David later became the King of the Jews by 1,000 BC, and won battles against the Philistines and others. King Solomon finally established a the peaceful and rich "Holy land of the Jewish people."

About thousand years later, in 70 AD, the Romans defeated the Jewish uprising against their oppressive rule and destroyed their Holy Temple. Thereafter-Roman Emperors renamed Israel "Palestine," which remained its name for many centuries.

By 1918 after World War I, the double-dealing British and scheming French leadership, carved-up the Middle East based on unscrupulous secret plans to reward the major war victors. Thereafter, the British controlled Palestine until World War II ended in 1945.

President Truman finally allowed a Jewish nation to be born (again) by two-thirds majority vote in the United Nations in 1948. Most of immigrating Jews called their newfound homeland

"Palestine." Years later, after many Jewish battles with Arabs, it was finally renamed the State of Israel.

When one has very bad neighbors who constantly carryout terrorist acts against you, there are only three choices:

1. Try to coexist with your neighbors by appeasement.
2. Build walls to separate your troubling neighbors.
3. Encourage the neighbors to relocate somewhere else.

It is important to realize that the majority of Shiite Muslims in Palestine and Syria, and Iranian Shia Persians, are not all evil actors. Nearly 30,000 Hamas terrorists maintain tight control over these two million somewhat moderate Muslims in Palestine. (Hamas stated they would not stop their terrorism until they have eliminated Israel from the face of this earth).

Israel also faces terrorists Muslims on their northern border controlled by Hezbollah leaders, who obtain weapons and financial support from terrorist Shia leaders in Iran. (Iran also supplies lethal weapons, including drones and rockets to Syria, its proxy, and lately to Russia in support of its war in Ukraine.)

The only "reasonable solution" to endless chaotic battles is to encourage Israeli's disadvantaged Palestine neighbors to relocate. Israel needs compelling "carrots and sticks" to actually accomplish such a challenging task. The "carrots" could be significant economic benefits. The "sticks" are consequences that are more negative if they refuse to move. Carrots might include a plot of land somewhere else, with WTO funds to buy land, build a house, and grow food, among other key benefits. If some continue to refuse to relocate, then you have to "make them an offer they cannot refuse."

Where can one move two million homeless Palestine people? There are less populated areas in Africa, Austrialia and major islands in the world. There are probably religious arguments against the Palestine people moving to any unknown foreign location. Nevertheless, Christians, Muslims and Jews have endured hardships and prospered in different foreign countries, including Europe, England, Canada, Americas, and the U.S.

The past U.S., EU and UN approach based on "appeasement" with endless billions in financial aid, has led to endless violent conflicts, and a waste of lives lost and finances. (Appeasement of Iran by U.S. releasing six billion dollars has hopefully been "refrozen" in the Arab banks.)

The Middle-East Future?

How might two million poor Palestine people survive when they are certain to double in population over the next decade? Unemployment rates are already well beyond tolerable levels. What about their basic needs for food, healthcare, education and jobs in this infinitesimal Palestine walled territory? After this 2023 Hamas terrorist war, they will be certainly far worse off than ever before.

Palestine families if given a chance to freely vote would likely decide that a future life for their growing families and greatly expanding Islamic faith is more essential than endless terrorist politics.

After all, the first Americans were immigrants from many different foreign countries, and they prospered well beyond their dreams.

"You reap whatever you sow!"

AUTHOR ROBERT &
SPOUSE MIRIAM

Robert Thomas Fertig is author of, *Culture Battles, Guardianship Reality, Best Interest of the Children, the Beauty and Wonder of Transcendent Truths, Guide to Universal Truths, the Software Revolution,* principal writer of *Waves of Change,* and *Gathering Storm in the Middle East.* He has traveled extensively to do research for this book, in Europe, the Far East, Israel, and America. Robert was President of Enterprise Information Systems, Inc., a Technology Consulting Firm in New York. Currently he is an Eldercare Guardian, responsible for assuring ethical clinical care for senior citizens. During the past five years, he and his wife, Miriam, were *Guardian ad Litem* volunteers, the objective "eyes and ears" of the court for abandoned, abused and neglected children.

www.ingramcontent.com/pod-product-compliance
Lightning Source LLC
Chambersburg PA
CBHW032146050726
47591CB00001B/97